ReVenge
UndOne

SENJA LAAKSO

REVENGE UNDONE
Book 1 in Revenge Series

ISBN 978-952-69809-0-4 (paperback)
ISBN 978-952-69809-1-1 (hardback)
ISBN 978-952-69809-2-8 (EPUB)

First published October 2021, by Stoorily

www.SenjaLaakso.com

Editor: Nick Hodgson
Cover: Stoorily

ReVenge UndOne

SENJA LAAKSO

TRIGGER WARNINGS

This novel contains graphic violence, gore, terrorism, manipulation, adult language, death, grief, loss of a loved one, addiction, smoking, alcohol, and PTSD symptoms.
Reader discretion is advised.

To my younger self,
who never gave up on her dreams.

Henry repeatedly shoved his hands in his pockets and yanked them out again. Thoughts raced through his mind and not even taking deep breaths calmed his nerves.

Out of all the places on Earth, why here?

His feet splashed in the water that had puddled all over the pavement from the morning rain. Seattle was still grey. Looking up at the sky, it was like being back in England.

Perhaps that was why *she* was there. Perhaps Seattle reminded her of home.

Henry wondered about other similarities between London and Seattle, but he wasn't in America for sightseeing. Not even to visit Washington's Sanctuary for Dragons.

For once in his life, he didn't have time for creatures. He was on a mission.

Walking past tall buildings, he scanned the numbers on the grey walls. He was nearing his destination, and his palms were sweaty.

His mission was to find her—his best friend. Leaving England hadn't been enough; she had left the continent too. He had waited for her call and had spent numerous movie nights alone until he had lost hope. But after everything, he was there to get the explanation he deserved.

It was time he took matters into his own hands. It had already been three years since she had left.

Henry expected her to be angry for seeking her out, but he hoped she would also be happy to see him. Even seeing her shocked would work for him. He wanted to see her—even if he was angry.

Henry spotted the block of flats he thought she lived in. He hoped he had the right place. Considering he had found it through a realtor who had sold Ciara's old—presumed—house, he couldn't be sure. Henry wouldn't have even found that house without his brother's address list for future wedding guests.

He was away from work for his trip. It was time for his annual summer holiday anyway, but his original plans hadn't involved Seattle. He hadn't been planning to fly to America until he had found her address.

America had been kind to him. He hadn't been there before, but so far his trip had gone well. He had no regrets about flying to the other side of the world, but a worry gnawed inside him. *What if she isn't there?*

Sighing heavily, Henry stopped in front of the tall building. He double-checked the number on the grey, textured wall before turning to look at the double glass doors.

He forced his feet to move, mixed thoughts building up in his head. Would he be angry with her for leaving him like that? Or happy to see her? Pulling at the door, he realised it was locked. And it required a code.

Of course he didn't have one, but it wouldn't stop him. Turning left and right, he made sure no one was nearby. He turned his attention back to the locked door and pulled out his wand. He focused his power, letting it flow through the stone core of the wooden stick. After a quick flick, the door unlocked.

He pushed them open while putting his wand back in his pocket. The doors slid close behind him.

What if she *was* there? Ciara, who had cut him out of her life. Henry hadn't seen her in so long that the possibility of seeing her still seemed distant. They had barely been adults when she had left.

But he hadn't come all the way to Seattle to turn around like a coward.

Taking a deep breath, he looked between the lift and the stairs. The latter gave him more time to think, and he needed that.

He had been meaning to walk, but after the second floor, he found himself running. He was halfway up when he decided there was no turning back.

He ran all the way up and stopped at the top of the stairs. Looking around, he didn't spot the right flat number. The corridor led left and right, but he couldn't tell which way to go.

He stood there long enough for someone to walk up behind him.

"My flat is over here."

Henry froze.

That voice.

He spun around to see his best friend standing a few steps below him.

His mouth hung ajar, and his eyes widened.

It was *her*, standing right there. Unless a spell was deceiving him—but it was unlikely. He didn't feel as if he was under any enchantment.

She had grown. Not taller, but she had matured. She looked skinnier but had gained some muscle—she must have been hitting the gym regularly. Her hair was longer and perhaps a shade darker.

The way she stood was different. Something powerful in her posture. Confidence, perhaps.

"Ciara."

She smiled at him. "Henry."

His eyes wandered down to her leg as she walked up to him. She was limping, only stepping lightly on her left foot. "Are you injured?"

Henry cursed himself. It was the stupidest thing to say. But it wasn't as though he had prepared a speech. He wasn't even sure whether he was excited or furious. Or both.

Ciara's smile lingered, and she glanced down at her leg. "Stupid accident." She shrugged. "I'll just have to be careful for a while."

His brows furrowed. Considering she could use magic, it likely hadn't been a mundane accident. Unless there had been non-magics around. Using magic in front of them was out of question and highly illegal.

"Do you want to come in?" Ciara gestured towards her flat door.

She seemed happy to see him, but distant. Almost unfamiliar.

It was as if he didn't recognise her anymore. His *past* best friend.

Henry nodded. "I'd like that."

Ciara led the way, limping to the door. She unlocked it by moving her hand for a spell. Then she snapped her fingers, and the doorknob twisted. Wandless magic. She was the only one Henry knew who could do that.

She slid the door open and let Henry go in before following.

He scanned the flat. It was minimalistic. A simple coatrack with a couple of coats hanging. The living area and bedroom space were one small room. Other than that there was just a mattress, a small chest of drawers, a desk, and one chair. From where he was standing, it looked as though the kitchen had just the essentials.

It wasn't a cosy flat—a place to call home. It looked like a cheap motel room, only cleaner.

"Very..." Henry wanted to be honest and polite, but it was impossible to be both.

"Empty?" Ciara offered and limped past Henry. "I know. I don't spend much time in here."

Henry continued to look around the flat, but spared a glance at Ciara. "So, you're at your boyfriend's flat or something?"

Ciara shook her head and glanced away from Henry. "No boyfriend, but I work a lot. I'm just suspended now."

Henry stopped looking around and turned to face Ciara. "Suspended?" His eyes fell down to her left leg—the one that was injured. It couldn't be just a sprained ankle. Magical healers had access to methods that could heal those in just a day or two. Unless the injury was so recent, it had to be something more serious.

Ciara nodded. "Too many near-death experiences, according to my superiors."

His brows furrowed. "Near-death experiences? What do you do for work?"

"I'm a hit witch." She smiled. "Well, sort of. I assisted with other tasks, too."

Henry knew exactly what a hit witch was. A hit wizard, except a woman. They were trained professionals who caught dangerous wizards and witches and put them behind bars.

He tilted his head to the side, giving himself time to gather his thoughts. "A-and you've had too many near-death experiences?"

She shrugged. "So they say."

He stared at the woman—his old friend—whom he no longer recognised. Ciara hadn't been reckless. Adventurous, maybe, but not reckless.

"I haven't gone insane. You don't have to stare at me like that."

"I didn't—"

Ciara smiled. "I know you, Henry. You actually seem very..." she looked him up and down "...unchanged."

He frowned. "Is that good?"

Ciara's smile widened. "I think so."

A smile crossed Henry's face and then vanished. "You've changed."

With a heavy sigh, she said, "It's been rough at work."

"So, you catch dangerous wizards and witches?"

"Well, on paper, yes." She walked over to her desk and leaned against it as if her leg was hurting.

"On paper?"

"I also do undercover and protector missions."

Eyes wide, Henry stupidly asked, "For real?"

She nodded, playing with the belt loops of her jeans. "Someone has to deal with the bad guys on the magical side."

Henry's forehead creased. "I know, but I never thought you would."

Ciara had always talked about becoming a curse breaker. Not a hit witch.

"I know it's dangerous. In fact, my job is so dangerous that I haven't seen my own mother. My job could put her in danger, too." She sighed, exhaustion shining through her eyes. "I just finished an undercover mission, and like I said, I'm suspended now."

It took a moment for that to sink in. In a weird way, Henry felt less sad about being left behind, knowing Ciara hadn't even seen her own mother. Yet at the same time, his heart broke thinking how lonely she had to be.

"How long will you be on suspension?" Henry asked.

"Six months at the very least."

It was a long time, and nothing appeared to be keeping Ciara in Seattle. It sparked the perfect idea.

"Come back to England." The words flew out of his mouth, taking both of them by surprise.

Ciara was at a loss for words.

"I mean it." And he did. He needed time with Ciara. He still didn't have an explanation to her disappearance, which she owed him.

"I...I don't know." Ciara rubbed her arm uneasily.

"Have you even thought about it?" Henry's eyes gleamed with hope, but it was soon ripped away.

"No."

He was disappointed. "Will you think about it?"

She avoided his gaze. "I don't know."

"Six months should be enough to visit old friends, even if you have other plans." Henry wasn't good at convincing people, but he was going to try hard for Ciara. "Everyone is wondering what happened to you."

"I have friends."

"Outside work?"

Ciara shrugged, making the answer clear. She didn't have many—if any—friends outside work.

Henry couldn't believe his best friend was such a workaholic.

"What about you?" Ciara asked, eager to change the subject. She sat down on the only chair in the flat and gestured for Henry to sit down on the mattress.

So he did. Leaning his elbows on his knees, he turned to face her. "What about me?"

"What do you do for a living?" She didn't know what he had been doing since graduation. It wasn't hard to guess what his job might involve, but she didn't want to *guess*, she wanted to *know*.

"I'm a creature trainer."

The corners of Ciara's mouth turned up. "Of course."

"I suppose it's not that hard to figure out."

"Nope."

The grin stayed on her face. She had always adored how much love Henry held for all magical creatures and animals. He was the type of person who would collect lost puppies and abandoned dogs. Or would have if he lived a non-magic life. But he didn't, and it wouldn't have been a surprise to learn that he had taken home a lost baby dragon.

"I'm not that surprised by your career choice either, now that I'm thinking about it." Henry was horrified—but not that surprised. "You've always enjoyed adventures."

Ciara smiled at him. "Well, you know me."

He couldn't control his tongue. "Do I? Because to me you seem so much more...mature. As if it had been a decade instead of three years."

"A lot has happened, that's all." She looked down at her hands and sighed. "Not all good."

"Like almost dying once in a while?"

Ciara smiled, but it didn't reach her eyes. "Others weren't so lucky."

Henry stared at her for a good minute, his eyes turning grim. "Someone died?"

"Many people have died." Ciara wagged her head, trying to shake off the memories. "It's just...I lived in Canada at first, you know." Her voice wavered, but no tears surfaced.

Henry remembered that side of her. How she hated showing feelings—especially negative ones—to other people. Even the people close to her.

"What happened in Canada?" Henry asked, hoping not to push Ciara over the edge.

"You remember Theo, right?" A smile crossed Ciara's face, quickly vanishing. "From the tournament back in our school years?"

"Theo Bouch or something." Henry remembered him. Ciara had been friends with the guy.

"Theo Boucher," Ciara said, nodding.

Then the tears came, glistening in the corners of her eyes. She blinked them away hastily.

"We became even better friends when we started working together after I moved to Canada. We had...a special connection." She paused to exhale. The tears were back. "But then he died on a mission with me." She wiped the escaped tears off her cheeks as if they were burning acid.

"I'm so sorry."

"It's been a while now."

Still, the sorrow in her eyes was clear as daylight. It hurt to see her that way.

"You know you could have called me, right?"

"I know." She turned away and paused before facing Henry again. "I know I could have. I just wasn't sure how you would react. Besides, I didn't want to put you in danger."

"I wouldn't have minded."

Ciara smiled and blinked away the last tears. "Well, enough of my tragic past years. How is your family?"

Henry's family had once been like a second family for her.

He smiled, happy to talk about them. "Mum and Dad are fine. They are having mid-life crises now that the others are growing up, but they should be okay."

Ciara chuckled. "They'll be just fine, I'm sure."

"Probably." Henry smiled wide enough for his teeth to show. "Anyway, Gabriel is about to finish his fifth year, and Polly and Poppy are finishing their third year."

They were all growing up so fast. Ciara had always seen them as little children, yet Gabriel was almost an adult already.

"Gabriel is also duelling in the school team like..." Henry stopped himself before his older brother's name slipped out.

"Like Liam once was." She didn't flinch—didn't even blink. "How is he, by the way?"

"Well, he's...he's back in England." Henry shifted in his seat. "And well...he, uh—"

"He's engaged." Ciara nodded. "So just spit it out and tell me how he is."

Henry cocked his head to the side. "Do you have a spy on him or what?" He paused, and it hit him. He pointed a finger at Ciara, shock fuelling his words. "If you tell me the two of you are in contact—"

"I haven't talked to him in years. And no, no spies, either. But he invited me to his engagement party."

"They, um...everyone assumed the invitation got lost in the mail."

"It didn't."

That hurt. Ciara could have come, even to see Henry for old times' sake. But she hadn't.

He swallowed, turning to look away from her. "You didn't want to come, then?"

"I would have come if the timing had been better."

Henry turned back to meet her gaze. "Meaning?"

Her jaw tightened, but she kept her eyes on him. "It was around the time of Theo's funeral."

That was an acceptable reason.

"Why won't you just come back to England now? Even for a visit."

Ciara shook her head, straightening her back. "I can't just leave everything."

"You're suspended for six months. What's keeping you here?"

She was silent, trying to come up with an answer, until she had one. "Well, nothing, I suppose."

Not with her suspension.

"Exactly!" Henry clapped his hands together. "So, it's decided now. You're coming back with me."

Ciara chuckled, shaking her head at Henry's excitement. "What would I do in England?"

"Meet old friends, of course."

"They probably think I'm dead by now."

"Exactly, and you're not," Henry said. "My family would love to see you."

Ciara sighed. "I won't make any promises on how long I'll stay."

"Then don't. Even if you come back for a week, I'll be happy."

"I suppose it's about time I came to visit."

"It is. Besides, you can stay at my flat, so you don't have to worry about getting a hotel room."

Ciara raised an eyebrow. "You have your own flat?"

"Yes."

"What about your girlfriend?"

Henry scoffed. "No time for a girlfriend. Creatures are the love of my life."

Ciara laughed. It was such a *Henry* thing to say.

"Alright. I'll stay for one week, but I'll make no promises on anything more than that," Ciara said.

Grinning, Henry asked her, "When do we leave?"

"Tomorrow?"

"It's set in stone!"

No more escaping. It was time to go back home. At least for a visit.

2

"It's so wonderful you could make it today, even though Iris couldn't," Mary Rossler said to her oldest son, William.

"We're separate people, even though we're engaged," William reminded his mother and smiled at her.

"Of course, of course," Mary said while counting down the plates on the table. She had already done so three times.

"So, what's so special about today's dinner?" William—or rather Liam—leaned against the kitchen counter, observing his mother.

She was often fussing around and making sure everyone was okay. But this time she was being *extremely* precise. The food had to be perfect, and the table had to be shining.

"Henry's coming over, too." Mary glanced at Liam in the middle of her preparations, and he saw the wide grin on her face. "He said he's bringing a special guest with him."

Liam raised an eyebrow. "He finally found himself a girlfriend?"

"What else could a 'special guest' mean?"

"I have no idea what it means, Mum."

"Exactly. It has to be a new girlfriend." She paused briefly, turning to face Liam. "He hasn't told you anything?"

He shook his head. "No."

"Maybe he went to the States with her," Mary wondered out loud, giving the plates a few more polishing touches.

"So, a romantic holiday in the States to test the relationship?" Liam smiled, humoured by the idea.

"Does it sound that absurd?"

Henry had never brought a girl home. It was going to be new for everyone.

"Guess not."

Knocking interrupted their conversation.

"Oh, my!" Mary squealed. She took a quick look around the room and turned to Liam. "Can you fill the glasses, please, dear?"

"Of course, Mum." He smiled, watching his mother glance around the house as if the Queen was coming for dinner.

Mrs Rossler rushed to the door, but not before checking herself in a mirror.

Liam shook his head and grabbed his wand. He flicked it in the air, energy flowing from within him all the way to the tip of the wand, and the glasses started filling with water.

"I can't believe it!" Mary's voice was a mix of shock and excitement as it rang through the house. It was followed by laughter.

Liam picked out his brother's laugh. But the other one was feminine. *Girlfriend*, he thought.

"It's been so long!" his mother said.

He froze. His mother knew Henry's girlfriend.

He turned around. The trio was standing just barely in his line of sight, still in the hallway.

And his jaw dropped. Henry had brought *her*.

The girl—or rather, young woman—wasn't Henry's girlfriend. Or so Liam hoped.

It was Ciara. Ciara Jareau, his ex-girlfriend.

Her hair was still brown, just longer and darker. Her build was slimmer, too. But she still looked like Ciara.

The same girl Liam had been in love with once.

"Why is it flooding in here?" Poppy asked her oldest brother, coming in through the back door.

Liam's eyes widened, settling on the flooded table. Water was running out of the glasses, pouring down all the way to the floor.

Poppy tilted her head and raised an eyebrow at her brother. "What distracted y—"

"Bloody hell! Ciara!" Polly—Poppy's twin—screamed with excitement. Loud stomping followed the scream as Polly rushed down the last few stairs.

Poppy's eyebrows rose, hearing Ciara's name. She turned to her brother Liam with a knowing look.

"Not a word," he hissed and hurried to make the extra water disappear using a spell. He flicked his wand, and the water vanished, leaving the surfaces dry.

"Polly!" It was *her* voice. Even after years Liam would have recognised it anywhere.

He turned back to see his brother and Ciara. Polly was hugging Ciara, and Poppy was waiting for her turn, which she soon got.

"What is all this noise?" Ray—Mr Rossler, or Raymond—walked down the stairs.

"Hello, Mr Rossler," Ciara greeted the man. They shook hands.

Mr Rossler smiled at her. "Blimey! It's been a while!"

Ciara smiled back at him. "I've been a little busy with work. But I have six months off now."

"Suspended for nearly getting herself killed." Words slipped from Henry's mouth like he was a little boy giving away his sibling's mischiefs.

"Killed?" Mrs Rossler shrieked.

"Henry is making it sound more serious than it is," Ciara

said, giving her best friend a long and hard look.

Ciara's words brought no comfort to Mary who was mortified. Her eyes were wide, and her hands covered her mouth. But Henry calmed her down.

Ciara's eyes scanned the room, taking in the familiar shade of green on the walls. The stairs had stayed the same— white lacquered wood. The scent of food coming from the kitchen must have been like stepping into a memory for her.

Her eyes settled on Liam while she was taking in her surroundings. He was standing a little further away, leaning against the wall near the kitchen doorway.

Ciara smiled at him. "Hi, Liam."

It was the first time they had talked since their break-up.

"Hi," Liam said with a matching smile.

"Alright then!" Mrs Rossler clapped her hands, deciding not to give room for an awkward silence. "The dinner is ready."

Mr Rossler called for Gabriel who was still upstairs. The others walked into the kitchen and sat down.

Henry grinned. "I am dying to get some of Mum's food!"

"I told you diner food isn't that good," Ciara said.

"Diner food?" Mrs Rossler asked. She set the food onto the table, flicking her wand in the air. The food floated from the kitchen counter to the table.

It was all made without magic. Food spells were beyond tough. But it wasn't because of that, because Mrs Rossler knew how to make food—with or without magic. She had just wanted to go through the effort of making it from scratch.

Ciara turned to face Henry. "You didn't tell them?"

Henry grinned, rubbing the back of his neck. "I didn't tell them I was going to see you. I said I was going to the States."

"What?" Mrs Rossler gaped. "I thought you were on a holiday trip!"

"As an adult, I'm allowed to do what I want without sharing all the details," Henry reminded his mother. "But yes. I went to see Ciara and now we're here." He leaned closer to Ciara with his head and then straightened back up.

The little gesture didn't go unnoticed by Liam. Ciara and his brother had once been best friends. Or was it more? Had it always been more?

Everyone started filling their plates with food. Meanwhile, Gabriel showed up. Ciara stood up from the table to hug him, too, and then they both sat down.

Everyone settled at the table once their plates were filled.

"How has America been, then?" Mr Rossler asked Ciara.

"Well, I wouldn't be the best tour guide, to be honest. I've been extremely busy with work."

"What do you do?" Gabriel asked.

Ciara smiled at the teenager growing up to be a young man. "I'm a hit witch. But I do whatever my boss tells me to do."

Gabriel's eyes widened, and his mouth twisted into a grin. "Wicked!"

Mrs Rossler had a different reaction. She frowned, eyeing Ciara worriedly. "Isn't that a little dangerous?"

"A little?" Gabriel looked at his mother in disbelief, shaking his head. "It's super dangerous."

"Exactly," Ciara said. "So, pick a better career path, Gabe."

"Listen to what she says. Those are some wise words," Mrs Rossler said, nodding.

Gabriel rolled his eyes. "Fine, whatever."

"Oh, I almost forgot," Ciara said, turning to look at Liam who sat on her left. "Congratulations on your engagement. I'm sorry I couldn't make it to the celebration."

Liam smiled at her. "Um, thank you. It's, uh, alright."

He was good with words, but seeing her after so many years made him talk like a teenage boy on his first date. It was silly. It was just Ciara.

But to be honest, he hadn't expected to see her.

Luckily for him, Ciara didn't mind if he was clumsy with his words. She just smiled. "Good."

"So, how long are you in England for?" Mrs Rossler asked Ciara.

Ciara smiled. "To be honest. I don't know. Anything from a week to six months, I suppose."

"What about your flat in the States?" Mrs Rossler had always been the type to worry, and she had once been like a second mother for Ciara.

"I was renting it, so right now I don't actually have a flat," Ciara said.

"She's staying with me." Henry flashed a smile and glanced at Ciara. "For however long she'll be here for."

Liam tried not to read too much into it. Henry and Ciara had been best friends forever. But something seemed out of place. Liam hadn't even been aware the two were talking.

All he had known was that Ciara was alive and living in North America, thanks to a spy he had hired to find out her whereabouts—and to know whether she was even alive. It had been after she hadn't replied to the engagement party invitation.

Liam stared out of the window, sitting at his desk and drawing in his sketchbook.

Henry and Ciara were outside, sitting side by side in the grass. Talking. Here and there, Henry said something to make Ciara giggle.

Liam couldn't focus on drawing. The pair was driving him insane with their stupid jokes.

At first, he felt silly for thinking that way. They were best friends. But it hurt to be left out. Both by his girlfriend and his brother.

Ciara sat down beside Liam on his bed. "You're being oddly quiet."

"So what?" He pretended to be reading the book in his hands to ignore his girlfriend.

"You're not in England that often. Can you please put the book

away so I can hang out with my boyfriend?" Ciara asked and smiled at him.

But Liam remained silent.

Ciara, not understanding something was wrong, got an idea. She snatched the book from her boyfriend's hands and stood up from the bed, holding it up.

"What is wrong with you?" Liam snapped at her. The mischievous grin on her face turned into a frown.

"Liam, I—"

"Can't you see that I'm reading?" he said, raising his voice. Getting up from the bed, he snatched his book back. "Go flirt with your new boyfriend!"

Ciara's brows furrowed. "What are you talking about?"

"There's something going on between you and Henry." Liam kept his eyes on the book. He opened it and stared at a random page.

"You can't be serious," Ciara said in utter disbelief. "Henry is my best friend. You know that!"

"Looked more like friends with benefits."

"You think I'd cheat on you?"

"Clearly it wasn't that hard," Liam hissed.

"I can't understand you."

"Well, I don't understand this stupid act you're trying to pull off right now. You can admit that you're in love with my brother."

Ciara wanted to scream at Liam. If they had lived in a flat of their own, she likely would have.

But she didn't want to scream in his family's house with everyone at home. So instead she grabbed her bag and threw all of her stuff in.

"You can call me when you come to your senses," Ciara spat at Liam and walked out.

He didn't run after her, even though he wanted to. Instead, he continued to stare at the book in his hands.

He already regretted his words.

"You're an absolute idiot!" Henry declared the next morning.

"Honestly, you are."

Liam didn't need to hear it. He already knew he was a jealous brat.

"Ciara would never cheat on you with anyone. She's crazy about you! And do you honestly think I'd do that to you?"

Liam sighed. "She's angry with me."

"She has every right to be angry. You barely see one another. And when you do, this happens. So go apologise."

"As in actually now?"

"You should have apologised yesterday!"

"Fine, fine." He sighed, shaking his head. "I'm an idiot."

Henry's mouth twisted into a teasing grin, one Liam was unfortunately familiar with. "I know."

Perhaps it was just Liam's imagination running wild again. Ciara and Henry had been best friends, never more than that.

But wouldn't Henry have told him if it wasn't that big of a deal? If they were still friends? The thought bugged him throughout the dinner.

3

"**N**ot that bad, was it?" Henry asked, leaning back on the sofa.

Henry and Ciara were at his flat, sitting in the living room. It was enormous—especially for one person—with two bedrooms and a living room big enough for a small party.

Ciara turned to smile at Henry. "It was actually nice to see everyone."

"Even Liam?" The thought slipped off his tongue. It had been the first time Ciara and Liam had seen each other since their break-up years ago.

Ciara nodded, unbothered by the question, and smiled at Henry. "Yes, even him."

Henry smiled back at her. "The lack of awkwardness positively surprised me."

Ciara rolled her eyes. "We're both adults. There's nothing to be uncomfortable about."

Henry raised an eyebrow at her as if to say it wasn't that

simple. "Adults who haven't seen each other in years. You were still dating the last time you saw one another."

It was true. Ciara hadn't even seen Liam when she had ended things. She had broken up on the phone.

They had been in a long-distance relationship. She could have waited for his next visit instead of calling him, but she hadn't.

Liam had been living in Peru for his job back then. They had become a couple on the day he had moved due to both of them lacking the courage to say anything until then. They had grown close during his last year at school, and he had moved to Peru right after his graduation—the same day they had finally admitted their feelings for one another.

"Well, clearly Liam has grown a lot, too," Ciara said.

"You mean the stubble?" Henry laughed.

Ciara shrugged, picturing her ex-boyfriend in her mind. His hair had always been longish, but it had grown over the past few years. The stubble was new, and it made him look a little older—more like a man, less like a boy. He was different, but still Liam.

"He was surprised to see you." Henry eyed Ciara to see her reaction.

"Wouldn't you be if you were in his shoes?"

Henry was quiet, weighing on the question. "Guess I would be."

"So, what is Iris like?"

"Are you asking because you're jealous or be—"

"Henry!" Ciara scolded. "I'm not jealous."

Henry raised his hands in surrender, smiling sheepishly. "I know, I know. You were the one to break up with him."

Ciara brushed off the comment. "Anyway, back to Iris. Is she the girl he worked with in Peru?"

Henry turned to Ciara, brows furrowing and forehead wrinkling. "She is." He glanced away from Ciara before his gaze settled back on her, the frown remaining on his face. "How did you know that?"

"I faintly remember hearing about her," Ciara lied.

No one had ever mentioned Iris. She had accidentally seen a letter from Liam to Henry back in school. Back then she and Liam had still been together.

Based on the letter, he had never cheated, but his interest in Iris had been obvious. The long-distance relationship had been tough, and Ciara had been holding him back. It had been better to end it. For both of them.

It had been the right call. He had found happiness.

"Iris is a healer. She worked as a medic on the field in Peru," Henry told.

"So she must be caring."

"I guess so." Henry shrugged. "Mum likes her, I guess. They work at the same hospital these days."

Ciara smiled. "Well, if your mother likes her, she has to be a good person."

"I suppose she is."

"You're not sure?"

Henry bit the inside of his cheek. "I don't know her that well. She works a lot of odd hours, so she's rarely at family dinners and gatherings."

"She's a healer. That's why," Ciara pointed out.

"I know, but I wish she was more present. I'd like to know more about the person my brother is planning to marry."

Ciara patted Henry's shoulder and smiled at him. "Then you have to make it happen."

Henry turned to face her. "What do you mean?"

"Plan something and invite both of them. It's not that hard, and I'm sure she'd appreciate it, too."

"Since when have you been a specialist in relationships?"

Ciara rolled her eyes. "It's just common sense."

"Right."

It had only been a few days since Henry had found Ciara in Seattle. He was excited to have Ciara back in his life.

At first their conversations had been tense and even awkward here and there, but things were returning to normal gradually. As if nothing had ever changed.

Except a lot had.

"So, how is England these days? Any news I should know about?" Ciara asked.

They had been talking about their past—their school years. But there was a lot they still had to talk about. Ciara had done everything to avoid talking about the elephant in the room—her sudden move to America and the three years she had stayed there.

Henry thought for a moment. "Nothing special comes to mind."

"Do you still hang out with people from school?"

"Sometimes."

"But not often?"

Henry smiled. "I'm sort of like you. I bury myself in work."

"If your job was anything other than what it is, I wouldn't believe you," Ciara said. "But considering that you work with magical creatures, that's easy to believe. You're a little predictable."

Henry chuckled. "Only because you know me so well."

He had always loved magical creatures. Be it adult or baby creature. Unicorn or forest fairy. Except both of those creatures were rare—nearly extinct.

Ciara eyed Henry, tilting her head to the side. "Do I still know you?" Neither of them was sure who the question was more for, Henry or herself.

"We have time to figure that out. Right?"

Ciara nodded. "We do."

His eyes turned solemn. "One thing's for sure, though. I haven't been through what you have."

Ciara went rigid, muscles freezing and her eyes stopping to stare at her hands. "We should talk about that another time."

"Promise?"

"I'll talk to you when I'm ready." She looked back up,

meeting his gaze. "I just...a lot has happened."

Henry nodded. "I get it. I don't want to pressure you. But I'm here for you as your best friend."

Best friend.

"I'm sorry for not being around as one for you." Ciara held his gaze, eyes full of hurt. "You've always been a great friend for me. Same can't be said about me."

Henry sat down beside Ciara. "Come on, spit it out. I can tell something's wrong."

"It's nothing," the brunette mumbled, hugging her knees.

"It's not 'nothing' if it makes you this sad."

"It's just stupid."

"I can be the judge of that. If you just tell me what's wrong, that is."

"You can't tell anyone." She turned to face Henry with a dead serious expression. "Okay?"

"I'll lock my mouth and throw the key to the bottom of the ocean. Now, will you tell me?"

Ciara smiled. But it was gone the moment she turned to look into distance. "I think I like Liam."

"You're friends. Isn't that ex..." His eyes widened. "Oh."

"Yeah, not just as a friend." Ciara sighed and buried her face in her hands.

"You have a crush on him?"

"Yes."

"And why does that make you upset?" Henry frowned, looking at the girl whose face was still buried in her hands.

"He's going to the ball with Mia."

"He asked Mia?" The disbelief shone through his voice.

"Yes."

"But Mia knows that—"

"She doesn't." Ciara's voice broke as she roughly wiped her eyes. "She's obsessed with him. S-she has a huge crush on him. She used to daydream about him and talk about him. Except now she doesn't

do that anymore."

Henry's mouth hung open. *"D-does she even know Liam?"*

Ciara rolled her eyes. But at last she turned to look at her best friend. *"Everyone knows Liam."*

"Does she actually know *him, though?"*

"I think they're dating now." Ciara wiped her tears away again. She hated crying in front of people—even if it was just Henry.

"What makes you say that?"

"Why would she no longer daydream about him otherwise? They're dating, and that's why!"

"Have you asked either of them if they're dating?"

"I don't want to talk to them."

"But—"

"Can we talk about something else?" It was time for her to stop crying over a guy. Even talking to Henry wasn't helping.

"Well, who are you going to the ball with?" Henry asked.

"I doubt I'm going."

"What?" Henry's eyes widened. *"Of course you are!"*

"I don't have a date."

"There are plenty of people going alone."

"Well, I don't want to, and you can't make me."

Luckily Henry had a solution. *"I'll take you to the ball as my date!"*

Ciara tilted her head to the side. *"You don't have a date?"*

"I was planning to go without one, but clearly I need a date. And there's no one else I'd rather go with." He grinned. *"So—"*

"I don't believe the last part."

"I want to go with you now."

"Who did you want to go with at first?"

"Doesn't matter. I promise we'll have fun. We always do, don't we?" Hope gleamed in his eyes.

Sighing, she admitted, *"We do."*

"So will you be my date?"

Ciara tried to hide her smile, but it didn't work. *"Yes."*

Henry grinned. *"Great!"*

"Thank you."

25

"I didn't have a date either."
"No, thank you for making me feel better."
"What are best friends for?"
"For taking their upset best friends to the ball?"
Henry rolled his eyes. "That's not what I meant. Besides, it'll be fun."
"You're right. It should be fun."
"But, fair warning: I'm not the greatest of dancers."
Ciara laughed out loud. "I think you've stepped on my toes so many times at practice that a few more will be nothing."

"Look, Ciara, I—"

A startling crash in Henry's bedroom ruined the moment. He jumped up from his seat, his eyes wide.

"What was that?" Ciara asked, but Henry was already in his room.

She ran after him. The air was thick with smoke, blocking her sight, and a fiery scent filled the room.

"Is something burning?" Ciara shrieked.

"Nope, nothing! Not anymore."

Ciara got rid of the smoke with a snap of her fingers. Magic was great like that.

As the air cleared, Ciara spotted a scaly red creature on Henry's bed. "When did you get a dragon?"

Henry smiled sheepishly, patting the small animal. "This morning. A friend brought it back. It was over at her place while I was in America."

"Is it yours?"

The dragon's red scales had bronze freckles on them, and its eyes were a shade of gold. It was beautiful.

"I'm taking care of him, so I took him home with me for my holiday. I won't be able to keep him here when he grows, though."

Ciara's eyebrows rose. "How quickly does he grow?"

Henry chuckled. "Don't worry, he'll fit through the door

when he leaves."

Ciara's eyes widened, making Henry laugh harder. "He'll be the size of a human?"

"No, smaller. Much smaller. But he *will* fit through the door."

"Good."

Henry stopped patting the baby dragon and turned to face Ciara, crossing his arms. "I'm a little insulted by your lack of creature knowledge."

Ciara shrugged. "Not my field of expertise."

"And what is?"

"Deadly curses and poisons?"

"I promise that by the time you return to America, you'll know a lot more about dragons and creatures."

The small beast grew annoyed at the lack of attention it was getting. It spit fire again, and the bed caught on fire.

"Oh, God! Roan!"

4

“Today we're having lunch with some friends,” Henry declared first thing that morning, walking out of his room.

“Do I know them?” Ciara asked, turning to face Henry, whom the baby dragon was following around.

Henry grinned. “Yes.”

The red dragon flew onto the sofa, taking a seat next to Ciara. She had a newspaper in her hands and had been reading it until Henry had interrupted her.

“So, who are they?”

Henry continued to grin. “You'll see.”

“But I want to know.”

“You'll see in fifteen minutes.”

“Fifteen minutes?” Ciara's eyes widened. “We're going to be late if—”

“It's the restaurant across the street. We'll be on time,” Henry reassured her.

“What about the dragon?”

Ciara turned to look at the red creature. As if on cue, it spit out fire. It didn't spit it at Ciara, but her newspaper lit up in flames and burned to ashes in her hands.

She gritted her teeth. "If he wasn't this cute..."

"But he is."

"He's lucky he is." She snapped her fingers, making the ash vanish from her clothes.

Henry gasped, and Ciara spun around to look at him. "I half-forgot about your wandless magic," he explained, grimacing.

Ciara rubbed her finger tips together, creating sparks. "Well, I've still got the gift. And before you ask, I still don't know how or why."

Henry nodded.

The dragon flew up, made a flip in the air and sat back down. Looking utterly innocent, it stared at Ciara with its big golden eyes.

"Can we even leave him alone in here?"

Henry nodded. "Yes. I have a sprinkler spell on. It should last long enough."

"If he burns anything I own—"

"He won't."

"He'd better not."

"Anyway, do you want us to go already or—"

"Yes, let's go!" Ciara stood up and grabbed her handbag. She could have just snapped her fingers and made it fly to her, but that would have been lazy.

"Are you more excited or nervous? I honestly can't tell right now."

"Both." She walked past Henry and opened the flat door. "You coming?" She turned to look at him, waiting in the doorway.

"Yup!"

They walked to the restaurant in just a couple of minutes, so they were early. It was a beautiful summer day in London, so they waited outside.

"Why can't you tell me who we're meeting here?" Ciara asked. There had been hundreds of people at school with them. She was dying to know who they were meeting.

"Because I—"

"Oh, my Merlin!" The familiar voice alerted Ciara and Henry. They spun around to see a trio of witches.

Mia, Evie, and Jenna—Ciara's friends from school.

"Ciara!" Jenna ran to hug Ciara with her blonde hair bouncing in the air and her glasses nearly falling off.

"Jenna!" Ciara wrapped her arms around her friend, happy to see her.

It took a moment for Jenna to let go. Stepping back, she fixed her glasses.

"It's been so long!" Evie smiled and hugged Ciara.

Ciara hugged her back. "Too long."

"Way too long!" Mia corrected, pushing past Evie to hug Ciara.

Ciara smiled. "Agreed."

Evie grinned at Ciara, clapping her hands in excitement. "You have so much to tell us!"

"Shall we go inside and get some food first?" Henry asked, gesturing to the restaurant's door.

Jenna smiled at him and nodded. "Yes."

The look they exchanged, still smiling to one another, was blatantly obvious. But Ciara kept her mouth shut and tried to control her smile.

Ciara hadn't seen her friends in so long.

They hadn't changed much, but there were a few things Ciara noticed. Jenna had let her hair grow. Mia had learned to embrace her curves, judging by the tight tank top she was wearing. She had also got a tan, probably from a holiday. The summer had enhanced Evie's freckles, matching her auburn curls, which she had cut shorter.

"So, how long did you stay in Seattle?" Mia asked Ciara.

"Five months, give or take."

"Let me tell you, she knows nothing about interior design," Henry said.

Ciara grimaced. "Oh, don't even start."

"What was the flat like, then?" Jenna asked, glancing between Ciara and Henry.

"She had a mattress and a desk. That was it," Henry said.

"I wasn't planning on staying in that flat for long," Ciara said, defending herself.

Jenna smiled. "Where did you live before Seattle?"

"Vancouver."

"Tell me your flat back there looked nicer," Henry pleaded.

Ciara smiled shakily, clutching her glass of water. "I had a house, and it looked a lot nicer."

"So, why Seattle?" Evie asked, leaning in closer over the table.

"I had more work in the States, but I wanted to stay close to Vancouver. Seattle seemed like the best option." Her mouth felt dry, so she jugged down a third of the water, trying to do it subtly.

Evie nodded. "What do you do for work?"

"I'm a hit witch. Mostly, anyway."

Mia slammed her hands on the table. "Whoa! What?"

Ciara smiled at Mia's reaction. "Is it that much of a shocker?"

"I always thought you'd become a professional dueller. Even a curse breaker, maybe, with your talent." When she spoke of Ciara's talent, she meant Ciara's wandless magic. It was a rare gift even amongst the witches and wizards—who only formed about one tenth of the world's population. "But I never realised a hit witch was an option," Mia said, a frown crossing her face.

"I wanted to be a curse breaker," Ciara acknowledged. "But becoming a hit witch seemed better when the time came."

"Considering how well you did in that tournament, I'm not surprised they accepted you as a hit witch," Jenna said, talking about a tournament Ciara had participated in back in school.

"I guess that helped." Ciara shrugged. "But enough about me. What are you doing these days?"

"I'm a journalist." Mia smiled proudly and leaned back in her chair.

Ciara smiled at her. "Really?"

"You can't say you're surprised."

"True." Ciara smiled and nodded. Mia had what it took to be a journalist. She was confident, relentless, and persuasive.

"I have a desk job at the Magical Bank of England," Evie said.

"Do you like it there?" Ciara asked.

"Surprisingly, yes." Evie chuckled, shaking her head a little. "It's clearly nowhere near as cool as your job. But I like it. Never thought I'd like maths so much."

"I could never do what you're doing. So it's just as important." Ciara was used to people telling her how her job was more this or more that. In her eyes, it was just another job—but with a more dangerous job description.

Evie shrugged. "Maybe."

Ciara smiled. "And Jenna?"

"I'm a research assistant."

"What kind of research?"

A grin made its way onto Jenna's face as she stole a glance at Henry. "Magical creatures."

Ciara looked at the two of them in turns. "You two are working together, aren't you?"

Henry nodded. "Not all the time, but we've worked together."

Ciara could swear she saw his cheeks turn slightly pink. As she turned to face Jenna, she noticed her blushing, too.

"I feel sorry for you, Jenna," she joked, grinning at the two.

Jenna tried to bite back her smile and failed. "The benefit of working with Henry is that I get to be a dragon babysitter."

"You were the one taking care of the little beast while Henry was in America?"

Jenna nodded. "Yes."

Ciara furrowed her brows. "Did he behave?"

"He burned Ciara's newspaper before we left," Henry said, mostly to Jenna.

Jenna chuckled and turned to face Ciara, a few strands of her blonde hair falling in front of her eyes. "He behaved just fine, considering how young he is."

The look of adoration in Henry's eyes didn't go unnoticed by Ciara. He was smitten with Jenna—and her love for creatures.

"Anyway," Mia said, turning her attention to Ciara, "did you apply to become a hit witch in America?" She leaned in, waiting for the answer impatiently.

"Actually, it was an offer I got before graduation."

Henry looked up from his plate, frowning. "Why did I never hear of this job offer?"

Ciara looked down, sighing. She had never told Henry—her best friend at the time. "I wasn't planning to accept at first."

"You could have told me, though." Disappointment washed over Henry's face, his forehead wrinkling. "I mean, you left for America out of nowhere. If I had known about the job…"

"I'm sorry." Ciara looked up. "I should have said something. But I didn't accept the job offer until the very last minute." She had acted wrongly and was ashamed of it, but she couldn't change what had already been done.

She didn't regret leaving, either. But she should have handled it differently.

"What made you accept?" Jenna's voice toned down, turning calm and quiet. She was trying to lessen the tension.

Ciara tore her gaze away from Henry who was still staring

at her. "The more I thought about it, the more it felt like an opportunity I couldn't miss."

Jenna smiled, but it wasn't as genuine as the previous ones. She kept glancing Henry's way, worry shining in her gaze. "I bet it did. Few get such a position at that age."

"And are you on your summer holiday now?" Evie asked Ciara, leaning her chin on her palm.

Henry snorted, placing his glass down on the table. "Ciara doesn't know what a holiday is."

Ciara nodded, looking at Evie. "I'm suspended for now."

"Suspended?"

"Yes."

"She nearly got herself killed," Henry said.

"What?" Mia shrieked.

"Multiple times," Henry added.

Ciara narrowed her eyes at Henry before turning to face the three others. "It's part of the job, nothing unusual."

Jenna's eyebrows squished together. "Why did you get suspended, then?"

"We finished an undercover mission. They needed me until it was over." Ciara paused, taking a deep breath. "Otherwise I would have been suspended earlier. My, uh..." Ciara shifted in her seat, trying to force the words out. But it was as if they got stuck. She refused to meet her friends' gazes and prayed they didn't notice how much she struggled. "My partner was killed in January, so they think I need time off."

"Like a police partner? Like in the movies?" Mia asked.

Ciara nodded. "Theo and I worked together on every case and mission until..." Cold filled her veins, and she shuddered at the memory. "Until his death."

Mia gasped. "I'm so sorry."

Jenna's mouth had fallen open, and her eyes were fixed on Ciara. "Theo as in...Theo Boucher?" Her voice was quiet, nearly hesitant.

Ciara eyes snapped up, meeting Jenna's gaze. "You

remember him?"

Jenna nodded. "Yes. He was always swooning over you."

A lump formed in Ciara's throat, and her hand flew up to her mouth. *Don't cry. Not here, not now.* Her eyes turned glossy, and she fought back the tears. She had to clench her other hand into a fist. Trying to focus on that, she breathed in and out.

Calm down.

Jenna lowered her voice even more, and her gaze softened. Her eyes turned watery from merely seeing Ciara's grief. "You weren't just working together, were you?"

Ciara blinked her eyes, making sure the tears stayed away. "We lived together." Her voice came out hoarse and low—not strong like she had intended.

Henry snapped his head to the side, his eyes growing wide. Ciara hadn't said anything to him. Not a word.

"He was your boyfriend," he breathed out. "When you said you two had a special connection, I thought..." His face twisted into a mix of shock and disbelief.

Ciara swallowed, her eyes fixed on the table. She couldn't look up to see her friends' pitiful eyes. "Fiancé, but yes."

The others fell silent. They stared at Ciara, either gaping or frowning.

"Why didn't you tell me when you told me about the whole...thing?" Henry asked.

Ciara's arms wrapped around herself. "I hate talking about it."

"We can discuss it another time with fewer people around," Jenna said, reaching out a hand to grab Ciara's hand, which rested on the table. "Let's talk about something else, huh?"

Ciara smiled at Jenna in appreciation. Then she turned to face the three girls, one by one. "How about each of you? Anyone special?"

Mia sighed. "Very single and very busy."

Everyone turned to look at Evie, waiting for her answer.

Her cheeks turned a soft shade of pink. "There's actually someone at work, but we're not really dating. At least, not yet."

Ciara grinned. "So, flirting phase or—"

"They're past the flirting phase!" Mia giggled. "They just need to make it official. And Evie should introduce us to Lola."

"She's shy," Evie insisted, but it was an obvious excuse.

"Well, we want to meet her. Besides, if you introduce us to her sooner rather than later, she might even have time to meet Ciara." Jenna grinned, gesturing to Ciara.

"How long are you in England for?" Evie asked Ciara.

"I don't know yet." She pushed a few strands of her hair behind her ear. "I'm suspended for at least six months, I guess, unless I figure out a way to convince my superiors otherwise."

"She promised to stay for a week. It's nearing its end, though," Henry said.

Ciara nodded. "I haven't thought about buying a plane ticket yet, so I suppose I'll stay until Henry gets sick of me."

Mia snorted. "Like he'd get sick of you."

"I can be rather annoying as a flatmate—don't you remember?"

Mia chuckled. "I think you were a great flatmate."

"I'm flattered."

"As you should be," Mia said light-heartedly.

Ciara smiled. "Anyway, Jenna, you didn't tell us anything about your love life."

Jenna shrugged. She tried to keep her focus on Ciara, but she kept leaning slightly closer to Henry. "There's nothing to tell, really."

"Nothing?" Ciara wasn't buying it.

"There's been a few guys around since you left, but none worth my time."

"I like the attitude."

Jenna chuckled. "Thanks."

Henry cleared his throat. "Since it sounds like you're dying for some girl talk, I'm gonna stop by at the men's room." He set his napkin down and stood up.

Ciara shot a grin at him. "Don't hurry back."

"Sure," Henry said and left the girls to talk alone.

Ciara glanced at Henry walking away, worried he was angry. But she pushed the feeling aside, returning her focus to Jenna. A smug smile formed on her face. "So, you like Henry."

Jenna's cheeks turned a fiery shade of red. "Is it that obvious?"

Ciara chuckled. "To me? Yes. To him? No."

It was nice to see her school friends. A lot had happened since graduation. They all had gone their own ways, and it was nice to catch up.

Once Henry returned to the table, the group finished eating, paid and left the restaurant, going their separate ways. Ciara and Henry headed back to his flat.

Nothing had burned, and the baby dragon hadn't set off the sprinkler spell. Ciara was impressed how well the little creature had behaved.

She sat down on the living room sofa, grinning a little. "That was fun." She looked at Henry who was petting the baby dragon near the flat door. "Thank you for the surprise."

Henry smiled. "I thought you'd like to see them."

"It was great."

"And now, can we talk about...well, everything?" Henry asked. He didn't have work, and it was barely afternoon. They had time to finally talk about all the things they had been avoiding since Ciara's return.

She exhaled shakily. "O-okay."

Henry shook his head as if trying to clear his mind. "I just...I'm confused. Why didn't you tell me Theo was more than just a colleague and a friend?"

37

"I thought maybe you realised. And if you didn't...well, I thought it didn't matter. It doesn't really change anything anymore. He's..." The words got stuck in her throat, so instead of continuing she looked down at her hands.

"You lived with him. You were *with* him. His death had more impact on you than a friend's death would have. So yes, it matters. You must be devastated." Henry's voice cracked. When Ciara looked up, she spotted his watery eyes.

She cleared her throat. "It's been five months."

"And how long did you live with him?"

Ciara sighed, sinking into the sofa. "One and a half years."

"See? That's huge!" Henry shook his head. He still couldn't believe Ciara hadn't told him. "How long were you dating?"

"Almost two years."

"That's a long time. Hell, even you and Liam weren't together for that long!"

"I know it is, but that doesn't mean I want to talk about it."

"Why?"

"I just don't." Ciara turned to look straight at Henry. "So, please, don't make me."

Henry had never seen that look in her eyes. It was utterly unfamiliar—unlike her. So vulnerable.

"I'm sorry," Henry apologised. "But you can talk to me about anything. I'm...I'm supposed to be your best friend."

"You are."

"Am I?"

"If you ask me, yes. But I can't speak for you. We haven't talked much the past few years, and that's on me, but not just anyone could have made me come back to England."

Henry nodded, letting her words sink in.

Ciara sighed, leaning her head against the back of the sofa. "I know I can talk to you. Trust me, I do. I just don't want to talk about it. Not with anyone."

"I know." He sighed. "I know."

The baby dragon observed the two people sitting on the sofa and made its way over. Jumping and flapping its wings, it moved to sit between Ciara and Henry.

Silence filled the room, but the little creature was oddly comforting. Even Ciara had forgotten all about her burnt newspaper from earlier.

5

"You don't have to come babysit them unless you want to," Henry said.

"I want to," Ciara insisted. "I really do." She grinned at Henry. "It'll be fun."

Henry rolled his eyes. "They're no longer children."

Ciara grabbed her bag from the sofa. "If I can handle the world's most dangerous criminals, I can handle a few teenagers, too."

Henry shrugged, grabbing his bag from the floor. "If you say so."

The baby dragon, Roan, was with Jenna again. Jenna had agreed to take care of it, because Mrs Rossler refused to let Henry take the dragon with him to the Rosslers' house.

To her surprise, Ciara already missed that little beast.

Henry's parents were going away for a spa weekend. They both had a summer holiday—and for once, at the same time.

Henry and Ciara had agreed to stay with his younger siblings at the house from Friday to Sunday. They wouldn't babysit anyone, considering all his siblings were teens nearing adulthood. They were just going there to ensure no one threw a party or burned the place down. Henry had also promised to cook for his siblings, so they wouldn't have to live on microwave food.

Ciara couldn't cook. When she had lived alone, all she had eaten was salad and takeaway food. She knew how to make a salad and even she couldn't burn a mix of lettuce and vegetables.

Ciara could have used her magic to make food, but it wasn't that simple. Making food taste like something with magic was hard. Usually the food turned out disgusting, because the texture and the taste were off. No one wanted to eat apples that tasted like fish.

Both Ciara and Henry were ready to go. Ciara moved her hand across the air, sparking her magic, and teleported herself and Henry to the Rosslers' home. The house appeared in front of them as Henry's flat faded away. Teleporting inside someone's home was impossible, unless you teleported out of there, which was why they had to walk in. They were fifteen minutes early, but it was better than being late.

"It's great to see you're still in England," Mr Rossler said to Ciara, heading for the door from having heard it open.

Ciara had already been in England for over a week.

"I might stay for a while." She owed that to Henry.

"Kids, remember to behave!" Mrs Rossler's voice rang out from the living room. Ciara, Henry, and Mr Rossler joined the others there.

Gabriel sighed, crossing his arms. "We're not babies anymore."

Mrs Rossler placed her hands on her hips. "That doesn't mean you always behave."

Poppy's focus shifted from her mother, and she grinned. "Ciara!"

Polly's face lit up, too. "You're still here!"

Ciara smiled and nodded. "Here I am."

The two younger girls had grown up with Ciara as their role model. Ciara had been like an older sister to them.

Mrs Rossler turned to face the freshly arrived pair. "Ciara, Henry, how great to see you both." She smiled sweetly at them. "I hope these three won't be too much trouble for you."

"I'm sure we can handle them," Ciara assured with a smile on her face.

"We'll be in our best behaviour with Ciara here," Poppy said, grinning. "Who would want to piss off a hit witch?"

Polly nodded. "Not us!"

Mrs Rossler rolled her eyes and pulled Poppy into a hug. Then she hugged the two other teenagers. "I'll see you all on Sunday. I love you."

"See you, Mum!" the three teenagers said in unison, smiling at their parents. "And see you, Dad!"

"See you, kids," Mr Rossler said and hugged his three youngest children, enveloping them in a group hug. Before he left the room, he ruffled Gabriel's hair.

Gabriel instantly fixed the damage done.

Both Mr and Mrs Rossler headed to the front door, Ciara and Henry trailing behind. His parents had packed their bags, and they were waiting for them by the door.

"There should be enough of everything in the fridge. And I prepared Liam's old room for you, Ciara. I hope that's fine."

Ciara smiled. "Of course. Thank you."

"Oh, and Iris might stop by here after work. She forgot her jumper here yesterday. It's on the desk in my and Ray's room."

"We'll give it to her if she comes round," Henry affirmed.

"Good. Call us if something happens."

"We'll be fine," Henry assured her.

"They'll be just fine, Mary." Mr Rossler placed a hand on his wife's shoulder and gave it a squeeze.

"Alright then." Mrs Rossler sighed. "I'll see you on Sunday. Be safe and eat whatever you like."

Ciara smiled. "See you, Mrs and Mr Rossler."

Henry handed his parents their bags. "Bye, Mum and Dad."

"Bye, bye." Henry's parents left. They waved at Henry and Ciara from the outside until Henry closed the front door.

He turned to look at Ciara. "Mum worries way too much."

Ciara chuckled. "You and Liam caused a lot of trouble for her in your time, so I'd blame you two."

"We weren't that bad."

"Clearly you were."

Henry rolled his eyes and shook his head. "If you say so."

"What's for dinner?" Gabriel yelled from the living room.

Henry and Ciara headed back to the room, staying near the doorway.

"How about homemade pizza?" Henry suggested, already knowing his siblings' answer.

"Sounds good!" Poppy exclaimed.

Polly nodded. "Agreed!"

Gabriel gestured to his sisters. "What they just said."

Henry decided he should start making the pizza dough straight away. Ciara joined him in the kitchen to keep him company.

"Do you need help?" she asked while Henry was gathering everything he needed.

"I think you'd burn the dough," Henry joked, winking at Ciara.

"Rude!" Ciara chuckled. "But not wrong."

The two best friends chatted while Henry prepared the dough. They had been talking for a while when someone knocked at the front door.

By then, Henry was covered in flour.

"I'll open it," Ciara offered and stood from her seat.

"You sure?" Henry eyed Ciara warily, knowing who was calling round.

Ciara nodded. "Absolutely." She walked to the door and opened it, revealing a blonde woman. Ciara smiled at her. "You must be Iris."

The woman eyed Ciara up and down. "Are you Ciara?"

Ciara nodded and offered her hand for Iris to shake. "Yes, that's me."

Iris shook her hand.

"Come on in." Ciara held the door open for the petite blonde woman and closed it behind her.

"I don't know if Mary said anything—"

"About the jumper, right?"

Iris smiled with slight uneasiness. "Yes."

"She mentioned it. Let me go get it."

Iris nodded.

Ciara walked into Henry's parents' bedroom down the short hallway. The jumper was on top of the desk like Mary had said. Ciara grabbed it and returned to the front door where Iris was waiting.

"Here," Ciara said, handing the jumper over.

Iris smiled, her uneasiness gone. "Thank you."

"No problem." Ciara returned the smile. "Oh, and congratulations on your engagement. I'm sorry I couldn't make it to England when you were celebrating."

Iris's smile widened. "Oh, thank you. And don't worry, I completely understand."

Henry had got most of the flour off his clothes and hair, so he finally walked to the door. He greeted Iris, "Hi."

"Hi, Henry." Iris smiled.

"The others are clearly too busy watching a movie to come and say hi," Henry said apologetically, gesturing towards the living room. The movie's noise sounded all the way to the front door.

"It's fine. I just saw them yesterday."

"Have you had dinner yet?" Henry asked. "Or is Liam waiting for you at home, so you can have dinner together?"

"Actually, he's going out with the boys tonight to have

drinks and dinner," Iris said.

Henry glanced at Ciara and then turned his gaze back to Iris. "Do you want to stay for dinner?"

"He's making pizza, and if he's as good as he used to be, it'll taste great," Ciara said and smiled at Iris.

Iris bit her lip. "I wouldn't want to bother you."

"I offered, so it's not bothering," Henry said.

Iris chuckled. "Well, if you insist."

"I do."

"Alright then." Iris took off her coat and set her jumper aside. She joined Ciara and Henry in the kitchen, and she and Ciara sat at the table.

"So, Ciara, are you on a holiday?" Iris asked.

"Actually, I'm suspended. A little less than six months to go," Ciara said. "My colleague died, and my superiors don't think I'm in the state to be working right now."

"I'm so sorry for your loss."

"Thank you."

Henry turned to glance at Ciara, worry written all over his face. Theo hadn't been just a colleague.

But considering Ciara and Iris had just met, Iris didn't need to know that. Even Henry understood that. Ciara didn't have to open up about her life tragedies to a stranger. But he couldn't imagine what she was going through in her head.

"So, did you drive here or what?" Henry asked Iris. It was a wonderful chance to get to know his brother's fiancée a little better.

"I teleported."

Henry grinned. "Then I have an idea. I'll be right back." He left the kitchen, leaving the dough unfinished.

Ciara and Iris turned to look at one another.

"What is he doing?" Iris asked Ciara as if she might have known.

"No idea. But clearly, he has an idea."

Iris chuckled. "Clearly."

Henry returned soon, holding up a bottle. "I have red

wine." He kept his voice low enough, so the teens didn't hear him.

Iris grinned and shook her head a little. "Oh, Henry."

"You don't have work tomorrow, do you?" he asked.

"No."

"So, wine it is."

"Just a glass or two."

"Well, it's a never-ending wine bottle," Henry said, placing the bottle down on the table. "I'll have enough time to persuade."

Ciara's eyes widened, and she turned to look at the bottle. "You have endless amounts of red wine?"

Henry flashed a smile at her. "Of course."

Iris stayed after they had finished eating. She and Ciara continued to talk after dinner, drinking wine. Henry had joined his siblings in the living room and was watching a movie with them.

Ciara was surprised at how easy it was to talk with Iris, considering the woman was engaged to Ciara's ex-boyfriend.

"I'm so glad I got to meet you." Iris looked at Ciara, setting down her wineglass.

Ciara smiled once she had taken a sip of her wine. "I'm glad we got to meet, too."

Iris smiled. "You know, I've always been a little jealous of you." She had drunk enough wine to be tipsy. The alcohol had loosened her tongue.

Ciara looked at Iris, raising her eyebrows. "Of me?"

Iris nodded, fiddling with her fingers. "Yes, jealous of you. I mean, everyone in Liam's family adores you. Even years later, they talk about you."

"I was Henry's best friend first and foremost. I've known the family for a long time."

"Perhaps." Iris shrugged. "But it has bothered me. I didn't like the thought of meeting you until I finally met you today.

In fact, I thought I wouldn't like you."

Iris was revealing too much. They had talked for a while, and Ciara liked her, but they barely knew each other.

"I didn't want to like you at first," Iris admitted. "But now that we've spoken, even if it's just for a couple of hours, I can see why everyone likes you. I feel bad for thinking so ill of you."

"It's alright. It's, uh, a natural reaction," Ciara said, hoping not to sound as uncomfortable as she felt. "And trust me, when you're not around, the family speaks very fondly of you."

Iris smiled, beaming with joy. "Really?"

Ciara nodded. "Yes. So, trust me, there's nothing to be jealous about."

Iris tilted her head a little and eyed Ciara, squinting. "So you don't like Liam anymore?"

Ciara chuckled and shook her head. "I've talked to him once in, like, three years. Whatever feelings I had in the past are long gone."

Ciara barely knew Liam anymore. She wasn't sure if she had ever quite known him.

She wasn't sad about how things had ended with him. Good things had come out of their break-up. Ciara would have never been with Theo, and Liam had also found happiness, even if it had been a little too fast for Ciara's liking.

She smiled at Iris. "So, are you planning the wedding yet?"

Iris sighed, running her hands down her face. "I'd like to have a festive wedding around December, but Liam keeps saying it's too soon. So, for now, we don't have plans."

"Perhaps you should just tell him how much it means to you." Ciara shrugged and took a sip. "Even though I might not be the best advisor. I've never been in your position."

"Engaged?"

"I was engaged, actually, but we never got around to

making any plans." Ciara's voice shook, and her mouth dried. She took another sip of her wine and prayed Iris wouldn't linger on the topic.

Iris, however, frowned, keeping her gaze on Ciara. "What happened?"

"He died." Ciara was blunt, because she wanted to keep the topic short. Iris wasn't the person she would pour her heart out to.

"I'm so sorry. That must have been..." Iris's eyes widened. "I can't imagine."

Ciara forced a smile. "It's been a while."

Iris nodded. "So, what are you doing tomorrow?" she asked, switching the topic.

"I'm looking after Polly, Poppy, and Gabriel with Henry all weekend."

"Could you take a few hours off?" Iris asked. "It'd be fun to have lunch with you tomorrow." She grinned at Ciara.

"Well, I—"

As he had shown many times before, Henry had the perfect timing. He walked through the kitchen doorway, saying, "Of course she'll take a little time off."

Ciara turned to look at Henry. "You sure?"

"Of course."

Ciara turned to Iris and smiled. "I suppose we could have brunch tomorrow then."

"Wonderful!" Iris squealed. "There's a cute little restaurant near where Liam and I live. Could you come over to our place around eleven o'clock? We can walk from there."

Ciara nodded. "Of course. I just need the address."

6

Ciara woke up early the next morning. The original plan for the weekend had been to stay at the Rosslers' house, so she had only packed the necessary clothes. The rest of them were at Henry's flat.

She emptied her bag on the bed—Liam's old bed.

Staring at the pile of clothes, she kept thinking she had nothing to wear. Ciara went through the pile, and it took a while for her to find a decent pair of jeans. She threw them aside, deciding to wear them.

She only had three shirts to choose from, so she picked the cleanest one.

Looking at herself in the mirror on the wall, her gaze fell on the room around her rather than on her outfit. That room had a lot of memories.

"I like that shirt on you."

"Of course you do," Ciara said. *"It's a crop top."*

Liam laughed. "Fine. I admit I enjoy seeing your skin." He drew a heart shape onto Ciara's bare stomach with his finger. "But it just looks great on you."

Ciara smiled at her boyfriend. "Smooth."

Liam laughed.

She turned to her side to peck his lips. "I love you."

"And I love you."

Ciara noticed him gazing at her and eyed him suspiciously. "What are you thinking about?"

"How much I truly love you," he murmured. He was gazing into her eyes as if she was the most wondrous thing in the world. For him, in that moment, she was.

Ciara blushed, unable to contain her smile. "You're so cheesy."

Liam shrugged and pulled Ciara into a hug. "Cheesy or not, I'm happy to be with you."

Those memories seemed so distant Ciara could hardly believe they were real. Being back in England had brought back memories she had once buried. She didn't fancy digging them up.

Theo had been the one to help her move on. He had been her anchor. Without him, diving so deep into her old life felt suffocating.

It didn't bring back just the memories she had from England. Constant questions were continuously reminding her of Theo's death, and it was driving her mad. She had revenged his death, but it brought her no joy.

"So, when are you leaving?" Henry asked.

He and Ciara were sitting in the living room. The teens were sleeping in. After all, it was a Saturday and their summer holiday.

Ciara checked the time. "In ten minutes."

"Isn't that five minutes early?"

"Rather early than late."

Henry grinned. "For me, it's better late than never."

"Timing is crucial with my job, so I'd rather be early no matter the occasion."

"It's still odd to think you're a hit witch. I mean, there's nothing surprising about it. You're a great dueller and a great spellcaster. I just don't like the thought of you doing...what you do for a living."

Ciara huffed. "I can handle myself."

"That doesn't mean there aren't any risks."

"Trust me, I know that."

"I know you do." He sighed. "Maybe you could have an entire year off?"

She couldn't. She would fight whoever tried to keep her from work for any longer than necessary. Even if she had already dealt with the monsters who had taken Theo away from her, there were more of people like them out there. People who needed to be put behind bars as soon as possible. She'd even prefer them dead rather than out in the world, roaming free.

"It's cute when you worry. But trust me. I'm more than capable of dealing with my job and whatever comes with it."

"I can still worry." Henry crossed his arms across his chest, leaning back into the sofa. "In fact, I *will* worry."

"Try to worry less for your own sake. I won't be working anytime soon."

"Thank God for that!"

Ciara smiled. It was refreshening to be around people who genuinely cared about her.

She had been close with many of her colleagues, but they all knew the risks from the beginning—even when they first got to meet each other. They were ready to lose one another from the first meeting, so it was different.

Ciara also hadn't seen Theo's family much after his death. His mother called Ciara sometimes, but that was about it. She hadn't stayed in contact with her and Theo's mutual friends outside work. It was wrong for everyone, including herself, but seeing them had reminded her of him. It had been too much.

At five minutes to eleven, Ciara knocked at the flat door. She spotted the surnames on the door, written in golden letters.

Lamont and Rossler.

Ciara didn't have to wait for long until someone opened the door. Someone who wasn't Iris.

Liam.

Seeing his stubble again was odd. Whenever she pictured him in her mind, she thought of the Liam she had dated. But he wasn't that person anymore—not on the outside, and likely not on the inside either.

"Hi," Ciara greeted him with a smile. "Is Iris ready?"

Liam blinked twice, as if surprised to see Ciara at his door. "She should be ready in a moment. You can come in and wait."

"Thanks," Ciara said, and Liam let her in.

Liam shoved his hands in his jeans pockets. "So, uh, how's England for you?"

He hadn't been alone—yet alone spoken—with Ciara since their break-up. It had been over three years, but that didn't make it any less awkward.

"It's nice to be back," Ciara said. "The weather isn't that different from Seattle."

In her mind, she dragged her hands down her face. She couldn't believe she was talking about the weather.

Liam didn't seem to mind. Or at least he was smiling. "It's a surprisingly warm summer."

Ciara nodded. "That's true."

"I'm so sorry for being late!" Iris's arrival startled Ciara and Liam. They both snapped their heads to the side to look at her.

"You're not late at all." Ciara flashed a smile. "I'm just a bit early."

Iris smiled back. "Oh, good." She turned to her fiancé and kissed his cheek. "I'll be back in a few hours."

Ciara felt as though she shouldn't have been looking.

"Take your time." Liam smiled at Iris, gazing into her eyes like a lovesick puppy.

It was *so* intimate. It was as if Ciara was intruding on something sacred—as if she shouldn't have been there.

She couldn't help but smile, though. She could *see* the love. Iris's eyes had that lovedrunk glow in them, and Liam's gaze just softened—nearly melted—when he looked at Iris.

She had once had that with Theo, too.

"I swear women have to wait for men more than vice versa!" Ciara called, faking the annoyance in her voice.

"I'm coming!" Theo ran to the front door with a duffel bag hanging on his shoulder.

"About time."

His expression turned into a grin, matching hers. "You know this takes time," he said, gesturing to his body.

Ciara didn't bother to hide how she checked out her boyfriend's bare muscled arms. "I know, I know."

Theo chuckled. "If you keep devouring me with your eyes like that, we'll never get to work."

Ciara shrugged. She tiptoed and pressed her lips on Theo's. Pulling back, she grinned again. "Let's go."

"We could be five minutes late. They wouldn't—"

"Theo." She reached for the doorknob. "Let's go."

"Fine. But when we get back from this mission..."

"I know."

Ciara looked away, the memories flashing through her mind were like a kick to her stomach. She didn't have that anymore. Theo was gone.

Iris grinned at Liam. "Alright. We'll be going now." She grabbed Ciara by the arm. "Bye!"

"Bye," Ciara said hurriedly, Iris pulling her out of the flat.

"Bye," Liam managed to say just in time before Iris shut the door.

"It's so wonderful you agreed to come with me!" Iris said when the two women walked down the stairs.

Ciara smiled. "Of course."

"It's also nice to see that you and Liam can be friends. Of course, I knew he no longer had romantic feelings for you. But what I mean is, I would hate to see you two hold a grudge or something. You know, arguing and fighting because of your history."

Ciara couldn't believe Iris was making sure she knew Liam was Iris's. Of course she knew. They were engaged!

But Ciara just nodded, choosing her next words carefully. "I would hate that, too. But we were friends before we dated. It would be weird to be fighting over something that doesn't matter."

Iris had to realise Ciara had no interest in Liam anymore.

But Iris kept going. "Didn't he have a crush on you for years before you two dated?"

Ciara shook her head and chuckled. "Trust me, he didn't. I was dating another guy before him, and he had girlfriends before me."

Iris nodded.

The restaurant was nice. Iris hadn't been wrong about that. They got a table the moment they arrived, and they didn't have to wait more than five minutes for their lunch.

It was a small, cosy restaurant. It wasn't noisy, but the atmosphere wasn't too intimate either. People were walking in and out, and the restaurant filled with mixed scents of spices from the kitchen. Black pepper and garlic were the dominant ones.

"Liam and I come here all the time," Iris said, poking at the food on her plate.

"I can see why. This place is nice."

"It is," Iris agreed and took a sip of her water. "Liam took me here for dinner right before he proposed."

Ciara smiled, turning her full attention on Iris. "How did he propose?"

Iris grinned, her white teeth showing. "You know that gigantic tree near the Rosslers' house?"

Of course Ciara knew it, having spent so much time at the Rosslers' place. So she nodded.

"We went for an evening walk, and that's where he proposed," Iris said.

"Did he go down on one knee and everything?"

A smile spread onto Iris's face, and she nodded eagerly. "He did. It was super cute. And so charming! But that's just how he is."

It turned out all Iris wanted to talk about was Liam—or their engagement. Ciara wished she could have just told Iris there was nothing to worry about, but it would have been inappropriate.

Ciara had nothing against Iris. In fact, she felt bad for her ill thoughts about her. So far, she had been nothing but nice—except a little annoying.

The topic didn't change even when Ciara tried to switch it. She wasn't interested in hearing about Liam and how charming he was.

He could be charming, but she didn't need to be told that.

"Oh! He just texted me!" Iris said, finishing talking about Liam's job.

"Oh." At that point Ciara didn't know what else to say.

Iris stared at her phone screen, her expression turning serious. "We need to go to the Rosslers'." Her voice was grim—as if something bad had happened.

"Is something wrong?"

"Not the way you think."

Ciara didn't know what that meant, but she figured she would find out. They paid for their lunch and left the restaurant.

Iris and Ciara let themselves in once they appeared outside the Rosslers' house. The voices were coming from the living room, and Iris rushed there with Ciara trailing behind her.

Mary and Raymond—Mrs and Mr Rossler—were home. Liam was there, too. The teens—Gabriel, Polly, and Poppy—weren't in the living room, but Henry was.

Iris ran to Liam's arms, and the couple embraced one another.

Everyone wore grim looks on their faces. Mrs Rossler's eyes were red and puffy, and her nose was runny. She held back her tears, sitting on the sofa, while her husband held her shaking hand. Mr Rossler's eyes were glossy, but he fought back the tears.

Ciara looked around, furrowing her eyebrows. She took in the scene, wondering what had happened.

"What's going on?" she asked, keeping her voice down.

Henry walked over to her. "Someone killed Mum and

Dad's friend." He kept his voice low, not wanting his parents to hear.

Ciara blinked, turning to look at Henry's parents. She didn't have time to say any comforting words, because knocking interrupted her thoughts.

"Henry, will you open the door for him?" Mr Rossler asked. He forced his voice to stay steady, but he was struggling to keep the tears away.

Henry nodded and left the living room to open the door.

Grief filled the room, replacing the air, and it was all too familiar for Ciara.

She remembered what it had been like at her home in Vancouver.

It was still fresh in her mind.

Ciara came back to her senses when Henry returned to the living room with an older man. She hadn't heard the front door open, she had been so deep in her thoughts.

Ciara had to take a second look at the man. No one else had eyes so icy blue, nor hair so black. And the wretched leather jacket was a sure sign. He *always* wore that jacket.

"Doherty?" Ciara gasped.

"I can't believe my eyes." Gregory Doherty smiled, but it didn't quite reach his eyes. His eyes were clouded with worry or grief; perhaps both.

"I didn't think I'd find you in England, Jareau."

Neither did I, Ciara thought, smiling at Doherty.

"Unless it's Boucher these days."

Ciara's smile dropped, an invisible force tightening around her throat. "Jareau. And, well, times change."

Doherty nodded. "Glad to have you here."

Mr Rossler looked at Ciara and Gregory. "You know one another?"

"Doherty was my mentor when I started," Ciara said, turning to Mr Rossler.

"She's my all-time best trainee," Doherty said proudly.

The grief on Mr Rossler's face turned into surprise for a

moment. "Impressive."

"Gregory." Mrs Rossler's voice was weak. She was still fighting the tears, forcing them to stay away. Her hands were shaking, and her lower lip was trembling. "Did Ellen make it?"

Doherty nodded. "She's protected."

"Is Ian her protector?" Mr Rossler asked.

Doherty nodded again. "He's the best I know, and trustworthy. I think we can all agree he's the best for the position."

Mr Rossler nodded. "He is."

"Ian Connell?" Ciara asked.

"Yes." Doherty turned to face Ciara. "Connell."

"How do you know everyone?" Henry asked Ciara, turning his head to the side.

"From work, of course."

Henry's eyes widened. "Y-you've worked with Ian Connell?"

Ciara nodded. "And?"

"And?" Henry shrieked. "He protects people from the worst of the worst."

"I'm aware."

"Looks like your boyfriend didn't want to learn the nature of your work," Doherty said amused. He crossed his arms across his chest, his gaze sliding from Henry to Ciara.

"Oh, we're not—"

"Henry's my best friend," Ciara said.

"I know." Doherty smiled a little. "Is Theo in England, too?"

He hadn't heard.

Shakily, Ciara exhaled. "Theo was killed in January." She forced the words out before they got stuck in her throat.

Doherty's smile dropped, and his eyes widened. "I'm sorry to hear that."

He had been Theo's mentor, too.

"Thanks."

Ciara's thoughts drifted to Theo—and his death. It had been exactly six months since Theo's untimely death.

Exactly. She hadn't realised it was the first of July already.

She had been planning to visit his grave, but she wasn't even in Canada. Vancouver was an ocean and a continent away.

She had utterly forgotten.

"Are you sure it was *them* that killed Byron?" Mrs Rossler asked Doherty.

Doherty nodded. "I'm afraid so."

Ciara didn't know who *they* were.

So she asked. "Who are we talking about?"

Doherty looked at Ciara. At first he didn't say anything, hesitating. "The witch hunters have expanded to Europe."

Witch hunters. In Europe.

"What?" Ciara breathed out. It felt like all air was kicked out of her lungs.

Doherty nodded, confirming she had heard right.

The witch hunters had killed Theo.

"We were told nothing in Canada, nor in the States." She had thought they were gone—except for a few remaining members.

Did her colleagues know? She knew her boss wouldn't have ever told her. Not after Theo's death.

She shook her head vigorously. "We destroyed their last base in May. There's three of them left in the States unless they've fled. They're no longer an issue."

They couldn't be. She had been fighting for so long to get rid of those terrorists. She had done everything to take revenge for what they had done to Theo. Those monsters had taken everything from her, and she had made them pay for it.

"They're no longer an issue *there*," Doherty corrected. "Because they've moved here."

She hadn't known.

Doherty sighed. "The magical government of Great

Britain refuses to do anything. They don't believe a group of sick believers caused the deaths. They blame it on individual murderers or just plain serial killers."

"That's why you came here."

They had moved Doherty to Europe from America. It had been sudden, and there had never been a reason announced for his transfer. But it finally made sense.

It was ridiculous she had found out more during her suspension than during her time at work. She was going to talk to her boss about that.

"That's why I left," Doherty confirmed. "We think their leader is located here, and someone needed to be here to try to stop them."

Ciara blinked as if she was trying to wake up from a dream. "But we killed Morell."

The memory resurfaced in her mind. She recollected all the blood in the room when they had finally ended him. A colleague of hers had cut his head off with a spell. Ciara had been washing the blood off her clothes for hours after that mission.

Doherty sighed. "He was just a middleman."

Ciara opened her mouth, but she couldn't form any words.

No... This isn't real.

"You've got to be joking," she eventually choked out.

She had believed the witch hunters had been dealt with already. She had been relieved to be finished with them.

But she had been wrong—about everything.

"We think there might be an infiltration in the States."

Ciara tilted her head to the side. "We?"

"We've done some research. Based on odd accidents and such..." Mr Rossler sighed. "Well, it makes sense."

Ciara looked between Doherty and Mr Rossler, mouth hanging open. Mr Rossler worked at a desk job at the Magical Ministry of the United Kingdom.

"Unofficial research?" she asked, cocking an eyebrow.

"Yes," Doherty said.

"We have a group of people working against the witch hunters," Mr Rossler revealed.

That was highly illegal.

"Because the government here refuses to do anything?" she asked.

Mr Rossler nodded. "Yes."

Highly illegal or not, Ciara wanted to be part of it. She was going to help. One way or another.

"I want to help."

"No!" Henry said.

Ciara turned to look at her best friend, gaping. "I've worked undercover within the witch hunters' group. You can't just tell me no. You don't know what I'm capable of."

She wouldn't accept a no. She had every right to do her part in getting rid of the witch hunters. She had lost people and suffered because of that sick terrorist organisation. After everything, she deserved justice.

Theo deserved justice.

"Ciara can help us." At least Doherty was on her side.

"She's suspended," Henry said.

Luckily her leg was already better, so he couldn't use that as an excuse.

"This isn't official," Doherty said. "In fact, it's illegal, anyway."

"I don't agree with this." Henry turned to face his parents. "Mum?"

Mrs Rossler looked at her son, wanting to agree with him. She didn't want Ciara to be in harm's way. But the young woman who stood her ground with such determination didn't seem like the old Ciara. She was a grown adult. Mrs Rossler only hoped she hadn't grown too tough with the life she had chosen.

"Ciara is an adult," Mrs Rossler said to her son.

Mr Rossler and Doherty, who were the founders of the group fighting against the witch hunters, agreed Ciara should help them. Mrs Rossler didn't like it, but she still agreed.

Henry, on the other hand, hated it. He was furious—but even more worried.

Liam and Iris had said nothing. Iris was a healer for the group, and she rarely took part in missions. She didn't see why her opinion would matter. Liam said nothing because he didn't know what to say.

He didn't like the idea of Ciara doing what he did for the group—fighting witch hunters. But clearly, she was already doing that at work.

He knew how cruel the witch hunters were. He had witnessed people die on missions.

Liam couldn't wrap his head around the fact that it was Ciara's job—seeing death and dealing with the witch hunters. She had worked undercover inside their organisation, and the thought made Liam shudder.

Perhaps it should have brought him comfort. At least Ciara knew how to take care of herself. Even so, knowing that didn't help.

It had nothing to do with his past relationship with Ciara. He cared because she was someone he had known for a big part of his life. They used to be close friends.

He was glad Iris and Ciara got along so well. It had surprised him to hear the two had become friends, but it was a pleasant surprise.

Liam hadn't known about Theo until Doherty had asked Ciara about him. If Liam had understood correctly, Ciara had been dating Theo before his death. Liam couldn't imagine what she had been through during her time in America.

"So, do you like that Boucher guy or what?" Liam eyed the guy who had just left their table. He felt compelled to glare after him.

"Theo?" Ciara asked.

Liam nodded.

"He's a great guy."

Liam's shoulders dropped. "So, you like him."

Ciara chuckled. "I don't have a crush on him, if that's what you're implying."

"Well, I—"

"You thought I was dating him?" Ciara couldn't contain her amused smile.

Liam scratched the back of his neck. "Uh, yes."

"Well, you'd hear about it if I was," Ciara said. "Theo's just a friend."

Liam nodded, with a hint of smile making its way onto his lips.

He hated that guy. He hated watching him make Ciara laugh. Theo Boucher wasn't the guy who had harboured a crush on Ciara for ages.

Liam was the one. He had never acted on his feelings. It was taking him so long to gather enough courage to tell her.

He feared he was too late, though. She spent a lot of time with Theo, and Theo was charming. Their connection was obvious.

According to her, it was just a friendship, but Liam was unsure. Theo made her laugh like no one else.

Still, Liam hoped it was platonic. He hoped they were just friends. That Ciara had told him the truth.

But Liam wouldn't ask about it again. It would have made his own feelings too obvious. He didn't want to reveal his feelings with the risk of Ciara liking Theo Boucher.

Liam knew his fiancée. If he had brought Ciara up, Iris would have become jealous. Ciara was just a friend—if even that. He didn't want Iris to misunderstand anything.

Iris didn't talk to him about Ciara. In fact, he felt as if Iris was already jealous. He knew how Iris had felt in the past whenever his family had brought Ciara up, even during

Ciara's absence.

But Iris had nothing to be jealous of. Even she knew Liam had chosen her over Ciara. Others did not—hopefully.

Liam's romantic feelings for Ciara were in the past. But that didn't mean he didn't care at all.

Liam craved to know more about Ciara and especially about her life in America. They hadn't talked in over three years, and it seemed as though a lot had happened in both their lives.

Still, he couldn't ask Iris, and Iris wouldn't tell him without asking.

Asking his mother about Ciara wasn't an option either. He doubted his mother or the rest of his family knew much more than he did anyway.

The person, who still knew Ciara better than anyone else, was Henry. The two of them were living together.

So Henry was Liam's best option.

8

Liam breathed in and raised his hand. Before it hit the wooden surface, he exhaled. He knocked three times and let his hand drop.

There was shuffling on the other side of the door. Then someone opened it, and it wasn't Henry.

Ciara was wearing a black tank top and a simple pair of jeans. Her hair was up in a messy bun that was nearly falling apart.

Liam smiled at her. "Hi."

Ciara smiled back, trying to fix her hair updo. "Hi, Liam."

"Uh, is Henry home?" He looked past Ciara but couldn't see his brother anywhere.

"He..." Ciara sighed. "Henry hasn't been here in a few days. He left on Saturday."

That was when Ciara had heard about the witch hunter situation in Europe, and it was already Wednesday.

"Really?" Liam hadn't heard from his brother after the weekend, because he had been busy at work.

Ciara nodded. "He's angry because of the whole witch hunter thing."

"He'll come around eventually," Liam reassured.

Ciara shrugged, unconvinced. "If you want to see him, I can tell you where he's staying with his dragon."

Liam raised an eyebrow. "His dragon?"

Ciara chuckled and nodded. "Yeah, he's taking care of it until he returns to work. It's a harmless little creature unless you don't want your newspapers turned into ash."

Liam laughed, seeing how Ciara was trying to hold back a grimace. "That sounds like Henry."

"For sure."

"I'm sure he'll be home soon."

Ciara smiled. "Always the optimist."

Liam smiled, too.

He had come to talk with Henry about Ciara. Instead, he had the perfect chance to talk with her.

"M-may I come in?" He couldn't believe he stuttered as if he had never talked to her.

"Of course." Ciara let him in and then closed the door.

He looked around the flat. Everything seemed as usual except for one open duffel bag on the floor. Inside the bag appeared to be Ciara's clothes.

"You haven't unpacked?" Liam asked, gesturing to the bag.

"I've repacked," Ciara corrected. "I'm going back to America."

Liam's eyes widened. "Already?"

"Just for now. Doherty and I will talk to a few people from work, so—"

"So it's a mission."

Ciara nodded. "Yes."

"Does Henry know?"

"I left him a message when he didn't answer any of my calls."

Liam nodded, fidgeting with his hands. "It's odd to

think that you work daily with the things we deal with only occasionally."

Ciara tilted her head to the side. "Odd?"

Liam shrugged. "I just never imagined you'd become a hit witch."

"I wanted to become a curse breaker originally."

Liam smiled, remembering how much Ciara had loved hearing about his work in Peru. "I remember."

"So, you work for the government now?"

Liam sat on the arm of the sofa. "I do." He nodded. "It's a little different compared to how it was when I worked overseas." Overseas he had dealt with ancient curses. Some of them even thousands of years old. In England, the curses were more recent and acute.

"More office hours?"

Liam chuckled. "Certainly."

It felt oddly natural, talking to Ciara. But he liked that. No room for uncomfortable silences. As if they had always been friends—as if they hadn't lost contact.

"So, America."

Ciara nodded. "What about it?"

"How is it?"

Ciara smiled and leaned against a wall. "At first it was exciting. New. A new job, a new country, new people. The training for the job was rough at first. The job became harder the longer I worked as a hit witch. And, well, now I'm here."

"You didn't work non-stop for three years. I'm pretty sure you had a personal life, too." He wanted to know about her life, not her job.

Even the thought of her doing what she did for a living was enough. He didn't want the details.

"Are you trying to subtly ask about Theo?" Her usually strong voice turned shaky, but her expression didn't waver.

Liam scratched the back of his head. "I just don't want to—"

"It's been over six months since his death." Ciara walked

to the sofa and took a seat.

Liam joined her but kept a friendly distance.

"I'm actually leaving a day early, because I need to visit his grave," Ciara said. "I also promised to visit his mother."

"You still see his family?"

"Rarely," Ciara said. "But she's been asking, and I have to explain why I won't be in Seattle."

Liam nodded. "So, you and Theo. How long were you two together?"

"Almost two years," Ciara said and smiled. "Officially anyway."

"And how are you?"

"I'll be fine."

Liam didn't push it. He could see Ciara's hands shaking. Even though he had never lost someone like she had, he could understand how hard it was for her.

And he knew—perhaps better than anyone—she hated talking about her feelings.

"How's your mother?" Liam asked, changing the subject.

"She's fine, but I haven't actually seen her in two years. She lives in Italy with her new husband."

Liam hadn't expected that. "Oh."

"With my job, it's impossible to keep in touch with her without putting her in danger. There are people who give me updates on her life here and there. I'd hear if something happened to her."

She had visited Liam's family, though.

But before she had known about the anti-terrorist group working against the witch hunters, she hadn't known the witch hunters were in England. She had thought those terrorists had been dealt with. Knowing about the group now, she knew his parents were involved with the witch hunters, anyway.

Her mother wasn't.

"Anyway, you know plenty about my past few years." Ciara smiled. "What about you?"

Liam shifted in his seat. "Well, I moved back at the beginning of 2015."

"With Iris."

Liam nodded. "Y-yes. With Iris."

"Did you start working for the government when you moved back?"

Liam nodded. "Yes. And, uh, Iris became a healer. She used to be a medic."

Ciara nodded. Even Liam could tell she had known about Iris's job. She was just being polite, not saying anything about it.

"Mum was overjoyed to have me back in England." Liam chuckled at the memory of her mother's reaction when he had come home, the corners of his eyes crinkling from the smile on his face.

"I bet she was."

"So, uh, how long will you be in America?"

"I don't know yet. Not three years, though." Ciara smiled, but it was a little forced. "I'm sure you'll hear when I'm back."

"And you're leaving today?"

"My flight leaves at eight o'clock."

"So, uh, how's Ciara?" Liam asked Henry.

It was like stepping on thin ice. He was already dating a new girl—Iris. Henry knew about Iris, but he was still Ciara's best friend. But he was also Liam's brother.

It was odd how no one had mentioned Ciara during Liam's stay. Usually Henry couldn't shut up about what he had been up to with Ciara.

"No idea." Henry's voice was harsh and cold. As if he didn't want to talk about his best friend.

"Don't tell me you two stopped hanging out the moment you graduated." Liam laughed. "You've been glued to each other for years. A friendship break-up right after graduation would be cliché."

"Well, that's basically what happened." Henry turned to look at

Liam, crossing his arms across his chest.

Liam's eyes widened. Letting it all sink in, his face twisted into a frown. "For real?"

"She left England and said she couldn't be in contact," Henry said. "I haven't heard from her since."

"That's an awful joke. Ciara would never—"

"Well, she did. It's not a joke."

Liam had never seen his younger brother so serious.

"So, if you want to hear how she is, go ask her Mum," Henry said.

"Have you asked?"

"No."

"So, you're angry with Ciara."

"Of course I am."

Liam pursed his lips together, wondering what to say. "I'm sure she'll be back with an explanation soon enough."

Henry shrugged, not saying a word.

"And Doherty will fly to America tomorrow?" Liam asked Ciara.

"His flight leaves tomorrow," Ciara confirmed, nodding.

"Does anyone else know about the mission?"

"I believe your Dad told most people already. Only a few of them have actually met me, though."

"So, Mum and Dad know."

"Yes, they do."

"Good."

Liam stayed talking with Ciara until she had to leave to the airport. He offered to take her, but she politely declined.

Liam felt content, having been able to talk with Ciara. The only thing left bothering him was that Ciara still felt distant.

"Did you know Henry hasn't been home for a few days?" Iris asked, pulling Liam out of his trance.

He blinked, coming back to the dining area from the corner of his mind. They were in the middle of eating dinner, and Liam had completely zoned out.

"I was looking for him at his flat," Liam said. "So Ciara told me."

"She left for America today, didn't she?" Iris asked and sipped her water.

Liam nodded. "Yes."

"She's leaving early to visit her fiancé's grave."

Fiancé? Liam thought. "Theo and Ciara were engaged?"

Iris nodded. "He died soon after, I think."

"Oh."

"Did you know Theo?"

"He was a contestant in the tournament in my last year."

"So he was representing Canada and North America?"

"Yes."

Iris furrowed her eyebrows and stopped eating. "Weren't you dating Ciara back then?"

"We started dating after the tournament."

"Do you think she liked him already back then?" Iris asked, twirling her fork in her food.

Liam pursed his lips together, letting the thought sink in.

Theo and Ciara had spent a lot of time together. Some days it had been as if someone had glued them to one another.

"I don't know."

Iris's eyes widened. "Maybe she moved to Canada for Theo!"

"I think she moved for the job."

Iris shrugged. "Or she's just telling everyone that."

"Who knows."

He wanted to believe Ciara had moved for her job. Still, Iris's words made sense.

A knocking came from the tent's entrance, gaining Liam's attention.

As he turned around to see who had cast a knocking spell, Iris—the beautiful medic—walked in. "Hey." She smiled sheepishly at him. "I'm sorry about the whole...uh, thing, you know."

He knew exactly what she meant. She had flirted with him and had then made a move on him.

"I misunderstood everything, and I had no idea you had a girlfriend in England." She grimaced, ashamed of her previous actions.

Liam smiled at her. "It's okay," he assured. "We actually broke up."

Iris's eyes widened. "Oh!" She blinked twice, letting it sink in. "I'm so sorry."

"It's fine." He was still smiling. "It didn't come as a surprise. The whole long-distance relationship thing didn't work for us."

Iris nodded. "And you weren't ready to move back for her?"

"My work is here."

She nodded again. A small smile made its way onto her face. "Well, if I ask you out for coffee in, like, two months, will you say yes?"

Liam offered her one of his most charming smiles. "I'd say yes if you asked me now."

Iris's eyes widened, glowing with excitement. "Really? In that case...would you like to get coffee with me some time?"

Liam grinned. "I'd love that."

"Wonderful!"

C iara sighed, finally getting herself a taxi. The queue had been long, and she had waited for hours.

She sat in the back seat of the car. Once she had given the driver the address, she let her muscles relax and leaned against the seat.

The ten-hour flight had felt like an eternity.

It was already late in Vancouver, but she was still heading to the cemetery. She wanted to visit Theo's grave. She hadn't been in the city in months, so she hadn't visited his grave either.

"Long flight?" the driver asked.

Ciara smiled. The driver saw her through the rear-view mirror, so she tried to look less tired. "Ten hours."

"That's more than enough."

"Yeah."

"You came from London?"

Ciara raised her eyebrow. "You know that based on the time?"

The driver shrugged. "A lucky guess from an experienced taxi driver."

Ciara didn't believe in lucky guesses. "How long have you worked as a taxi driver?"

"Years." The driver chuckled, throwing his head back, his eyes barely staying on the road. "I've lost count."

Ciara forced a smile. "A long time, then."

"Indeed."

"You live in the city?"

"Lived here my whole life."

"What a relief!" Ciara forced a smile onto her face. "You know the fastest way to the cemetery then."

The driver nodded. "I do."

Ciara continued to smile. "The church in the middle of the cemetery is beautiful in the summer, isn't it?"

"It sure is. One of the most beautiful ones I've seen."

"Undoubtedly."

Except there was no church in the cemetery. Anyone who had been there knew that. The driver was lying, and Ciara had a good guess about what was going on.

"So, you're familiar with the city?" the fake taxi driver asked.

"Somewhat."

"You have family here?"

Ciara nodded. "Something like that."

"Are you staying long?"

Ciara chuckled, faking it. She was lucky she was experienced in acting thanks to her job. "I don't know yet."

The driver nodded. "I see."

Ciara kept her eyes on the driver, so she didn't miss the slightest of movements. She was in danger. It was only a matter of time before the driver attacked.

She wasn't sure if the driver was even heading for the cemetery. They were still driving the right way, but it could have been a coincidence.

She couldn't tell if the driver was a witch hunter or

someone from her past cases. She tried to look for a tattoo on him. The witch hunter mark—a flame-like symbol with a wand in the middle of the fire. From where she sat, she couldn't spot tattoos on him, but that didn't mean there weren't any.

The car was nearing red lights. Ciara inhaled quietly, eyeing the road ahead and the driver in turns. She prepared herself to deal with the driver—before he dealt with her.

Just when they were about to stop at the red lights, the lights turned green. The driver sped up, and Ciara lost her chance.

Soon there were red lights ahead again. The car slowed down, and Ciara was ready to strike. She was about to raise her hand to cast a spell, but a wand appeared out of nowhere. It pressed against the side of her neck, halting her movements.

"Don't even think about it." A rough male voice. Unfamiliar.

Someone had been hiding in the the boot of the car. Ciara hadn't spotted the man, even though there was an open space between the back seat and the boot. A rookie mistake. She should have checked.

The car stopped. Another wand—the driver's wand—pointed at Ciara.

There were two of them. They had to be witch hunters.

The man sitting in the boot laughed darkly. "Going to see your dead boyfriend?"

Ciara gritted her teeth and clenched her hand into a fist. No one talked about Theo like *that*.

"I think you hit a soft spot." The driver let his gaze slide to the other witch hunter for a moment.

"I sure did."

Theo was sitting on the sofa, unable to stay still. He was shifting in his seat. "I'm worried, Ciara." A frown darkened his features.

Ciara was in the kitchen, having made herself a cup of tea. She left the cup on the kitchen counter and walked to the living room. She sat down beside her boyfriend. "Everything will be okay," she said and brushed her fingers against Theo's cheek.

He looked pale, looking into Ciara's eyes. "I worry about you."

Ciara took Theo's hand in hers, giving it a reassuring squeeze. "Nothing will happen to me."

Theo pulled Ciara onto his lap, wrapping his arms around her and burying his face in her hair. "I love you so much."

"I love you, too, Theo," she murmured. "We'll be fine. We always make it out just fine."

"You got injured last time." He shuddered. "I thought I was going to lose you." He shook his head, his forehead creasing. "Ciara, I never want to go through that again." He looked back up into her eyes.

Ciara cupped his face and leaned her forehead against his. "And you'll never have to."

🍁 🍁 🍁

The memory made Ciara's heart ache. One of her last moments with Theo. But she couldn't dwell on the grief. Not when she was in danger.

She needed to get out. She didn't have back-up. The witch hunters shouldn't have known she was in Canada.

She had naively assumed she was safe.

She was alone with two wands pointed at her. Either of the witch hunters could have flicked their wand and killed her. It didn't look good for her.

She had to get out.

She wasn't finished with the witch hunters like she had once thought. Her revenge wasn't over until they were gone for good. There was no way she was going down before them.

She also had to go see Theo's mother who had been asking for her to visit for so long.

She also had to fix things between her and Henry again. She owed him that. In fact, she owed him a lot after how harshly she had originally left England.

And she hadn't seen her own mother in years. There was no way she would die before seeing her.

She hadn't had the chance to talk with Liam, either. Not properly. She hoped they could be friends again, like they used to. That would never happen if she let herself die.

She had to take a risk. Her only option was to attack the men. Even if it cost her life, at least she wasn't going to die without a fight.

But the bootlid flew open. The wand dropped from Ciara's neck onto her lap, and the man flew out of the boot, screaming.

Ciara didn't turn to see what happened behind her. She focused on the other witch hunter and disarmed him.

She moved her hands, casting magic. She knocked out the driver, making him bash his head against the window hard enough to crack the glass.

Grabbing both wands, she rushed out to see what was happening. Someone had come to her rescue. That someone had also dealt with the other witch hunter who lay unconscious on the street.

Bald head and dark skin. It was her American colleague, Joshua Talbot.

Ciara grinned on seeing Josh. "Just in time." Ciara sighed in relief. "Thank you."

Josh returned the smile. "No problem. Wanna help me take these two in for questioning?"

She was on suspension, but she doubted anyone would mind if she helped. After all, the two morons had attacked her.

Ciara nodded. "Let's do it."

The pair used floating spells to take the two witch hunters in for questioning—to the interrogation rooms of their Vancouver base.

They put the witch hunters under surveillance in separate rooms. Using binding spells that would last throughout the interrogations, they tied them up and then headed to their boss's office.

Alan Torres, Ciara's boss, welcomed her with a tight smile. "Welcome back."

Alan was an experienced hit wizard with notable successes under his belt.

Ciara smiled. "If it were in different circumstances, boss, I'd say it's good to be back."

Alan nodded. "I understand. I spoke with Doherty. In fact, thanks to someone in England, we knew we had to save you tonight."

"I could have handled myself. Although, I prefer how things went now."

He nodded. "You could have." He had seen her in the field. "That's not why you're suspended."

"I know."

"We brought the witch hunters in for interrogation, boss," Josh said.

"Good." Alan nodded. "Go see if someone is working late. Have them assist you with the interrogations, will you?"

"Right away, sir." Josh nodded. Then he turned to hug Ciara. "It was good to see you."

"You, too, Josh," Ciara said and flashed him a smile.

He left, having work to do.

Alan gestured at the empty chair. "Sit, please."

Ciara sat down, relaxing her muscles.

Alan took a seat on his side of the desk. "Doherty told me you're aware of the British group."

Ciara nodded. "That's what I'm here for."

Alan's expression turned serious. "Are you sure you're... capable of working like that?"

"It's not official work." It wasn't even legal, but her American colleagues didn't care what happened on the other side of the Atlantic—especially not when it helped them.

"I know. But I also know it requires having to put yourself in dangerous situations." Alan sighed. "You buried yourself in work after Theo died. I'm afraid you haven't dealt with your grief yet."

"I'm working on it. But I would never do anything reckless."

Alan smiled a little. "Unless it would save someone."

"Then I would see it as necessary action. It would have nothing to do with Theo's death."

Alan nodded and leaned back in his chair. "If you say so. I know you put others before yourself."

A curse headed for Josh.

Before it could hit him, Ciara intercepted, and the curse hit her instead.

The pain was excruciating, sending electric shocks through Ciara's entire body. She screamed in agony, and her knees gave out.

Josh turned to see Ciara. His eyes widened, but he couldn't get to her. He had a witch hunter to deal with first. "Hang in there!" he yelled desperately.

Ciara heard him only faintly as she fell onto the ground. She lay there, writhing in pain. She couldn't tell what the curse had done, but the pain was agonising.

"I've never regretted saving anyone. It has always been worth the cost."

Alan sighed. "Doherty has requested for your transfer to England."

Ciara opened her mouth, but no words came out. Doherty hadn't said anything to her. She hadn't expected such news. "What?"

Alan nodded. "You heard right."

Her eyes widened. "Really?"

"Yes."

"But I live in the States. I don't live in England anymore. I—"

"But would you like to?" Alan asked. "It's something to consider. You'd be a great help for the British magical government. You have the skills and the knowledge they need there."

"I mean...maybe, but there's paperwork and everything."

"You've gone through the paperwork before," Alan reminded her.

"True."

Ciara hadn't thought about moving back to England. She had only planned to stay for a visit. With the witch hunters in Europe, though, the transfer made sense to her.

Anything to avenge Theo.

"What about my suspension?" she asked.

"It stands, nonetheless, so take your time in considering the offer."

Ciara nodded.

"I'd like to have you stay here. You've done splendid work here in America." Alan offered Ciara a brief smile. "But I agree that they may need you more in Europe."

Ciara smiled at her boss. "I'll think about the offer."

"Good." Alan cleared his throat. "You're still suspended. But would you mind helping analyse the interrogations? If you have somewhere to be or—"

"I can help." Ciara nodded. "I promised to meet Theo's mother in the morning, but I'm free until then."

Alan stood up from his chair and gestured to the door. "Shall we?"

Ciara stood up. "We shall."

10

Ciara stood in the driveway of a blue house. She smiled, letting all the memories resurface.

She remembered how she and Theo had first come to visit his mother. Ciara had been scared his mother wouldn't like her, and Theo had tried to calm her nerves. Still, Ciara and his mother had instantly become best friends. His mother had always been welcoming of her.

They had hosted barbecues in the backyard. It had been a year since the last one.

The house held a lot of memories. Wonderful memories, but they brought back the painful ones, too.

Ciara didn't mind. She didn't want to forget Theo, even though it hurt to think about him.

Exhaling, she walked to the front porch. She raised her hand and knocked three times like Theo had always done.

Soon Estella Boucher—Theo's mother—opened the door for her. "Ciara!" The older woman beamed with joy, pulling the younger woman into an embrace.

Ciara hugged her back. "It's so good to see you, Estella."

They were on a first name basis. Estella had always preferred for Ciara to treat her as family. And Ciara had nearly become her daughter-in-law.

If only things had gone differently...

"As it is you, dear," Estella said and released Ciara from her embrace. "Come on in." She ushered Ciara inside, closing the door behind.

Ciara shrugged off her coat and hung it on the coatrack. She followed Estella to the kitchen, where they sat down at the island.

"How was your trip?" Estella smiled at Ciara.

Ciara grimaced. "Eventful, unfortunately. But I'm fine, so no worries."

Estella's smile turned into a frown. "What happened?"

"Two witch hunters attacked me. Josh was there to save the day, so I'm fine."

"Be more careful." Estella sighed. "I mean, of course you are careful. It's just...after Theo—"

Ciara reached for Estella's hand to hold it. "I know."

"He wouldn't want anything to happen to you." Estella's voice faltered. "He loved you so dearly."

Ciara had to blink back tears. "I know."

"Did you visit his grave yet?" Estella's voice went quiet.

"I was going to, but then there was the attack. I'll visit his grave later today." Ciara fidgeted with her hands. "I haven't visited in a while."

Estella smiled, though the sorrow was visible in her eyes. "I know you're thinking of him, even if you don't visit his grave all the time. There's nothing to feel guilty about."

Ciara had always been easy for Estella to read. But Ciara had nothing to hide from her. Estella was like another mother to Ciara. She would have been a fantastic mother-in-law.

"I wanted to visit his grave on the first of this month, but then...well, I was in England, and I couldn't come here. I nearly forgot about it."

"It's just a date on the calendar," Estella said, placing a comforting hand on Ciara's shoulder. "It doesn't matter when you visit his grave. What matters is how much you think about him. And I know you think about him."

"Of course I do." Ciara swallowed, feeling as if there was a lump forming in her throat. "I loved him."

That was it—all it took for her to break. Tears cascaded down her face, and she tried to hold in the sobs.

Estella rushed to hug the young woman breaking into pieces in front of her. It wasn't the first time Estella had seen her break.

Ciara wouldn't cry. Despite losing control over her tears, she had kept her sobs in check during the funeral.

She was glad she hadn't worn mascara. The tears would have smeared it all over her face even before the funeral.

Her heart had been breaking. It was as if it had slowly cracked into small pieces. Staring at his coffin had caused her physical pain. Her legs had nearly given out. She had wanted to vomit from the physical pain the grief caused her.

But she hadn't let it show—except through the tears.

Until she and Estella were at Estella's house. The door was barely closed when Ciara's legs gave out and the sobs began.

It took Ciara a while to gather herself again. Estella hugged her and tried to soothe her through the worst of it before making some tea for them. Ciara continued to breathe in and out, trying to calm the storm of feelings inside of her.

She still missed Theo. *So much.*

She tried not to let it show, but she wasn't made of stone. She was more like thin ice.

Soon the room filled with a light scent of herbs and spices, meaning the tea was ready. Estella handed her a teacup, and

Ciara curled her fingers around it, comforted by its warmth.

"Ciara." Estella's voice was soft. "Haven't you let yourself grieve?"

Ciara looked at her tea. "I don't know how to."

"There's no right way," Estella said. "But grieving will help you move forward." The brown-haired woman sighed and sat down beside Ciara. "I think you won't let yourself grieve because you're afraid of moving on."

"I don't want to move on. I want to go back to that day in January and prevent *it*."

Estella smiled sympathetically, looking at the heartbroken girl. She pushed Ciara's hair behind her ear. "There was nothing you could have done differently, dear. It wasn't your fault."

Ciara furrowed her eyebrows, still staring at her tea. "I don't want to leave him behind."

"You're not doing that. He'd want you to move on. To live your life to the fullest."

"Even looking at another guy makes me feel like I'm cheating on Theo."

"You're not cheating on him. He'd want you to be happy. And I want you to be happy."

"But I wanted to be happy with Theo." Ciara's words were hollow. Theo was gone, and no amount of longing and anguish was going to bring him back.

"He's gone, dear."

Those words hurt Estella as much as they hurt Ciara. It was like a cracked glass shattering from the final hit.

"I know." Ciara's breathing became shaky. "I just wish nothing more than to have him back."

She didn't cry this time. But there was a clenched aching around her heart.

"Me, too."

They were both silent—deep in their own thoughts. Ciara was drowning in hers. She had to get out of the depths of her mind to catch her breath.

"How have you been, then?" Ciara took a sip of her tea and turned to look at Estella.

Estella sighed, also taking a sip of tea. "I'm dealing with it. I'm back at work."

"That's good."

Silence filled the room again, but it didn't last long.

"I'm sorry I haven't been around as much as I should have," Ciara said.

"You've been around enough."

"But if you ever need anything, you can ask me. Okay?"

Estella smiled. "Of course, Ciara. You're like a daughter to me. No matter what happens. I hope we can still stay in contact."

"I'd like that."

Estella's smile widened. "So, how is England? Have you met any old friends?"

"Some of them," Ciara said, nodding. "I've been staying with my best friend, Henry."

"I remember hearing about him. A decent boy, according to Theo."

Ciara smiled. "Henry's great."

"Anyone else?"

Ciara shrugged. "Some friends from school. We were a group of four girls back then. We had lunch together. Well, Henry tagged along. He was the one who set it all up." Ciara couldn't contain her smile, thinking about how great her friends were. "I think he's crushing on one of my old friends, Jenna. They both work with magical creatures, so I suppose it's no surprise. Henry adores people who love animals, and Jenna does."

"Sounds like they'd make a perfect couple."

Ciara grinned. "They would."

"How did everyone react to your return, then? I bet most were excited."

"I suppose they were. Especially at first." Ciara furrowed her eyebrows. "Now, I'm not so sure. Some of them are starting to remember how angry they were when I left."

"They'll come around," Estella reassured her.

"I hope so." Ciara sighed. "It's just that Henry hasn't spoken to me for a few days. He doesn't like that my work includes dealing with the witch hunters."

"Henry's just worried. He's lost you once and doesn't want that to happen again."

Ciara nodded. "Maybe."

Estella took Ciara's hand into hers and squeezed it. "You'll be just fine. I'm sure he'll come around."

Ciara smiled. "You're still the best at pep talks, it seems."

"Thank you."

Ciara was glad she was reminded of how much she appreciated having Estella in her life. Estella was like family. Like a second mother—sort of like Mrs Rossler.

Ciara was lucky that way, but she still missed her own mother.

"Did you meet your ex-boyfriend?"

Estella knew about Liam, but she didn't know everything.

Ciara nodded. "Yes, I did. He's engaged now. He even invited me to their engagement party in January, but I didn't go."

Estella's eyebrows rose. "Oh."

Ciara looked down and nodded. "It's the girl he began dating before I moved to Canada."

"Oh, I remember hearing about her." Estella sounded mildly angry.

"She's actually nice."

"She is?"

Ciara nodded. "I've hung out with her. Even alone."

"You're not angry with her?"

Ciara shook her head. "But hanging out with her is still odd."

"Odd how?"

"She doesn't want me near Liam. Liam and I have barely talked since I went back."

"I thought she was nice."

"She is. It's just that she seems jealous of me. She even told me she was jealous."

Estella smiled. "Well, I'm sure you'll get a chance to talk to Liam."

"I hope so. It'd be great to be friends with him again."

"So, no old feelings have resurfaced?"

"He's engaged," Ciara said. "Besides, I'm not over Theo's death. It would be highly inappropriate, and—"

Estella smiled gently. "But you didn't deny it."

Ciara's eyes widened.

"You can't control your feelings. You left him because you loved him so much that you simply wanted him to be happy. It wouldn't surprise me to hear that you never actually got over him."

"I got over him," Ciara insisted. "I didn't love him when I loved Theo. And I still love Theo."

Estella nodded understandingly. "I know you loved Theo, and I believe you still do. But there is nothing wrong with moving on."

"I'm not ready to move on." Ciara's lips thinned, pressing together. "And I would never try to move on with someone who is engaged."

"I know. Just don't suffocate your feelings. It's okay to feel. Both bad and good things."

"Still reading me like an open book, I see." A small smile crept onto Ciara's face.

Estella smiled, revealing her perfect set of pearly white teeth. "I know you so well."

"I know you do."

A look of worry replaced the smile on Estella's face. "You have to take care of yourself."

"I will and I have."

"But you always put others before yourself."

"My boss thinks so."

"No wonder." Estella's voice was serious, but her eyes

were kind, and her lips had curled into a smile.

"It was selfish to leave England the way I did. I want to make up for it."

Estella shook her head sharply. "It wasn't selfish. You came here for work, and your work has saved countless lives."

"But my motive was to run away from my life in England."

"There's nothing wrong with taking a break."

"It was three years long."

"That's life," Estella said, offering Ciara a soothing smile. "I'm sure you're not the only person that has happened to. Please, Ciara, stop feeling so guilty. Start thinking about yourself before others."

Ciara smiled. "Thank you for being there for me when I need you."

"I'm always here for you," Estella assured, smiling.

The two women finished drinking their tea and continued to talk.

It was late into the afternoon when Ciara left. She couldn't say when she would visit again, but she promised to stay in contact.

Next it was time to visit the cemetery. It had been too long since Ciara had last visited Theo's grave.

On her way, she stopped by a flower shop. She bought a bunch of red roses as a sign of her love.

Making it to the cemetery at last, she walked between the gravestones until she found the right row. She made her way to the dark gravestone with her fiancé's name on it and stared at the carved name for a good while before she set down the flowers.

Ciara sat down on the grass. It probably looked ridiculous to some people passing by, but she didn't care. She wanted to sit there for a moment. Simply being there was comforting.

She missed Theo a lot.

Estella had been right. Ciara hadn't let herself grieve. She was holding onto the past, dying to linger there a little longer.

Her eyes watered, and the thought of moving on nauseated her. No one could ever be what Theo had once been for her. She still wasn't sure how to live without him.

"The next guy to win your heart will be so lucky."

Ciara's head whipped around, and she met Theo's gaze. "What did you say?"

He smiled, reaching for his glass on the coffee table. "You heard me."

"Did I hear correctly?"

"Yes." He held her gaze, a soft, subtle smile making its way to his face. "Just make sure he's worth your time."

Her cheeks heated. "And are you?"

Theo's hand froze mid-air, his wineglass stopping inches from his lips. "What?"

"You heard me," Ciara said, imitating his earlier words.

"I thought..." He blinked. "You told me you didn't want a relationship." He set his glass back down, his eyes staying on her.

"A month ago."

"You changed your mind?" He was undoubtedly biting the inside of his cheek and still failed to hide his smile.

Ciara nodded. "Maybe that kiss convinced me."

He let out a breathy chuckle. "Was it that good?"

She shrugged. "Don't get cocky now."

"Can I convince you with another kiss?"

"Go ahead."

He moved closer to her and brought his hands up to stroke the sides of her face. He took his sweet time leaning in until their lips finally touched.

Ciara sat alone, staring at the gravestone for hours. Seeing his name on the wretched stone made her lower lip quiver. She stayed there, staring at the engraved letters, until she was ready to go.

She stood up and walked away from the gravestone, only to see Doherty waiting for her at the end of the grave row. "Doherty."

"It's good to see you, Ciara." Doherty gave Ciara a nod. "Theo deserved a longer, happier life."

"He would have."

"I'm sorry you witnessed him dying. No one deserves that."

Ciara exhaled shakily. "At least he wasn't alone."

"Does that bring you relief?"

"Not really."

Doherty nodded.

Ciara gave the gravestone in the distance one last look before she and Doherty walked away. Every step was heavy, but it eased when they made it to the main path—the wider path leading out of the cemetery.

"I spoke with Alan already."

Ciara nodded. "So did I."

"I'm glad nothing happened to you last night."

"Me too."

"Henry went through the flight information from Great Britain to Canada, just in case. He found out there were two witch hunters on the earlier flight." Doherty's eyes turned thunderous, and his lips thinned. "I contacted Alan immediately."

"You possibly saved my life," Ciara said. "I would have made it out without help only with luck. Josh coming to my aid was possibly life-saving."

Knowing she could have died didn't startle either of them. That came with the job. She had handled enough dangerous witches and wizards.

"You have to thank Henry. Looks like his worrying turned out to be a good thing."

Ciara smiled. "I'll thank him for worrying later."

"Good." Doherty straightened. "I'm afraid we have plenty of work to do now."

"We do."

11

Liam and Henry were having a brothers' night at Henry's flat. It was Friday, so they were drinking and watching a game of crashball.

Crashball was a magical sport that resembled volleyball.

Neither Liam nor Henry liked volleyball, but they loved crashball. It was so much more interesting with the magic involved. The players weren't allowed to touch the ball. And if they did, the ball vanished with a puff of smoke and the other team won.

"Ciara still has no idea when she'll be back?" Liam asked Henry.

Liam had been thinking about asking for a while, but asking Ciara wasn't an option. He didn't have her number. And not even his parents had mentioned anything about Ciara.

"Nope." Henry sighed and paused. "But I haven't even spoken with her."

Liam raised his eyebrow at Henry. "What?"

"Mum and Dad are in contact with Doherty every other day. Ciara and Doherty are working together, so all the information comes that way."

"You haven't even tried to call her?"

Liam usually thought his brother was smart, but sometimes Henry acted like an idiot.

Henry shook his head. "No. She's being selfish the way she's putting herself in danger all the time. She should realise there's people who care about her."

"You're worried about her. You shouldn't be angry for something so silly. She's your best friend, for God's sake!"

"Whom I didn't see for three years."

"She came back, didn't she?" Liam gave his brother a pointed glance. "She got an excellent job offer. Wouldn't you take a job offer like that?"

"I wouldn't cut ties with everyone. Especially not my best friend." Henry reached for his beer on the coffee table. He brought it to his lips and took a sip.

"I thought she apologised."

"An apology won't fix everything."

"Did you ask her why she never contacted you? Or anyone else?" Liam asked, turning his focus away from the crashball game.

"She's avoiding questions like that." Henry took another quick sip of his beer. "But claiming it was to protect anyone is just an excuse."

"Are you sure? Because she has a reason. If not that, then another good one."

"You're such an optimist."

Liam smiled. "She said the same thing."

Henry's eyebrows rose, and he turned to face Liam. "You two talked?"

"A little. I came here, but you were at Jenna's place. It was mostly just catching up." Liam furrowed his brows and reached for his beer. "It was...sort of weird."

"Not what you expected?"

"She feels distant," Liam said, nodding. "I mean, yes, we used to date and we haven't spoken much since the break-up. It's just...I'd like to be her friend again, maybe."

"And what would Iris think of that?"

"Iris is her friend."

Henry didn't want to argue, even though he doubted his brother's fiancée would have appreciated Liam and Ciara being friends. "Fair enough," he ended up saying.

Talking about Iris brought a conversation back to Liam's mind. "Iris suggested Ciara went to the States for Theo."

Henry turned to Liam. "Why would she think that?"

Liam shrugged.

"Ciara said she didn't know she would be working with Theo until she met him at work." Henry paused, his brows knitting together. "Are you sure someone doesn't have hidden feelings for my best friend?"

Liam scoffed and shook his head. "Of course I don't. Not romantic ones. I love Iris. We're in the middle of wedding planning."

Henry brushed the topic aside, deciding it was wrong to question it further. Instead, he hung onto the topic of the wedding.

"So, December wedding it is, huh?"

Liam nodded. The movement was slow, as if his brain was weighed down with too many thoughts. "December wedding it is." His voice was monotonous, lacking any excitement.

"You're gonna have to hurry with the planning."

Neither brother focused on the game anymore. Their conversation was far more important.

"Iris has most of it planned already."

"You don't want to have a say in anything?"

"I don't care about napkin colours."

"Well, I'm not a wedding expert, but I think there are other things that need to be planned for a wedding."

"I know." Liam sighed.

"Tell me you got to choose your best man at least."

"I asked Hugo."

"And how did Shawn take it?"

Shawn and Hugo were Liam's best friends. They had known each other since their school years.

"Shawn was fine with it. I let Iris decide between the two, so no one felt offended."

"What?" Henry's eyes widened. "You let your bride decide on your best man?"

"In a way, but it was still my—"

"It was her decision," Henry said. "Don't tell me otherwise."

"Her decision was good."

"I suppose."

Liam sighed. "But?"

"Just thinking. Because a while ago, you said you weren't even ready to get married yet." Henry furrowed his eyebrows, looking at Liam. He couldn't believe his brother was about to let his wedding be taken over by his bride. "You said you wanted to be engaged for a little longer. So, what changed your mind?"

"Iris wants this."

"Iris wants this? And you're gonna let her make every decision?"

"Not every decision, of course. But honestly, I don't see any downsides in this whole wedding thing."

"Downsides? It's your wedding! You should be excited and planning it. You don't feel you're ready."

"There's plenty of time to get used to the idea," Liam said. "Besides, I love Iris. I'm happy to do this for her. And most importantly, with her."

A sigh passed Henry's lips, and he nodded. "As long as you're happy."

"Trust me, Henry, I am."

A silence filled the room, and the two brothers turned to watch the crashball game again. They both sipped their beers, unsure what to talk about.

"So, how about you and Jenna?" Liam asked, breaking the

silence. He turned to face his brother, and a smirk formed on his lips.

"Oh, don't start," Henry groaned and took a gulp of his beer as if in a hurry to drink it.

"Oh, come on, Henry. I know you like her. In fact, you might be a little obsessed with her," Liam teased.

A blush crept onto Henry's cheeks. "She's amazing," he admitted dreamily.

Liam's smirk only widened. "And it took you this many years to figure that out?"

"Well, I might have had a small crush on her in school." Henry's blushing got worse, painting his cheeks bright red. "I've just got to know her better recently. You know, without Ciara there as the mutual friend."

"So something good came out of Ciara's absence. You found yourself a girlfriend."

"We're not dating."

"Yet."

The corner of Henry's lips twitched. "I asked her out already."

Liam's eyes widened, and he grinned as if he had just received world-changing news. "When and where?"

"We're having dinner tomorrow. At a restaurant."

"Cute."

Henry rolled his eyes, briefly turning to look at his brother rather than the game. "Don't tease."

Liam raised his hands in surrender. "I'm not teasing."

"Oh, please!"

Liam chuckled. "Alright, fine. I was." He smiled, happy for his brother. "Are you nervous?"

Henry wished he could escape the questioning. He wondered what spell would make the soft cushions swallow him whole. Nothing came to mind.

He ended up nodding. "A little." Cocking his head to the side, he looked at Liam. "How did you woo Iris? With flowers?"

"No. She asked me out when I was still dating Ciara. I declined."

"But you went out with her right after the break-up."

Liam had written to Henry about Iris back then, so he couldn't deny it. He nodded, unsure what to say.

"I always wondered why you dated another girl so soon."

"Was it too soon?" Liam had thought about it before. But Ciara had been the one to break up with him.

Henry shrugged. "It felt soon to me. But I guess the whole long-distance thing had already made you and Ciara drift apart."

"I think it had."

"Does Ciara know the entire story?"

Liam shook his head. He stared at the television screen without focusing on the game. "I don't think so. And I hope she doesn't find out."

Henry nodded. "It would hurt her feelings."

"Exactly." And Liam didn't want that.

Time flew by in England. Liam was busy at work for the following week. He even worked the weekend.

A government official had been cursed by an unhappy citizen. As it turned out, the citizen had known her way around curses, so breaking the sickness curse had turned out to be a struggle.

On another day, there was a cursed house with dead witches and wizards inside. The officials insisted it was just a group of misfits. Liam doubted that. What sort of misfits went around killing people mindlessly? It had been the witch hunters, without a doubt, and the government refused to accept that after the horrors Canada and the United States had gone through in the hands of those terrorists.

A lot of horrible things had happened, and those cases involved curses that had to be dealt with.

It was clear as daylight that the witch hunters were

growing more dangerous. They were causing more and more harm. More people got hurt. Some even killed.

After the talk Liam and Henry had had, Liam felt guilty for having to work so much while Iris was planning their wedding. But still, he was glad he didn't have to think about napkin colours when there were mindless murderers on the loose.

It was late by the time Liam finished work that Sunday. He was excited to be heading home. The following day would be his day off.

He was about to leave and go home when he received a message.

They needed him at his parents' house.

He sighed in frustration. For a moment, he wanted to smash his phone.

But then he grabbed his wand and hurried to teleport himself to the house. Once he was there, standing outside, he knocked at the door. He hadn't realised it was raining, having spent the entire day inside.

The second his father opened the door for him, he could see the chaos inside. He had heard none of it outside, thanks to an enchantment.

The house was full of people. They were all part of the anti-terrorist group. There were only about twenty or thirty members, but it was enough to fill the house. Most were family friends or people who had suffered in the hands of the witch hunters. Most importantly, all of them were people who weren't going to accept the government's inability to accept the problem. Even if their actions were illegal, they were going to fight the witch hunters.

Liam's father explained the situation to Liam. Witch hunters had killed one of them in the man's own house and had severely injured another. Those terrorists had tracked down the address and had attacked.

Iris was tending to the injured woman in the bedroom. Or so Ray told Liam, but Liam didn't go to see. He knew he shouldn't distract Iris when she was working. She was probably trying to save a life in there.

Liam found his mother and tried to comfort her. She was upstairs crying. She didn't want all the other members to see her break down, so she had gone to Liam's old room.

It became a long day—or a night. It was rough for Liam, but he couldn't imagine what his fiancée was going through, tending to the injured woman.

Next day was Liam's day off.

Finally.

But he didn't get to enjoy it. Instead, he spent his time planning the next mission. They had to repay for the attacks. They needed a plan on how they would handle the situation—and the witch hunters.

Despair was growing within the group, and the members were coming up with more and more desperate ideas—some of them even impossible. They couldn't track the witch hunters with a spell, like Liam's father's friend Eric had suggested. Liam could understand the desperate need to find any kind of solution—possible or not. It had been Eric's brother who had died the previous day.

People were impossible to trace with magic unless they knowingly left a magical trace to be followed. Tracking an object could have worked if they had got a piece of any object the witch hunters had. But they had nothing.

Iris was also busy that day. She was checking up on the injured woman once every other hour. The injuries could have turned fatal if it hadn't been for her. Thanks to Iris, it was looking like there wouldn't be more death.

Liam was proud of his fiancée. She was such a caring person. She worked hard in order to help others, and she was a great healer with her knowledge of healing potions and spells. Although healing spells were rather limited. Injuries couldn't be completely healed with a spell, but the pain could be eased and the healing process could be sped up.

No matter where Liam went, he had to deal with witch hunters. Most of the curse breaking at his work resulted from something the witch hunters had done. He recognised their curses and methods. He was all too familiar with them.

The government still refused to believe any of it. They refused to admit there was a witch hunter organisation—a terrorist group—loose in England. They still thought the problem was in America.

The witch hunters' message had been clear in America when they had been wreaking havoc across the continent. They wanted equality between the magical and the non-magical—no matter the cost. Those terrorists wouldn't stop killing until magical governments stepped out into the daylight and made themselves seen to the non-magical side of the world.

Even in European countries, showing magic to non-magical people was highly illegal and punishable. The witch hunters had expanded to Europe to get their message across. The magical government in the UK had to be blind not to see that.

If Liam could have, he would have knocked some sense into the government officials. Unfortunately, he couldn't do that.

On a Friday evening, there was a meeting at Liam's parents' house. A lot of the members, Liam included, were attending.

"We need to do something," was the most used phrase of the meeting. The members kept repeating it over and over again. Especially Eric who was driven by revenge after his brother's death.

"We need information before we do anything. Right now we have nothing to work on," Ray said, raising his voice. He made sure everyone heard him. "Doherty and Ciara are in America for that. Once they're back, we will get information. Then we can do something about this situation."

"We don't know when they'll be back," a male member argued. Liam recognised him as one of his parents' friends, but he couldn't remember his name.

"What do you suggest we do, then?" Henry asked, crossing his arms. "We have no information to work with. Even the government is against us rather than on our side."

"Doherty is working on that, too," Ray said.

"Oh, please! He's been working on it for ages now," a black-haired woman called Hannah scoffed. "It's useless." She was the one Iris had been treating after the last witch hunter attack on the group. She had made it.

"What kind of information are we expecting to get?" Eric asked.

Ray sighed. "We don't know yet."

Liam didn't have to be a seer to know how the conversation was going to end. Even the calming shades of green and beige on the living room walls weren't enough to keep any members calm. They were all shifting in their seats.

He trusted Ciara and Doherty. They would bring back any information they could.

"How do you know the information will help us?"

"Any kind of information will help us," Henry said.

"Well, we've been waiting for the information for a month now." It was Hannah—the black-haired woman—who spoke. "How much longer are we supposed to wait?"

"She's right," Eric said. "We've waited for too long. We've watched the witch hunters kill more and more. They've killed innocents. And our own, too. We need the information now!"

"Just give them a few more days," Liam said. "It's not like

we can do anything else."

"We need that information now!" another man demanded.

It was no surprise the members were growing irritated, considering the situation. Their friend had been recently killed, and another one had been severely injured. Even if Hannah was already better, it had been a close call.

The group wanted revenge. They needed to plan a mission.

But they couldn't plan a mission yet. With no information on the witch hunters, it would have been foolish, even suicidal, to rush into action.

"We do—"

Just in time, someone opened the front door. There was a soft thud, but it was loud enough to make everyone fall silent.

Doherty appeared in the doorway of the living room, scanning the room to see who was present. "I didn't think I'd need to knock," he said as an apology for his sudden appearance.

"Finally!" Once again, it was Hannah.

The other corner of Doherty's mouth turned upwards a little. It was half of an amused smile. "I see you've all become impatient during my absence. I understand why." His smile became full, both corners of his mouth curling up. "But I bring good news."

"It had better be!"

Doherty had a knowing look. He knew the information he had was good enough to make every irritated member satisfied. "The government seems to have realised the threat in our country is as real as it was in the States and Canada."

First silence hit the room. Then after the initial shock, whispers filled the space. Liam didn't join in, but he observed the other members.

"Ciara, whom some of you have met and some have yet to meet, has convinced the British head of the hit wizards,"

Doherty said.

Liam snapped his head at Doherty, his eyes widening. He couldn't believe Ciara had done *that*. He wasn't sure if it was her influence or her persuasion skills, but it was impressive.

"But this isn't just good news for us," Doherty said. "If we want to continue our work, we have to do a better job at hiding our missions. Our actions would be considered even more illegal now that the government will have their own people working on this."

"Where is Ciara?" Henry asked.

"Signing her transfer papers," Doherty grunted.

"Transfer papers?" Liam swore he saw his brother's eyes fill with a hopeful glee.

"She's moving back to England."

Liam hadn't expected that. No one had. Ciara had just come back for a visit.

Henry was excited. He had an apology to make for walking out on her when she had joined the group, but after that he would have his best friend back in his life.

Liam couldn't deny he was happy too. At least he would have time to talk everything through with Ciara, because she wasn't leaving.

The meeting didn't end there. In fact, it seemed never-ending. The members wondered how the government would deal with the situation and with the witch hunters. It was just guessing, but it still went on for hours.

Even with those few hours spent talking, they didn't get anything done. The members agreed they would meet the following week. Ciara would have more information by then. Information they could use against the witch hunters, like their possible whereabouts or any leverage they might have on the terrorists.

C iara sighed heavily. She had just left the London headquarters.

It had been quite a meeting. And not just a meeting, but a long day.

She had managed to convince the British head of hit witches and wizards that there was a real problem in Great Britain. She wouldn't have been able to convince anyone without all the proof she had. Luckily, she and her colleagues had got information out of the two witch hunters in Canada. She also had some more proof to offer thanks to the British group of volunteers who had gathered evidence—potions, blood samples, and such—on their missions.

Having been transferred to England, Ciara's new boss was Doherty, like back in the old days. It was going to be great. Both she and Doherty worked for the—illegally active—group. They could deliver information if the government failed at their task, so they still had a back-up plan.

Even though Ciara had convinced the head of the Hit

Department, there had been no actions to convince her yet. Nothing had been proven, and Ciara refused to get her hopes up.

She hoped there would be proof soon. There wasn't time to waste.

The sky was dark, and the streets were quiet.

Ciara hadn't spoken with Henry since before her mission. In fact, Ciara hadn't spoken to anyone other than Doherty— and her American colleagues. Still, she wouldn't stay with Doherty.

He had done enough for her. The man had been the one to offer her the job as a hit witch. She had been one of the first hit witches ever in Canada. Even still, most of her colleagues were men.

Doherty had never treated her differently for being a woman. He hadn't gone harder or easier on her, like many others had. She had been equal to her colleagues in his eyes—something she would never forget.

But even if Doherty hadn't given her special treatment, he had spoken highly of her when she had earned it. Without him, she would have never got the chance to play a part in bigger missions with the more dangerous criminals.

She could have asked Doherty if she could stay on his couch for a little while, but she didn't want to be a bother. She needed a hotel room.

To her luck, she found a hotel that wasn't fully booked. The second she got a room, she rushed in there. A little later she had taken a shower and was ready to get some sleep.

She hadn't had a decent night's sleep in weeks.

Ciara's morning was not off to a good start from the moment her phone rang. She sleepily reached for it. Declining the call was tempting, but she saw the caller was Iris.

She didn't want to seem rude. She cleared her throat, hoping she wouldn't sound sleepy, and picked up the call.

"Iris? Hi."

"Ciara! Hi!" Iris sounded frustratingly cheery. "It's great to hear your voice. It's been so long. I was told you're back in England."

"Yes, I'm in London."

"Wonderful!"

If it had been anyone else, Ciara would have hung up.

"There's something I need help with at my flat," Iris said. "Would you mind coming over?"

Yes, I would mind, she thought. "Right now?"

"As soon as you can."

Ciara checked the time. She wanted to stay in bed for the rest of the day. "I should be there in less than an hour. Is that okay?"

"That's perfect! See you soon."

"See you."

It wasn't the type of wake-up Ciara had expected. And she should have at least asked what Iris needed help with. Did it have something to do with the witch hunters and the group?

Ciara had been away for weeks. She didn't know what had been going on in England.

In forty-five minutes, Ciara stood at Iris's flat door. She knocked, and soon enough the smiling blue-eyed woman opened the door for her.

"Ciara! It's fantastic to see you!" Iris said and hugged Ciara.

Ciara smiled. "It's great to see you, too." She stepped inside and closed the door.

She was so glad she had used magic to throw on some makeup. At least she didn't look like a zombie. Except perhaps compared to Iris.

Iris had her blonde hair in waves. She was wearing shimmer eyeshadow, and she looked full of energy. In fact, she was beaming.

Iris grinned. "How was America? Anything exciting?"

"You'll hear plenty about it at the meeting next week. It was just a work trip."

"Not even a bit of free time?"

"I visited Theo's grave and met with his mother." Ciara swallowed, an uncomfortable sensation washing over her from thinking about Theo again. "Otherwise, it was just work."

Iris nodded. "I see." She gestured for Ciara to follow her and led her to the kitchen.

A pair of unfamiliar women were sitting at the table. Soon enough Ciara found out they were Iris's friends.

"So, what did you need help with?" Ciara asked. "It seemed somewhat urgent."

Iris grinned, revealing her perfect set of pure white teeth. She had undoubtedly had them whitened. "I'm sort of in the middle of planning a wedding. Liam agreed we should have a December wedding at last."

Ciara looked at the blonde with her mouth agape for a second. She recovered from her initial shock and smiled. "Congratulations. So what can I help with?"

If Iris asked Ciara to help with the security at the wedding, she would be happy to assist.

"Liam doesn't seem to care about the theme colours and such," Iris said. "He said I can do the planning for him."

It wasn't going the way Ciara had expected.

"So, I started thinking." Iris smiled at Ciara. "You know Liam almost as well as I do, so I'd like to have you help me. Well, us." She gestured to her two friends. "I'd really appreciate the help. Unless you mind, of course."

Ciara didn't want to plan her ex-boyfriend's wedding. She had a lot more important things on her mind. She was dying to tell Iris that.

But she couldn't say no, seeing how excited Iris was. She put on a smile and agreed.

The four women went through theme colours, napkin colours, and flowers. It was tiring, and Ciara began to regret her decision to help.

She could have said no. In fact, she *should* have.

She didn't even know anything about flowers. She was there just because she knew Liam. Or, rather, had known Liam.

And it was just plain odd for Ciara to be helping with her ex-boyfriend's wedding. It made her uncomfortable, and she couldn't wait for it to be over.

Ciara wasn't sure what the worst part was of helping plan the wedding. Either it was the fact that they were planning her ex-boyfriend's wedding, or it was the fact that she would have been planning her own wedding if Theo hadn't died.

She lasted an hour before she came up with an excuse so she could leave. She claimed to have promised to meet a friend.

Iris walked her to the door while her two friends remained at the dining table. "So you're staying in England now? For good, I mean."

"You found out already?"

Iris nodded. "Doherty told everyone."

"Oh."

"And, well, since you're staying...would you mind helping more with the wedding? It'll just be little things, I promise. I already have bridesmaids and a maid of honour, but I would appreciate a little help."

"I don't know how busy my schedule will be in the upcoming months. But if I have time, then sure."

Ciara hoped the upcoming months would be busy for her. She didn't want to help, but she didn't know how to tell Iris no. After Theo's proposal, she had been excited about the idea of marrying him one day. Ciara could understand how Iris felt.

"Great! Thank you so much. You're such an angel."

Ciara smiled. "No problem."

They said goodbyes, and Ciara left. When she heard Iris close the door, she sighed, relieved it was over—and exhausted from it.

Ciara took the stairs rather than the lift. She went through her handbag, looking for her phone, when she heard someone say her name.

She looked up to see a familiar hazel-eyed man standing two steps below her. "Oh, hi." Ciara smiled at Liam and stepped down one step, so she was only standing one stair higher than he was.

"Hi." He smiled back at her.

"I heard you set your wedding date," Ciara said.

"Oh, yeah." Liam ran a hand through his long hair. "Well, Iris wanted a Christmas wedding, so I agreed."

Ciara nodded. "It means a lot to her."

"Yeah, I suppose it does." Liam nodded, too. "Um, do you have a moment?"

Ciara had lied to Iris about meeting a friend. She had to lie to Liam, too. "Actually, I have to meet a friend." She forced a smile, knowing it worked when she had to lie for her job.

"Oh."

Liam was disappointed, which Ciara noticed. But she didn't know Liam could tell she was lying. Her small, polite smile gave it away.

"But I promised to help with your wedding whenever I can, so I suppose I'll be around here and there," Ciara said. "Unless you mind. It's your wedding, too. I mean, Iris asked, so—"

"No, of course I don't mind," Liam said. "It's, um, nice to have you back in England."

Ciara smiled. "Nearly forgot you already know."

"Doherty told at the meeting."

"Iris told me that."

"So—"

"Um, I'm sorry," Ciara said, dying to get out of the

building. "I really have to go now or I'm gonna be late."

"O-of course." Liam nodded. "Have fun."

Ciara smiled. "Thanks. See you around."

"See you."

They both smiled at one another, and with one last glance, Ciara hurried down the stairs. She had to pretend she was about to be late for a meeting with a friend.

13

On Monday it was time for the meeting. It was at the Rosslers' house, as usual. The meeting would start at six o'clock, so Ciara made sure she was early.

Ciara made it to the Rosslers' place at half past five. Mrs Rossler nearly crushed her in a hug, so excited to see her. "It is so wonderful to have you back from America."

Ciara smiled. "It is wonderful to be back, Mrs Rossler."

"Oh, it's Mary to you, dear." Mrs Rossler—Mary—smiled at Ciara.

Ciara smiled back and nodded. "Alright, Mary."

Ciara caught a glimpse of the younger Rosslers before their parents forced them to go upstairs. They were too young to be involved with the group—too young to deal with the horrors of the world.

Doherty arrived early, too, only a little later than Ciara. "You ready?" was the first thing he asked, not bothering with greetings.

"Of course." Ciara nodded. "It's just a meeting."

"Oh, it'll be an exhausting one." Doherty sighed and headed to the living room.

Little by little, the house filled with witches and wizards. Mr Rossler introduced them to Ciara, but she forgot most names. There were too many to learn so fast.

It was only five minutes to six. Everyone was already sitting in the living room. The ones missing were Henry and Liam—and some who had said they wouldn't make it, like Iris. But Henry and Liam were supposed to be there.

Liam arrived two minutes later. He spotted Ciara, who was still standing outside the living room, and walked over to greet her. "So, your first meeting."

Ciara looked up and smiled. "It is."

"How early were you here?"

Ciara couldn't help but chuckle. "I came thirty minutes ago."

Liam smiled, shoving his hands in his pockets and taking a quick look around. "Of course."

"Better early than late." Ciara liked to live by that. She had to, with her job.

Liam couldn't see his brother anywhere. "Try teaching that to Henry."

"Once he starts talking to me again, I will."

Liam turned to look at Ciara again, his brows furrowing. "You're not staying with him?"

Ciara didn't have a flat in England. At least he doubted she did.

"I haven't talked to him in weeks. So, no."

"Where are you staying, then?" Liam asked.

"A hotel. It's—"

"Henry will come late!" Doherty said and stood up. "We need to begin now."

It was six o'clock.

Liam and Ciara stood in the doorway, not bothering to squish between other witches and wizards sitting on sofas, benches, and chairs.

Doherty turned to look at Ciara. "Would you mind telling us what you know, Ciara?" he asked and sat back down.

Ciara looked around the room. Everyone was staring, dying to hear what she had to say. "Well, uh, as some of you might know, I've been working to defeat the witch hunters for quite some time. We've been able to either catch or kill nearly all the witch hunters in America," she said. "But, unfortunately, some of them escaped to Europe. Great Britain seems to be their target now. We thought we had identified their leader, but we were wrong. It turns out their organisation has more levels. We don't know who the actual leader is, but there are people working to find that out. We also haven't figured out how many mid-level leaders there are. It's likely their organisation is more complex than we first assumed."

"So, you're telling us you know nothing?" A snort followed the words. Ciara remembered the man—Harry Edmonds.

"No," Ciara said, unbothered by the way the man presented his question. She was used to dealing with people like him. "It looks like at least thirty witch hunters have come from America to Great Britain. More witch hunters are scattered elsewhere in Europe. For example, we could locate two in France, and the local officials already caught them."

Liam had never seen Ciara talk like that. There was so much determination and strength in her tone. She spoke like a leader. An inspiring leader.

"As far as we know, there are six more witch hunters somewhere in Europe. Or more. So far, they've evaded the authorities," Ciara continued. "In America, we caught two witch hunters. Both originally from America, but they had moved to Great Britain earlier this year. We were able to get some of this information by interrogating them. Even so, they were rather tight-lipped, and we weren't able to get as much out of them as we would have liked."

"What happened to them?" The woman who spoke was Diana Adams or Diana Adamson, Ciara couldn't remember which.

"They were dealt with in America."

"*Dealt with*?" The woman raised an eyebrow. "You mean killed?"

"Once we were sure we wouldn't get more information from them, we delivered them to professionals who handle people like them," Ciara told. "As far as I know, their memories are erased and they don't know who they are. They are in a prison of sorts."

"How can you be sure they have no more information?" This time another woman spoke.

"Well, first of all, experience. They would have had more information, but they would have never given it to us. We use a potion to make sure that's the case. There's no point trying to gain more information after the confirmation."

"Is it fail-safe?" Harry Edmonds asked.

Ciara nodded. "It is."

Mr Edmonds nodded, but he didn't seem convinced.

"Anyway, it looks as though thirty witch hunters have come here. It's likely they've gained more followers during their time here, too," Ciara said. "According to our calculations, there could be over seventy witch hunters in Great Britain right now."

"Whose calculations?" Mr Rossler—Ray—asked.

"A colleague of mine from America. He's the best at what he does."

"You trust him?"

"Absolutely."

Ray nodded. "That's good enough for me."

Ciara smiled in appreciation. Ray openly showing his trust for Ciara would help Ciara gain more trust inside the group. So far, the members had been rather sceptical and doubtful.

"We also know the possible whereabouts of some of the witch hunters."

Gasps and whispers filled the room upon this revelation.

Liam wondered if Ciara had practised her speech. It was smart to leave the juiciest parts towards the end.

"We should send out people to make sure this information is correct," Doherty said. "People who won't be seen. We can plan an attack after we have confirmed the locations."

"I already agreed to check one of the locations unless someone objects," Ciara said.

The room went silent. Everyone waited to see if anyone would object, but no one did.

Doherty stood up, gaining everyone's attention. "We need seven more volunteers."

"I volunteer," Liam said, stepping forward. He earned a displeased look from his mother, but he ignored it.

He wanted to help, and for once Iris wasn't there to stop him. She was working.

Once Liam had volunteered, more people followed suit. In the end, there were eight volunteers, including Ciara and Liam.

Each voluntary member was assigned a location. The task was to see if there were any witch hunters in the location. They had until the morning.

After the meeting was over, Doherty stayed behind to talk with the volunteers. "I need each of you to be finished by morning. And I want to hear from you when you're done, so I'll know if anyone runs into trouble."

All the volunteers agreed. Six of them left the house to do their part.

Henry was still a no-show.

"Are you going to leave right away?" Liam asked Ciara.

She nodded. "I want to be finished on time."

"Be careful."

Ciara looked him in the eyes. "You, too."

"Of course."

Ciara said her goodbyes to everyone and left. Mary, who scolded Liam for volunteering, held him back a little longer. But after the one-sided discussion, he left to finish the task.

The location assigned to Ciara was an old house. An elderly woman was supposed to live there, but Ciara feared that someone had killed her.

Ciara used a hiding spell and blended herself into the tree. She was sitting on a branch, spying on the house. She could see shadows moving inside, but the curtains were closed. There was no way to make out what was happening.

Ciara was glad she didn't have to go inside—at least not yet. She dreaded the thought of what had happened in that house.

She had witnessed plenty of horrors thanks to the witch hunters. They killed innocents whenever they benefitted from it. A life could be worth less than a house for them. No one was safe from them. They didn't always target specific people. Sometimes their victims were random, selected for something they had—like a house.

Ciara doubted she could finish before the morning. She wasn't excited about spending a night on a tree branch, but she couldn't go around wandering if there were witch hunters. Not alone.

That was the tough part of the task, even though it seemed rather simple. If the witch hunters saw Ciara, it would likely be the end of her. Even if she managed to escape, the rest of the witch hunters would have found out their whereabouts had been uncovered. There was no way Ciara would let that happen.

So she sat in the tree and even surprised herself with her own patience. For two hours she just sat there. During those two hours, nothing happened.

Her patience was thinning. In fact, she was planning to switch her hiding spot to another, even though it was risky.

But, as if on cue, the front door opened. A man walked out, carrying a rubbish bag.

Ciara could see his tattoos from where she was hiding.

He was a witch hunter. He even had a tattoo of their symbol on his shoulder. An outline of a flame with a wand in the middle.

Was he alone? Ciara had seen shadows move inside, but she couldn't be sure if it had been just one or two people. If the man was alone, Ciara could attack on her own.

That man deserved to die for what he and the rest of the witch hunters had done. They had killed Theo.

Ciara's eyes flickered between the windows and the man. A flood of adrenaline rushed through her, and her heart raced.

There was no movement inside.

Is he alone? Could I beat him?

Ciara hesitated too long. After taking the rubbish out, the man walked back inside.

Ciara had already done enough. She had confirmed there were witch hunters in the house. Still, she stayed in the tree.

She wanted to find out what had happened to the owner of the house—the woman who had lived there.

Eventually, her decision to stay and watch a little longer turned out to be a good one.

She found out there were two witch hunters. Both were around thirty years old and male.

Ciara didn't find out anything about the owner, though. She couldn't risk being seen, so she couldn't go around snooping.

Perhaps she was better off not knowing about the poor woman's fate, anyway.

But she didn't have anywhere to be the following day, so she stayed observing the house until it was five in the morning. She gained little more information, but at least she had done everything she could.

She used magic to teleport near her hotel, exhaustion hitting her, and made her way inside. The first thing she did was get to the lift, even though she would have preferred stairs because of a past accident. She stepped inside, pressed her floor's button and waited.

She leaned against the lift wall and stretched her neck. Her eyelids felt heavy, and she had to force back a yawn.

Before getting any sleep, she would have to call Doherty.

The lift doors opened, and Ciara stepped out. She walked to her hotel room.

Just as she had got her hands on the key card in her pocket, she looked up and saw the door was already open—ajar.

14

Ciara shoved the key card in her pocket and slowly pushed the door more open. She was expecting someone—or something—to attack her, but she didn't see or hear anyone.

Staying at the door, she reached for her phone and called Doherty.

It didn't take him long to pick up the call. "Are you ready?"

"Come to my hotel room now," Ciara said and hung up.

She didn't have time to talk with Doherty if someone was in her hotel room. Someone just had to know something was off. Because if something happened, Doherty would be there to figure it out.

Ciara stepped inside. She listened carefully but couldn't hear anything. Keeping alert, she checked behind the door. Nothing.

She reached for the wardrobe door. Holding her hand on the handle, she stopped moving and listened, then yanked the door open. No one in there.

Ciara eyed the corridor, leading to the bedroom part. She couldn't see or hear anyone. She turned her attention to the bathroom door.

Clenching her hand into a fist, she pushed the door open. She opened her fist, sending an air blast into the bathroom, and stepped in. No one in there, either.

With her air blast, Ciara had broken the mirror. By only moving her hand, she fixed it with magic.

She was aware how heavy her breathing was. Her heart pounded so loud she could hear it. Exhaling, she stepped out of the bathroom, closing the door silently. As she walked along the short corridor, her heartbeats only grew louder.

She walked around the corner.

There was no one. Not anymore.

But her clothes were no longer neatly folded in her bag. They were in the bag, but someone had thrown them back in there.

She strode over to see if anything was missing. She went through her belongings, but she couldn't figure out what was missing. It looked like nothing was.

She also couldn't see anything out of place or any items that weren't hers.

"Ciara!" Doherty had been quick. He was already at the hotel room door.

Ciara walked to Doherty's line of sight, noticing he wasn't alone. "Someone's been here," she said and returned to investigate her bag.

Doherty, along with Henry and Liam, followed her.

"Liam, look around and make sure there's no one spying on us. Also, check for any spells," Doherty instructed.

Liam nodded and got to work.

"Someone has gone through my stuff, but nothing is missing," Ciara said.

Henry furrowed his eyebrows. "How do you know someone went through your stuff then?"

"Everything was folded and set neatly in my bag before.

The hotel room door was also open when I came here. Not just unlocked, but actually open."

"Do you think it's one of the witch hunters?" Doherty's eyes clouded with worry, and he observed Ciara.

"I have no idea." Ciara sighed. "I've made a fair share of enemies. Not all of them are witch hunters."

Doherty nodded. "You're right."

"Well, you can't stay here," Henry said and turned to face his best friend—to whom he hadn't talked in weeks. "You have to come stay with me."

"You don't mind?" Ciara asked.

"Of course not."

A knock at the door startled Ciara, Henry, and Liam. The latter two turned to face the door and grabbed their wands, pointing them at it.

"Calm down. It's Diana." Doherty walked to the hotel room door while the two wizards lowered their wands.

"What is she doing here?" Ciara asked.

"She should be able to tell who has been in here," Henry said, pocketing his wand. "She has an ability. Runs in the family."

"Oh."

Doherty returned to where Ciara and Henry were standing with the woman Ciara had seen at the meeting. Diana was looking around the room. Everyone else stared at her, eager to know what she would find out with her ability. Ciara supposed it was a special gift like her wandless magic.

"I'm afraid I won't be able to help you much," Diana said and turned to face Ciara. "Whoever was here, she or he was powerful."

So someone powerful was after Ciara. Another confirmation she wasn't safe to be around.

"Pack your stuff," Doherty ordered. "You're going with Henry."

Ciara nodded and threw everything in her bag. There wasn't much to pack. She only had to grab a few things from the bathroom and make sure nothing was left on the bed or the tables.

"Whoever was here, they left no trace." Liam sighed. He had searched through the entire room but had found nothing. He couldn't even sense any hiding spells.

Doherty nodded and turned to Ciara. "Check out of the hotel. Then go with Henry."

Ciara nodded.

Doherty turned back to Liam. "Go with them in case there's still someone nearby. Diana and I will wait a moment and then leave, so we'll be here if someone is waiting for Ciara."

Liam nodded.

Henry grabbed Ciara's bag. "Let's go."

The trio left the hotel room after quick goodbyes to both Doherty and Diana. They didn't spot anyone on their way to the lift.

"So far, so good," Henry mumbled.

"Whoever it was is long gone by now," Ciara said.

She knew how dangerous witches and wizards were, but it was unlikely they would attack with everyone on alert. They would have had a better chance when she had been unaware and alone.

"You're probably right," Liam said. "But let's not take any risks."

Ciara signed out of the hotel while the brothers kept an eye on the surroundings—and Ciara. There was no one suspicious around. Ciara had been right. Whoever had been in her hotel room was already gone.

Once Ciara had signed out, the trio walked out. The air was humid, but the morning sun was warm.

The trio walked to a quieter spot and then used magic to get to Henry's flat. All three of them were exhausted, having stayed up all night.

Without Ciara having to ask how Liam and Henry had ended up with Doherty, Henry explained everything.

Henry had been stuck at work, so he had been late for the meeting. Doherty had explained everything to him later when he had finally made it to the house. Then there had been an emergency with a volunteer. The witch hunters had spotted him, so Henry and Doherty had gone there to help.

Once they had come back, Liam had finished and gone to his parents' place.

After Ciara had called Doherty, he had explained the situation. Both brothers had demanded to tag along.

"Are you okay?" Liam's brows furrowed with concern, and he placed a hand on Ciara's shoulder.

"I'm fine." She forced a brief smile. "That wasn't the first time someone's broken into my hotel room."

The latter didn't bring Liam any comfort. He let his hand drop from Ciara's shoulder and nodded. "G-good."

Henry looked between his best friend and older brother before looking solely at Liam. "Iris is probably worried and waiting for you."

"You're right." He glanced at Ciara. "Just call me if either of you needs anything."

Henry patted his brother on the shoulder. "Will do."

"Bye," Liam said, walking to the door.

"Bye," Ciara and Henry said before Liam left.

Once the door shut, Ciara sat down on the sofa. She leaned against the soft cushions, closing her eyes. All she wanted was to sleep.

Henry was still standing in the middle of the living room. He had only set Ciara's bag down so far. "I'm sorry."

"It's okay," Ciara said, meaning it. "But...do you mind if we get some sleep before we talk?"

Henry yawned and nodded. "You can have the bed."

"No, the sofa is fine. I'm already here anyway," Ciara said, not bothering to open her eyes.

"Are you sure?"

"Yes."

"Alright then." Henry nodded, even though Ciara couldn't

see that. "Good night."

"Good night, Henry."

Meanwhile, Liam opened the door to his and Iris's flat. He was ready to get some sleep.

Iris hurried to hug her fiancé. "I was so worried!" She cupped his face with her tender hands and looked up at him with worry clear in her eyes.

"I'm fine," Liam said. He pecked his fiancée's lips and gave her a comforting smile.

"I thought you'd be back earlier." Iris stepped back to let Liam put his coat away.

"I wasn't done until early in the morning." Liam removed his coat and hung it on the coatrack. "Then Ciara called Doherty. It seemed like she was in trouble. Someone had been in her hotel room."

Iris furrowed her eyebrows. "I didn't know she was staying at a hotel."

"Me neither. She's staying with Henry now."

"So, she's safe?"

Liam nodded. "She should be."

"Good."

"Do you have work?" Liam asked Iris.

"In an hour."

"Do you mind if I get some sleep?" Liam's eyes were burning, and he had a massive headache brewing.

"Go ahead." Iris kissed his cheek. "I love you."

"I love you, too."

15

Ciara had been asleep since seven in the morning, then woke up around noon. She didn't feel tired despite getting only five hours of sleep.

She freshened up in the bathroom and then cooked scrambled eggs. Henry wouldn't mind a good breakfast.

Except she had only tried cooking scrambled eggs once before, and it hadn't gone well. She was planning to make eatable scrambled eggs this time.

And she did. They turned out to be digestible at least.

Ciara grabbed a plate and a fork and started eating her half.

"You cooked?"

Ciara nearly choked on the food in her mouth. "Henry!" she gasped out, coughing.

"Sorry." Henry grimaced, watching his best friend.

Ciara stopped coughing. "No worries. I, uh, cooked us breakfast."

"That is a miracle. Is it edible, too?"

Ciara laughed. "Try it."

Henry sat down. Ciara had already set a plate for him. He filled it with scrambled eggs and began to eat. First, he only tried a mouthful. "It's good," he said once he finished eating the food in his mouth.

"Surprisingly."

Henry chuckled. "Yeah."

The two ate in silence for a little while. When it became too much, Henry started talking.

"I'm unbelievably sorry for being an ass." He didn't know how else to say it.

"It's okay."

"No, it isn't." He shook his head. "I was stupid because I worry about you. But I should also trust you. I know you've been doing these things for a while now. You know what you're doing better than most."

"I forgive you," Ciara said. "It's okay to worry."

"It's not just that."

She pushed aside her plate. "What do you mean?"

Henry shook his head, sighing. "I don't want to lose my best friend again."

She reached over the table to squeeze her best friend's hand. "I'm sorry I left. I am. It's never going to happen again, I swear."

Henry pulled his hand away, looking down. "It's not just that."

"I don't understand."

"At school, we used to be there for each other. For everything. Whether one of us needed help with something or a date or...anything."

"I needed you more than you needed me."

Henry smiled. "Maybe. But what I mean is that then Liam came into picture. Then you started dating him. And for a while, I felt shut out."

Ciara's eyes softened. "I didn't know. Henry, I swear, if I had realised—"

"Well, then you broke up and everything seemed to go back to the usual. Except then there was this weird tension between me and you, as well as me and my brother."

Ciara nodded. She could only picture what Henry had felt like. "I never meant to put you in such a position."

"I know. But the least you could've done is told me about leaving. You just left out of nowhere. You walked out on me."

Ciara swallowed. "I know, and nothing I say is going to fix that. I needed a break, and that's no excuse, but it's the reason I left. America and the job and everything, it was fresh air for me. But I had no right to walk out like I did. I didn't leave because of you, and to be honest I missed you like hell. If you could ask Theo, he'd tell you."

"Ciara—"

"No, just let me finish." She looked straight into her best friend's brown eyes, hair hanging on her face. "I'm sorry, and no number of apologies is going to fix anything. But from now on, I'll do better. I promise I will. Henry, you are the greatest best friend one could have, and I'm the worst. If it counts at all, I'm back now and I'll do whatever it takes to earn your friendship back. You mean a lot to me, and I never want to lose you again. I'd literally be dead without you. You saved my life by figuring out that those two witch hunters were in Canada for me."

Henry smiled, the corners of his mouth twitching. "I like to be the hero."

Ciara chuckled. "Knew it."

"So, are we good? For real good?" Henry asked.

"On my behalf, of course. I can't stay angry with you. Especially now that there's nothing to be angry about."

Henry's smile grew brighter on hearing those words. "Good. Because I forgive you. For everything."

Ciara grabbed her fork and pointed it at Henry. "But I won't leave all the work for others. I'm going to do my job."

Henry nodded. "I wouldn't expect anything else."

"Good."

"So, how was America this time?"

"Busy as usual. It was just work."

"But you visited Theo's grave, right?"

Ciara nodded, an ache clutching at her heart. "Yes, I did. And I visited his mother."

"How is she?"

"She's moving on. Little by little." Ciara smiled. "She's such a sweetheart. I mean...she's almost like another mother to me."

"You seem to make a good impression on your boyfriends' mothers."

"It's a habit."

"Well, Mum adores you."

"I was your best friend before I was anything with Liam, though."

"Still."

Ciara smiled.

"So, did you hear about the wedding yet?" Henry asked, changing the subject. It was fair to tell Ciara.

"I did." Ciara nodded, fighting back a grimace. "Iris already asked for my help."

Henry raised an eyebrow. He looked at Ciara as if she had just said something unheard of. "Really?"

Ciara nodded. "Really." She sighed at the mere thought of wedding planning. "It's kind of odd, to be honest."

"I bet!"

Ciara bit her lip. "Yeah. But I couldn't just say no to her."

"Why not?"

"Iris was so excited. And I'm sure she means well. She just wants help with the biggest day of her life."

"Still," Henry said, shaking his head in disbelief. "Planning your ex-boyfriend's wedding is weird."

"It is. I'm hoping I'll be able to come up with good excuses most of the time."

"So, you're being kind and polite by lying," Henry said.

Ciara nodded. "Is it wrong?"

"Not in this situation."

"Did Liam ask you to be the best man?" Ciara asked Henry.

"Nope. I'm his brother and that's enough," Henry said. "I think he asked Hugo Stiller. Remember him?"

"Of course."

She hadn't seen Hugo in years. The last time she had seen him had been before she and Liam had been dating. It had been Liam's last year—and Hugo's too.

"They still hang out?" Obviously they did, but Ciara couldn't believe how everyone was still hanging out with their old friends from school.

Henry nodded. "And Shawn, too."

"Wow." Ciara remembered Shawn.

"They started hanging out again after Liam came back to England," Henry said.

"That makes sense."

"Oh, and I should tell you about one thing."

"Why that tone?"

Henry tilted his head. "What tone?"

"You talk about your crushes with that tone," Ciara said.

"How do you still know me that well?" Henry asked, his mouth hanging open.

"I'm your best friend forever," Ciara said and smiled. "So, is it Jenna?"

Henry blushed. "Well, y—"

"I knew it!" Ciara grinned in victory. "Finally! And official for how long?"

"A week." Henry's cheeks turned a deeper shade of red. "We've gone on one official date and then a couple of lunch dates."

"So cute!" Ciara squealed. "When are you going to propose?"

Henry rolled his eyes, but he was smiling. "Give me a year at least."

"Fine," Ciara said and sighed dramatically. "But no more

than that."

Henry chuckled. "You're more excited than I am."

"I just think you two will be the cutest couple ever."

"Well, looks like you'll be around to see us together."

"I can still go back to America if you want me to, but—"

"It's good to have you back for good," Henry said, cutting Ciara off mid-sentence. "I've missed you. Everyone has."

"It's nice to be back for good now," Ciara said, nodding. "And don't worry, I'm already looking for a flat, so I'll try to move out as soon as I can."

"No hurry," Henry said. "I don't mind you staying here. Especially now that you might be in danger."

"Henry, I have plenty of enemies. I'll always be in danger. But I can take care of myself."

"I'd feel less worried if I knew someone was there to look after you, though."

Ciara knew what Henry was implying. The familiar ache reappeared in her chest. "I'm not ready for a new relationship right now."

Henry nodded. "I can understand that. Maybe you should get a dragon. Like a guard dog, but a guard dragon."

Ciara laughed. It was an absurd idea. Dragons couldn't be domesticated. They belonged in the wild unless they needed special care. For that, there were sanctuaries like the one Henry worked at. "That'd be something. But if I got a dragon, you'd never leave my house." Not that she would have minded. Henry was her best friend.

"You got that right."

"What happened to your dragon?"

Henry smiled. "I still see Roan at work every day. He's growing fast, so I can't keep him here anymore."

"So he's healthy and well?"

"He is." Henry nodded.

Ciara couldn't help but smile. "That's good to hear." Somehow, she had grown fond of that dragon.

"You didn't have to come with me," Ciara said to Henry when the two of them walked into the school hall.

They had turned the hall into a ballroom. It was beautifully decorated. There was sparkle and glitter floating in the air to make the hall look even more magical. Flower decorations were scattered around. The blue curtains had been changed for beige ones with golden stripes.

Everyone had put on their best attire. The girls wore beautiful long gowns, and the guys wore their best suits.

Henry smiled at Ciara. "I wanted to come with you."

Ciara was still looking around the decorated hall, mesmerised by the beauty of it, when her gaze landed on a couple. Liam and Mia were already there. Mia was talking to Liam enthusiastically, and he was smiling at her.

It was his usual smile. The soft smile that reached his eyes, lighting up his entire face. Ciara was all too familiar with it. She could only daydream of being in Mia's position—of causing that smile.

Henry's eyes followed Ciara's gaze, landing on the couple. He knew the look on his best friend's face. He wanted both of them to enjoy the school ball, and that wasn't going to happen if she was sad.

"How about we dance?" Henry said, hoping to get Ciara's mind off his brother.

Ciara grinned. "Don't step on my toes."

"Never again."

Liam spotted his brother—hand in hand with Liam's long-time crush. He was jealous, watching his own brother lead Ciara to the dancefloor.

Liam had asked Ciara to go with him, but she had declined and chuckled as if it was a poor joke.

It had hurt.

Seeing her with Henry brought Liam a spark of hope. Ciara would never have ditched Henry. Not for anyone. If they had agreed to go together before he had asked...

Perhaps Liam still had hope.

The ball felt endless.

Mia was nice, but Liam was growing tired of her constant rambling.

Ciara rarely rambled. She was more focused. Quieter, too, but she wasn't shy. She just liked to keep to herself more than some people—people like Mia.

Mia was a tad clingy too. But Liam would never admit that out loud. Mia was one of Ciara's closest friends. Liam also liked Mia as a friend. He just seldom had to endure her endless rambling. Ciara probably put up with it more.

Ciara was all Liam had been thinking about the entire night, filling his thoughts. He couldn't stop sneaking glances at her either.

At one point, Mia excused herself to go talk with Jenna who had been waving at her. It was the perfect timing, because Henry had just left Ciara to go get drinks.

Liam saw his opportunity and walked past the crowd and over to Ciara. "Hi," he said, standing right behind her.

Ciara spun around with her dark hair bouncing in the air and the hem of her dress flowing like waves. Liam could smell her perfume. He was convinced she only used it on special occasions. It was a fresh, floral scent. It suited her.

A wide smile spread across Ciara's face. "Liam, hi."

"You look beautiful," Liam complimented, gesturing to her bright red dress. It matched her bold red lipstick.

"You don't look too bad yourself," Ciara said, smiling. She thought Liam looked rather handsome in his dark blue suit with a beige bow around his neck.

"Thanks," Liam said with his usual soft smile.

Ciara took a quick look around. "Did you lose Mia or something?"

"She's somewhere with Jenna."

"Oh." Ciara blinked. "She was excited about coming here with you."

Ciara could only hope the disdain in her voice didn't show as much as she feared.

Liam furrowed his eyebrows. "Mia's just a friend."

Ciara's eyes widened. "She is?" The words flew out of her mouth.

Liam smiled, happy with Ciara's reaction. "Yes, she's a friend."

"Why didn't you ask someone else then?"

I asked you, Liam thought. But he couldn't say that out loud. "Like who?" he asked instead.

Ciara shrugged. "Trixie?"

Liam scrunched up his nose and shook his head. "No."

"She's obsessed with you."

"A little too much," Liam said, grimacing.

Ciara couldn't help but chuckle. "True."

Liam spotted Henry caught in a conversation with two of his friends. "Looks like your dance partner is being held back," he said, turning his gaze back to Ciara.

Ciara turned to see what Henry was up to. "Clearly."

"Well, since both our partners are busy with their friends...can I have this dance?" Liam offered Ciara his hand.

She couldn't contain her smile. "Of course."

As Liam led Ciara to the dancefloor, she felt a blush creep up onto her cheeks. She could only hope she was wearing enough makeup to cover it. The blushing got worse once Liam placed his hand on her waist and pulled her closer.

Blushing or not, she liked it. It was a total cliché, but she felt like she could forget about everyone else in the room. Her focus was solely on Liam—and not stepping on his feet.

The dreaded night turned out to be wonderful after all.

16

"I've talked with each of our volunteers now," Doherty said.

Doherty, along with most members of the British group, was sitting in the Rosslers' living room for yet another meeting. According to Doherty, it was unheard of to have a meeting only two days after the previous one.

But they needed to act fast. They knew some witch hunters' locations, but there was no guarantee they wouldn't pack and leave. The group couldn't risk losing track of them. Not when they were so close.

Ciara was dying for action. She wanted to wipe out those terrorists for everything they had done to her.

And to others.

Under the orders of the British government, the officials were barely working on the witch hunter case. They weren't even intensifying the training for the hit witches and wizards. The officials only did something when the witch hunters killed someone, even though it wasn't enough. They didn't do anything to prevent the attacks.

"We have five confirmed locations, two false locations and one unsure location," Doherty explained with all the members listening to him intently. They were all dying to get answers.

Most of the group's members were witches and wizards who had already lost someone because of the witch hunters. But there were also people who merely wanted to help.

"But there's a problem," Doherty said to the members who were shifting anxiously in their seats. "The witch hunters are living in five of the confirmed locations, and we don't know how many witch hunters to expect. It's likely there's one house with only two witch hunters, and there may be one with three. But that's purely based on what we could find out over one night, so we can't be sure."

"We need to deal with the witch hunters before they flee," a member said, pointing out the obvious.

But it wasn't that simple. Some of the members wanted to run into fights before thinking everything through. Some of them were blinded by grief and anger. It wasn't a good, nor a safe, combination. People often lost rationality when they experienced such powerful emotions.

"First, we have to come up with plans for each location," Doherty said. "We can't risk mistakes, and we can't take any unnecessary risks."

"We need teams for all the locations," Henry said. He and Ciara were standing near the doorway, side by side.

"And back-up in case something goes wrong and we have underestimated the number of witch hunters in the location," Ciara said.

"The back-up can wait here," Ray said. "Once they get the alert, they'll teleport to the right location. If they were already on scene, someone could see them. We can't take that risk."

"Any volunteers?" Doherty asked.

Ciara was about to offer, but Doherty saw it coming.

"Ciara, I want you as part of the back-up team, okay? You'll be more helpful if or when things go south. You know what to do in tough situations."

Ciara knew Doherty was right, so she agreed. "Alright."

But she didn't like it. She would have preferred to be out there fighting—getting revenge on her fiancé.

Liam tried to volunteer, but his mother was quick to disagree. Eventually he ended up in the back-up team with Ciara. Iris volunteered for the back-up team, too.

The said team ended up being bigger than most of the location teams, but they split it into pairs. Iris and Liam were one pair. Henry was with his father. There were other pairs, too, but Ciara was left by herself. Doherty wanted to send her wherever she was needed most.

Ciara was one of the few professionals in the group. It didn't mean she was better, but she had more experience.

The missions—the attacks on the locations—were going to take place the following day. Everyone needed to be well-prepared and well-rested, so there was no point executing the missions until then.

Once the meeting was over, everyone headed home. Little by little, the house became less and less crowded.

"You'll be late for your date with Jenna if you don't leave soon," Ciara told Henry, her voice low as they stood in the living room, watching people leave.

Henry's eyes widened, realising what time it was. "You're right!"

Ciara chuckled, amused. "You'd better hurry."

"Uh, I'll be home late."

"Or tomorrow?" Ciara said, wiggling her eyebrows at Henry.

"I'll see you later anyway," Henry said before running out of the room. He said his goodbyes and vanished, teleporting to Jenna's place.

Right after, Mary walked into the living room to talk with Ciara. "Is everything okay with Henry?"

"Oh, yes." Ciara smiled at Mary. "He just realised he's about to be late."

Mary's eyebrows rose, and she looked intrigued. "Late for what?"

"Well, I bet you've noticed how he can't stop staring at his phone."

Mary's eyes widened. "He's dating! Finally!"

"But I didn't tell you that."

Mary smiled. "Of course not. Do you have any idea who it might be?"

"I'm afraid I can't tell, but ask Henry about it," Ciara said. "I can try to convince him to bring her here, too."

"Do that!" Mary's smile was so broad her teeth were showing. "You know her, don't you?"

Ciara smiled and nodded. "I do, and I think she's perfect for Henry."

Joy lit up Mary's eyes. "I believe I'll like her, too."

"I bet you will." Ciara was already excited about the idea of Mary meeting Jenna.

"Did Henry leave already?" Liam was standing in the doorway of the living room, looking around with a confused frown.

"He was late for his date, so he just left," Ciara told.

Liam bit his lip but couldn't contain his smile. "Of course he did."

"You knew?" Mary asked in disbelief. "Why didn't I know until now?"

Liam raised his hands in defence. "He asked me not to say anything."

"Ciara said nothing either, but at least she gave me a hint!" Mary, of course, wasn't upset with Liam, even though she was looking at him disapprovingly.

Liam rolled his eyes. "Men don't do hinting, Mum."

Mary sighed. "Oh, my boy."

Ciara smiled, amused, and took one step towards the exit. "I think it's time for me to head home."

"Are you sure? Do you have dinner prepared?" Mary asked.

Ciara smiled. "Yes, I have food waiting for me in the fridge." She looked at Liam and Mary in turn. "I'll see both of you tomorrow."

"Rest well," Mary said. "And don't forget to eat well. It's important you have enough energy tomorrow."

"Of course, Mary." She glanced at Liam then. "See you tomorrow."

"See you," Liam said and smiled at Ciara.

"See you," Mary said, too, before Ciara left the living room.

Ray was talking to two other members who had yet to leave. Ciara chose not to interrupt them. Instead, she walked over to Iris to say goodbye to her.

"See you tomorrow."

"Are you leaving already?" Iris asked.

Ciara nodded. "I need to rest before tomorrow."

"Ah, I see." Iris nodded. "Do you think you have any time off later this week? I'm looking for a wedding venue, and I'm going to visit a couple of places this week. I'd love to have you come along."

"I can't promise anything yet, but I'll keep you updated on my schedule." Ciara dreaded the idea of tagging along with Iris, but she didn't let it show. Instead, she smiled.

"Wonderful!" Iris squealed.

"See you tomorrow then."

Liam and Iris were the last ones to leave, because they stayed for tea. Mary had wanted to talk about the wedding with them. They ended up being home by nine.

"So, Ciara has been helping you?" Liam asked Iris once they were sitting on their own sofa. Liam was watching a television show, but he wasn't paying much attention to it. Iris was reading a wedding magazine.

"Oh, yes. Just a little for now, but I asked her if she could help more and she agreed. She might come see some of the venues with me."

Liam furrowed his eyebrows. "Why didn't you say anything about that earlier?"

"What do you mean?" Iris set down the magazine and turned her full attention onto Liam.

"I mean..." He hesitated, but he knew he had to say it. "Isn't it odd that she's helping with our wedding? So far, she has done more than I have."

"She's your friend, isn't she?" Iris said. "Besides, you're busy at work, so it makes perfect sense that she's helping. She knows what you like and so on. I mean, I do too, of course, but it's nice to have someone there to confirm my thoughts."

"If you want my input on the wedding, we could wait one more year. You want a festive December wedding, but December comes every year." Liam sighed. "Especially with the witch hunters and—"

Iris's eyes widened, and blood drained from her face. "Are you having second thoughts?"

"No." Liam took his fiancée's hands into his. "I just... planning a wedding in a rush might be the wrong choice. I could help if we waited. It could be safer in a year, too."

"Is this about Ciara being back?"

"Why would this be about Ciara?"

"She *just* came back and now you're suddenly thinking about changing our wedding date." Iris pulled her hand from Liam's hand and crossed her arms across her chest.

"It's not about her. It's about my input on the wedding. And the witch hunters. I've barely even talked with Ciara."

"Yet you came home at seven in the morning because of her," Iris said accusingly.

"You know it wasn't like that. I was working for the cause. I went there as back-up. If someone had been there, they might have needed my help." Liam sighed and shook his head. "There's nothing to worry about."

"Oh, please!" Iris spat. "Even your Mum adores her!"

"Why does that matter? We're getting married. You and me, Iris. It has nothing to do with her," Liam said, his voice soothing. "My mother knew her way before I even had a crush on her. She's Henry's best friend."

Iris sighed.

"I love you, Iris."

Iris turned to look at her future husband, letting her arms drop. "I love you, too."

"I was surprised when you asked me out yesterday," Iris confessed to the tall, handsome man beside her. He was walking her home after their first date.

Liam smiled. A soft chuckle passed his lips. "I suppose it was sudden."

"It's nice, though." Iris couldn't help but grin. "I've had so much fun today."

"I could say the same thing. You seem like someone I'd like to get to know better."

"I'm sure that can be arranged," Iris flirted.

"So, I will get a second date with you?"

"Give me a time and place, and I'll be there."

"Dinner this Friday?" Liam suggested.

Iris smiled widely and nodded. "You pick the place."

Liam returned the smile. "Will do."

17

Ciara was waiting for the hours to pass. She had nothing to do until it was time to go to the Rosslers'.

Henry was at work. He was going to go to his parents' house straight from there.

It meant Ciara had to wait alone. She tried to watch a television show to pass the time, but it ended up being more boring than just doing nothing. She longed for action. Even the mere thought of fighting the witch hunters made blood rush in her veins.

Her luck seemed to change when heavy banging at the door interrupted her. She clenched her hand into fist, wondering who it could be. Witch hunters? The idea excited her.

She reached for the doorknob, ready to strike. Pushing it open, she revealed a man. But he wasn't a witch hunter.

"Doherty."

"No time to talk. Grab your jacket and wand. We need to go. There's been an attack." His voice came out in a blur, so

Ciara knew to be fast.

She grabbed her jacket from the sofa. Her wand was in her jacket pocket, specially designed for a wand to fit in. She was ready within seconds. "Let's go."

With a flick of Doherty's wand, he and Ciara disappeared from the living room. He teleported them to a street Ciara didn't recognise. They stood in front of an old yellow house.

The street was empty. Quiet. Even though there was a house nearby, there were no lights and no movement.

They walked to the porch and to the sloppily painted door. Based on the name tag on the door, the house belonged to someone named Tubbs. Ciara didn't remember ever hearing that name.

Doherty was the one to knock—first twice and then three times. Meanwhile, he gripped his wand in his other hand.

Ciara's hand went to her wand, but she kept it in the pocket. Not that she actually needed the wand with her gift of wandless magic, but sometimes it drained less of her energy to use a wand on missions.

The silence was intense. Ciara could hear her own breathing, and it made her muscles tense. It was like waiting for someone to come and kill them.

She didn't know if that was the case. Doherty hadn't bothered to explain. She didn't know what they were doing there.

But she remained calm. She had been under a lot more pressure at work. It was nothing new for her.

And she trusted Doherty. He also trusted her. They were a great team. After all, he had taught her everything in the beginning when she had become a hit witch. From techniques to strategies, he had been the one to teach her all of it.

Like he had taught Theo, too.

The sound of footsteps broke the silence, making both Ciara and Doherty hold on to their wands tighter.

The steps weren't hurried, nor were they slow. But they

were approaching the door without hesitation. Each step was louder than the previous one.

Ciara was about to pull out her wand when the door opened, revealing a shaking woman. All colour had drained from her face, making her look like a ghost. The sorrowful look in her eyes aged her by years.

Doherty's shoulders relaxed, and he sighed in relief. "Imogen."

Imogen Tubbs, Ciara noted.

"Gregory, he's dead!" The woman's voice came out as a bloodcurdling scream. Her knees gave out, but Doherty caught her, not letting her fall onto the porch.

That was when Ciara saw red staining Doherty's clothing. Imogen's shirt was wet and sticky with blood. There was a deep wound running across her stomach.

Ciara grabbed a scarf from around her neck. She tied it around the poor woman's torso to put pressure on the wound, her hands working fast. She had done it many times before.

"Go get Iris," Doherty blurted. "It's an emergency."

Ciara didn't have time to speak before Doherty teleported away with Imogen. She shut the front door and left the scene, using magic to go to Iris's and Liam's flat.

She appeared in front of the building and ran inside. Running up the stairs, she hurried to the right flat door. She didn't bother with knocking. Using a spell, she unlocked the door and walked in.

Doherty had asked for Iris, so he wasn't going to take Imogen to the hospital. It had to mean he didn't want the attack to be handled by the useless officials. He wanted the group to take care of it.

The engaged couple was having dinner when Ciara walked in. When they heard her, they both stood up and turned to see what was happening.

Liam's eyes widened, spotting the blood covering Ciara's hands, arms, and clothing. "Are you injured?"

Ciara brushed off the question and turned to face Iris. "You need to come right now. It's an emergency."

Iris didn't question it. She grabbed her wand. Without saying a word to Liam, she and Ciara teleported to the Rosslers' house.

They rushed inside.

"What's going on?" Iris asked Ray who was standing near the front door.

"In the bedroom," Ray instructed.

Iris nodded and rushed to the bedroom. Ciara followed her but stopped at the doorway.

Mary was already treating Imogen, but she had her hands full. Doherty was standing near the bed, trying to calm Imogen down. Imogen still seemed to be conscious, if barely so.

"What's going on?"

Hearing Liam's voice, Ciara shut the bedroom door to give the healers some privacy as they were trying to save the injured woman. She joined Liam and Ray in the kitchen.

"Imogen Tubbs is being treated. They nearly killed her. Ciara and Doherty made it just in time," Ray said to his son.

Ciara furrowed her eyebrows. "Someone died."

Ray turned to look at Ciara with a grim look and nodded.

"A member?"

"Yes, he was," Ray confirmed.

"We need to search the house. There could still be witch hunters," Ciara said. "Besides, we can't leave anyone's body in there to rot."

"Doherty will come up with something," Ray said.

"Well, he's busy now," Ciara said.

"Imogen will probably pass out soon. From medicine or blood loss," Ray said.

"Oh." Ciara wasn't a medical expert, even though she knew the basics. Ray, however, had learned something, being the husband of a healer.

Liam looked at Ciara. Disturbed by the sight of the blood,

he walked over to her. Grabbing his wand, he cleaned the blood off.

"Thanks." Ciara had hardly acknowledged the blood that had been covering her hands, arms, and clothes, but she was glad to be rid of it.

"What were you and Doherty doing?" The look of concern remained on Liam's face, and worry filled his voice.

"He appeared out of nowhere and told me to grab my wand. We went to the house and found Imogen Tubbs injured. He brought her here, and I came to your flat. The rest you know. It happened just as fast as it sounds like it did."

Liam opened his mouth, but then the three of them heard the bedroom door open. They turned to see Doherty walk into the kitchen.

"We need Iris here now, so she won't be part of the back-up team," Doherty said. "It looks bad for Imogen."

"Is she dying?" Ray asked.

"She has a slim chance of surviving," Doherty said grimly.

"Why not take her to the hospital?" Liam asked.

"Mary says it would make no difference, and I trust she knows what she's doing. And this way we can work without having to worry about getting caught."

Liam nodded, trusting her mother knew the best.

"So, what about the house?" Ciara asked, jumping straight into action. "We need to search it."

"I'm taking you off the back-up team," Doherty said, pointing at Ciara. "I need you to search the house."

"Alright."

"She can't go alone," Liam blurted. "It's way too dangerous. There could still be witch hunters there."

Doherty looked at Ciara and Liam in turn. He shrugged. "Go with her then."

Liam nodded. "I will."

"I don't want you to just run in," Doherty said to both Ciara and Liam. "It's likely there's still a witch hunter in there. Could be more than one. I need you to monitor the house until you know it's safe to go in."

Ciara nodded. "We'll send a signal once we've made sure the house is secure."

"Good. Also, send an alert if you run into trouble," Doherty said. "The next house on the street is empty right now. You should be safe watching from there."

Ciara nodded and turned to face Liam. "You ready?"

Ciara used a spell to teleport her and Liam to the house Doherty had mentioned.

Without wasting a second, she walked in and went to the window that offered the best view to the Tubbs's house. She saw both the front and the back door from her spot.

"Straight to work, I see," Liam said, heading to the kitchen. He grabbed two stools for him and Ciara and set them down by the window. Then he sat on the other one.

Ciara hesitated at first but eventually sat down. "I'm not used to wasting time, I suppose." She kept her eyes on the house the whole time in case there was something to see.

"I can tell." Liam's primary focus was on the house they were watching, but he couldn't help but sneak glances at Ciara.

She looked determined. He doubted he had ever seen her look as driven by anything. It was probably how she was at work.

"I can also tell you're quite determined." He felt stupid for saying it out loud, but by then it was too late.

"I want to get rid of the witch hunters." Ciara still wouldn't even glance at Liam. "They've caused enough trouble."

Liam bit his lip, falling deep into his own thoughts. He should have focused on their mission, but all he could think about was Ciara.

He wondered how Theo had died. No one had ever told him. Yet it seemed like Ciara held a grudge against the witch hunters. The fight against those terrorists seemed personal for her.

"They killed him, didn't they?"

"What are you talking about?" Ciara furrowed her eyebrows, but her gaze was still fixed on the house.

"They killed Theo."

Ciara inhaled sharply. "Yes, they did."

"I'm sorry."

"Thanks."

Ciara's eyes softened, and sadness glazed over them. No matter how focused she was, the look in her eyes turned distant.

"I saw it happen." Ciara's eyes widened, as if admitting it out loud surprised her.

"I wish you hadn't."

"Me too."

"Are you okay?" Liam's attention was no longer on the house. Instead, it was on the young shaking woman sitting beside him.

He worried about her. He knew how hard it was for her to talk about her feelings. She held most of it in, not letting anyone know how she felt.

"I've come to terms with it," Ciara said. "It's been over seven months."

"But you're still mourning his death."

"I suppose." Her lips pursed together, but she didn't even glance at Liam. She was watching the house keenly, not letting her focus falter.

The two of them were silent for minutes. They watched the house, even though they couldn't see anything there.

"Talking with his mother helped," Ciara confessed.

"That's good," Liam said, glancing at Ciara. "How is she?"

"She's doing well." Ciara sighed. "Considering she lost her only son. She's slowly moving on with her life."

"You are, too."

"I wasn't for a while, though."

"There's no right way to grieve," Liam said.

Ciara smiled faintly, but her eyes remained on the house. "I see you still have the right words for every situation."

Liam couldn't help but chuckle at that. "You always said that."

"Only when it was true," Ciara said. "Which was often."

The faint smile was still present on her face. It didn't quite reach her eyes, but her frown had eased. The look in her eyes was no longer distant, and the sadness in them was fading.

"Were you and Theo engaged?" Liam couldn't help himself. He had to know, and he wanted the answer to come from Ciara.

"Yes," Ciara said, nodding. "But he died soon after."

"Really?"

"Yes."

"That's horrible."

Ciara nodded.

"So, did your feelings for him start at the tournament?"

Liam wasn't sure if he should have asked, but he couldn't help himself. They hadn't had time to catch up. Now that they were stuck in a house, Liam thought it was a great chance for him to talk with her.

"What?" Ciara said, both surprised and amused by the question. She turned to look at Liam briefly before turning her gaze back to the house. "Of course not. I started dating you right after the tournament, remember?"

"I remember. And even back then you were close with him."

Ciara smiled. "Not like that. He was a friend back then. He was just a friend for a long time, even in Canada."

Liam raised his eyebrow, even though Ciara wasn't looking at him. "Really?"

She nodded. "Yes. We met again in July once I had moved to Canada, but we didn't start going out until the following March. He even helped me get over you."

"That couldn't have taken long. You were the one to break up with me," Liam said bluntly, a hint of hurt shining through his voice.

"You were the one who wanted out of the relationship," Ciara said defensively.

Liam turned his gaze on to Ciara. "What are you talking about?"

"I know you liked Iris before we even broke up."

Liam's eyes widened. She wasn't supposed to know that. Henry had promised Liam he wouldn't mention it to Ciara.

"Did Henry say—"

"No." Ciara shook her head. "I accidentally saw a letter you had written him and I read it."

Liam opened his mouth but struggled to find any words. "You've known all this time?"

Ciara nodded. "That's why I broke up with you."

Hearing that left Liam gaping. "For real?"

Ciara nodded but kept her eyes on the house. "Yes, for real." She smiled a little. "Clearly it was the right decision. You and Iris seem happy together."

Liam was baffled. Ciara had known the whole time. Despite his greatest efforts, he had hurt her feelings. He had tried to keep the information from her, so her feelings wouldn't be hurt. He had already felt bad, but knowing the truth, he felt worse.

Liam had always thought that the long distance between him and Ciara had ended their relationship. He had been wrong. It had been *him*.

"I'm sorry."

"Don't be," Ciara said. "Because I'm not upset. I was sad at first, but that was years ago. I was holding you back, and it would have been wrong of me to continue that."

"It wasn't your fault. There was nothing wrong with you."

Ciara nodded. "We just weren't meant to be," she said, clearly finishing the conversation.

18

Liam and Ciara sat in silence for over an hour, watching the house. They both had a lot to think about.

After observing it for two hours, they finally decided to head to the house. So far they had seen no movement inside.

They placed the stools back in their original spots. With a snap of Ciara's fingers, she sent a signal to the others.

They left, keeping their eyes on the Tubbs's house. Walking closer, Ciara kept eyeing the windows. She and Liam were out in the open. If there were witch hunters in the house, they were at risk of getting hurt. Anyone could see them.

As they neared the house, Liam grabbed Ciara by her arm. "Stay behind me, will you?"

They could already see the front porch.

Ciara frowned, glancing at Liam, before looking back at the house. "I'm—"

"I know. Just as my back-up," Liam said, obviously lying.

There was a hidden reason. One he wouldn't tell her. But his pale face was enough for her to give in.

Ciara sighed and nodded. "Lead the way."

They both had their wands in their hands when they approached the front door. The wood under their feet creaked, almost making them jump.

Ciara spotted blood on the front porch. It was from earlier.

Liam looked at her as if to ask about it. Without having to say anything, nodding her head, Ciara let Liam know it was nothing to worry about.

Liam nodded and turned to face the door. He reached for the doorknob, and she held her breath. He twisted it and slid the door open.

They both pointed their wands at the empty hallway. They couldn't see anyone, but something was off.

The sun was no longer high in the sky. It was setting behind the trees, and the last of the sunlight didn't help them see any better. To make it worse, the lights were off.

They couldn't turn the lights on. If it was a trap, it would have alerted the witch hunters. Using spells for light wasn't an option either because of the same issue.

The thought of a killer possibly waiting around the corner made their hands sweat.

Ciara wouldn't have been anxious if she had been alone. But she was with Liam, and the thought of someone hurting him sickened her. She had already lost Theo. She couldn't handle more loss.

Liam and Ciara stood in the doorway, listening. The house was silent. There wasn't even creaking. Nothing.

They would have to go in and check the house.

Liam reached for Ciara's hand and held onto it. "Stay close to me," he mouthed.

The two of them peeked into the first room. There was no one in there. They stepped inside and searched behind the curtains and everything but still didn't find anyone.

Ciara shuddered, turning to look at the dark hallway again. Liam noticed and squeezed her hand.

They left the first room, looking into the pitch-black darkness. The house was eerily silent, and the temperature had dropped. They had left the front door ajar, and the cool air got in.

Ciara had been in similar situations dozens of times, but her heart was still pounding in her chest. She was anxious.

Normally she would have been in the situation with a colleague or on her own. This time she was with Liam.

She hadn't orientated her mind to think of Liam as a colleague who could die any day.

They tiptoed, trying to prevent the old floor from creaking. The next room's door was slimmer than the previous one. It looked like a basement door.

Neither one of them liked the thought of a dark basement.

Liam reached for the doorknob with the hand his wand was in. He silently pushed the door open, revealing what was inside.

It wasn't a basement.

It was a tiny storeroom. There were old books in baskets, clothes in boxes, and tools on shelves that covered the walls.

No one was in there.

They shut the door and continued on.

The next room's door was closed, and Liam grimaced, reaching for the doorknob.

Just like last time, Liam slid the door open, trying to keep it from creaking. Seeing a man sitting on a chair startled both Liam and Ciara. They raised their wands, and Liam was about to hex him.

But they realised there was no point.

He was dead.

Liam dared to shine a little light in the room from the tip of his wand to see what had happened. Instantly he wished he hadn't.

The dead man's eyes had turned pure white with the

pupils gone. His mouth was open, and his eyes were wide. It only made the corpse a more horrifying sight. His skin had turned a mix of blue and white. His veins had come to the surface of the skin, and they were dark grey.

Cuts covered the body along with the dried blood all over it. The room was as bloodied as the corpse. Crimson fluid had dried onto the room's floor and the walls. Blood splatters were all over. There was even blood on the ceiling.

"Mr Tubbs," Ciara breathed out.

He had died a horrible death.

Except for the corpse and the chair, the room was empty. But it looked as though it hadn't always been empty. There was an outline of a sofa on a wall.

But at least there weren't any witch hunters lurking behind any furniture.

Once Liam and Ciara recovered from their shock, they moved onto the next room, sparing dead Mr Tubbs one last glance. The sight was revolting.

They searched the entire house, one room at a time. They went through every inch of it but found nothing.

Knowing no one was there, Liam dared to let go of Ciara's hand.

Sending a magic signal, Ciara informed the others. She and Liam walked back to the front door, but they stayed inside waiting.

Neither one of them was ready to revisit the murder scene. Neither of them wanted to talk about it either.

The door was ajar, so Doherty and Ray walked straight in, lighting up the hallway with their wands.

"The body is in the living room." Ciara's voice was hoarse. "There was no one here when we came."

Doherty nodded and headed to the living room.

"How did the missions go?" Liam asked his father.

"Two more injured, but they should recover," Ray said,

glancing at Doherty who disappeared into the darkness. "We killed four witch hunters."

"A victory for us," Liam said. But it didn't feel like a victory. Not after seeing the murder scene.

"They'll be more dangerous now. More careful, too," Ray said.

"And we will be better-prepared," Liam said. Somehow he could still find the optimistic side in himself.

Doherty returned to the hallway, having seen the corpse. He looked grim and, from what could be seen in the dim light, all colour had drained from his face. "Liam and Ciara, you can go now. You've done enough."

"Call if you need anything," Ciara said.

Doherty nodded. "Of course."

"Henry is waiting for you," Ray told Ciara. "He refuses to go home before he sees you."

Ciara nodded.

"Iris is still there, too," Ray said to Liam.

"Will Imogen make it?" Ciara asked.

"For now, it looks like she might," Ray said, smiling.

Ciara smiled, too, from hearing such good news. "That's good."

"I'll see you later, Dad, Doherty," Liam said, first nodding at his father and then at Doherty.

"See you," Ciara said.

Liam took her hand and teleported them to the Rosslers' house. They appeared at the front door. Liam opened it and let Ciara walk in first, following right behind.

Henry rushed to hug his best friend the second he spotted her. "Thank goodness you're okay!"

"Oh, please. It was mostly sitting and staring at a house." Ciara chuckled, embracing her best friend. "It was the easiest task tonight, I bet."

"There was the possibility of danger." Henry loosened his arms around Ciara before dropping them down.

"I know."

Henry turned to look at Liam. "Iris just left. She was exhausted after treating Mrs Tubbs."

Liam nodded. He turned to glance at Ciara, letting his gaze linger, and then turned back to face Henry. "I suppose I should go check on her."

Henry nodded. "Good idea."

"Good night, Ciara," Liam said, turning to her.

Ciara smiled at him. "Good night."

"Bye, Henry."

"Bye."

Liam disappeared, using magic to go home.

Henry furrowed his eyebrows and looked at Ciara. "What did you two talk about?" He had sensed the weird atmosphere around the two. Something had happened on their mission.

Ciara sighed. "Nothing."

Henry let it slide for the time being. He saw how exhausted Ciara was, and not just physically. He didn't want to add onto that.

Despite how exhausted Ciara and Henry were, they stayed for tea.

The company of Henry's younger siblings had cheered Ciara up, but she was still tired. The exhaustion hit her when they made it back to Henry's flat.

Still, she wasn't sure if she could sleep. Her mind kept drifting back to her conversation with Liam. She tried not to think about it, but so far it wasn't working.

The murder scene also bothered her. It had reminded her of Theo's death. It had brought back terrible, gruesome memories.

She wished she had got a chance to fight the witch hunters, but the house had been empty. Those bastards deserved to die for what they had done.

Henry stayed silent when he hung his coat onto the

coatrack near the door. But after that, he said, "Something's bothering you."

Ciara was just hanging her coat, too. "I can't talk about it right now," she said, shaking her head. "Please."

"Can't or won't?"

"Can you let it be for now?" Ciara pleaded.

Henry nodded, seeing how distressed his best friend was. "Of course."

"Can you give me a hug?"

Henry had never heard Ciara say that. Those words were enough to tell how serious it was. She wasn't okay.

He wrapped his arms around his best friend and hugged her. Ciara wrapped her arms around Henry, clinging on to him. She had never needed a hug so desperately.

19

"*L*iam!" *the dark-haired girl shrieked in excitement, running down the street into the arms of her boyfriend.*

Liam had to take a step back from the force of her embrace. "Whoa there!" He chuckled. "You'll knock us both over."

"I don't care," Ciara said, holding onto him.

They hadn't seen each other in nearly a month. She hadn't known about his visit. It had been a surprise.

Liam couldn't help but smile, holding his girlfriend in his arms. He inhaled her fresh scent.

A surge of happiness washed over him. He had missed her so much when he had been in Peru. He always counted down the days until his next visit.

This time Ciara hadn't known he was coming. He had kept it a secret to surprise her. Thanks to a little help from Henry, it had been possible.

Liam's heart was doing flips. Merely seeing her face was so intoxicating, enough for happiness to overtake his entire being. He loved her.

And she needed to hear that.

"I love you."

It was the first time he had told her that. He had thought about it numerous times, but he hadn't been sure until then, not sure if it was infatuation or love. But finally he knew for sure.

Based on the bright smile crowning Ciara's face, she liked what she heard. "I love you, too." Her voice was breathy and soft. Her eyes, gazing into Liam's eyes, were glowing with passion.

His smile widened.

No girl had ever made him feel warmth like that.

He had known Ciara for years and had hoped to have her in his life for the rest of it. But having her there as a friend was no longer enough. He wanted her there as his girlfriend. And eventually, when the time was right, as his wife.

For minutes, the couple stood there in silence, as if they were alone in their own little bubble. Then he could no longer keep himself from kissing her.

His lips hovered over hers, teasing, before he finally pressed them against hers. His hands slid up to the sides her neck, and he stroked her face with his thumbs. Her hands flew up to his collar, pulling him closer.

It wasn't their first kiss, but Liam couldn't remember any of the other kisses feeling like that one. He held onto Ciara as if she would vanish otherwise. As if it wasn't real.

The joy filling his insides, without a doubt, was unreal.

Liam's eyes opened, and he blinked lazily, adjusting to the darkness in the bedroom. He turned around in his bed, expecting to see a dark-haired woman beside him.

Instead he found a blonde woman sleeping beside him. His fiancée.

Iris. That's Iris.

It had all been a dream.

Liam's eyes widened, and his breath got caught in his throat.

No way.

Dreaming about Ciara wasn't startling.

What stunned him was that he had forgotten that visit. The one he had dreamed about. He hadn't remembered the moment he had relived in the dream.

Except it wasn't just a dream. It was his memory. An actual memory he hadn't been able to remember for years. As if it had never happened.

But it had. All the details were back in his mind. The scent of her hair, the softness of her touch—all of it was back.

Liam ran his hand through his hair. Were there more memories he had forgotten? He hoped not.

How had he ever forgotten it? One of his most precious memories.

He blinked rapidly, his hands shaking, until out of nowhere realisation hit him. He jumped out of the bed and hurried to the bathroom in desperate need of a cold shower.

It didn't feel real. He couldn't believe he had thrown the memory away so thoughtlessly.

His head was spinning. Thoughts were twirling around in his head. Even the cold water hitting his bare skin wasn't enough to clear his head.

He had been in Peru, working on a case. There had been an old cursed vault he had been investigating, and he had promised his boss he would get it open. He had wanted to impress his boss.

It hadn't been worth the cost. Nowhere near worth it.

There had been text on the side of the vault. A solution for breaking the curse. An enchantment that could only be triggered by a memory.

Of course Liam had read it.

It had required him to choose one of his memories in exchange of a future memory that would show him how to open the vault. It had sounded so simple back then.

He had thought of all the memories from his childhood and school years. Picking a memory had been too hard. He hadn't wanted to part with any of them.

He had been careless and had let the enchantment take

any memory from his past. And it had been the memory of the moment he had realised he was in love with Ciara.

If the memory was back—and it was—the vault had to be resealed. The old curse had to be in place again. The excavation had to be over, unless someone had shut the vault by accident.

Once Liam finished in the shower, he wrapped a towel around his waist and walked out of the bathroom. Seeing it was only five in the morning surprised him.

He hadn't realised it was so early. Nevertheless, going back to bed wasn't an option. Instead he got dressed and made himself coffee.

Time passed slowly, even though he could have sworn he had drunk the coffee within three minutes. On any other day he would have sat down and enjoyed the moment for at least ten minutes.

He couldn't get his mind off the dream—the memory. It still hadn't sunk in, but it was real. It had to be.

He couldn't stop thinking about Ciara.

He needed to get the memory out of his head. *Her* out of his head. A run sounded like a fantastic way to get himself back together.

Pulling his long hair into a ponytail, he headed out.

"Where have you been?"

Liam looked up to see Iris while removing his trainers. "I went running."

Iris raised her brows. "For how many hours?"

"Two," Liam said, as if it were normal for him. Then he stood straight.

"Is everything okay?" Iris's voice filled with concern. She could tell something was bothering Liam.

"It's just..." He hated what he was about to say. "It's the murder scene from last night. I wanted to clear my head," he lied.

Guilt hit him instantly. He wasn't the lying type, but this time he couldn't tell the truth. His entire relationship with Iris had only ever begun because he had given away *that* memory.

"Was it that bad?" Iris asked, pushing a loose strand of his hair behind his ear.

"It was bad." He sighed. "But I'll be fine."

He and Iris would be fine, he thought.

Iris nodded. "You know you can talk to me, eh?"

Liam smiled, appreciating how sweet his fiancée was. "I know."

Iris smiled, too, when she saw Liam smile. "Good."

He took off the hoodie he was wearing, placing it down on the sofa. Then he pulled off the ponytail.

"Should we do some wedding planning today?" Iris asked with a hopeful glimmer in her eyes.

"I..." He sighed, hating he couldn't be as excited as Iris.

"We don't have to." Iris reached to touch his forearm. She ran her fingers up and down. "We can just watch a movie and relax. Does that sound good?"

Exactly what he needed. "Perfect."

"But first, you need a shower," Iris said, pointing to the bathroom. "You stink."

They would be fine. Or so Liam kept telling himself.

20

"**S**ince you were so down yesterday, I have a surprise for you!" Henry declared, joining Ciara in the living room.

Ciara looked up, raising an eyebrow in question. "A surprise?"

Henry sighed, crossing his arms. "Could you at least try to act like you're excited? Or even mildly interested?"

"I don't know anything about the surprise. I can't be excited about something I know nothing about," Ciara pointed out.

"Alright, fine." A grin appeared on Henry's face. "Jenna and Mia are coming over."

Ciara's frown turned into a smile. "That sounds like a great surprise."

"There's also another surprise coming."

"Another surprise?"

"You can thank Mia for that."

Ciara's eyes widened at hearing Mia's name. "Please, tell

me it's nothing bad."

"I don't know what it is."

Ciara groaned, covering her face with her hands. "So, it is bad."

"We'll see."

"When are they coming over?"

"Any minute now."

Ciara looked down, checking her outfit. Jeans and a top. At least she didn't have to rush to change.

Mia's surprise was a mystery, but Ciara had multiple worst-case scenarios running through her mind. She knew how Mia could be.

Long minutes passed before someone finally knocked at the door. Henry jumped up and rushed to open it.

As expected, it was Jenna and Mia. Jenna's face lit up upon seeing Henry, and even more so when he pulled her into a loving embrace.

Mia smiled at the couple. Ciara stood up from the sofa and couldn't help but smile, too. They were so cute together.

"Hi," Ciara said to her friends when Henry and Jenna let go of one another.

Mia rushed to hug Ciara with a wide smile on her face. "It's so great to see you."

"Exactly what she said," Jenna said. She hugged Ciara right after Mia stepped back.

"It's great to see you both."

Mia laughed. "You'll change your mind soon."

Ciara turned to look at her, raising her eyebrows. "What is that supposed to mean?"

"You two are going speed dating." Jenna moved to stand beside Henry who snaked his arm around Jenna's waist.

Ciara stared at Jenna with her mouth open. Then she turned to face Mia. "Speed dating?"

She had never tried speed dating. Hadn't even considered it.

She hadn't dated anyone after Theo. His death still

plagued her mind. She wasn't ready to move on, and there was no way she would seek comfort in another man's arms.

She still loved Theo. Moving on was hard enough. She wouldn't be able to move on to another relationship anytime soon.

"Unless you're still mour—"

"No, it's not that," Ciara said, cutting Jenna off.

Except it was. Although speed dating didn't mean she was off to marry a new guy, she wasn't ready.

But if she said that out loud, Henry would worry.

"Wonderful!" Mia grinned. "I don't want to go alone, and you're the only single friend I have."

Ciara grimaced. "The only one? Really?"

Mia nodded, but it wasn't enough to convince Ciara.

"B-but I don't have anything to wear," Ciara said, despite knowing excuses were useless with Mia.

"We're going shopping," Mia said and grinned from ear to ear. "The speed dating event starts at seven, so we have time to find the perfect outfits, get our hair and makeup done and get there."

Ciara looked at Mia with a baffled expression on her face. "I can't believe I'm being forced to go speed dating."

Mia laughed. "It'll be fun!"

"You've tried speed dating before?" Ciara asked.

"She hasn't," Jenna said, answering for Mia.

"But I trust it'll be fun," Mia said, still smiling.

Ciara wasn't so sure. Biting her lip, she said, "Let's hope so."

Jenna joined Ciara and Mia for the shopping part. After that, she would head back to Henry's flat. Then Ciara would be left at Mia's mercy.

Ciara couldn't believe what she had got herself into. Trying on new outfits in a fitting room felt stupid—pointless. Trying one dress after another was silly.

She should have been out there trying to find the witch hunters. They were still wreaking havoc across Great Britain and they needed to be stopped. Ciara still hadn't avenged Theo's death.

She couldn't believe she was going to a speed dating event. For once, she should have known how to say no.

She suggested quitting, but Mia and Jenna were having none of it.

It took the trio an hour longer than expected until they found outfits for Ciara and Mia. Mia had a flowery summer dress and stylish trainers, complementing her personality.

Ciara didn't want to go too overboard. She ended up with beige trousers, a tight top, and some heels. Simple, but at least she looked as though she had put some thought into it.

After clothes it was time for the makeup and hair. Jenna walked Mia and Ciara to the salon, but then she left.

While the hairdressers and makeup artists were working on Mia's and Ciara's makeup and hair, they had time to catch up while still talking with the lovely ladies at the salon. Ciara had nearly forgotten how fun hanging out with Mia could be. For a moment, she even forgot to think about the witch hunters and her revenge.

Once the work was finished, Ciara had some lip gloss and dark eye makeup. For her hair, she had a high ponytail. She looked quite beautiful—in her own opinion, too.

Mia had warm eye makeup with bright coral lipstick to match her new dress. Her hair was curled to complement her flowery look.

By six o'clock, it was time to head to the event. Both women looked beautiful, and even Ciara was warming up to the idea of speed dating. Talking with Mia had eased her mind, and somehow she had realised she was in need of a break. She hadn't had one in months.

Not since Theo's death.

It was a beautiful summer evening, and Ciara and Mia agreed to walk to the venue.

"I can't remember the last time I had my hair and makeup done," Ciara confessed when they were walking along the pavement. "In fact, I think I've only ever done this for work. Like an undercover job."

"Well, it's a wonderful thing that you have me. We are going to have so much fun!" Mia was beaming, thrilled to try speed dating.

Ciara smiled. "It is. I'm actually warming up to the idea."

Mia's eyes widened. "I wish I had recorded that." She gaped at Ciara. "I can't believe you said that."

Ciara chuckled. "Well, I said it."

"I know! But I still can't believe it."

"Take your time adjusting."

"So are you planning to go home with someone or..."

"I don't even know what kind of men there will be."

"I hope there's at least a few smoking hot guys," Mia said, twirling her hair between her fingers.

Ciara chuckled, amused by Mia. "So, are you looking for a one-night-stand or a long-term guy?"

"Either suits me."

"Feeling *that* single?"

"You got that right." Mia's smile turned into a frown. "Are you sure you're okay with this?"

Ciara knew what Mia meant by that. "He would want me to move on."

Mia nodded. "He would."

Speed dating wasn't for Ciara. Three minutes per guy was either not enough or too much.

She noticed right away when the man was the arrogant type. She could also tell if the guy was there for easy sex.

Still, Ciara chatted with a few men who seemed nice. But even if they were nice, she didn't feel any connection.

Mia seemed to enjoy herself. Ciara could tell she had eyes on at least two candidates by the time they had met ten men.

Towards the end, Ciara had come to a conclusion. Speed dating wasn't for her.

The next guy strode over to her table. "Oh, my goodness! I almost didn't recognise you."

Ciara looked up, at last paying attention to the guy. Her eyes widened, staring at her ex in shock. "Jesse Kingston?" Her voice filled with disbelief, and her smile grew. The coincidence—running into him—was almost too good to be true.

Jesse—Ciara's ex-boyfriend from her teenage years—sat down, chuckling. "I'm glad you still recognise me."

"Well, you've changed a lot," Ciara said, admiring Jesse's physique. "In a good way."

He had gained muscle since graduation. He had to be hitting the gym at least five times a week to have his arms look like that.

Jesse smiled at Ciara—a smile she had seen hundreds of times. "It's been a while."

"It has." Ciara chuckled a little. "I mean, it's been years."

Jesse nodded, still smiling. "I'm surprised to find you here. I thought you moved across the ocean. America, right?"

"I did, but I just moved back. For now, I'm staying with Henry while I look for a flat."

"Are you back for good?" Jesse asked.

"I don't know yet. But I'm back for now."

"So, you like America? Had fun there?"

"More or less, but I'm happy to be back." Ciara smiled at Jesse. "What about you? What have you been up to?"

"I have my own flat, and I own a gym."

Ciara's eyes widened. "You own a gym?"

Jesse chuckled and nodded. "Yes. It's right below my flat, too, which is great."

"So gym music every hour of every day?"

Jesse laughed. "Thank goodness, no! I made some renovations, and the flat is now soundproof both ways."

Ciara grinned. "I'm sure your ears thank you."

"And my head. I'd lose my mind if I'd have to hear that music all day every day."

"I bet."

"So what made you try speed dating?"

"This is Mia's surprise for me," Ciara said, gesturing to the table where Mia was talking enthusiastically with a blond guy.

"Oh, I see," Jesse said, nodding.

"She didn't want to come alone, and she said I'm her only single friend."

"It's nice to see you two are still friends."

Ciara smiled. "We've reconnected since I came back."

Jesse nodded.

"What brought you here then?"

Jesse shrugged. "I saw the event on Facebook, and I thought I'd try it."

"And is speed dating working out for you?"

"Actually—"

The bell rang, informing them that another three minutes had passed.

"Alright, this was it! Now you'll have time to converse freely before we end the event. I hope you all enjoyed your time," the host declared.

Jesse turned to smile at Ciara. "Wanna get out of here?"

"You don't want to continue with any girl?" Ciara asked, grabbing her handbag.

"I do. With you," Jesse flirted.

Ciara chuckled, taken aback by the bold change in Jesse's demeanour. "Alright."

Ciara let Mia know she was leaving with Jesse, and they left the venue.

The ex-couple ended up going to a small bar. Jesse had ordered and paid for both of them like a gentleman.

169

They were sipping their drinks and catching up.

"So, what do you do for living?" Jesse asked.

Ciara smirked. "You won't believe me."

The corner of his lip moved up. "Try me."

"I'm a hit witch."

Jesse's eyes widened, and he gaped at Ciara. His expression was unreasonably exaggerated as if he wasn't surprised in the slightest bit. "For real?"

"For real."

"Wow. That's...wow." Jesse grinned, his eyes turning playful. "Although, if you can ride a dragon, like you did at the tournament back at school, you can do anything."

Ciara smiled, remembering the dragon-riding task. "That was fun."

Jesse shook his head. "I doubt that."

"Maybe you should try."

"No, thanks."

"It was terrifying at first," Ciara admitted.

Jesse laughed at her confession. "I bet it was."

Ciara smiled at Jesse and took a sip of her drink. She was having fun catching up with him. They hadn't talked in years.

"If you don't mind me asking," Jesse began, "when did you and Rossler break up?"

"After he met his current fiancée," Ciara said.

Jesse gaped at her. "He cheated on you? I didn't take him as that type of guy."

"He didn't cheat. He didn't kiss her or sleep with her or anything. But I found out he liked her, so I decided it was best to break up."

"Oh."

"It was years ago, so it's all good now. I'm even friends with his soon-to-be wife."

Jesse raised his eyebrow. "Really?"

Ciara chuckled. "Yes, really. Sometimes it's sort of weird and awkward."

Jesse smiled. "I bet."

"Yeah."

"So, any guys after that?"

"I was engaged."

"Really?"

"You remember Theo Boucher? He was in the tournament, too."

"You and him?" Jesse said, his eyes widening. "Engaged?"

Ciara nodded.

"I have to admit, I always thought he had a thing for you."

Ciara chuckled. "Recently I've been hearing that from everyone."

"No doubt about that." Jesse cleared his throat. "So, uh, what happened?"

Ciara took a sip of her drink to prepare for her next words. "He died."

"He died?" Jesse repeated. His mouth hung open. "I-I'm *so* sorry, Ciara."

"Thanks."

"How are you?"

"Moving on."

"Good." Jesse nodded. "That's good."

Ciara grimaced, seeing that Jesse was at a loss for words. "I ruined the moment, didn't I?"

"No, of course not." Jesse smiled. "So, did you move to America because of him?"

"No. I got a job offer in Canada. I needed a fresh start, so it was the perfect timing. Theo and I worked together, and that's how we met again."

"I bet you made a great couple."

"I think we did."

"Looks like remeeting guys is a thing by now. Just a lucky coincidence?"

"Seems to be. But it's nice to see you after so long."

"I could say the same thing."

With Jesse, talking was easy. There were no weird, tense

silences. Unlike with Liam.

Ciara and Jesse had so much fun catching up. Jesse was especially interested in Ciara's years in America. They didn't talk nearly enough about his past years. He was so intrigued by her life.

Ciara and Jesse stayed at the bar until midnight. Towards the end of the night, the conversation had taken a turn. They had ended up flirting for an hour straight.

Right before it would have been the time for goodbyes, Jesse had the guts to ask Ciara to spend the night with him. She said yes, and they headed to his flat. They barely made it to the lift leading from his gym to his flat before the first layer of clothes went off flying.

21

Worry gnawed at Henry's insides. He had been trying to reach Ciara without an answer. Even Jenna had already left to have lunch with her friends.

Henry had called Mia in the morning to ask about Ciara. Mia had just told him Ciara had left the event with a guy.

It didn't make Henry feel any better. He was sick with worry, running through possible scenarios in his mind.

He couldn't wait much longer, or he would be late for lunch with his family. But he refused to leave before Ciara showed up—or at least answered her phone.

If he went to see his parents in that mental state, they would notice how worried he was. Then he would have to explain. He didn't want to worry everyone like that.

Perhaps he was worried for nothing. He prayed he was.

To his luck, the flat door opened, and Ciara walked in.

"Where have you been?" was the first thing to leave Henry's mouth while Ciara closed the door.

Water dripped down her hair. She didn't have any makeup on, so she had likely washed it off. She looked good for someone on a walk of shame.

"You don't want to know," she said, shaking her head. "Just know that I slept in."

Henry couldn't tell whether she was grinning or grimacing.

"Actually, I do want to know," he said, walking up to her. "You never sleep in."

"Where are you going?" Ciara asked and gestured to the button-down Henry wore. She was trying to change the subject on purpose.

"I'm having lunch with my family."

Ciara nodded.

"Do you want to come?" Henry would be late if Ciara agreed to come, but he didn't care.

"No, not this time," Ciara said and shook her head. "I need a nap."

Henry scrunched up his nose, wondering how his best friend could be so tired. "You just said you slept in. What did you do last night?"

Ciara walked to the kitchen. "Let's agree I didn't just sleep with my ex." She grabbed a glass from a cupboard. "Tell everyone I said hi."

"Um, will do!" Henry said goodbye before he left in a hurry.

He couldn't believe Liam had cheated on Iris.

Liam was at the family lunch, too. It was uncomfortable for Henry. But at least Iris was stuck at work.

Henry tried to look for a chance to talk with Liam. He was planning to ask about his and Ciara's night together, but he never got the opportunity to chat in private with his brother.

If his mother heard, she would freak out.

Henry had to wait through the lunch. When Liam was

about to leave, Henry came up with an excuse to leave, too.

"I thought you would have stayed longer," Liam said as he and his brother walked away from the house.

Henry tilted his head in confusion, but soon realisation hit him.

"Don't tell me you were planning to see Ciara," Henry hissed, pointing a finger at his brother.

Liam's eyes widened. "How did you—"

"I know!"

Liam looked alarmed, his eyes still wide. "A-about what?"

"I know you slept with her."

The alarmed look on Liam's face twisted back into a frown. "What?"

"She told me."

"She told you I slept with her?" Shaking his head, he continued, "Ciara told you that?"

"Well, aren't you her ex? Where did you two spend the night? And how could you do that to Iris?" Henry couldn't believe his brother and best friend had done that.

Henry wasn't the biggest fan of Iris, but he couldn't tolerate Liam cheating on her. Besides, Liam was still going to marry Iris, and Ciara wasn't someone he should have toyed with.

"Last night?" Liam shook his head, confused by Henry's words. "I was home with Iris last night."

Henry opened his mouth to yell at his brother. Before any sound came out of his mouth, he processed the words.

"But Ciara..." It all dawned on him, and he realised his mistake. "Oh."

"What?" Liam asked, not understanding Henry's thought process.

"She slept with Jesse Kingston." First his eyes widened. Soon, though, his expression turned into a grimace.

"Jesse Kingston? They're still in contact?"

Henry shrugged. "Or they met at the speed dating event."

Liam's eyebrows knitted together. "Ciara went speed

dating?"

"With Mia, yes," Henry said and crossed his arms across his chest. "Which has nothing to do with you. So, why are you so interested?" He observed his brother, raising an eyebrow.

"I'm not," Liam snapped.

"You're not telling me something."

Standing straight, Liam clenched his jaw. "There's nothing to tell."

"Except?"

"Nothing."

"I don't believe you."

"Then don't!" Liam sighed in frustration, shaking his head. "I need to go. See you later." And with that, he flicked his wand and vanished.

⚜ ⚜ ⚜

Liam had sunk low. He had gone out for a drink, because his ex-girlfriend was sleeping with her other ex-boyfriend. Jesse Kingston, out of all the men in the world.

He was sitting in a pub with a whiskey in his hands. He kept his gaze on the golden-brown liquid in the glass, swirling it.

He was an idiot. It had been his fault his and Ciara's relationship had ended at all, because he had given away his most treasured memory. He had forgotten how much he loved Ciara only to impress his stupid boss.

Despite not acting on his feelings, he felt as though he was cheating on Iris. He loved Iris and never wanted to hurt her.

But he could no longer deny his feelings for Ciara. Feelings that were wrong.

He didn't know how to get rid of them, and he was growing desperate. He had even considered trying to find an enchantment to forget again. But those enchantments were rare.

His work files would have helped him find an enchantment

like that. But the risks were too high.

Enchantments weren't that simple. There were side effects. In the worst case, he would forget everything, including his family and Iris. Perhaps even himself.

Liam rarely needed someone to talk to, but now was one of those moments. The problem was he didn't know who to talk to.

Henry was out of question. It would have been wrong to put him in that position. Henry would see Iris at family gatherings, and he lived with Ciara.

Liam also didn't fancy the idea of talking to his friends about his problem. They were more or less Iris's friends, too. One of them might accidentally blurt it out to Iris when they got together for drinks.

Liam considered telling his mother, but he chose against it. Liam's father wasn't an option either.

Naturally he couldn't talk to Ciara, either.

He had no one to talk to.

Liam sighed, staring at the empty glass in his hand. He tried to tell himself he could work it out. After all, he loved Iris, and they were planning their wedding.

But he hadn't figured out how to get Ciara out of his mind.

22

A week passed by with little happening. The witch hunters stayed quiet. Ciara kept jokingly thinking they were having a summer holiday.

She didn't believe that was the case, though. Whatever was going on, she doubted it was good. Her best guess was that the witch hunters were plotting their next move. Probably something big.

Some members agreed with her. In fact, most did.

Since Henry's summer holiday was over, Ciara needed someone else to hang out with. She had started visiting Jesse—sometimes even when Henry wasn't working. Jesse had given her access to his gym for free. She insisted on paying, but he refused to take her money.

She went to the gym almost daily. It was the perfect excuse for skipping wedding planning with Iris who had been asking for Ciara's help more and more often.

It was Saturday. Ciara had finished her workout, and she was hanging out at the counter with Jesse. They were mostly flirting.

Her ringtone interrupted them.

"Let me guess," Jesse said, already laughing. "Iris."

Ciara looked at her phone screen and sighed. "Yes, it's Iris."

Jesse cocked his head to the side, looking between Ciara and her ringing phone. "Are you going to pick up?"

She sighed again. "I guess I have to." She tapped the green phone icon on the screen and raised the phone to her ear. "Hi."

"Ciara! I've been trying to call you for hours!"

"I've been at the gym all morning. I'm sorry I didn't notice."

"All morning?" Iris asked, surprise evident in her voice. Ciara could only imagine her checking the time, too.

Ciara chuckled. "It's a long story."

"Oh," Iris said. Ciara could hear from her voice that she was smiling. "So, what are you doing later?"

"Um..."

She had just wasted her chance for an excuse. Wrong move.

"I would appreciate your help." Iris sounded desperate, which made Ciara feel bad about her excuses.

"What time do you need me?"

"Five o'clock. Does that sound good?"

"Five o'clock at your flat?"

"Yes. Liam is going out with the guys tonight, so it's just us two."

"I'll be there at five."

"Wonderful! See you."

"Bye." Ciara ended the call and turned to look at Jesse.

He read her expression. "Wedding help?"

"Looks like it." Ciara ran her hands down her face, letting out an exasperated sigh. "I don't know why she doesn't ask her friends."

"Maybe they're tired of doing Liam's work," Jesse

179

suggested. Even he had grown tired of Ciara doing Liam's work.

"Good point."

"And Iris knows they don't know Liam as well."

"That's true, too." Ciara nodded. "So, do you want me to plan your wedding? It looks like I'm about to become a full-on professional," she joked.

Jesse laughed. "Oh, yes! I'll make sure to ask you."

Ciara grinned. She enjoyed hanging out with Jesse, because it was easy. He didn't ask her about the witch hunters. Instead he had questions about her everyday life. It was a fresh change to have someone who didn't constantly remind her of Theo's death.

Ciara stopped by at Henry's flat. She needed a shower and a fresh set of clothes after her workout.

It was five o'clock sharp when she walked up the stairs of the block of flats, on her way to help Iris with all the wedding planning. She had had an accident with lifts in the past, so she preferred to take the stairs.

It was already one minute past five by the time Ciara reached the right floor. She picked up her pace, so Iris wouldn't wonder why she was late. After all, Ciara was always rather early than late.

She walked towards the flat door, but then stopped, seeing a man leave the flat.

He was shirtless. In fact, he was just pulling his shirt on when he closed the door.

Ciara continued to walk, hoping the man wouldn't acknowledge her sudden halt. He didn't need to know which flat she was heading to.

The man nodded at Ciara as they passed by one another. Based on the sound of his footsteps, he was heading for the lift, but Ciara didn't turn around to see.

She pretended to be heading to another flat while she

hoped that whoever lived there didn't open their door. When she was standing at a random flat door, she turned her head to the side. The lift doors opened, and the man stepped in.

Once the lift doors slid closed, Ciara walked to the right door. She raised her hand to knock. But before her hand hit the wooden door, she froze.

Iris had cheated on Liam.

Unless Liam was still home, and it had been a threesome.

Or perhaps the man had borrowed a washing machine to wash his shirt. Except that sounded absurd.

Ciara tried to think of reasons. Anything but cheating. But the thought of Iris cheating on Liam kept repeating in her head.

She didn't know what to do. She couldn't call Liam. He would never believe her. If she told him, he would think of her as a jealous ex-girlfriend. Meetings would be awkward after that.

Ciara's thoughts were racing. She didn't want to see Iris, but she was already late. She raised her hand again and knocked at the door.

She hoped Liam was home, and the trio had just had a threesome.

Iris opened the door for Ciara right after she knocked. For a few seconds, she looked at Ciara wide-eyed but then faked a smile. "Hi! I didn't even realise it was five already. Come in."

"Hi." Ciara forced a smile and stepped inside.

She couldn't see Liam anywhere.

And Iris's hair had never looked so messy. It was all over the place. As if she hadn't brushed her hair in days.

Iris was cheating.

It wasn't just the hair that gave it away. She was standing up straight, and her shoulders were tensed.

She also kept biting the inside of her cheek. She seemed worried. Worried that Ciara had seen the man leave. She had seen that, but Ciara mentioned nothing and made sure Iris didn't notice anything odd in her behaviour.

She didn't want Iris to suspect anything, so she stayed for a couple of hours. A couple of *endless* hours.

Eventually Iris relaxed and became her normal self—her normal secretly cheating self. She even tried to have Ciara stay longer, but Ciara came up with an excuse.

Ciara couldn't stand being around the woman. She wouldn't spend any more time with Iris than necessary. Ciara had never hated Iris. She had never had hard feelings for her, even though Liam had picked Iris over her. They had been friends, even if Ciara hated helping with the wedding planning.

But Ciara could no longer stand the woman.

She tried to think of other possibilities besides cheating, but the evidence seemed clear. Iris was a cheater.

Ciara was so deep in her thoughts she didn't realise she was stupidly standing at Henry's flat door, staring at it. She snapped back to reality when she heard someone say her name. She spun around to see Henry.

"Did you forget your key?" Henry asked, gesturing to the locked door.

"No. I..." Ciara blinked. "Nothing."

Henry opened the flat door, eyeing Ciara worriedly, and they both walked in.

"So, uh, where were you?" Ciara asked Henry.

"I had dinner with Liam and his friends."

Ciara wanted to grimace, but she kept it in. "Oh. So guys' night?"

"Guys' day," Henry corrected.

Ciara nodded. "All day?" she asked, making her way to the sofa.

"We went bowling at two," Henry said and sat down beside Ciara.

"Oh."

"What were you doing today?" Henry asked.

"I was at the gym, but Iris called, so I went to help her."

She wondered if she should tell Henry about the shirtless man.

"So, anything new?"

"What do you mean?" Ciara asked, turning to face Henry.

"With the wedding planning?"

"O-oh." Ciara exhaled. "No, nothing new."

"You got nothing done?"

"Not that much."

"Oh."

Ciara was dying to tell Henry about the cheating. But in the end, she couldn't bring herself to tell him.

She doubted herself. Perhaps the whole thing was a misunderstanding. Just her imagination playing tricks on her.

It had to be her old feelings rekindling.

It wouldn't have made any sense for Iris to be cheating on Liam. They were planning a wedding, and Iris was excited about it.

A truth spell would have revealed everything, but using one was out of question. It would have been wrong to use such a spell on Iris, even if she was cheating on Liam.

"What's on your mind?" Henry asked, pulling Ciara out of her thoughts.

"Just thinking. It's about the wedding planning," Ciara lied. "Nothing to worry about."

23

Liam was drinking tea in his parents' kitchen with his mother. His siblings were outside doing whatever teenagers did on a beautiful summer Sunday, and his father was at work.

Iris hadn't been able to come early with him. She was hanging out with her friends but would try to make it to the meeting. She and her friends had made the plans long ago, so cancelling wasn't an option.

Liam had come for a meeting, but he was early on purpose. It was the perfect chance to spend some time with his family.

He had already tried sunbathing with his sisters, but the heat had been too much for him. He and Gabriel had also built a Lego spaceship. Gabriel had been collecting Lego sets since he was a child. It was a tradition for Liam and Gabriel to assemble all his new Lego sets. Ever since Liam had been old enough, they had added magic to make their Lego even more fun.

Before his father had gone to work, Liam had also helped with fixing his car. With a few spells, it didn't take long.

They only used the car when they had mundane errands. Like when Liam's parents went grocery shopping. Otherwise, teleportation was more convenient—and time-saving too.

"So, how is the wedding planning going?" Mary asked her eldest son, bringing her teacup to her lips.

Liam cringed, staring at his own cup of tea. "Uh, it's…"

"Are you having second thoughts?" Mary set down her tea and furrowed her brows.

"No." It came out like an automatic message.

"Are you going to marry Iris?" Mary asked with a rephrased version of her earlier question.

"Yes." His mother would have heard the uncertainty even if he had tried to hide it, so he didn't bother.

He still hadn't stopped thinking about Ciara. It wasn't that he hadn't tried; he had.

And with those feelings resurfacing, he wasn't sure what to do about the wedding. Could he marry Iris when he also had feelings for Ciara?

Mary's expression softened as she smiled at her eldest son. "You know you're still very young, don't you?"

"I'd hope so. Being twenty-two and everything," Liam said and smiled at his mother.

Mary smiled back. "Almost twenty-three now. It's only three weeks until your birthday."

Liam grimaced, shaking his head. "Oh, don't remind me."

"But that's not my point," Mary said, adding seriousness to her tone. "What I meant is that it's not too late to have second thoughts. If you don't want to get married yet, tell Iris. She has to understand and value your opinion."

"She'd be wrecked if I told her that." Hurting Iris was out of question. She deserved only the best, and he wanted to give her that.

Mary placed her teacup down. "You have thought about calling off the wedding."

Liam sighed. "I have." The words came out in a slow blur, and they barely felt real. "I want to stay with Iris, so it's not about that. I love her. There's just so much going on now. With the witch hunters and everything."

Mary nodded. "There's nothing wrong with feeling that way. But you have to tell Iris before the wedding has been set up and paid for. It wouldn't be fair to leave it until last minute."

"I know."

"Will you call off the wedding then?"

"I'll have to think about it."

"Think fast," Mary advised. "Just remember, even marriages might not be permanent."

Liam smiled with amusement. "I'm not getting married just to get a divorce, Mum."

"Of course not. But if that's what is bothering you, remember that it's not as final as it may seem. Or it doesn't have to be."

Liam smiled. "Thanks. I don't know if it's some Mum superpower or whatever, but you always manage to help me out."

Mary smiled fondly at hearing those words. "Of course, dear."

Iris couldn't make it to the meeting. She was still stuck with her friends and had texted Liam about it, so he told the others.

Thirty minutes before the meeting, people were arriving. Ciara and Henry were among the first ones.

"Hey," Liam said to both of them.

"Hi," Ciara said and turned to look away, seeming to be lost in her thoughts.

"Hi," Henry said, smiling. "Iris isn't with you?"

Liam turned his attention back to Henry. "No. She's stuck with some of her friends." His gaze flew back to Ciara. He could have sworn he saw her flinch.

Henry sighed. "I should have stayed with Jenna."

"Iris hasn't seen her friends in a while, so—"

"I know, I know. No worries. I'm sure we'll be just fine without her here. Besides, she's often away from meetings for work. It's not any different now." Henry patted Liam on the shoulder.

Liam smiled at his brother and gave him a slight nod.

"I'm gonna sit down," Ciara said. She didn't even glance at Henry—or Liam—before she headed to the living room.

Liam stepped closer to his brother. "Is everything okay with Ciara?" he asked, lowering his voice. He didn't want anyone other than Henry to hear.

"She's been acting a little odd," Henry admitted. "I'm sure it's nothing, though."

Liam nodded and turned to glance towards the living room where Ciara had gone. Whatever was wrong with her, he hoped it wasn't bad.

🍁🍁🍁

The meeting was short and uneventful. The witch hunters hadn't resurfaced with any recent attacks, so there was little to report.

Once the meeting had ended, Liam left for home. Iris came home a little later, and they decided to spend a nice evening together.

They were watching a romantic movie when Liam's thoughts drifted to the conversation with his mother. His mother had been right. He needed to talk to Iris about the wedding.

He didn't even know how the wedding planning was going. And it was *his* wedding.

"Iris."

"Yes, honey?" Iris turned to face him with her beautiful blue eyes. She was completely oblivious to what Liam was planning to say.

At first he hesitated, but then he forced the words out. Before the words left his lips, guilt already gnawed inside him. "A-are we rushing into things?"

"You mean the wedding?" Her full attention was on him, concern clouding her eyes. "Are you having second thoughts?"

Seeing the hurt in her eyes made his heart ache. "I love you and I want to marry you, but I'm not sure if it's the right time."

It wasn't. Not when he still harboured feelings for another woman.

And with witch hunters undoubtedly plotting something, the wedding didn't sound ideal. He still wanted to marry Iris, but waiting seemed like the best thing to do.

Iris didn't say anything, still letting his words sink in.

"What if we wait another year? Would you consider that?"

"Of course I would," Iris said. "But I'd rather not. I mean, I love you, Liam, and I want to marry you."

He wanted to make her happy. She deserved that.

"I want to marry you, too."

"Then why won't you?" Iris asked and smiled at him, taking his hands into hers. "I don't mean to push you into marriage. I don't want you to feel like this is rushed. But I don't see why we should wait. Is there a reason?"

"It's just the witch hunters and everything else going on right now." If only she knew...

"They could be a problem ten years from now."

"True. But we're so young, too. I—" Their age wasn't the problem; it was just an excuse.

"It's not like we're going to be much older a year from now." She continued to smile at him. "Liam, I want to do this with you, and I hope you want this too."

He was being silly. He wanted to marry Iris.

"But you're still having second thoughts?" Iris asked.

Liam stayed silent. His eyebrows furrowed as he thought it through. Even if he still had old feelings for Ciara, he loved

Iris and was engaged to her. Letting those old feelings affect his relationship with Iris wasn't fair. After all, with or without those feelings, he wasn't leaving Iris.

"It's okay to be nervous. I am, too. But if that's holding you back, we'll be engaged forever."

Liam chuckled. "Would that be so bad?"

"No, but I'd rather call you my husband." Iris smiled at him. "I love you."

"I love you, too. And I..." Liam's voice drifted off, and he looked at his gorgeous fiancée.

"And what?"

A smile brightened up his face. "I'm no longer having second thoughts, I suppose."

Iris's eyes widened, and her face brightened. "You want to get married this year?"

Smiling at Iris, Liam nodded. "Yes."

The following week went by with Liam hardly seeing Iris. She was working long hours, and they only saw each other briefly before heading to bed.

Even though Liam hated it, he was okay with it. It wasn't Iris's fault. It was her job to take care of the sick and the injured. Liam was proud of what she did for a living. Yes, he would have preferred to see her more. But knowing the situation was temporary made it alright.

It helped to be back at work, too. His summer holiday was over, and he no longer had as much time to think about Ciara. In fact, he spent more time thinking about his future with Iris.

Perhaps his rekindled feelings had only been the cause of the threat—the witch hunters. He had merely been worried for Ciara and had misread his own feelings.

He was going to marry Iris, and it was the right decision.

189

Two weeks passed, and there weren't any meetings. By the time the next meeting took place, the end of August was nearing.

Just like the previous time, Iris couldn't make it. She was busy at work. That was why Liam had gone to his parents' house early again.

To his surprise, Ciara, Henry, and Jenna were there, too. It was the first time Henry had brought Jenna with him. Everyone was having dinner when Liam arrived, so he joined them. He hadn't eaten since lunch, anyway.

Liam knew Jenna back from the school years. She had been one of Ciara's best friends.

Everyone was eating the vegetable pie Mary had cooked. Liam's parents and siblings were busy talking to Jenna. They hadn't met her properly before.

The only ones, who weren't talking non-stop, were Liam and Ciara. As he kept stealing glances at Ciara, he couldn't help but wonder what was going on in her life. He had heard nothing from either Henry or Ciara recently.

He could no longer keep himself from asking. "What have you been up to?"

Ciara turned to Liam. Her expression softened, and she smiled. "Gym."

Liam raised his eyebrows. "Gym?"

"She lives there," Henry said, joining the conversation.

"She goes there in the morning, and sometimes she won't be back until late," Jenna added.

"I'm also helping around, so it's not just working out," Ciara said.

"You know the owner?" Mary asked.

Ciara turned to face her and nodded. "From school, yes."

Mary's eyes widened as she grew intrigued. "Do I know her?"

"Him," Henry corrected.

"Him?" Mary moved her gaze on Ciara. "New boyfriend?"

Ciara chuckled and shook his head. "The opposite. Ex-boyfriend."

"His name is Jesse Kingston," Henry told his mother. "Remember him?"

"Oh, yes," Mary said and turned to face Ciara again. "You were dating before the tournament."

Ciara nodded. "Yes, that's him."

"Are you working with him now?" Ray asked.

"No. I'm just helping around," Ciara said and smiled at Ray.

Liam wished he hadn't asked. He had never been a fan of Jesse Kingston, and that wasn't about to change. Something was off with that guy and had always been.

Fortunately, Henry's teasing pulled Liam out of his thoughts. "How does it feel becoming old?"

He scoffed at his younger brother. "I doubt twenty-three is considered old in most scales."

"You sure?"

"Quite certain, yes."

"Old enough to get married," Henry said and shoved his fork in his mouth.

From the corner of his eye, Liam spotted Ciara moving her gaze to her plate and her shoulders tensing. Something was still going on.

"I'm pretty sure I've been old enough to get legally married for a few years now," Liam said, pushing aside any thoughts of Ciara's odd behaviour.

"Fair enough," Henry said, his mouth full of food.

"Will we celebrate your birthday before school begins?" Poppy asked Liam.

"Liam agreed to have birthday dinner with us on Wednesday," Mary said, answering for Liam.

Gabriel sighed, dropping his fork onto his plate. "I don't want to go back to school."

"Then you won't get a cool job," Ciara said, flashing a smile at Gabriel.

The bored look on his face turned into a small smile. "I

mean...it can't be that bad."

"All your friends are there," Liam said.

"Boarding school would be a nightmare without friends," Gabriel said and grimaced at the thought.

Polly sighed. "Such a drama queen."

"Polly!" Mary scolded.

"Sorry!"

Before the meeting began, Liam spotted Ciara near the living room doorway. She was standing alone, so he made his way over.

When she noticed him, her shoulders tensed. It seemed like a habit of hers. He didn't know what it was about, but he was hoping to find out.

"Are you okay?" Liam asked, no longer caring if he was too straightforward.

Ciara's eyes widened at first, taken aback by his bluntness. Soon her expression turned into a frown, though. "O-of course. Why wouldn't I be?"

Liam shrugged.

The two went silent. Liam pondered on ways to make Ciara spit out the truth, but she interrupted his thoughts by continuing to talk.

"So, are you having a party or just dinner with Iris for your birthday?" she asked, changing the subject.

"I think we'll have a lazy day at home."

Ciara smiled, but it didn't quite reach her eyes. "Still not a fan of your own birthday?"

"I don't hate it, but I don't see the point in having an enormous party." Liam couldn't help but smile, pleased to know Ciara remembered his quirks.

Ciara nodded. She was looking around, avoiding Liam's gaze.

"When was the last time you celebrated your birthday?"

"Last year with a nice dinner at home," Ciara said, smiling.

"But I bet you still don't fancy the idea of celebrating your birthday by partying."

"I don't fancy the idea of any parties," Ciara admitted.

"So, you—"

"Gather around!" Doherty shouted, making his voice louder with magic. It was like using his wand as a microphone, channelling his voice through it. "We have a meeting, you know!"

People hurried to the living room. The first ones in the room took a seat. The rest remained on their feet—some leaning against the walls—because there weren't enough seats for everyone.

Liam stayed standing next to Ciara. She was listening to what Doherty had to say, as if he was telling them about a secret spell that could make the witch hunters disappear.

There was that familiar concentrated look on her face, and her eyes stayed fixed on Doherty's face. She was forcing herself to focus harder than she needed to, and Liam had no idea why.

I ris had asked Ciara to help plan Liam's surprise birthday
party, but Ciara had kept herself busy. And eventually
Iris had given up.

It was already the day of the party—the second of
September. Liam's official birthday was the following day,
but it would have been a Sunday, and Saturday worked
better for a party.

Ciara should have been getting ready, but instead she
was cleaning gym machines with Jesse. She wanted to be late
to avoid Iris.

"Shouldn't you be heading home?" Jesse asked. He knew
about the party, because Ciara had told about it.

"She's cheating. I don't know how to act normal if I have
to see her and Liam in the same room."

"Play a role, you'll be fine."

"Until Henry sees right through me."

"He'll be busy talking with Liam's friends that he hasn't
seen in a while."

Ciara sighed. "Maybe. And he'll have Jenna there, too."

"And they'll be busy snogging."

"I wish I could take a plus one."

Jesse chuckled. "You'd take me with you?"

"Yes!" Ciara said, stating the obvious.

Jesse smiled. "I'd come with you, to be honest. Free booze sounds fun."

"Maybe I should fake a stomach ache," Ciara thought out loud.

"And Henry won't see right through that?"

"Good point." Ciara sighed. "Again."

"Look, you'll be fine. You can leave somewhat early, claiming that you're tired," Jesse said, wiping a treadmill clean.

"I hope so."

"You should go, you know."

"But—"

Jesse stood straight, playing with the rag in his hands. "I'll be fine. There's not much to do. Then I can call it a day." He gestured to the clean gym machines. "Go home and get ready as slowly as you wish, but at least get ready."

"Fine." Ciara handed the wipe in her hands to Jesse. "If tonight becomes a disaster, I'm blaming you."

"I want to hear all about it on Monday after your hangover."

"Not planning to have a hangover."

Jesse smirked. "Good luck."

"Until Monday!" Ciara waved her hand and grabbed her bag.

It was eight by the time Ciara made it to the party. She sneaked in with no one paying much attention to her late arrival. She had bought a gift together with Henry and Jenna, and they had already given it to Liam, so she didn't have to worry about that either.

They had changed the flat using magic. Instead of the somewhat small living room, there was a vast hall. It reminded Ciara of a nightclub, but there were more lights.

Ciara regretted not helping with the party. It didn't look like Liam's ideal birthday celebration. Not even close.

"Ciara Jareau?"

Ciara twirled around, coming face to face with one of Liam's friends—Shawn Sears.

She smiled. "Shawn. It's been years!" The music was blasting loud, and she hoped Shawn could hear her over the noise.

Shawn smiled back. "It has. I heard you were in America."

"I was, but I'm back now."

"Are you here to stay?"

Ciara shrugged. "I'm here for now."

Shawn nodded. "I see, I see."

"What about you? How's life?" Ciara asked—not just to make small talk but to find out.

Shawn chuckled. "I have a boring desk job."

"Shawn Sears has a boring desk job?" Ciara said, acting shocked.

Shawn smiled but rolled his eyes. "Who would have thought, right?"

"Well, you're not the first shocker. Jesse Kingston works at a gym."

Shawn's eyes widened. "Really?"

"He owns it."

"I expected him to become a hit wizard or something."

"Surprised me, too."

Shawn sipped whatever was in his cup. "I bet." He paused for another sip. "Didn't you two date in school? Before you and Liam were a thing?"

"We did."

"And you're dating again?"

Ciara laughed, shaking her head. "No."

Shawn wiggled his eyebrows a little. "But?"

"I'm helping him with the gym, that's it. I'm suspended from work, so it's nice to do something."

"And you haven't slept with him recently?"

"Just once."

Shawn grinned. "There's always that one time."

Ciara rolled her eyes.

"Anyway, it looks like you are missing a drink. Should we get you one?" Shawn offered his arm out like a gentleman.

She gripped onto it. "That'd be nice."

It had been a while since the last time she had been at a party of that size. Theo had still been alive. It had been his friend's birthday party.

"What do you think about the party?" Shawn asked, leading Ciara through a crowd of people.

"A little crowded." It was too much like the previous party she'd been to. The entire situation brought back too many memories. It was overwhelming.

"Not Liam's style, for sure," Shawn said.

"Unless he's changed his preferences."

Shawn led Ciara to the drinks table. "I doubt he has."

"You two still hang out?"

"At least twice a month." Shawn picked up a mojito in a can and handed it to Ciara. "Is that good?"

"Perfect. Thanks," Ciara said and opened it.

Shawn leaned against the table and sipped on his own drink. "So you've been helping Iris with the wedding."

Ciara grimaced and brought her drink to her lips. "I have. It's weird she asked, but I didn't want to let her down."

"Did she tell you Liam almost called it off?"

Ciara's eyes widened. Her focus was solely on Shawn, as if the music and the drinking people in the background had disappeared. "The wedding? Really?"

"Yeah. Guess he's having a quarter-life crisis." Shawn shrugged.

"Already?"

"Apparently."

"I hope I won't be around to see him in his fifties."

Shawn laughed. "Oh, it'll be terrible!"

"Yep!"

"You know, you need to drink faster to get drunk." Shawn nodded at Ciara's mojito can.

"Who said I want to get drunk?"

"Are you afraid you'll try to hit on Liam because of old feelings?" Shawn teased.

"No, of course not. That'd be awful."

"So, what is it?"

"It's a secret." One big secret that could ruin a relationship.

"Who else knows about it?" Shawn asked, tilting his head.

"Only two people here, I think." *Me and Iris.*

"Two people? You and who?"

"Not telling you."

"So, have you seen Liam yet?" Shawn asked.

"No. I came late, so—"

"Get ready to sing him a birthday song then," Shawn joked.

"Hi."

Ciara turned around to see Liam, smiling at her. She smiled back. "Hi and happy birthday. I won't sing like Shawn here suggested. Just to save your ears."

Liam's smile widened. "Thanks. Shawn sang already, so I think my ears have done enough bleeding for tonight."

"Hey!" Shawn scolded.

"Liam!"

Liam turned to see who was calling for him. "I gotta go," he said apologetically. Turning to Ciara, he added, "I'll see you later."

Once Liam had walked away, Shawn turned to look at Ciara. "You sure you're not into him?"

Ciara's eyes widened. "What?"

"He seems happy about you being back."

"What does that have to do with my feelings? Besides, he was my friend before—"

"I'm going to be very blunt now," Shawn warned. "I think you and Liam are unfinished business."

Ciara glanced the way Liam had gone. "I broke up with him so he could be with Iris."

Shawn, who had just taken a sip, spit it all out onto the floor. "For real?"

"Yes, for real."

"Well, I think he's regretting his decision now."

"Hardly. They're getting married."

"Because Iris wants to get married. If you ask me, I'm team Ciara."

"There's only team Iris."

"Ciara!"

Without much of a warning, Henry wrapped his arms around Ciara's neck, hanging off her.

Ciara hugged him back, noting he was drunk. "Hi, Henry."

Jenna trailed behind him. "He's like a big baby."

"Every time he drinks," Ciara said.

"If this is girl talk, I know why guys hate it so much," Henry mumbled, stepping away from Ciara. He returned to Jenna's side, wrapping his arms around her.

"Henry!" Shawn returned with new drinks for him and Ciara, his face brightening. He handed Ciara's drink to her and turned to Henry. "I was looking for you earlier."

"Looking for me?" Henry slurred.

Shawn nodded. "I need you, to be honest."

"Okay."

"Do you think your brother is into Ciara?"

Jenna's eyes widened, and she turned to look at Ciara.

Ciara shook her head. "Shawn is crazy."

"Crazy, right, for sure," Henry said and turned to face Ciara. "Why else would Liam be so concerned about your recent behaviour?"

"He hasn't been—"

"He just hasn't said that to you," Henry said, cutting Ciara off.

A smug smile made its way onto Shawn's face. "See?"

"Not funny," Ciara said. "There are people around us. You could ruin a wedding with false information."

"Except it's not false," Shawn said.

Ciara rolled her eyes. "He loves Iris. They're perfect together. I didn't break up with him just to get back together years later. End of story."

"I'm still team Ciara," Shawn said.

"There's no such thing," Ciara hissed.

"Henry and Shawn, how about beer pong?" Jenna asked, noticing Ciara's frustration.

"I'll be back soon." Ciara handed Jenna her drink and turned around. She walked through the crowded room and left the party.

25

With a snap of her fingers, Ciara teleported a cigarette from Henry's flat into her hand. She brought it to her lips. Snapping her fingers again, a small flame appeared on her fingertip, and she lit the cigarette.

She wasn't a smoker. She had stayed away from cigarettes until Theo's death. Then she had tried one. Smoking had helped soothe her nerves. For a while, she had been addicted, but since her return she had only smoked whenever she was stressed.

Shawn and Henry made her stressed.

Shawn should have kept his mouth shut. Ciara felt bad for Iris and guilty because of Shawn's words. There was no team Ciara, only team Iris. Shawn, as one of Liam's best friends, should have known that.

"I didn't know you smoked."

Ciara spun around and saw Liam standing a few feet from her. She blew out the smoke. "When I'm stressed."

Liam stepped closer. "Smoking kills."

"A lot of things kill." Ciara brought the cigarette back to her lips.

Liam furrowed his eyebrows, a mix of disapproval and concern on his face. "What did Henry say?"

Ciara hated the softness in his voice. It still worked on her, soothing her. Hell, it was better than the cigarette.

"Why do you think Henry said anything?"

"You were talking to him before you walked out."

Ciara prayed Liam hadn't heard anything. "He didn't say anything," she lied. She finished the cigarette and got rid of it with a snap of her fingers.

"If it wasn't Henry, it was Shawn." Liam was eyeing Ciara, and she was painfully aware of it. And aware of how close they were standing.

Ciara shook her head. "It's nothing."

"And nothing makes you stressed enough to walk out and smoke?" Liam shook his head, not believing one word. "I've seen you in stressful situations, yet I've never seen a cigarette in your hand. Not until now."

It made Ciara think about the night at Tubbs's house with Liam. She wished he hadn't reminded her of it. Somehow thinking that night made her feel guilty. She had held a soon-to-be married man's hand, and she wasn't entirely sure if it had been just a friendly gesture.

"Shouldn't you be at your party?"

Liam ran his fingers through his hair, letting them linger at the back of his head. "It's a little too crowded."

Ciara felt like an idiot for wanting to run her fingers through Liam's hair. It was longer than it had been when they had been dating.

The longer style suited him.

"Well, someone's likely looking for you already, so—"

"Why are you trying to push me away?" His brows knitted together, and his lips thinned into a line.

Ciara opened her mouth to answer, but she couldn't get

the words out.

At first she had kept a distance, so Iris wouldn't be jealous. But then she had seen that shirtless man. Ciara wanted to tell Liam, but she didn't expect him to believe her.

If he had been just a friend in her eyes, she would have told him without hesitation. She didn't want to accept she saw him as anything more than a friend. Not so soon after Theo's death.

"So, you are doing it." He paused. "You're avoiding me. It's not just my imagination." Hurt laced his voice.

Ciara would have preferred him to be angry. Anything but hurt by her actions. "Look, I don't mean to avoid you or whatever."

Not at first, she hadn't. But the more her feelings grew to be a tangled mess, the more she preferred to stay away. The cheating thing didn't make it any easier, either.

"Then why are you doing it?" Liam sounded desperate.

Ciara sighed. "I don't know. I guess it's just weird."

"Being around me?"

Ciara shook her head. For a moment she processed her thoughts, so she didn't say anything she could have regretted. "It's weird being shoved back into my old life when nothing is the same."

Liam tilted his head to the side and furrowed his brows. "You think it's weird being my friend?"

"In a way." Right after the words slipped past her lips, she cursed herself in her mind. It was too easy to talk to Liam, and she had to learn to keep her mouth shut.

They were both silent—Ciara cursing herself and Liam deep in his thoughts.

"So, do you still—"

Ciara didn't want to hear what Liam was about to say. "It'll take some time to get used to everything. I've only been back a bit over two months. Minus the weeks I was in America."

"You'll have time to readjust."

Ciara shrugged, wrapping her arms around herself. "I suppose."

"What is that supposed to mean?"

"I'm staying for now. It doesn't mean it's final."

Liam's eyes widened. "You're thinking about leaving already?"

"Not anytime soon. I'm staying until we deal with the witch hunter problem."

"And then you'll leave?"

"I've considered it," Ciara admitted.

Liam gestured towards the building where Henry was likely playing beer pong. "Does Henry know?"

"There's nothing to know. I'm not about to leave yet."

The frown remained on Liam's face, as if permanent. "What do you have in America that you don't have here in England?"

"Work."

"You transferred."

"It can happen again."

Liam opened his mouth, but it took a moment for the words to come. "So, you'd rather live in the States or in Canada?"

"I don't know."

They both went silent. To Ciara's surprise, it was comfortable. Not awkward like it had recently been.

Eventually, Liam started talking. "Iris said you've been busy. With Jesse?"

"I've been helping at his gym."

Liam raised an eyebrow. "He doesn't seem like the type to own a gym."

Ciara smiled. "I know. Who would have thought back in school."

"Yeah."

"I'm not dating him, though, if that was your real question," Ciara clarified.

"I was thinking about it," Liam admitted. "Iris said you've

been super busy with him, so I naturally assumed..." He sighed, turning to gaze up into the night sky.

"Nothing like that." *Unless you count sex.*

Liam hesitantly turned his gaze back to her. "Will you still help Iris with the wedding planning?"

"I'm not saying no." Ciara turned to face Liam. "But you should be the one helping her. It's your wedding, too."

"You think I don't do enough?"

"You don't," Ciara said. "I think Iris thinks so, too. Sometimes she wonders whether you even care about the wedding. And you should care about your own wedding."

"I'll try to do better."

"Good." Ciara was glad the wedding conversation was over. It would have become uncomfortable if it had gone on.

"You still don't have a flat?"

"I'm going to go see one next week," Ciara said. "Jesse's friend is renting one, so we set up a meeting for Tuesday."

"Is it far?"

"No."

"Should we expect a housewarming party soon?" Liam asked. "I hope it's not this crowded, though."

Ciara could tell Liam didn't mean to say the last part, but she didn't mind. Instead she smiled at the comment. "Let me at least see the flat first."

Liam smiled back. "Alright then."

"Should—"

"Could you stop avoiding me now?" Liam looked straight into Ciara's eyes.

The gaze was intense, and Ciara swore her breath hitched in her throat. An overwhelming feeling of warmth washed over her. And she hated it.

She cleared her throat. "I can do that."

Liam smiled so brightly it reached his eyes. "Good."

Ciara noticed Liam was about to continue. He had a concentrated look on his face—as if he was pondering whether he should open his mouth.

Ciara didn't want to hear what was on his mind. She didn't want him to ruin everything. "We should go back upstairs, don't you think?"

Liam let out a small, disappointed sigh. "You're right."

Once Liam and Ciara made it back to the flat, Iris pulled Liam away. Shawn appeared at Ciara's side within a second, instantly apologising for his behaviour.

Ciara told Shawn to relax. She wasn't annoyed at him anymore. The fresh air and the cigarette—and the talk with Liam—had done wonders.

She glanced at Iris and Liam, seeing them hug one another, and wondered if she should have told him about the shirtless man. She should have, but she couldn't bring herself to do that.

He was happy with Iris. He wouldn't believe Ciara.

26

On Sunday afternoon, Doherty called Ciara, asking her to meet him. She asked what for, but he didn't give the details over the phone. Ciara didn't have a hangover unlike her flatmate and Jenna, so she agreed.

Knowing Doherty, they weren't meeting for fun. She had to go there prepared for a mission.

The address he had sent her turned out to be an empty car park in the middle of abandoned warehouses. It was in England, but a little farther away from London.

"Out of all places, this is a weird one. Even from you." Ciara smiled, shoving her hands in her pockets. "So what's up?"

Doherty's lips turned up into half of a smile. "You can still back off. This is going to be half-official, half-unofficial."

"For me, unofficial then." Ciara had been transferred to work in Great Britain, but she was still suspended. Even Doherty couldn't work around that.

"Exactly." Doherty's smile dropped, his expression

growing grim. "As it's official on my behalf, I didn't want to alert the group. The head of the department won't fire you for helping, even if you're suspended."

"But the others would go to prison if we got caught." Ciara nodded. "Yeah, I know. What's the mission?"

"One of my team members, Theresa, found a new witch hunter location with her hacking talents. I'm going to search it. You can still say no and leave."

"When have I ever said no to a fight with those fuckers?"

"Never."

"Exactly. I'm staying."

Doherty nodded. "Good. I was counting on it."

"Any idea how many witch hunters to expect?"

"A few."

"Anything else I should know?"

"Be careful."

"As always. And that's it?"

Doherty pulled his wand out of his pocket. "Grab my hand."

Ciara did as she was told. The moment she grabbed Doherty's hand, he teleported them to a warehouse. The area looked similar to the car park, and Ciara assumed they hadn't teleported far. There were grey warehouse buildings all around them, and the sight was quite depressing.

"You okay?" Doherty asked, his voice lowered. "If this is too much after everything—"

"I'm fine." Ciara gave him a long look. "Let's do this."

"I'll take the front."

Ciara nodded. "I'll take the back."

Just like good old times.

They split up, heading to the different ends of the building. At the back of the building, Ciara found two doors. Both small but still possible escape routes for witch hunters inside. There was no way she was letting even one of them slip through her fingers.

Blood rushed in her ears, thinking about how she would

kill any witch hunter who crossed her path. She wouldn't let them walk out of there.

They hadn't given Theo a chance, and for that they were going to pay. She didn't care if it was his actual killer or another witch hunter. They all deserved to die for their crimes.

And for everything they had taken from her.

Ciara sealed the other door shut, melting the door into one block of metal. Once it was done, she headed straight in through the other door, hands clenched into fists at her sides.

"Hey, we got company!"

Two men and a woman jumped up from their seats, cards scattering around as they dropped them. They had been waiting for something—but not Ciara.

The woman ran for the sealed door—oblivious to the fact she wouldn't get out that way.

Meanwhile, the men charged at Ciara. Two against one didn't seem fair, but she didn't mind. As long as she got to kill witch hunters.

An image of Theo's pained face just before his death flashed through Ciara's mind right before she sent a laceration spell at the other witch hunter. It didn't hit the man, dressed in all black, but he had to create a shield.

Ciara turned to her next target, the man in a white t-shirt. The man shot a spell at her, magic flashing in the air, but she raised her hands and shielded herself with magic. Bringing her shield back down, she shot two laceration spells back at him. Both hit their target, thanks to her swiftness.

The man grunted, stepping back. His hands flew to his wound, and the liquid pumping out painted his shirt crimson.

The man wearing black got close enough to grab Ciara by her hair. Next his hands were on her neck. Pushing with her feet, she tackled both herself and the man onto the ground. He lost his grip. To her luck, she also managed to stay on top.

Straddling the man in the most killer like way, she snapped her fingers. Her knife flew from her boot to her hand.

Behind her the woman screamed out in frustration, likely realising there was only one door leading out. Ciara's lips curled up in satisfaction.

Before Ciara would handle the woman, though, she had another target. Blood pounding and ears roaring, she slashed at the man. His eyes turned wide for a split second. Just in time to realise he was dying. And at last, he croaked out his last breath, going limp.

Footsteps approached Ciara from the back. She jumped out and opened her fingers wide, sending a slicing spell at her attacker. The man she had already cut with a laceration spell froze. A clean line formed on his neck before his head fell. The body followed, crumpling down.

Dead and headless. Blood pouring out of the body like melted chocolate in a dessert fountain.

"Ciara!" Doherty's voice echoed through the warehouse. Ciara's muscles tensed, and her attention slipped for a second.

A flash hit her, sending her flying against the concrete wall. Air knocked out of her, and her hand flew up to cover for the next spell. The shield formed just in time.

"I'll kill you!" the woman screamed at her.

Her head was fuzzy from hitting the wall. But not having time to sort it out, she forced herself up and threw her knife. She added force to it with a spell. The knife plummeted all the way to the woman standing across the enormous room.

It hit its mark on the woman's chest, and the body hit the ground. Then, thanks to Ciara's spell, it came back flying like a boomerang. Ciara grabbed it, sheathing it in her boot.

Doherty!

Ciara had never known her own father. But out of all the men in her life, Doherty came the closest to a father figure. He had been more than a mentor or a boss for Ciara. There was no way he would die on her watch.

Not after Theo. Losing more people would shatter her.

She dashed to the next room. Empty. Then the next. One by one, she ran from room to another until she made it to the enormous hall at the front of the warehouse.

Doherty was there, but he wasn't alone. One body was left in a pool of blood, but two witch hunters—both men—were still alive. Both throwing spells at Doherty.

Ciara jumped at the other one. Her fist connected with the witch hunter's face. With her forearm, she pushed the man against the wall, pressing on his throat. Peeking from beneath his shirt was the witch hunter mark. A flame with a wand in the middle.

Theo's killer had one of those, too. The exact same one.

All she could see was white rage. Images of dying Theo flashed through her mind. Without him there, they had no leverage on her. Nothing to keep her from killing all of them, and she would kill every last one if she got the chance.

The man in her grip would never hurt anyone again.

She grabbed the man's hair, bashing his head against the wall. Blood poured out of a new wound. She didn't even blink, snapping her fingers. The blade from her boot flew to her right hand.

She stabbed him. The blood coated her hands in an instant, and she watched the dying man collapse with a thud.

"Ciara."

She spun around to be met by familiar eyes.

"Lower your knife."

Her gaze trailed down to her raised hand, still holding the blade. Eyes widening, she let it drop.

"Ciara."

Doherty had gagged the last witch hunter and tied him to a pillar. There was no blood on him or his clothes.

Eyes narrowing, Ciara turned to her old mentor. "You didn't kill him."

"We need answers." Doherty's gaze moved from her to

the body behind her. "And I think this warehouse has seen enough blood for a moment."

She turned around to see her own handiwork. Her hand had carved an inches deep hole into the man's neck.

"Do you want to talk about it?" Doherty's voice lowered, turning unusually soft.

"No!" Ciara snapped. She grabbed her blade from the ground and wiped it clean with a spell before sheathing it back in her boot.

It took a moment for it all to hit her. Her clothes were soaked in blood. As if she had stepped into a bathtub filled with blood. She hadn't even realised despite the clothes clinging onto her skin. Like the warm blood was embracing her.

Had she gone too far? Those fuckers deserved to die for what they had taken from her.

"How do I stop?" Ciara croaked out.

"Get your motives straight." He didn't show any pity. He never had, because she didn't need that. She needed someone to knock some sense into her.

Ciara nodded.

"I need to call my team. They don't know you're here."

It was time for her to leave. "I won't let this happen again."

Next time she would use her head, not her heart, like Doherty had taught her. She knew better than to let her emotions cloud her mind.

As she was about to head out, Doherty reached a hand out, squeezing her shoulder. "Ciara."

"Yes?"

"You've been through more than you ever should have to go through." His voice was foreign. It wasn't the voice of the ruthless hit wizard Ciara knew him as. For once, there was worry clear in his words.

"I'll deal with it."

"Ciara."

She turned to look at him, refusing to let her eyes water

despite the burning in them. "I have to move on."

He nodded, agreeing.

"And I will. From now on, I won't let my emotions drive me." Ciara pressed her lips together, forming a thin line. "I'll do better. I won't turn into one of them. Into a mindless killer."

"You're nothing like *them*, Ciara." His voice turned sharp as her blade. "You have every right to feel what you do. Just don't let it cost you your own life. Nor your sanity. Theo wouldn't want that."

He was right. As always.

"I'll get better." She had to if she wanted to do her job.

Doherty raised an eyebrow. "Where is this sudden optimism coming from?"

"Guess Liam has a bad influence on me."

Doherty nodded, knowing it was best to leave it at that. "So—"

His own ringtone cut him off. Looking at the screen, he said, "You should go. Will you be okay?"

Ciara smiled at Doherty. "I'll be fine. Thank you for trusting me."

Doherty looked up and smiled, too. "Take care of yourself." With one last look, he picked up the call and brought the phone to his ear.

It was Ciara's cue to leave.

Making a quick stop at an empty alley, Ciara used a cleaning spell to get the blood off her clothes and calmed herself. When she was done, she went home. Henry was the only one there, because Jenna had gone to get food.

There was a distinct smell of alcohol that made Ciara scrunch up her nose. Henry was lying on the sofa, suffering from a hangover. He asked Ciara where she had been when she joined him in the living room. She told him she had been with Doherty.

Henry didn't need the details. All he had to know was that she met Doherty and then he had to rush to work. It wasn't a lie.

"He's busy with work then?"

"Yes."

Henry nodded. Changing the subject, he said, "You talked with my brother last night."

"I did."

"And when will we talk?" Henry asked.

"About what?"

"What's going on with you and Liam?"

"We're friends, I guess." Ciara shrugged. "And he's my ex-boyfriend."

"What about you and Jesse?"

"Friends."

"Just friends?"

Ciara rolled her eyes. "Friends with benefits *if* we feel like it."

Henry's eyes widened. "You're sleeping with him?"

"I'm pretty sure it was a one-time thing."

"Remember when you said you had slept with your ex, and you meant Jesse?"

Ciara nodded. "What about it?"

Henry grimaced. "I thought you meant Liam."

"What?" Ciara exclaimed, her eyes widening.

Grimacing, Henry continued, "I even asked him about it."

"You what?" She opened her mouth, staring at her best friend in horror. "Henry! Do I look like a home-wrecker to you?"

"No, but I can see the tension between you and Liam."

Ciara rolled her eyes. "There's no tension."

She refused to have feelings for another man so soon after Theo's death.

Henry gave her a look. "Whatever makes you happy."

"He's about to get married and—"

"And it bothers you."

It would bother you, too, if you knew Iris was cheating on him.

Henry raised his voice. "She's what?"

Ciara's eyes widened, realising she had said it out loud.

"Iris is cheating on Liam?" Henry repeated.

"I—"

"How do you know? For how long? What the hell?" Henry rambled.

"Wait, wait, wait," Ciara said, trying to calm Henry down.

"I need to tell Liam!" As if his hangover had vanished, Henry jumped up from the sofa with newfound energy.

"On his birthday?" Ciara shook her head. "No."

"She's cheating on him!"

"Just sit down, dammit!" Ciara pointed to the sofa. "Let me explain what I know first."

Henry sat down, facing Ciara. "Tell me."

"I went to see Iris for wedding planning. When I went there, I saw a man walking out of the flat."

"Maybe it was her friend or—"

"Well, her friend was shirtless. Or he was just pulling on his shirt when he walked out," Ciara said and sneered at the memory. "Iris seemed strange when I finally knocked at her door and—"

"She doesn't know that you know?"

Ciara shook her head. "No. I keep telling myself I misunderstood something or—"

Henry cut Ciara off again. "So, you'd think it was normal if a shirtless guy walked out of Jenna's flat?"

"Well, no."

Henry had a good point. Ciara would have done something about it if she had seen a shirtless man leave Jenna's flat. She would have told Henry in an instant.

"You still like Liam."

Ciara bit the inside of her cheek to keep a straight face. "Why wouldn't I like him?"

"You have feelings for him," Henry clarified. "That's why

215

you're doubting what you saw. You think you're making it up."

Ciara buried her face in her hands. "Fuck."

"That's a mood."

"You can't tell Liam! About anything," Ciara blurted, raising her head from her hands.

"You don't want him to know Iris is cheating on him?"

"No, it's not that," Ciara said. "I just...I don't want him to be hurt for no reason if it's just my imagination."

"I doubt you're making all that up." Henry shook his head with his eyes fixed on Ciara.

"Still!"

The front door opened, and Jenna walked in with a bag of food. Sensing the tension, she asked, "What's going on?"

Ciara was hugging herself, staring at Henry with desperation clouding her eyes. Henry's eyes were wide, and his face was white. It was easy to tell something was wrong.

"Iris is cheating on Liam," Henry said.

"Henry!" Ciara exclaimed.

"She's what?" Jenna said in disbelief, setting the food down on the table. Based on the spicy scent, it was Chinese takeaway.

"Or I'm just making things up," Ciara said and stood up.

Henry jumped to his feet, too. "I doubt that."

They all sat down at the kitchen table. For a moment, the flat was silent. No one touched the food.

"So what happened?" Jenna asked eventually.

"Ciara saw a shirtless guy walking out of Liam and Iris's flat when she went to see Iris," Henry said.

"He was pulling on his shirt," Ciara clarified.

"Did he have bed hair?" Jenna asked.

Ciara furrowed her brows, picturing the man in her head. His hair had, in fact, been haywire.

"Possibly." Ciara grimaced. "Iris certainly did."

Henry sighed. "And Iris always has her hair brushed and styled."

"She's cheating," Jenna stated.

"We can't tell Liam now," Ciara said. "It's his birthday. And someone has to do it face to face."

"I'll tell him," Henry said.

"How will you make him believe you?" Ciara asked.

"You saw it," Henry said. "He'd believe you, so he'll believe it when I tell him."

"I'm his ex-girlfriend. He'll just think I'm jealous."

"Are you?"

Ciara gaped at his best friend. "You think I made the whole thing up?"

"No." Henry pointed a plastic fork at her. "You think that."

Ciara sighed.

"Alright," Jenna said, hoping to end the conversation. "Someone, probably Henry, will tell Liam. But for now, I'd like to eat."

"I'll tell him tomorrow," Henry said.

Ciara nodded, even though she feared Liam would think she was lying. Even if he believed it, Ciara was going to ruin his relationship.

27

"**A**re you excited about the flat?" Jesse asked when he and Ciara were cleaning the gym machines on Tuesday.

After they finished at the gym, they were going to see the flat.

She smiled. "I am. I like staying with Henry, but I'm pretty sure he and Jenna would prefer some privacy."

Jesse chuckled. "I bet. Besides living alone has its *benefits*."

Ciara dropped the wipe in her hands, startled by her phone ringing. She picked the wipe back up and placed it down before grabbing her phone that had been resting on top of the machine—because she didn't have pockets in her gym tights.

"What is it?" Jesse asked.

"I need to take this," Ciara said and headed to a quieter spot. Doherty was calling her. She picked up the call. "Ye—"

"It's an emergency! Get to Rosslers' immediately!" Doherty shouted into the phone before hanging up.

Ciara's eyes widened. She ran back to where Jesse was. "Do you think the flat can wait? It's an emergency."

Jesse stopped cleaning, observing Ciara's colourless face. "Of course."

Ciara nodded. "I'm so sorry, but I need to go now."

"Call if you need anything."

Ciara forgot to say goodbye as she rushed to grab her bag. Gripping her phone and bag, she snapped her fingers and teleported to the Rosslers' house.

She ran straight in, not bothering to knock. She dropped her gym bag near the front door and headed to the living room.

Liam walked out of the room, his jaw slackening, and stopped her midway. His hand brushed against her upper arm, and his wide eyes were fixed on her face, scanning every bit of her. "Can we talk outside?"

Ciara furrowed her eyebrows, glancing past Liam, but nodded. She let Liam lead her outside. They didn't go far from the front porch, and Ciara kept eyeing the front door.

"What's going on?"

"The witch hunters attacked a few of us," Liam said, his eyes fixated on Ciara. "Mum and Iris are helping the injured, but some didn't make it."

Ciara squeezed her eyes shut as the thought of Theo's death invaded her mind again. Who had died this time? Opening her eyes, she let out a shaky breath. "Why are we here then? What—"

"Once Doherty comes here, I need to go with him."

Ciara turned her full focus on Liam, no longer wondering what was going on in the house. "I'll come with you."

"No." His voice was stern, but panic shone through.

Ciara examined his face, taken aback by his odd behaviour. Worry was written all over his face. Worry for *her*.

"If it has you this worried, you'll need help."

Liam shook his head. "We'll call for back-up if we need to."

"But—"

"Please, stay here," Liam pleaded, his eyes gazing deep into Ciara's.

She had *never* stayed behind. She sighed, shaking her head. "Liam."

"I've been thinking about you a lot," Liam confessed.

Ciara looked straight into his eyes. Something about the look on his face was painfully familiar to her.

"I need to tell you something."

"Liam—"

The front door flew open, revealing Doherty. "We need to go! Finish up!" he ordered and walked back inside.

Ciara stared at the front door for a few more seconds before turning back to face Liam. "You should go."

"But Ciara—"

"You can tell me later," she said seriously. She looked straight into his eyes. "Once you're back from this...mission. Once you're back in *one piece*, okay?"

"I need to tell you now, Ciara. I—" Liam was about to reach out to touch her face, but she stopped him mid-air. She held his hand in hers, giving it a light squeeze.

"Not now."

Liam froze. He had no words.

"You need to go now," Ciara said. Because if he didn't leave soon, she wouldn't let him go.

Liam nodded. His eyes didn't leave Ciara's for a second. "Yeah."

"Be safe."

"Of course."

That was it. Ciara wanted to hug Liam, but she couldn't.

With one last look at Ciara, Liam went inside. Once he was out of her sight, terror invaded her mind. If anything happened to him...

Ciara stayed outside in the windy weather. It helped clear her head a little.

She wasn't sure what had happened between her and

Liam. But her feelings were back. This time it was different, though. More painful.

This time she wouldn't have him. Not in the end.

Taking a deep breath, she headed inside.

"Ciara, I need help!" Mary shouted from the main bedroom.

Ciara ran there, but she froze at the door. Covering her mouth, she stared at the two people lying on the bed—Henry and Jenna.

Had someone attacked Henry's flat?

He wasn't moving—other than his chest rising. A witch hunter had cut his stomach open. If it had been any deeper, Henry would have already been dead.

Jenna was struggling to stay conscious, blinking. Her clothes were bloody, and Ciara couldn't pinpoint where all her injuries were. There was so much blood.

"Why aren't they in hospital?"

"To keep the officials out of this. They would figure out our involvement, and we would all go to prison." Mary cursed under her breath.

"What can I do?" Ciara's voice was shaky, but she tried to keep her nerves in check.

"Try to clean Jenna's wounds, please," Mary said, her voice breaking while she was tending to her unconscious son's wound.

If Mary could do that, Ciara could do her own part. She grabbed what she needed and started cleaning the wounds. She wasn't a healer, but she wasn't useless with cuts.

Jenna's wounds weren't as severe as Henry's, but there were more of them, as if she had gone through a shedder.

Ciara shuddered but continued to tend to Jenna. For a while, she stayed focused on the small wounds covering her friend's body, not letting anything distract her.

She made a mistake and looked at Henry. He looked pale, his lips a shade of bluish purple. It was unimaginable what Mary was going through. They were going to lose Henry if he lost much more blood. And if Henry survived, it would be thanks to his own mother.

Ciara forced her attention back to Jenna.

Everything was beginning to make sense. Liam had originally been worried that someone had attacked Ciara, too. He had been overwhelmed with worry—but not out of love. It had nothing to do with his feelings. He didn't have those for Ciara.

However, it wasn't the right time to think about Liam or the dangerous mission he was on. Ciara needed to focus on Jenna so Mary could save Henry.

Ciara couldn't lose him.

Ciara hated blood. Especially when it was her friend's blood, not her enemies'. It didn't make her vomit or faint, but she hated how it felt on her skin and clothes. It turned sticky as it dried, and the smell of iron was nauseating.

The iron stench brought back so many memories. They were like flashbacks.

The worst was the memory of her holding Theo's lifeless body as he bled out onto the floor. She had been dragged out of that place. She had been forced to leave his body.

The memory made nausea hit her.

Mary noticed it. "Take a break," she said sternly.

"I-I'll be back." Ciara's voice nearly gave out before she rushed out of the bedroom and into the bathroom. She turned on the tap and scrubbed her hands as if the blood covering them was toxic. The water turned red and splattered all over the sink.

She had to close her eyes to keep the memories away. It wasn't the right time to suffer from post-traumatic stress symptoms. Mary needed her help. She should have been in the bedroom treating her friend.

She hadn't even lasted two hours in that room. She had been tending to Jenna the entire time. Ciara had sewn shut the worst wounds, but only thanks to magic. She had been nowhere near finished with Jenna's injuries when she had rushed out.

She turned off the running water and opened her eyes. A mix of blood and water smeared the edges of the sink, but Ciara left it there. She couldn't bring herself to look at it any longer, so she walked out.

An ear-splitting scream filled the house.

Henry.

Ciara sprinted to the bedroom. It had been Henry's scream, but he was unconscious when she ran in.

Jenna was unconscious, too, but she had passed out from the pain before Ciara had left.

However, Mary had turned sickly pale. Her hands moved unbelievably fast, tending to Henry.

Henry. Ciara's eyes scanned over his body. His wound had reopened.

"He needs blood!" Ciara said. "I'm the same blood type."

"Sit down." An order, not a question.

Ciara sat down.

"You'll feel dizzy after this," Mary warned, working with needles and tubes so she could get blood from Ciara.

"I don't care. It'll help save Henry." Her eyes were fixed on her best friend. *Anything for him.*

28

Ciara sat on a kitchen chair. Mary had told her to lie down, but she refused to. She was already useless enough. Mary had assured she could handle tending to both Jenna and Henry after the blood transfer. But even so, Ciara longed to do something.

Her hands were shaky and her vision kept going blurry whenever she tried to get up. Nausea washed over her. At some point she rushed to the bathroom and tripped onto the floor. Despite being nauseous, she didn't vomit.

She had drunk water and eaten biscuits like Mary had ordered her to. It didn't make her feel much better.

She was going to be the worst back-up if someone needed help. And that terrified her.

Liam and Doherty had already been on their mission for over three hours, and Ciara was sick with worry. She was afraid something had happened.

At least the younger Rosslers were already at school, so they weren't there to witness all the horror—witness Henry nearly die. It would have been too much for them.

Ray wasn't home, either. He had gone with a couple of other members to search the attack scenes. He had been planning to join Doherty and Liam after, but Ciara didn't know if he was with them.

Ciara had never been so powerless. Instead of helping, she was sitting on a freaking chair while others were fighting for their lives.

She should have been out there, too.

A thump from the hall alarmed her. She jumped up from the chair. Her vision blurred again. She stood still until she recovered. Then she walked out of the kitchen.

Liam and Ray were there. Liam's arms and face had cuts all over them, and dried blood covered his skin. Dirt and dust blanketed his clothes and hair. His father looked the same, except there weren't as many cuts on him.

Ciara let out a small sigh of relief. They were alive.

But then her eyes settled on what was behind the two. Lying on the floor was a body.

The sight was revolting. The wounds ran so deep she could see muscle tissue. The stench of iron slowly filled the room. The once red fluid had turned into a crimson coat on his skin. His eyes were lifeless, as if staring into endless nothing. The skin—like a canvas for the dried blood—was sickeningly pale, nearly white, with shades of blue and purple pushing through.

His chest wasn't moving.

Ciara blinked, and her legs buckled underneath her. When her eyes opened, her knees hit the floor.

"Ciara!" Liam ran to her. He wrapped his arms around her waist and pulled her close to his chest, trying to shield her from the sight. Her tears coated his shoulder, and her body shook under his touch.

"Take her upstairs," Ray said. He didn't bother to talk to Ciara. She wouldn't have registered his words. Not in her state.

"I'm going to carry you, okay?" Liam whispered to Ciara. He didn't get an answer, but he scooped her up into his arms and carried her away from the corpse that was seeping blood onto the floor.

Gregory Doherty was dead.

Ciara stared without seeing. Grief clouded her eyes. She clutched onto Liam's jacket as if it was the only thing keeping her grounded.

Liam carried her to his old room and set her down on the bed. She sat there, staring into nothing. The tears still cascaded down her face, and her hands shook. In fact, her entire body was shaking, and she didn't try to fight it.

Liam knelt in front of her and enveloped her hands in his. "Hey," he breathed out, hoping to pull her away from whatever dark corner of her mind she was in.

"H-how?" she croaked.

Liam didn't want to tell Ciara, because it would break her. She didn't need to know the details.

"It was a trap," he said, keeping his voice soft. "He insisted on going in alone. We couldn't get to him before...before..."

Ciara stayed unmoving for a good minute. Once the words sunk in, she nodded. It was a small but noticeable movement.

"How's Henry?" Liam's voice became breathless. He would have preferred not to bring it up, especially with the state Ciara was in. But he had to know if he had lost his brother, and he didn't want to leave her alone to go find out.

"Henry's unconscious. He lost a lot of blood, but we gave him more. Your mother said he'll make it." Her voice was distant, and she talked monotonously, as if in a trance.

"He got more blood?" Liam furrowed his eyebrows. His mother's blood type didn't match Henry's, and Mary wouldn't have stolen blood from the hospital.

"I'm the same blood type." Ciara's voice reached barely above a whisper, but Liam heard her.

He froze, staring at her. "Thank you." A simple thank you

didn't cut it. Not after she had saved his brother's life. But he had nothing else to offer.

"There's nothing to thank—"

"You might have saved his life."

"I've been having more PTSD symptoms than I've done helping. I've hardly saved anyone," Ciara argued.

"You've done plenty."

"I should have come with you. I—"

"No!" Liam squeezed her hands. "Someone could have killed you out there."

"What if I could have saved him?" Ciara said, her voice breaking.

Liam gripped onto her hands, dying to take the pain away. Looking into her eyes, he said, "I wouldn't have let you put yourself in that kind of danger."

Ciara looked at him through her tears, processing the words.

Liam let go of her left hand and reached his hand up to wipe away her tears. "Are you okay?"

It was a stupid thing to ask, but he needed her to talk to him.

She looked down at her lap. "I just...I thought enough people had died and now..."

The pain was all over her face. It was as if she was radiating pain, and Liam was dying to take it away. *If only there had been a way.*

"He was like family. I don't...I just..." she choked out.

Liam stroked the back of her hand. "Everything will be okay."

He moved to sit beside Ciara, still holding her hand. They stayed like that in silence.

Ciara clenched her jaw as if fighting the pain. She was trying to hold back the tears, struggling with the grief. Her eyes were glossy, but no tears had formed again.

The shaking didn't stop, but it eased. Her breathing remained uneven.

Liam wanted to end her pain. She didn't deserve any of it.

Ray walked in, interrupting the silence. At first, Liam was about to tell him to go away, but then Ray told the good news. "Jenna is awake."

Ciara whipped her head to look at Ray. "I need to see her." She stood up fast, having forgotten she had donated a lot of blood. Her knees nearly gave out, but Liam rushed to steady her just in time.

"I'll help you," he offered.

She nodded.

Ray walked ahead while Liam ended up carrying Ciara downstairs.

When they made it to the first floor, Liam set Ciara down. Despite her dizziness, she rushed to the bedroom. Running to Jenna, she pulled her into a hug. "It's so good to see you awake," Ciara said and burst into tears again.

"Ciara!" Jenna's voice filled with surprise, and she threw her arms around Ciara.

Henry wasn't in the room anymore. Ray told them Mary had taken Henry to his old room. Henry was still unconscious, even if his condition was stable, and Mary was keeping an eye on him.

"I was so worried," Ciara said, still clinging onto Jenna.

Ciara wasn't the type to talk about her feelings lightly, so hearing those words meant a lot.

"I'm fine," Jenna said and smiled. "According to Mary, you were a big help."

🍁🍁🍁

Ciara had fallen asleep on Mary and Ray's bed with Jenna. They were both asleep when Liam checked on them.

His mother was still up with his father. They were keeping an eye on Henry in case there were any complications.

Liam sat alone in the living room.

It had been a crazy day.

When he had heard about the attack at Henry's flat, he had thought first about Ciara. He had assumed she was there, too. Even though the worry for his little brother and Jenna had left him feeling sick to his core, he had been relieved to see Ciara alive and fine.

More relieved than he should have been.

At first the members had suspected the witch hunters had kidnapped Ciara or even killed her. When Liam had heard that, he had nearly lost his mind. He couldn't bear the thought of losing Ciara.

It was wrong for him to care so much. He was about to marry another woman.

Liam didn't even know if Iris was home or not. He hadn't heard from her after she had gone to tend to the other injured members. He had told her he wouldn't be home until morning.

He sat alone with those thoughts for a long while before he made his way upstairs to his brother's old room. He opened the door, and his parents turned to face him.

"How is he?" Liam asked, turning to look at his pale, unconscious little brother lying on the bed. Henry was breathing, but other than that, he wasn't moving.

"He'll be fine," Mary said. Her eyes barely stayed open, but some colour had returned to her cheeks.

"Will he wake up soon?"

"Probably tomorrow."

"We'll let you know right away," Ray said. "Go home and get some rest."

Liam nodded. "Ciara is asleep with Jenna."

"Let them get some sleep. They need it," Mary said. She had already heard about Doherty and everything that had happened. She knew what Ciara had been through.

"Sure." Liam nodded and turned to look at his brother again. "Call me when Henry wakes up, okay?"

"Of course," Mary said, nodding. "Try to get some sleep."

29

Ciara woke up beside Jenna.

Jenna was still asleep. But she wasn't running a fever, and her breathing was steady. Knowing Jenna was fine, Ciara dared to get up. She walked to the bathroom and washed her face with cold water.

After that, she headed upstairs to see how Henry was. She was glad to find Ray watching over Henry. It had been a long night for Mary.

"Good morning," Ciara whispered, not wanting to startle Ray.

He looked at her and smiled. "Morning."

"How is he?" Ciara asked, remaining near the doorway.

"He should be fine. I told Mary to get some sleep. She was exhausted."

"I bet." Ciara nodded. "But I bet you're tired, too."

"I'll be fine."

"No, I mean it. I got enough sleep last night. I can watch over him now." Ciara glanced at her slowly healing best friend. "Yesterday was rough for all of us."

Ray sighed and nodded. "Alright." He stood up. "If you insist."

"I do."

"Wake us up when he wakes up," Ray said. "We'll be in the twins' room."

There was plenty of room in the house, even with the injured guests there, because the younger Rosslers were staying at school. The magical school in Great Britain was a boarding school of sorts, and the students even spent some of their weekends there.

"Of course," Ciara said, and Ray left the room. She took a seat beside the bed, watching her best friend.

It was like reliving a nightmare. Ciara was numb from inside, and she knew that feeling all too well. From January, when Theo had died. Except it had been worse, because she had been alone in their house. Every piece of that house had reminded her of him.

Ciara reached for her phone and began typing. She needed to tell Jesse she couldn't make it to the gym.

Once she sent the message, all she could do was wait.

Looking down, she realised she was still wearing her gym clothes from the previous day. But that was the least of her worries.

She worried about Henry, even though he was going to make it. He looked better already.

Still, the thought of what could have happened made her shudder. It made her sick to her very core.

Ciara was prepared to wait for hours. But to her surprise and relief, Henry woke up in less than an hour.

His eyes fluttered open. He blinked a few times, adjusting to the light. Then he turned to look at his best friend.

Ciara cupped his face. "You're awake."

"Hi there," Henry mumbled groggily. A shaky smile made its way to his face.

"Hi." A grin spread across Ciara's lips.

"W-what happened?"

"You were attacked at the flat and—"

Henry's eyes widened. "Jenna!"

"She's fine. Just asleep. You had it worse."

Henry sighed, his muscles relaxing.

"There were other attacks, too, targeted at other members. A-and there was a mission. You'll hear about those later," Ciara said. "I should wake up your parents."

Henry furrowed his eyebrows. "Wait, wait. How long have they been sleeping?"

"Your father went to sleep an hour ago, but I'm not sure about your mother."

Henry nodded. "Do you have to wake them up?"

"I doubt they're getting much sleep. They were extremely worried."

"Fair enough."

Ciara stood up. "I'll be right back." She left the room and made her way to the twins' room where Henry's parents were. She tried to wake up the two exhausted parents without startling them. "Henry's awake."

Mary burst into tears. She scrambled up and ran out of the room. Ray followed right behind her. Mary's sobs sounded all the way from Henry's room, filling the house.

Ciara couldn't imagine their joy. They had nearly lost their son.

She wanted to let Henry and his parents talk alone. So she walked downstairs to go check on Jenna who woke up when Ciara opened the door.

Ciara smiled and walked over to the bed. She let Jenna know Henry was awake, and Jenna demanded to see Henry, so Ciara helped her up the stairs.

Jenna rushed to hug her boyfriend with her newfound strength. They clung onto one another as if the other would vanish otherwise.

"Someone needs to inform Liam!" Mary realised, watching her son and his girlfriend hug.

"I'll take care of that," Ciara said, knowing no one wanted to leave Henry. She didn't want to leave, either, but she also didn't mind.

Mary looked at her and smiled. "Thank you, dear."

"I'll be right back," Ciara said and left the room.

Once she was out, she used magic to teleport. Appearing in front of Liam and Iris's block of flats, she hurried inside, up the stairs and to their flat door.

"You were there until five in the morning!" Ciara heard Iris scream inside when she was about to knock.

"Yes! I was looking after my brother and his girlfriend who were both severely injured!" Liam yelled back at Iris. "What else would I do there?"

"Ciara was there, wasn't she?" Iris's voice was thick with accusation.

Eavesdropping made Ciara feel guilty, even if it was accidental, but she didn't dare to knock. Not yet.

"You honestly think I would cheat on you?" Liam asked, disbelief shining through his voice.

Ciara was livid. Iris had no right to accuse Liam of something he hadn't done when she was cheating behind his back. That was where she drew the line.

She raised her hand and knocked, having heard enough. The flat went silent, and soon Liam opened the door.

"Henry is awake."

Liam had had a deep frown on his face, but his eyes widened upon hearing the news. His muscles relaxed, as if someone had lifted a heavy weight off his shoulders.

"Go." Iris had her arms crossed across her chest and her lips pursed together. She showed no sign of going with Liam.

Without another word, Ciara and Liam teleported to the Rosslers' house. Liam rushed straight to Henry's old room with Ciara right behind him. Kneeling beside the bed, Liam pulled his younger brother into a bone-crushing hug.

Ciara stayed in the doorway, smiling.

But her smile dropped when she felt her phone vibrate

in her back pocket. She left the room and walked downstairs, picking up the call. "Hi," she said to Jesse.

"Hi. I got your message, but I thought I'd check up on you. Did something happen?"

"Thanks. And yes, something happened." Ciara exhaled. "H-Henry and Jenna were attacked and, well, a lot happened."

"Attacked? A-and are they okay?"

"They will be. But it didn't look good at first."

"Was it the witch hunters?"

"You know about them?" Ciara asked, her feet halting.

"Of course. I mean, they've been on the news lately."

"Oh." Ciara wasn't good at keeping up with the news outside work. "Well, it was them."

"Where did they attack?"

"Henry's flat."

"You could have been there."

"I know."

"You need a new flat for sure. It's not safe there."

"You're right. It just looks like there will be a funeral and a few other things to arrange before I can think about a new flat."

"So someone died?"

"My..." Ciara struggled to get words out. An invisible force tightened around her chest. "My old mentor." The words were like burning hot pieces in her throat.

"I'm so sorry."

"Thanks."

"You should stay with me," Jesse said. "I have a guest bedroom. You can have it for as long as you need. For free, too. You've helped so much with the gym."

"Are you sure?" Ciara asked. "For real?"

"Of course. I'd like to know you're safe."

Ciara bit back a smile, even though Jesse couldn't see it. "You worry about me?"

"I would."

Ciara hummed. "I...I'll have to talk with Henry, but I'll

234

consider it."

"Of course."

Someone cleared their throat behind Ciara, and she spun around to see Jenna.

"Uh, Jesse, I have to go," Ciara said. "I'll call you when I can, okay?"

"Okay. Stay safe."

"I will, thanks. Bye."

"Bye."

Ciara hung up and shoved her phone in her pocket before turning to face Jenna.

Jenna smiled. "Jesse, huh?" Her voice was teasing, but her smile seemed genuine.

"Yes."

"He's worried about you?" Jenna asked, grinning.

Ciara rolled her eyes. "I told him there was an attack, so he got worried, that's all."

Jenna nodded. "Well, Mary and Ray think the flat's no longer safe."

"They're probably right."

"You and Henry need a place to stay. I mean, Henry could stay at mine, but my flat is so small and—"

"If Henry can stay with you, then I have a place to stay."

"You do? You got a flat?" Jenna asked, dumbfounded.

"Not yet. I was supposed to go see one yesterday, but that didn't work out for obvious reasons."

"Oh."

"But Jesse offered to let me have his guest room."

Jenna raised her eyebrows. "Jesse wants you to live with him?"

"It's not like that."

"Romantic or sexual?" Jenna asked, wiggling her eyebrows.

Ciara groaned. "Oh, my goodness, Jenna!"

Jenna giggled, even though the movement made her wince because of her wounds. "So, which one describes your relationship with Jesse better?"

"The s-word."

Jenna laughed again, even though she tried to hold it in. "Ciara! What are you? Five?"

"I've slept with him once."

"After your break-up, you mean," Jenna said. "So, what is he like these days?"

"He's matured a lot," Ciara said. "He's polite and laid-back, but also caring. Plus, he has a better sense of humour these days."

"That is a must." Jenna's grin widened again.

"What's with the face?"

"Nothing."

30

"That flat is no longer safe," Ray said.

Everyone—Ray, Mary, Henry, Jenna, Liam, and Ciara—gathered around in Henry's old room where Henry was still on bed rest.

"You'll have to move out," Ray said, talking to Henry and Ciara.

Ciara nodded, agreeing with him. "Henry has room at Jenna's flat, and I have a place to stay. So that's sorted."

"A place to stay?" Henry blinked, staring at Ciara.

"Jesse offered me his guest room."

Henry raised an eyebrow. "Jesse?"

"Yes."

"Oh."

"But we need to get everything from the flat," Ciara said.

"We should do it today. You'll have to go to the flat anyway," Ray said, gesturing to Ciara's gym clothes. "It's better to take care of it now."

"*Now* now?" Liam asked.

"I can't even walk yet," Henry said. "I can't—"

"We'll do it without you," Ciara said.

"But—"

"Jenna can take your stuff to her flat," Ciara said, and Jenna nodded.

Henry sighed. "Fine. Just make sure you don't accidentally forget something."

"Sure thing."

Ciara, Jenna, Ray, and Liam went together to see the flat. It was safer to go as a group, because the witch hunters could be watching the place.

Ciara packed her own things. She used magic to make one of her bags bigger from the inside, while it remained the same on the outside. It helped her fit everything in one bag.

She didn't have much to pack. Just clothes, makeup, and other essentials.

Once she had finished, she helped Liam in the kitchen. They were using magic to teleport everything to Jenna's flat. They had moved some of the furniture to the Rosslers' house, because the bed, the sofa, and the table wouldn't fit in Jenna's flat.

"So, you and Jesse?" Liam asked while he and Ciara were casting items to Jenna's flat.

"Not dating."

Liam furrowed his eyebrows. "Don't you think it'll be weird? Living with your ex-boyfriend, I mean."

Ciara shrugged. "Would it be weird if we lived in the same flat?"

"I don't think so."

"I'll let you know if it's weird living with Jesse," Ciara said, continuing to cast the items.

"So I'll know to never move in with you?" Liam asked, amusement sparking in his eyes.

Ciara chuckled. "Exactly."

Moving all the furniture and other items from Henry's flat to Jenna's place took most of the day. Once they were finished, Jenna, Liam, and Ray were going to head to the Rosslers' house for a late dinner.

Ciara considered joining them, but she had already called Jesse and told him she would go to his flat soon. So she said goodbye to the others and teleported outside Jesse's flat.

Jesse had already prepared the guest room. He had even made the bed. He had also made dinner. Just pasta with pesto sauce, but it was way better than anything Ciara could have cooked.

"As far as I know, you still can't cook," Jesse said when they were eating.

"That hasn't changed."

Jesse smiled and looked up from his plate. "So, rule number one, you stay away from the stove and the oven."

Ciara chuckled. "Sounds like a plan. But I can deal with the dishes then."

"Well, I won't argue with that."

Ciara chuckled. "No surprise there."

Jesse raised two fingers up. "Rule number two, warn me *before* you bring anyone here."

"I'd rather not walk in on you and some girl having sex on the sofa, either. So, the same goes for you?"

"Deal."

"Rule number three, I pay rent," Ciara said. "How much?"

"I already told you, no rent." Jesse shook his head. "You can help at the gym."

"Are you sure? Because I can—"

"I am sure."

Ciara nodded. "Fine."

Ciara didn't have time to help Jesse around the gym at first. She was helping others plan Doherty's funeral. He didn't have any family, so there were no relatives to arrange anything.

Jesse understood, assuring Ciara it was okay. He offered to help her, even by listening, but she kept to herself. The more he tried to make her talk, the further away she pushed him, and eventually Jesse gave up.

Ciara was locked in her own headspace until the funeral. Even the ceremony was a blur for her.

She kept staring at the coffin throughout the funeral. The thought of Doherty's corpse lying inside felt unrealistic. She had a hard time accepting it.

Theo's funeral had been worse, but it was still a rough experience. Doherty had been like a father figure for Ciara. She couldn't believe she had lost him, too.

She struggled to say goodbye and let go. She couldn't get any words out at the ceremony, and it didn't help her move on.

There had been too many funerals already. Each felt more and more surreal. As if they were an endless nightmare.

Doherty was gone, but Ciara was struggling to bring herself to accept it.

It was tough for others, too. Some members had known Doherty even longer than Ciara had. Some of them had been part of the group because of their friendship with Doherty, and they left the group after his untimely death.

The group became smaller—close to non-existent. Ten members remained—Ciara, Henry, Jenna, Liam, Iris, Mary, Ray, Eric, Hannah, and Tony. There hadn't been more than one meeting since Doherty's death. He had been their leader—the uniting force of the group, and there was no one to take his place.

Ciara was lost without the group, and she was on suspension until the beginning of December. She wasn't sure how to keep hunting down the witch hunters.

But giving up wasn't an option. Nothing could keep her from tracking down those terrorists.

The fight was personal. The witch hunters had already taken too much from her. Dozens of co-workers, then Theo and Doherty.

Ciara could get information from her old co-workers in the States and in Canada. With their information, she hoped she could continue to fight.

No one else had to know. She didn't want anyone to risk their life. She had already lost enough.

This time she would fight alone.

31

I t was a Saturday evening, five days after the funeral.
Mary had decided that, after everything, it was time
to have a big family dinner. Even the twins and Gabriel
were home from school for the weekend. The timing
couldn't have been better.

Mary had also invited Ciara. Ciara thought she might
be intruding, but Mary had assured her she was almost like
family. After all, she was Henry's best friend.

Ciara arrived early, before any of the other guests.

"Ciara!" the twins squealed when Mary let her in. The
girls were thrilled to see her after so long. Somehow, they
had heard about Jesse and they were dying to hear more.

Ciara tried to tell Polly and Poppy that Jesse was just her
friend, but neither twin was buying it.

"Ciara and Jesse sitting in a tree—"

Ciara rolled her eyes, and the twins started giggling.

Ciara had also caught sight of Gabriel and Ray briefly
before they had left outside to fly a magical kite that they

had built the evening before.

After talking with the twins, Ciara went to help Mary in the kitchen. She stayed away from the oven, but she helped with setting the table.

"You still hate cooking?"

Ciara smiled and glanced at Mary. "I wouldn't call it hate. I just prefer not to burn anything."

Mary chuckled. "Oh, Ciara."

Ciara smiled, setting the plates on the table.

"But I don't see why you'd have to cook," Mary said, smiling. "You'll just have to get yourself a man that can do it for you."

Ciara grinned. "Well, from now on I'll ask about cooking skills on every first date."

"You're not seeing anyone?"

Ciara shook her head. "No."

"But you're looking for someone to date?"

"Not really."

"What about Jesse? You're not interested in him, either?"

Ciara chuckled slightly. "It's not like that with him. He's a good friend, but that's it. We're just friends. Although, I'll admit, he has matured a lot since school."

"Is it odd being friends with him?" Mary asked.

"Not really." Ciara shrugged. "It's sort of like with me and Liam."

Mary nodded with a hint of a smile on her face, the amusement reaching all the way up to her eyes.

Ciara tilted her head to the side. "What?"

"So you and Liam are friends."

Heat rushed to Ciara's cheeks, and she prayed Mary didn't notice. "I suppose so."

Mary smiled and nodded, looking at Ciara, before she turned back to the oven. "I think he still cares about you a lot. Whether it's platonic, I can't tell."

"He's happy with Iris," Ciara said, setting down the glasses.

Mary turned to glance at her, eyebrows raised. "So you

still love him?"

Ciara sighed. Denying her feelings, even from Mary, would be pointless. "Love is a strong word."

"But?"

Ciara trusted Mary. Even if she was Liam's mother, she wouldn't tell Liam—or Iris. After all, Mary was like a second mother to Ciara.

Ciara turned to look at her and smiled. "I'm happy for him."

Mary looked back at Ciara, and her face twisted into a sad—almost pitying—smile. "I'd call that selfless love."

"It doesn't matter. Everyone's happy now." *Everyone but me.* But Ciara couldn't be happy after all the loss. She needed time to heal.

"I suppose so." Mary nodded. "But even if you won't be officially part of the family, I'll want to see the next guy to win your heart."

Ciara smiled. "I'll bring him over once I find him."

Mary smiled warmly. "Oh, you'd better."

The two women heard the front door open and close. A moment later Liam stepped into the kitchen, lingering in the doorway. "Hi, Mum," he greeted his mother and then turned to face Ciara. "Hi, Ciara." He smiled at her.

Ciara smiled back at him. "Hi," she said, folding the light green napkins.

"It's so good to see you, dear!" Mary said, beaming at her son. "I'd hug you, but this cooking won't wait." She gestured to the stew she was stirring.

Liam smiled. "I'd hate for it to burn."

Mary smiled and tried to peer behind Liam. "Did you come alone? Where's Iris?"

"She should be here later. She has some errands to run, but she promised to come."

Mary smiled and nodded. "Good, good."

The twins walked downstairs and spotted their eldest brother in the kitchen doorway. "Liam!" Poppy squealed and rushed to hug Liam.

Then it was Polly's turn.

"How's school?" Liam asked the twins after the greeting hugs.

"Polly has a date in a week," Poppy revealed with a triumphant grin.

"Poppy!" Polly screamed at her twin, her eyes growing wide. "It was supposed to stay a secret!"

"Polly has a date?" Mary shrieked with both surprise and excitement—and perhaps a bit of worry.

Poppy grinned at Polly and shrugged. "Too late now."

Liam crossed his arms. "So, who is the guy? Do I need to give him a few rules before or—"

"Please, don't!" Polly cried out. Her cheeks were glowing red, and she looked mortified.

Liam couldn't help but chuckle.

"I'm sure Poppy will make sure he's a decent date. Right?" Ciara turned to look at Poppy.

Poppy smiled and nodded. "Of course!"

"I hate all of you," Polly muttered, crossing her arms. She pouted and glared at her family members.

"So, when will we get to meet this guy?" Mary asked.

"Mum!" Polly shook her head. "Stop teasing!"

"Alright, alright," Mary said and smiled at her daughter. "Just wait until your father hears."

Polly, who had just relaxed a little, looked mortified again. "No! No, no, no."

To Polly's luck, the front door opening interrupted the moment.

"Hello, everyone!" came Henry's voice before he and Jenna walked into the kitchen.

"It's so good to see both of you here!" Mary said and smiled at them. "How are you two?"

"Almost running late because of this one," Jenna said, nudging Henry.

Mary sighed but smiled. "Oh, it's always the men we have

to wait for."

Henry rolled his eyes.

"So, you two still haven't killed each other now that you're living together?" Liam teased the freshly arrived couple.

Henry and Jenna had decided it was best for them to live together, even though they hadn't been dating for long. Neither one of them saw any point in Henry looking for a new flat when they would spend most of their time together in one place anyway.

"We haven't even fought once," Henry revealed and smiled proudly. "You can't top that, I bet."

"Oh, just wait," Liam said.

Soon Gabriel and Ray came inside from flying their magical kite—which had been a success. It was just in time for the dinner.

Iris still hadn't shown up, but there was a seat saved for her at the table. Ironically, the empty seat was between Liam and Ciara.

Everyone continued to eat while chatting until Mary asked Liam about Iris. Liam excused himself to call his fiancée. When he returned to the table, it turned out she hadn't answered his call. Liam tried to come up with an excuse, saying Iris's phone was dead or she had lost track of time.

But Ciara feared it wasn't that.

She turned to look at Henry and Jenna. Henry looked uneasy and slightly pale.

He had never got the chance to tell Liam about the cheating. The day he had been planning to tell, Iris had been with him and Liam the entire time. Then there had been the attacks, Doherty's death, and the funeral.

Henry had eventually forgotten to say anything.

Ciara had tried to make sense of the cheating. But none of it made any sense, considering how in love with Liam Iris was. Their wedding was nearing, too.

Liam kept shifting in his seat. He seemed uneasy, but not

for the same reason as the others. He was worried about his fiancée.

Worried enough to leave right after dinner.

"I hope everything's okay with Iris," Mary said, her forehead wrinkling with worry.

Ciara was cleaning the kitchen with her. Henry was outside with Gabriel. Ray was taking a nap. And Jenna was braiding the twins' hairs. Everyone had something to do.

"Liam will call soon if something's wrong, I'm sure," Ciara said, trying to comfort Mary.

"Unless someone attacked their flat."

"There are strong protection spells guarding it," Ciara reminded her.

After the attacks, every member—or former member—had put up guarding and protection spells around their homes. None of them felt safe, and none of them *were* safe. But the spells helped, and they were made to last for weeks, if not months.

Mary sighed. "You're right. Perhaps I shouldn't worry so much."

"It's okay to worry about your children. After everything that has happened, I would worry, too."

Mary nodded.

"I think Iris might have been running some errands for the wedding," Ciara said, trying to reassure Mary. "I mean, she's so excited. It would be no wonder if she lost track of time."

Mary smiled and nodded, feeling relieved. "You're right."

Ciara smiled back and set a pile of plates in the sink.

"It's quite surprising that the two of you are friends."

Ciara looked up at Mary. "I have nothing against Iris. She seems like a wonderful person."

The moment those words left Ciara's mouth, she wanted to take them back. Her thoughts drifted to the shirtless man who had walked out of Iris and Liam's shared flat.

32

Once Ciara got home to Jesse's place from the Rosslers' house, she ran to her room, threw on another set of clothes and added eyeliner. She had agreed to go see a film and have drinks with Jesse.

It wasn't a date. Not a romantic kind, at least. It was just two friends hanging out. It had been Jesse's idea. He claimed Ciara needed a fun night out after the funeral. But even more so, he seemed to think she needed to get wasted so she could forget everything for one moment.

The film was an action movie with horror elements. Both Ciara and Jesse liked it. Neither one was the type to watch sappy comedies.

When the film finished, Jesse took Ciara to a small pub. It wasn't too crowded, but there were customers scattered around. It was perfect for the occasion—getting wasted.

Jesse and Ciara had just stepped in and hadn't even walked up to the bar when Jesse spotted a familiar face. "Isn't that William Rossler?"

Ciara turned her head, and her eyes landed on Liam. He was alone at the bar with a whiskey in his hands. His eyes were fixed on the glass. In fact, he was staring at it rather intensely.

Ciara furrowed her eyebrows. "Uh, yeah. That's Liam."

"Should we go check on him?" Jesse asked, eyeing the lonely man. "It looks like he's drinking his sorrows away."

Jesse was right. Liam didn't seem to be expecting company. It looked as if he was there to get drunk and drown his sorrows.

Ciara forgot to answer Jesse, walking up to where Liam was sitting. Jesse followed her. She sat down on a stool beside Liam, and Jesse stayed standing right next to her.

"Hi," Ciara said, making Liam look up. He hadn't noticed her until then.

His eyes were red, and his movements were slow. It was obvious he was wasted.

"Hi."

Ciara barely made out what Liam said as he slurred the word.

"How much have you been drinking?" Ciara asked and took the whiskey glass from his hands. She set it down on the table further away from him.

She had never seen Liam so drunk.

"*A lot*," he mumbled.

"We should probably get him home," Jesse said.

Liam turned to look at Jesse, to whom he had paid no attention until then. He muttered something that neither Ciara nor Jesse could understand, then turned to stare at the glass on the table.

Liam was about to pick it up, but Ciara was faster. She grabbed his hand to stop the movement. Liam's gaze settled on her, and he stared at her in silence. Then he intertwined their fingers, making Ciara's eyes go wide.

And like that, the glass was forgotten.

"Look, we're going to take you home, okay?" Ciara said.

"Can you walk on your own?"

Liam nodded.

But it turned out to be a struggle. Even with both Jesse and Ciara helping him stay upright, it was hard to get him out of the pub. Once they were out, they used magic to teleport to the front of the block of flats. It was a pain in the arse to get Liam up the stairs and to his and Iris's flat door.

Ciara went through Liam's pockets, while he swayed drunkenly, and eventually found his keys. She twisted the key in the lock and opened the flat door. They walked in, and Liam threw up on the floor.

The disgusting stench filled the room. Ciara scrunched up her nose and made sure not to step in the mess. There were no lights on, so Ciara flicked her fingers to turn them on.

"Iris?" Ciara called out, but she got no answer.

"She—" Liam threw up again, adding onto the mess.

"I'll help him to the bathroom," Jesse said and walked Liam towards the bathroom after Ciara pointed the right way.

"I'll clean this up," Ciara said, cringing at the orange mush on the floor. Even the smell made her gag.

Once Ciara had cleaned all the vomit off the floor and the furniture, she grabbed her phone and dialled Henry. He didn't pick up.

Sighing, Ciara shoved her phone in her pocket. She went to check on Liam and Jesse. Liam was hovering over the toilet, retching and vomiting.

"This might go on for a while." Jesse grimaced and glanced at Liam.

"Yeah." Ciara sighed, looking at Liam. She had never seen him in that state.

"Iris doesn't seem to be home," Jesse said, lowering his voice.

Ciara nodded. She had noticed, too. "I wonder where she is."

"Should you try to call her?"

Ciara bit her lip, thinking. "I don't know. She didn't show up for the dinner today. Something's going on."

"Maybe they had a fight. That would explain everything," Jesse said, gesturing to Liam.

"So I won't call her."

"Perhaps a good idea."

"I tried to call Henry, but he didn't pick up."

"Well, Liam seems to be in terrible shape."

Ciara could only imagine Iris's face, coming home and finding Ciara there. It didn't sound ideal, but it seemed like the only option.

"I'll stay with him. You don't have to."

"Are you sure?" Jesse asked. "You might need help. Like, with carrying him or something."

"I can handle this."

"If you say so."

"Go get some sleep or go have a drink," Ciara said.

"We will have drinks some other time."

Ciara smiled and nodded. "That's a plan."

Jesse grinned. "Good luck with him."

"Thanks."

Once Liam stopped vomiting, Ciara helped clean his face and hair from the puke. She helped remove his shoes, jacket, and shirt, which were all covered in vomit.

Helping Liam to the bedroom was a struggle, considering Liam was taller and weighed more than Ciara. With a little effort, she got him to the bedroom and made him sit on the bed. He didn't stay sitting, though. He fell back, lying down with his legs dangling off the edge.

Ciara sighed.

"Thanks," Liam mumbled out, about to pass out. And he

did.

Ciara didn't think it was okay for her to undress Liam any more than she had, so she tucked him in and turned off the bedroom lights.

Even though Liam was in bed and asleep, Ciara didn't feel like she could leave him. She went to the living room and looked around.

She had cleaned up the vomit, but there was still a mess. A broken photo frame lay on the floor, shards of glass scattered around it. Ciara cleared the glass away before she lay down on the sofa.

33

Liam's head was pounding, and he had a foul taste on his tongue when he woke up. He was starving.

He didn't remember leaving the pub or making it home. Not to mention making it to bed. It was a miracle he had even got the flat door open.

Somehow he wasn't sleeping on the duvet, either. Instead, it was on top of him. But he was wearing clothes except for shirt, jacket, and shoes. He had no idea how he had got them off—especially the shoes.

He moved to sit on the edge of the bed. Groggily, he got up and headed to the bathroom to clean his teeth.

After freshening up and returning to the bedroom, he heard noise from the kitchen.

He grabbed a T-shirt and pulled it on. "Iris?" He went to see who was in the kitchen.

It wasn't the blonde woman he had expected; there was a dark-haired woman making eggs. *Ciara.*

"Morning." She turned to smile at him. "I, uh, thought it

would be okay to make you some eggs. They're said to help with hangovers."

"Ciara?" Liam blinked, having a hard time trusting his sight.

Ciara nodded. "Yep, it's me. You don't remember much about last night, huh?"

Liam's eyes widened, and his cheeks heated in embarrassment. "Not really."

"Jesse and I were going to have drinks, and we ended up in the same pub as you." Ciara moved the eggs around in the pan. "You were wasted. You could barely speak."

Liam cringed.

Ciara smiled. "At least you couldn't say anything you might regret later."

That brought a smile to Liam's face.

"Anyway, Jesse and I helped you out of the pub and then here. When we got in, you threw up on the floor. Twice. But I cleaned it up, so no worries. Jesse helped you to the bathroom, and he left after I told him to get drinks by himself. Then I helped you to bed," Ciara told. "You were in such a terrible shape that I didn't dare to leave you alone, so I slept on the sofa. I hope you don't mind."

Liam pressed on his temples, his headache worsening as he processed the words. "Of course not. I'm sorry I ruined your night with Jesse."

"Don't worry about it; I'm sure you didn't ruin Jesse's night. He's probably home with some girl."

Liam blinked. "You're seriously not dating him?"

Ciara chuckled. "I thought I've told you that like a hundred times by now. No, I'm not dating him."

"I'll try to remember from now on," Liam mumbled.

"Good idea." Ciara turned off the stove, finishing cooking the scrambled eggs. "Anyway, where do you keep your plates?"

"I'll get those," Liam offered. He opened a cupboard and grabbed two plates along with two forks from a drawer.

They sat down, and Liam looked past Ciara to see a broken photo frame—minus the glass—still on the floor. A reminder of his and Iris's fight.

"Are you okay?" Ciara asked.

Liam froze, staring at his plate. "Yeah."

"And the genuine answer?"

Liam stayed silent. He would have preferred not to talk about it.

"I've never seen you that drunk. I doubt you've ever been that drunk before."

Liam furrowed his brows, raising his gaze from his plate. "Iris has been cheating on me."

Ciara's eyes widened, and colour drained from her face. "So she was cheating," she spluttered.

Liam squinted. "What do you mean?"

Ciara set down her fork and looked down in shame. "I...I saw someone leave the flat, and it wasn't you. But I just..."

"Blond hair? Striking blue eyes? Ripped abs? Super muscular?"

"Yes." Ciara didn't raise her gaze from her plate, avoiding making eye contact with Liam. "He was pulling on his shirt at the door. I, uh, pretended to be going to a different flat until he left."

"It's not your fault."

Exhaling, Ciara looked back up and met his eyes. "Well, I should have said something. I mean, I wasn't sure what it meant, but I suspected that...you know."

"Still, not your fault."

"H-how did you find out?"

"I suppose one loses track of time when busy in bed," Liam said bitterly.

Ciara's eyes softened, but her jaw clenched. Pity for Liam, and hate for Iris. "They were here?"

Liam nodded. "Yep, in the bedroom."

"So, where is Iris?"

"I told her to leave. I suppose she's at the guy's place now,"

Liam said and shrugged. "Honestly, I don't care."

Ciara opened her mouth, but then closed it. She wasn't sure what to say to make it better for Liam.

"I'm calling off the stupid wedding."

"You've already thought everything through."

"She has been cheating on me since July."

"I'm sorry."

"It has nothing to do with you."

They were silent until they finished breakfast. Ciara offered to wash up, but Liam insisted he would do it later.

"Thanks for the eggs," he said.

"You should thank me for not burning down the entire building," Ciara said, trying to lighten the mood.

Liam chuckled. "Well, you didn't even burn the eggs."

"This time."

Liam smiled.

"Anyway, I suppose I should go." Ciara looked straight into his eyes. "Will you be alright?"

Liam nodded. "Thanks again."

Jesse woke up when Ciara went home. He had gone out for drinks on his own, but he hadn't brought anyone home with him.

"So, how is Liam?" Jesse asked, sitting in the living room with Ciara.

Ciara leaned her back against the sofa. "He found out Iris was cheating on him. Him getting drunk resulted from that."

"Oh. So, he's heartbroken."

Ciara nodded. "Yes."

"And you?"

"What about me?" Ciara asked, dumbfounded.

"Well, you have feelings for the guy. What are you thinking?"

"I'm angry at Iris for what she did," Ciara said. "I feel sorry for him, and I also feel guilty for not telling him before."

Jesse patted Ciara on her shoulder. "You don't know whether he would have believed you even if you had told him."

"I know."

"Is he going to call off the wedding?"

"He said he would, but he was angry and hurt."

Jesse nodded. "So you're not getting your hopes up yet."

"I'm not getting my hopes up at all." Ciara shook her head. "First of all, he's heartbroken. He doesn't need a girlfriend, and especially not an ex-girlfriend who's still not over him. Second, I wouldn't want to be his rebound girlfriend. Third, calling off the wedding doesn't mean that he's giving up on Iris. They could get through this."

"So what are you going to do?"

"Nothing."

Henry called Ciara later that day—closer to the evening.

"I have horrid news." That was the first thing that came out of Henry's mouth when Ciara picked up, the shock apparent in his voice.

"About what?" Ciara's mind went to the witch hunters, and her heart pounded in her chest. Adrenaline rushed through her veins, readying her for a fight.

"Liam found out about Iris cheating on him."

A weight lifted off Ciara's heart, and her muscles relaxed. She breathed out in relief. "I actually heard already."

"Already?" Henry's voice rose.

"Jesse and I went to the same pub as Liam. He was wasted, so we took him home. I stayed the night to make sure he was fine."

"He got drunk?"

"No, he got wasted."

"He rarely drinks."

"I know." Ciara sighed, remembering the shape Liam had been in. "But wouldn't you react irrationally if you found out that your fiancée had been cheating on you for months?"

"Good point."

"We should have told him," Ciara said.

Henry sighed. "I was thinking the same."

"Do you feel guilty?"

"Yes. You?"

"Yes."

"But it's not our fault. It was Iris who did it."

"I know, but that doesn't ease my mind," Ciara said.

"Liam wouldn't be mad."

"He wasn't when I told him what I had seen. At least he claimed not to be."

"So he knows."

"He knows I know," Ciara said. "I said nothing about you and Jenna."

Henry exhaled heavily. "Mum was furious when she found out. I think she's over at his place right now."

"No wonder."

"Yeah. I hope he's okay." Henry hummed. "I wish I had told him the second I found out."

"I should have told him," Ciara insisted.

"*We* should have told him."

34

The flat Jesse's friend owned was still available. Ciara got another chance to see it and she fell in love with it. It had the perfect view, and it was the perfect size for her—not too big, nor too small.

There was a spare bedroom. Ciara didn't need it but didn't mind having one for special occasions.

Ciara and the flat's owner agreed on the rent right away. The owner told her to move whenever she wanted to, so she packed everything and moved. It was easy, because she only had one enchanted bag full of her belongings.

But she had to buy furniture, because she didn't have any. She only bought the essentials at first, such as a mattress, a sofa and so on. She had lived with the bare necessities before, and she liked having space.

Jesse's friend had given Ciara the permission to paint the walls or put up paintings. She didn't like the dark grey wall, so she painted it sage green.

Ciara finished with the wall and was heading to the bathroom, her hair and clothes covered in paint, when the doorbell rang.

It was early, and she wasn't expecting guests. It could have been anyone. Witch hunters included.

She approached the front door, ready to strike if she had to, and opened it.

Her eyes widened, seeing Liam at her door. "Liam."

She hadn't seen him in nearly two weeks. She had been busy at the flat, and it wasn't her place to intrude.

Henry had told her that Iris had gone back home to her and Liam's flat. Ciara didn't want to see Iris, and the feeling was probably mutual.

"Um, hi." Liam rubbed the back of his neck. "Henry, uh, mentioned your new address, and I—"

Ciara smiled. "Come on in. I'm sorry it smells like paint."

Liam smiled and stepped inside. "I could tell that you've been painting." He gestured to the paint on Ciara's clothes and hair.

Ciara chuckled, pushing the flat door closed. "Yeah. I was just about to have a shower."

"Oh. I can, uh, come back later or—"

"No need," Ciara assured. "Unless you have a tight schedule or something, make yourself at home. It won't take me long."

Liam smiled and nodded. "Alright."

Ciara grabbed some clothes and rushed to the bathroom.

Meanwhile, Liam looked around the flat. There was tons of room, and lots of light came in through the enormous windows. The colours and tones were warm and earthy, giving the space a cosy feeling.

Ciara showered as quickly as she could. In ten minutes she stepped out of the bathroom—dressed and without paint in her hair.

She joined Liam in the living room, sitting down beside

him on the sofa.

He smiled at her. "I like the flat."

"Yeah, me too."

"Are you going to stick to the minimal furnishings?"

"I already have more stuff than I did in Seattle," Ciara said. "But I'll probably get a coffee table."

"And what about a housewarming party?"

Ciara shrugged. "I haven't thought about it yet."

Liam nodded.

"Um, how have you been?" She hated bringing it up, but she had been thinking about it for almost two weeks. She had been thinking about Liam a lot.

His jaw clenched, and his eyes hardened. "Well, Iris came back last Saturday."

Ciara nodded, urging Liam to continue, even though she wasn't sure she wanted to hear more.

"She was basically begging me not to call off the wedding." He sighed, trying to keep his cool. "She asked for another chance. I agreed for her to stay at our flat."

Ciara picked at her cuticles absentmindedly and chewed on the inside of her cheek.

Of course, she thought. Iris and Liam were in love and still engaged.

"I took the sofa," Liam said. "Then this morning she started begging again, asking me to rethink and so on."

Ciara's eyes fixed on Liam. "A-and?"

"I ended things with her for good." His brows furrowed, and he paused. Taking a deep breath, he turned to look at Ciara, and his gaze softened. "Then I came here."

Ciara's mouth made the shape of an O. She was the *first* person he had come to.

"And what about your shared flat?"

"I want to sell it. Iris refuses to. That's actually why I'm here." He ran his fingers through his hair.

Ciara raised an eyebrow. "Really?"

Liam nodded. "I was wondering if I could live here.

Only temporarily. Henry said you have a guest room, so I thought—"

"Of course." Ciara didn't hesitate at all, despite being surprised. "There's plenty of room."

Liam smiled. "Would you mind if I brought my chest of drawers and a few other things here? Again, temporarily."

Ciara smiled back. "Of course not."

"Are you sure? I can pay half of the rent or more. And I can—"

"Yes, I'm sure. I would have to pay the rent anyway, so don't worry about that either."

"Are you sure?"

"For the second time, yes, I'm sure."

Liam's face brightened. "Thank you."

Liam moved in that day. Henry and Jenna helped move his stuff, and there was more than just one chest of drawers. All his clothes, linen, a bookshelf, tons of books amongst other things. It all fit in nicely, blending in with Ciara's furniture.

"I would never have thought you two would live together!" Henry said.

He, Jenna, Liam, and Ciara were having some wine. It was a Friday night, and they had just finished moving everything.

Ciara rolled her eyes at Henry. "I have more extra space than anyone else."

He gestured to their surroundings. "Because you only have, like, a sofa and a chair."

Ciara pointed at her television. "I bought that."

"Fair enough."

"It's more than I had in Seattle."

Henry laughed, leaning back. "Oh, I know."

"I felt like a hoarder when I was here the first time," Jenna said, looking around.

"Only Ciara could live with so little stuff," Henry said.

"It's all I need," Ciara said in her defence.

"It's still insane."

Jenna grinned. "And when is the housewarming party?"

"I asked her the same thing." Liam held up his wineglass. "She claims she hasn't even thought about it."

Jenna turned to look at Ciara. "You have to have one! You will, won't you?"

"Eventually, I suppose."

"Not good enough." Jenna shook her head. "You should have one in...like, a week!"

Ciara's eyes widened. "In a week? Who would I even invite?"

"Us." Jenna gestured to herself, Henry, and Liam. "And Evie with her girlfriend. Mia, of course. Oh, and Jesse. Maybe his friends."

"Shawn would be happy to see you again," Liam said.

"You could invite someone from Canada or the States, too," Henry added.

Ciara shook her head. "I doubt anyone has the time with a week's warning."

Jenna grinned. "Fine. If you have it closer to the end of the month, you can have a Halloween theme."

Ciara raised her eyebrows. "A theme party?"

"It would be fun!"

"I think it's a great idea," Henry agreed.

"Liam, please, tell them it's silly," Ciara pleaded.

Liam chuckled, amusement reaching his eyes. He shook his head and smiled at Ciara. "Actually, I think it sounds like a plan."

Ciara looked at Liam first, then at Henry, and last at Jenna. "But—"

"No but." Jenna grinned and sipped her wine. "Besides, we'll help set everything up."

"I have a bad feeling about this."

Jenna scoffed. "Nonsense. You're just trying to be a party pooper."

"It's set!" Henry declared. "The party will be on the last

Saturday of this month."

"I thought that was my decision to make," Ciara said.

"Three against one, so you're outnumbered," Henry said, smirking at his best friend.

Even days later, Ciara was thinking the Halloween party was a bad idea. She was busy painting walls and decorating the flat to make it look decent.

Luckily, Liam had moved in with his furniture. The flat looked a lot more like home, because it was no longer empty.

Liam had also brought a big painting. He had told Ciara she didn't have to hang it, but she did, anyway. It fit perfectly on an empty living room wall with its shades of green, gold, and black.

Ciara had bought a few items for the flat, too: a stand mirror near the door, and some pillows and a blanket for the sofa. She had even bought a few plants, but she was unsure how long they would survive in her hands.

She was falling in love with the place. It felt like a home, and no place had felt like a home for her after Theo's death.

Ciara and Liam ate takeaway that Liam had brought on his way home from work.

While eating, his eyes settled on the piece of art Ciara had hung on the wall. "I see you hung the painting."

Ciara glimpsed at it but then turned back to face Liam. "Oh, yeah! I should have asked you, but—"

Liam turned his gaze on Ciara, smiling at her. "It looks great."

Ciara's cheeks warmed, and she smiled. "It does."

Liam turned to his food briefly, eating a mouthful. "Have you thought about your costume yet?"

Ciara stopped eating and tilted her head to the side. "My costume?"

Amusement glittered in Liam's eyes. "For the housewarming party."

"I didn't realise I needed a costume." She sighed. "Why did I agree to this?"

Liam smiled. "It'll be fun."

Ciara shrugged, poking at her food.

"Did you send the invitations yet?"

"I did. But I wouldn't have if Jenna hadn't threatened to send them herself."

"Would that have been bad?"

"Who knows who she would have invited." Ciara shook her head. "There could be everyone from school!"

"Like one of those school parties?" Liam grinned, clearly thinking back to his memories.

Ciara grimaced, remembering them too. "I think we had enough of those."

35

Liam enjoyed living with Ciara. He loved coming back home to see what she had done or whether she had bought anything new. He found his habit of checking on Ciara every morning he left for work oddly soothing. She was usually asleep—sometimes even on the weekends, when he went out to get breakfast for them.

The flat was usually filled with laughter or chatter, and Liam found himself enjoying the simple things with Ciara. Even watching television, even though they didn't always agree on what to watch. The small, everyday events became meaningful.

But it was too soon for it to be anything more than two friends living together. Liam wasn't ready for a new relationship—not even a rekindled one.

Besides, he wanted to make it right this time. He wanted to remember every bit of it all the way to the tiny, silly details.

It was the night before the party. An October Friday night.

Liam had hoped to spend time with Ciara and watch a movie with her, but she wasn't home. He hadn't seen her since the morning when he had left for work. Even then, she had been fast asleep.

Jenna and Ciara had decorated the day before, and Jenna and Mary had promised to do the baking. So everything was prepared.

But Liam was worried about Ciara. She hadn't even told him where she was, but had texted him, saying she was busy and would be home late. Even though no one had worked on the witch hunter case recently, the old members could still be in danger.

Liam hadn't heard from Ciara in hours, and it was nearing midnight.

In the midst of his worrying, he also wondered if Ciara could be with a guy. But he had no right to be jealous, because they weren't dating. They just lived together.

Liam hadn't looked for a flat as much as he should have. Ciara hadn't said anything, and Liam kept thinking perhaps she liked having him around. And that fuelled his hopes.

Liam stared at the television, unable to focus. He lost track of what show was on, falling deep into his thoughts.

Worry clouded his mind, and there was no way he could sleep before Ciara came home. So he kept staring at the television.

At two in the morning, the flat door opened.

Liam jumped up from the sofa and rushed to see Ciara.

She closed the flat door and turned around. "Liam?" Her voice was quiet and fragile, but surprised. Her hair was messy and dripping water. Mud covered her coat, and there was dirt on her jeans and boots.

Liam looked her over. "Are you okay?"

She opened her mouth, but then closed it, her expression turning into a frown.

His stomach twisted with worry. "I know I—"

"I'm fine." Ciara shrugged off her coat, keeping it in her hands, and kicked off her boots. Her hands were shaking when she grabbed her boots, too. "I'm, uh, going to shower."

She walked past him, and he wanted to reach out for her, but he forced his hands to stay at his sides. He had to clench them into fists to keep himself from reaching out.

"Good night, Liam." She only glanced at him before walking to the bathroom.

Something was wrong. Liam knew it, and he wouldn't let it slide.

He paced back and forth in the living room, waiting for Ciara. It took a while. She *never* took more than twenty minutes in the shower.

Except it took her forty minutes to step out of the bathroom. She only had a towel wrapped around her naked body.

Liam's gaze fell on the fresh bruises covering her arms. He strode over to her, his eyes widened. "What happened?" He brushed against her still wet skin, tracing his fingers over the red marks.

Ciara's eyes widened as if she had been caught doing something wrong. "It's stupid." She was still shaking, no matter how hard she tried to hide it.

Liam gave her a long look. "You're covered in bruises. Whatever that means, it isn't stupid." His voice remained soft but stern.

"Can you just let it slide this time?" Ciara wrapped her arms around herself and refused to meet his gaze.

"What?" Liam breathed out. "Someone hurt you, Ciara. What happened?" He raised his voice the tiniest bit, fuelled by anger. No one had the right to hurt her.

"Liam—"

Liam's brows furrowed, and he stared into Ciara's eyes. "What's going on, Ciara? If this is some guy or—"

Ciara's eyes widened. "What? No, it's not like that."

"Then what is it?" Liam asked, begging to know. "You're

acting oddly. You're quiet. I can tell you're trying to keep your composure, but you're slipping. And you're covered in bruises."

"I didn't stop when the group stopped," Ciara whispered unsteadily.

"Ciara," Liam choked out her name.

She stared at the floor, still hugging herself. Her shoulders were hunched, and she was shaking. She looked nothing like the confident young woman she usually was.

Liam's mouth tightened. "W-what happened?"

"I've been tracking *them* for a while now with the help of some old colleagues." Her voice was weak, but it was the only sound in the entire flat, so Liam heard her fine. "I can't stop. After everything they've taken from me, I *can't* stop." Her face was pale, and her voice was shaky.

"You've been going after them alone?" Liam's stomach twisted with worry. He didn't want to spare one thought to Ciara fighting against those monsters on her own.

"Not until today." Her voice was hollow—empty of feeling.

"What happened today?"

Ciara's eyes glistened with tears, and her bottom lip quivered. "T-they killed a child," she choked, struggling to get the words out.

Liam froze, his eyes widened. He had never seen witch hunters kill a child, even though he knew how cruel they were. They killed for attention—for media coverage to get their message across.

His heart broke, seeing Ciara in that state. He wanted to comfort her, but he wasn't sure how. He had no words. So he wrapped his arms around her.

Her tears wet his shirt, and quiet sobs followed. She was struggling to steady her breaths. She had been through so much. She had lost too much.

Liam wanted to make it better. He couldn't even comprehend what she had witnessed. Even if she was tough, it was going to haunt her for a while.

It took a moment for Ciara to calm down. Even then, the tears cascaded down her face. Liam let her cry for as long as she needed to and then led her to her room.

They didn't say a word. They didn't have to, not even when Ciara changed. Liam turned around, giving her privacy. He didn't turn back around until Ciara touched his arm.

Their eyes met.

"Stay." Her voice was fragile, and her eyes were red from crying.

Liam took her hand in his, squeezing it lightly. "Okay."

They lay down on the bed under the duvet. Ciara avoided Liam's eyes, but she didn't turn her back on him. She still tried to fight the tears. Longing to comfort her, Liam snaked his arms around her and pulled her closer.

It was comfortable, even though it had been years since they had shared a bed.

Soothing.

"Your mother will freak out," Ciara hissed when Liam pulled her into his room.

Liam chuckled, making sure no one heard. "Oh, please. Not that long ago she talked to you and Henry about protection."

Ciara's cheeks heated, and she bit her lip. "She told us not to share a bed. I don't—"

"We're old enough to share a bed. I live abroad most of the time, and I'm allowed to share a bed with my girlfriend when I finally can," Liam said, determined, caressing his girlfriend's face.

"You're impossible."

Liam grinned at her. "I know, but you love it."

Ciara smiled.

Liam pulled her to his bed—his childhood home bed. He still used his old room when he visited England.

"This is nice," Ciara murmured, resting her head on Liam's

chest. His arms wrapped around her, and the heat of his body warmed her skin.

"Agreed," he said with a content smile.

"I missed you." And she had. But no amount of distance would be enough to drive them apart. They were made for one another. They challenged one another when there was need for it, and then supported each other when it was rough. Their future plans were clear as daylight, and they couldn't wait for Ciara to graduate. He was her home, and she was his.

"I missed you, too."

36

Ciara woke up to a rush of cold air. She blinked, adjusting to the sunlight filling the room. She turned to glance at the door just in time to see Liam walk out and close the door behind him.

She listened to his footsteps, heading to the bathroom. After a brief silence, he turned the shower on.

Then she got up. She changed into a pair of joggers and a tank top, deciding she would dress up for the party later.

It was past noon, meaning Ciara and Liam had slept in. It didn't surprise her after the previous night. She still wasn't over what had happened, and even thinking about it drained her energy.

Feeling hungry, Ciara tried to cook something. The only food she had previously had luck with was scrambled eggs, so that's what she tried again.

Just as she finished and moved the pan off the stove, Liam walked into view, stopping in the kitchen doorway. "You can cook?"

He only had a towel wrapped around his waist, revealing his muscled chest and abs. Ciara's eyes wandered down to where his towel was covering him before she realised she was checking him out. Blushing, she blinked and looked back up into his eyes.

"I even surprised myself," she admitted with a chuckle. "Do you want to try it?"

"Of course." Liam flashed a smile. "Just let me get dressed first."

"I'll get the plates ready."

"Thanks," Liam said and left for his room.

Ciara set the table with plates and cutlery. She grabbed two glasses and juice and set them on the table. She put down a pot stand and placed the pan on it.

"You sure you didn't poison it accidentally?" Liam teased.

Ciara turned to see him walk into the kitchen. He was wearing a white top with joggers, no longer shirtless.

"Hope not."

Ciara and Liam sat down at the table. Ciara tried her scrambled eggs first, surprised by the taste.

She turned to look at Liam, watching him take a bite.

His eyes settled on her, noticing the nervous face she was making. He swallowed the mouthful and smiled at her. "It's great."

Ciara bit her lip. "You sure?"

"Of course," he said and continued to eat.

Ciara smiled. She had never understood why people became so happy from others complimenting their food, but it slowly began to make sense.

"Are you sure you haven't just been trying to trick everyone into believing you can't be allowed in the kitchen?" Liam asked, grinning.

"Oh, trust me, this is like the third time I didn't have to put out a fire while cooking something."

Liam smiled. But there was a hint of pain in his eyes, probably left from the previous night.

Ciara didn't want to talk about it, so she asked, "What is your costume going to be?"

Liam smiled. "You'll see."

Ciara raised an eyebrow, intrigued to find out what Liam's costume might be. "Are you going all out?"

"Not really." He shook his head. "It's a fairly simple costume." He looked up, meeting her gaze. "What about yours?"

"You'll see," she said, copying Liam.

Liam chuckled. "Of course."

"How did I even agree to this party?" Ciara wondered out loud, leaning back in her chair and looking around.

The flat was decorated. There were warning signs with changing texts scattered around the walls. They had enchanted plastic spiders to move like real ones, and they were crawling on the ceiling. Fake spiderwebs adorned the corners. There were floating witch hats and floating candles scattered around, not yet lit. They had also enchanted fake skeletons, fake bones, and some pumpkins to float in the air. The decorations were magical in every sense of the word.

"It'll be fun." Liam smiled at Ciara. "Besides, you don't have to worry about much more than your costume. Not even the baking. Although, I'm beginning to think you could have handled that surprisingly well."

Ciara shook her head. "I'd burn the flat down if I tried to bake something."

Finishing a mouthful of scrambled eggs, Liam said, "Have a little faith."

"In my cooking skills, yes, a little. In my baking skills, nope."

Liam chuckled. "So when is Jenna coming over?"

"I don't know the exact time. I suppose she'll be rather early than late," Ciara said and ate a forkful of eggs.

"Well, at least someone is making sure Henry won't be late."

Ciara grinned. "Oh, he'll never be late with Jenna around."

The two finished their breakfast. Ciara was about to clean the table and wash up, but Liam insisted on cleaning up, because Ciara had made the breakfast.

Ciara was about to disagree when the doorbell rang.

"That's probably Jenna and Henry." Ciara headed to the door and opened it.

Her guess had been correct.

Jenna and Henry were carrying endless amounts of cakes, cupcakes, cookies, cake pops, and such. Thanks to magic, they could carry everything in tall piles without accidents.

"Hi." Jenna grinned. "Time to get ready."

"How did you get Henry up already?" Liam asked Jenna from the kitchen, placing dishes in the dishwasher.

"Hi, Liam." Jenna smiled and walked to the kitchen, floating most of the baked goodies behind her while dodging the floating decorations. "As you probably can tell, it wasn't an effortless task."

"I bet."

Henry rolled his eyes. "Isn't my girlfriend supposed to be on my side?" he whispered to Ciara, leaning closer.

Ciara chuckled and patted Henry on his shoulder. "Come on. Get those last cakes on the table, will you?"

"At your command," Henry said theatrically, walking to the kitchen.

Ciara closed the flat door and followed.

"Has anyone declined the invitation?" Jenna asked Ciara, while filling the table with the cakes and other baked goods. The ones that needed to be kept in cool temperature had cooling enchantments on them.

Ciara shook her head. "No, no one."

"Wonderful! It'll be a full house then!"

Ciara nodded. "Mia will have a friend or two tagging along."

"It's good we have plenty of cake then," Jenna said and smiled.

"Did you make most of this yourself?" Ciara asked,

gesturing to what Jenna had brought.

"Mum did a few things, but Jenna made most of the baked goods," Henry said.

"So, what do I owe you?" Ciara asked Jenna.

"Nothing," Jenna assured, smiling. "This was my idea, and I wanted to do the baking."

"You sure?"

Jenna nodded. "Yes. Just enjoy the party and it's fine."

"If you're sure—"

"I am."

"Alright."

Jenna finished with setting everything on the table. "But now, we need to go get ready." She wrapped an arm around Ciara. "So, boys, make sure you're ready on time, too."

Ciara's costume was a fortune-teller. She had a midi-length skirt with a white shirt and a dark corset, and she wore sandals. Jenna did her hair to match the costume's vibe. The entire costume had been Jenna's idea, and she had even bought Ciara the rings and bracelets and a tiara-like headpiece for it.

Jenna's costume was a rock star, inspired by the eighties. She wore a black top and black boots with electric blue leather trousers and a matching leather jacket. She had even replaced her eyeglasses with contacts.

"So will Henry's costume match yours?" Ciara asked as Jenna was finishing Ciara's makeup.

"Sort of. He has more black and more denim, but he's supposed to be an eighties rock star, too."

Ciara grinned. "Cute."

"But so are you and Liam."

Ciara raised an eyebrow. "Me and Liam?"

"Yes, matching with your joggers and everything. I'm surprised you're not together yet."

Ciara rolled her eyes at Jenna. "He's my ex."

"Who you share your flat with."

"He's looking for a new flat. Iris still hasn't agreed to sell their old one."

"Still, I can see you stealing glances at him." A smile appeared on Jenna's lips. She finished with Ciara's makeup and turned to finish her own eyeliner.

"It's one-sided."

Jenna frowned, pausing, and turned to face Ciara. "What makes you think that?"

Ciara sat down on her bed. "He just broke up with Iris. Not that long ago. And they were supposed to get married soon. Besides, he fell for Iris when he was still dating me. I doubt it will work the other way around."

"He and Iris were dating when you and him were dating?" Jenna asked, gaping. "What the...I seriously want to curse him right now!"

Ciara shushed Jenna. "It was years ago. Besides, I was the one to break up with him."

"That doesn't make it any better," Jenna hissed. "He was cheating on y—"

"On an emotional level. I don't think he ever acted on his feelings. Not until I told him we were done. He didn't even know I knew about all this until last summer."

"Clearly he chose the wrong girl."

"See? The point is that he already chose her over me. I don't stand a chance."

Jenna's eyes widened, anger written all over her face. "I didn't know he was such a—"

"Calm down." Ciara smiled at Jenna. "It was ages ago."

"But—"

A knock interrupted them.

"Come in," Ciara said.

Henry opened the door and peeked in. "It's almost seven."

"And we're done!" Jenna said, finishing her makeup.

The two women cleared the makeup bags from the bed and then joined the two brothers in the living room.

Henry matched with Jenna's costume. They looked great, standing together with their arms wrapped around one another.

Liam's costume was a pirate. He wore a pair of black trousers and a half-unbuttoned white shirt. The sleeves were rolled up to his elbows, revealing his forearms. He looked good as a pirate.

Ciara couldn't keep her eyes off him. She tried not to make it too obvious, only checking him out subtly.

"So who do you think will be the first to arrive?" Jenna asked.

"It could be anyone but Mia."

Jenna laughed. "True."

Ciara's eyes widened, realising she had forgotten the drinks. "Wait, the drinks aren't—"

"In the fridge, and the rest are in an ice bucket on the table." Liam smiled at Ciara. "So no worries."

Ciara sighed. "Thank you."

"No problem."

"You are such a worrier." Henry said, shaking his head. "Haven't you ever had a housewarming party?"

"Not on my own." Ciara's voice drifted off, and memories of Theo and their housewarming party plagued her mind.

Luckily, the doorbell rang.

37

Ciara opened the door for her colleague from Canada. "Josh!"

Josh smiled and wrapped his arms around her. "Hi. Looks like I found the right flat just fine." He paused. "Isn't that how you say it here in England? 'Flat'?"

"Yes, perfectly British." Ciara smiled and nodded. "Was your trip alright?"

"Oh, it was."

"Great."

"Anyhow, I brought you a little something." Josh handed Ciara a small present. "I hope you like it."

Ciara smiled. "Thank you."

Josh took off his coat and hung it on the coatrack. Underneath it, he had an American prisoner costume.

Ciara grinned. "Love the costume."

Josh laughed. "I couldn't help myself. I had to try one of these."

"Those are *actual* prisoner clothes?"

"Yes."

"Impressive."

Ciara led Josh to the living room to meet everyone and made the introductions.

Then the doorbell rang.

"Make yourself at home," Ciara said to Josh and hurried to open the door again, placing the present on a chest of drawers on her way.

This time it was Evie and her girlfriend.

Ciara smiled at them. "Welcome."

"It's so good to see you." Evie hugged Ciara and gave her a present.

"You, too."

Evie turned to her girlfriend. "Ciara, this is Lola."

Ciara smiled and shook Lola's hand. "I've heard a lot about you."

"All good, I hope," Lola said and smiled.

"Absolutely all good," Ciara assured.

Evie and Lola matched with their identical costumes. They were both wearing skeleton dresses with skeleton tights. They both had frizzy, curly hair, so the matching costumes were perfect. The only difference was in their hair colour and skin. Evie had auburn hair and pale complexion, and Lola had dark hair and skin.

Ciara barely made it to the living room with Evie and Lola when the doorbell rang again. She placed the present down and hurried to the door.

This time it was Shawn, dressed as a Jack Daniels bottle. He had the logo on the shirt, and his hat looked like a bottle top.

After Shawn, Jesse and his friend Max Salters arrived. Jesse was dressed as a cowboy, and Max as a military zombie.

Only a little after their arrival, the rest of Ciara's American colleagues—Brody, Alec, and Charlie—arrived.

Once the greetings were over, all three men took off their coats and hung them up, revealing their Halloween costumes. Brody was dressed as a lifeguard, wearing shorts and a lifeguard's top. Charlie wore a Superman shirt, which was peeking from under his blazer. Alec's costume was a devil, with horns and a fancy suit.

It was only quarter past six and everyone but Mia and her friend had arrived.

"Ciara has saved my life so many times you wouldn't believe if I told you about all of them!" Josh said, gesturing to Ciara with a glass of sparkling wine in his hands. "One time she stepped in front of a curse for me. There's no one as stupidly brave as she is."

Ciara shook her head. "Josh, you're exaggerating. Besides, you've repaid the favour."

Josh turned to the others. "She's just being modest."

Henry nodded, bringing his glass closer to his lips. "She always is."

Then the doorbell rang.

Ciara grinned. "Perfect timing."

"I didn't finish with the stories yet," Josh warned.

"Sure, sure," Ciara said and headed to the door. She opened it for Mia and her friend.

What surprised Ciara was Mia's friend, Trixie Archer. Ciara knew her from school. Trixie had been in Liam's year, and she had had an obsessive crush on Liam back in school. But so had Mia and plenty of other girls.

"Trixie?" Ciara said, regaining her composure.

"Hi, Ciara!" Trixie grinned widely and pulled Ciara into a hug. They had never been friends, so the cheeriness took Ciara aback.

"Hi." Ciara smiled. "I didn't know Mia was bringing you. Didn't even know you were friends." She turned to look at Mia.

"Oh, right!" Mia said and grinned. Clearly she hadn't realised Trixie had never been friends with Ciara. "Trixie is also a journalist," Mia explained. "We've worked together here and there."

Trixie turned to smile at Ciara. "I hope you don't mind that I tagged along."

"Of course not." Ciara shook her head and smiled. "It's nice to see familiar faces."

"It's great to see you, too. Mia has told me so much about your job. It's so cool!"

"Thanks."

Mia's costume was a sexy explorer, with short shorts and a crop top. Trixie was dressed as a Barbie doll, with a Barbie shirt and a pink miniskirt.

Once they had hung their coats and handed Ciara their present, Ciara led them to the living room to meet everyone.

"Hi, guys!" Trixie said, grinning.

Jenna's eyes widened. "Trixie...hi."

Ciara placed her last present on top of the chest of drawers. Jenna walked over to talk to her in privacy.

"Trixie?" Jenna asked, raising an eyebrow.

"I had no idea Mia would bring her," Ciara whispered. "But she seems alright."

Jenna shrugged. "I guess. Wasn't she, like, obsessed with Liam back at school?"

Ciara nodded. "Wasn't everyone, though?"

"I wasn't. But Mia sure was."

The baked goods and snacks were a success. Jenna and Mary were both excellent bakers.

"When will you start dating that roommate of yours?" Brody inquired, keeping his voice low, when he and Ciara walked in the kitchen to get drinks.

Ciara chuckled, walking to the fridge. "He's my ex."

"And future boyfriend?"

Ciara rolled her eyes and pulled the fridge door open. She grabbed a beer can and handed it to him. "Oh, Brody."

"So you're still not over Theo. Is that it?" Brody asked, his voice softening.

"No." Ciara shook her head. She grabbed a canned cocktail from the fridge and pushed the door shut. "I'm not completely over his death and I don't know if I ever will be." Ciara sighed, popping her can open. "But I'm moving on."

She had promised Doherty she would move on. But it didn't mean she was going to give up on her revenge. After losing Doherty, she was even more determined to wipe out the witch hunters.

Brody nodded. "Theo would want you to move on."

"That's what I keep telling myself."

Brody stepped closer and placed his hand on Ciara's shoulder. "It's the truth. He wouldn't want you to spend your life mourning him. He'd want you to live."

Ciara sighed and leaned against Brody. "You're right. It's just not that easy."

"Well, I think he'd give his blessing to that ex of yours."

Ciara chuckled and shook her head. "You're impossible, you know that?"

Brody smiled. "Nah, just a love expert."

Ciara crossed her arms but grinned at Brody. "Yet you have no girlfriend."

"Actually, I've gone on two dates with someone now. Expecting to go on a third one." A proud smirk crossed over Brody's face. "We'll see where it goes."

"Hope it goes well."

"Yeah, she seems great."

Ciara pointed a finger at Brody, poking his chest. "Then call her and take her out on that date."

"I will."

Ciara and Brody returned to the living room. Josh was once again telling stories about Ciara's heroic acts. Jenna, Henry, and Jesse were listening to him keenly. Max and Alec were chatting, and Shawn was sitting with Evie and Lola. Trixie had ended up hitting it off with Charlie. And Mia was busy flirting with Liam.

When Shawn spotted Ciara, he walked over. "So are you

going to let your friend steal your man?" he whispered in Ciara's ear.

"Not you, too."

"Your costumes almost match. You both have the same shade of red, some black and—"

"Not on purpose."

Shawn shot a grin at Ciara and winked. "So it's destiny."

"Ciara!" Josh called from his seat. "Remember the time you had to beat up that guy without magic?"

"The non-magic guy?" Using magic in front of non-magical people was illegal. In some countries it was even punishable by death. Even in the countries that didn't support death penalties, the consequences were severe.

"That murderer, yeah," Josh said, nodding.

"I remember. I'm not doing it again," Ciara said, cringing.

"But it was badass!" Josh exclaimed.

"I can't imagine Ciara beating up a guy." Henry's eyes widened, and he turned to grimace at his best friend.

"Yeah, he was big," Brody said. "Pure muscle."

"The guys are exaggerating. Again," Ciara said.

"Even so, you never tell these stories," Jesse said, grinning. If Ciara didn't know better, she would think Jesse had a crush on her. He never stopped with the questions and was always dying to know more about her and her life.

"It's just work," she said, shrugging. She sounded modest, but it was the truth. It was just work for her.

"Your work sounds exciting."

"Well, last time it was Josh who saved *my* life," Ciara said and started telling the others about it.

Liam tried to listen to Ciara, but Mia was talking to him non-stop. "How did you pick the costume? It looks great on you."

Liam shrugged, looking down at his clothes. "It was the easiest costume I could come up with."

"Well, it looks good."

"Thanks." Liam smiled awkwardly. He didn't know how

to get rid of Mia. For years, he had gone to parties with Iris. He wasn't used to being single.

"And how is everything at work? You're still a curse breaker, eh?" Mia leaned against the wall and twirled her hair between her fingers, trying to seem attractive.

"Yes. It's partially a desk job now that I'm in England." Sometimes Liam missed getting to spend all of his days actually breaking the curses. He had more paperwork in England, and sometimes it was tedious.

"You like it, though?"

Liam nodded. "I like it in England." Subconsciously, he stole a glance at Ciara who was chuckling at something Josh had said.

"More than in South America?"

"It's different, but yes."

"What is South America like? I bet it's beautiful."

Liam, once again, glimpsed at Ciara. "Uh, yes, it's beautiful there."

Mia was persistent. Liam had to excuse himself to the bathroom to get rid of her.

When he came back, he spotted Ciara walking to the balcony and followed her. He lingered in the doorway.

She leaned against the wall, choosing a spot no one could see from the inside. She snapped her fingers, and a cigarette appeared between her fingers. With another snap of her fingers, she lit it up.

"Don't do that." Liam walked up to her and snatched the cigarette. He dropped it onto the balcony floor and stomped on it.

Ciara looked up at him wide-eyed, like a teen caught doing something illegal. "Liam."

"Why are you stressed?"

"I'm not."

"You told me, at my birthday party, that you only smoke when you're stressed," Liam said, recalling that night.

Ciara sighed, leaning her head against the concrete wall.

"It's nothing."

It wasn't true, but Liam didn't push it. Not after the previous night. He didn't want to ruin the party for her.

"Quite the stories Josh is telling," he said, changing the topic.

Ciara smiled, turning to face Liam. "He's exaggerating most of it."

"I like his theory better. You're just being modest." The corners of his mouth turned up, and he gazed at Ciara.

Ciara's cheeks turned pink. "You're taking his side, huh?"

"I didn't know there were sides." Liam chuckled, his eyes fixed on Ciara's face.

Ciara looked down, still flushed. Her eyes settled on Liam's hand. "You've forgotten your drink."

"I think Mia might have poured love potion in it, so I'll grab a new one." Liam was joking, but the idea didn't sound absurd to either of them.

Ciara hummed. "She's had a huge crush on you since school years. I bet she's elated to know you're single now."

"Well, I guess I have to—"

"Here you are!" Jenna peeked through the balcony doorway. "I know you used to do these balcony meetings at school parties, but I didn't know they were still a thing," she teased. "Anyway, come inside. Everyone's wondering where you two disappeared to."

"Coming," Ciara said. She and Liam headed inside, and Liam grabbed a drink from the fridge on his way.

"Henry was just telling us about how you rode a dragon in the tournament!" Alec's eyes were wide with excitement, and he was grinning. "How have I never heard about that?"

Josh grinned "I have!"

"It was ages ago," Ciara said. "But it was fun."

"It didn't look fun," Evie said, grimacing. "I was horrified!"

Jenna raised her drink. "Ciara came first, though. Theo finished second."

"I completely forgot Theo was in that tournament, too."

Alec scratched his chin. "I bet it was a tough one between you two," he added, facing Ciara.

Ciara smiled. "Well, I won."

"You sure he didn't just let you win?" Brody teased.

"Highly doubt that! He was so competitive," Josh said and smiled at the memory of his deceased colleague.

Ciara smiled fondly at the memory of Theo. "Josh is right. He was hell-bent on winning."

Ciara made her way to a nearby balcony. It was cold outside, but she needed a moment of privacy. She had got through another tournament task earlier, and people had been celebrating since then. She hadn't had a moment to catch her breath.

"Are you trying to catch a cold?"

Ciara spun around to see Liam had followed her. He walked over and offered her a smile.

"I won't be here for long," Ciara said.

"Well, you have an exam on Monday, so..." Liam pulled off his jumper, leaving him in just a T-shirt. "Take this," he said, handing it to Ciara.

Ciara hesitated. "But you're gonna freeze."

"I'll be fine."

There was no point in arguing. If she didn't take the jumper, they would both freeze. She took it and pulled it on.

His scent was all over the jumper. Ciara would have recognised it anywhere. Fresh, sort of lemon-like, but with hints of something warmer—perhaps cinnamon.

She smiled. "Thanks."

Liam smiled back at her. "You were incredible today."

Ciara heard how impressed he was, and she couldn't help but blush. "Thanks...again."

"Henry was impressed by your beast-taming skills."

Ciara chuckled. "He hasn't shut up about it all night!"

"I bet," Liam said, amused.

"He's hoping I'll change my mind on my future career choice."

"Will you?"

She shook her head. "No. I want to be a curse breaker. Although I have to admit, riding a dragon was fun."

"Fun?" Liam said in disbelief.

Ciara chuckled at his reaction. "After it calmed down, yes."

"You're one of a kind, Ciara."

She shrugged.

"Try to keep dragon-riding stories to a minimum during the holidays, by the way. Mother will freak out if she hears," Liam warned.

"I'll keep that in mind."

"So are you still up for tutoring on Wednesday?" Liam asked.

Ciara nodded. "Of course."

"Great."

"You've told Professor Tennant what an incredible job you've done, right?" Ciara checked. Liam had spent so much time helping her, he deserved credit for it.

"I've told him what an incredible job you have done," Liam said.

"All thanks to you," Ciara pointed out.

"Should I give you another talk about giving yourself more credit?" Liam asked, cocking his head to the side.

"I'd say it's my turn to give you one of those."

"No need." Liam smiled gently.

"Don't forget to give yourself credit then."

Liam nodded. "I'll try not to."

A certain brown-haired best friend of Ciara's pushed the balcony door open. "Here you are! I've been looking all over for you! There are some guys who want to hear about today's task. Theo's friends, I think. Come!"

"But—"

Ciara didn't have time to say goodbye before Henry pulled her back inside.

38

The night went on, and people got more and more drunk. Brody had had quite a few drinks and had been talking with Jesse for some time. Jesse seemed to get along with all of Ciara's American colleagues, and she had hardly had the chance to talk with him. So, Ciara made the mistake of joining the conversation. After finding out Ciara and Jesse had dated in the past, Brody wouldn't stop bugging them about it.

"And when was the last time you slept together?" Brody asked, first looking at Ciara and then turning to Jesse. The smug grin on his face widened, seeing their faces.

Ciara's eyes grew wide. "Brody!" she scolded.

Jesse raised his hands up. "No comment."

"You slept together, didn't you?" Brody said, the stupid grin on his face widening.

"None of your business." Pointing to the kitchen, Ciara said, "Go get yourself another drink and stop talking."

"Wait," Brody said, holding his finger up and turning to

face Jesse. "Next time I come visit England, I have to see that gym of yours."

"It's a deal," Jesse said, grinning.

Brody grinned. "Now I'll get that drink." He stood up and headed to the kitchen.

Ciara turned to face Jesse, grimacing. "Sorry."

Jesse chuckled. "All good."

Liam was in the kitchen, talking with Shawn. They had both just grabbed cans of beer from the fridge.

"When will you tell her?" Shawn asked, lowering his voice.

Liam furrowed his eyebrows and popped his can open. "Tell who and what?"

"Tell Ciara about your feelings," Shawn whispered. Except he didn't know how to whisper when he was drunk.

To Liam's bad luck, Brody walked in. The smirk on his face told enough; he had heard Shawn. "You like Ciara?" he asked, his voice drunkenly loud.

Liam glared daggers at Shawn while Brody grabbed himself a canned cocktail from the fridge. Then Liam turned to Brody, trying to think of an excuse for Shawn's words. "It's, uh—"

"A secret." Brody nodded. "Don't worry, it's safe with me." He patted Liam on the shoulder and winked. "Unless you don't tell her soon."

Shawn grinned and turned to face Liam. "See? Even Brody agrees."

Liam shook his head. "She's not even over Theo. She—"

"Let me correct you there," Brody said, interrupting Liam with a more serious tone. "She still misses him, yes. She blames herself for not saving him, too. The way she lost Theo was horrendous, and that leaves eternal scars. But she's moving on. And honestly, you seem like a good guy."

Liam smiled a little, with appreciation and unease, and nodded. "Thanks."

"Just tell her," Brody said. He gave Liam a thumbs up

before he walked out.

"See?" Shawn said, grinning again.

Liam glared at Shawn. "I see you should keep your voice down," he hissed. "She's still upset about Theo's death. I'd feel as if I were taking advantage of her...state."

"Brody just said—"

"He wasn't here last night." Liam shuddered from the memory. Brody was right about Theo's death scarring Ciara. But there were no scars yet, just wounds. What Liam had witnessed the night before had proven that. Ciara wasn't ready.

Shawn furrowed his brows, turning serious. "What happened last night?"

"She came home upset. She talked about losing Theo and...other stuff. She, uh, asked me to sleep with her in her room and—"

"You two slept together?"

"We didn't have sex."

Shawn nodded, holding back a grin until he could no longer hide it.

"What?"

"You're so into her." Shawn shook his head and tried to hold in his chuckles. "I knew it."

"Knew it?"

"You liked her even before you and Iris called things off, didn't you?"

"I—"

"I'm not judging, just saying." Shawn raised his hands with his palms facing Liam, and a smile spread onto his face. "I ship it."

Liam rolled his eyes.

"Here you are!" Both guys turned to the kitchen doorway to see a grinning Mia walk in.

Liam wanted to either let out a long sigh or hide. But being polite, he didn't do either.

"Hey, Mia!" Shawn said, grinning, as if he had read Liam's

mind. "I have something I need to ask about your job as a journalist."

"Oh," Mia said, her eyebrows raised. "Ask away."

Liam saw his chance. He gave a quick, grateful smile to Shawn and walked—or ran—out of the kitchen.

Jesse and Max were the first guests to leave, around midnight. Evie and Lola left a little after them. They had all had only a few drinks, while most others had drunk double that or more.

"Wait, so you came here, like, super early," Shawn said, gaping at Josh.

"It was ten in the morning in Vancouver when I came here," Josh said, nodding.

"So, it's only half past four for you?"

Josh nodded.

"That's crazy." Shawn blinked, staring wide-eyed.

Liam's eyes sparked with amusement. "He's drunk."

"Seems like it," Brody agreed, unable to contain his laughter.

"I'm not that drunk!" Shawn argued. "I'll prove it. In a drinking game!"

"You sure?" Liam asked, eyeing Shawn. Shawn had already had plenty of drinks.

"Hell yes!" Shawn grinned. "Who's playing with me?"

Shawn, Liam, Brody, Jenna, Mia, and Josh gathered around the table to play.

Ciara, Henry, and Alec stood nearby, observing the game with mild worry. Meanwhile, Charlie and Trixie were still talking on the sofa. They had been chatting together for most of the night, having hit it off pretty well.

"Never have I ever is the game!" Shawn announced, earning both horrified and excited reactions from the others.

The questions started with everyday things, but little by little they became more personal.

The game went on for a while before Ciara started worrying about how it would end. It looked like it wouldn't end until someone vomited.

Ciara turned out to be right. The game ended when Jenna dashed to the bathroom, Henry rushing after her. At the same time, Shawn passed out at the table.

"That was fun," Mia said, slurring.

Trixie realised how drunk Mia was and told Mia it was time to head home. Mia almost fell off her chair. At least Charlie had the perfect excuse to tag along with Trixie—and Mia.

"I don't want to go." Mia tried to get out of Trixie's grip to wrap her arms around Liam who moved his chair further from Mia as a precaution.

It took a while for Trixie and Charlie to get Mia away from Liam so the three of them could leave.

Soon after Alec, Brody, and Josh left, too. Jenna and Henry were still in the bathroom.

Ciara walked back to the dining area. Liam was still sitting there, staring at the passed-out Shawn. When Ciara sat down, he turned his gaze to her.

"I don't think Shawn will wake up anytime soon," he said, gesturing to his friend.

Ciara tried to shake Shawn awake, but he didn't open his eyes. She checked he was breathing fine, and he was. Using magic, Ciara helped him onto the sofa. She grabbed a blanket and placed it on top of Shawn to keep him warm for the night.

Meanwhile, Liam had somehow stood up. He was leaning against a wall near the sofa, swaying.

"You can still stand?" Ciara teased once she had tucked Shawn in. "You drank quite a bit."

Liam smiled at her and shrugged. "I can do a lot of things."

Ciara chuckled. "Like what?"

"Like—"

"Actually, don't answer that," Ciara said. "Let me get you to bed before the alcohol kicks in."

"You want to get in bed with me?" Liam asked, his words coming out as a slur. His eyes were glassy, and his breath reeked of alcohol.

Still, Ciara blushed at his comment. "Confirmed, you're drunk."

Liam's face turned into a pout. "I drank too much, didn't I?"

Ciara walked closer to him. "A bit."

"I'm sorry." He was like a child apologising for eating the last biscuit.

Ciara smiled at him, amused by his drunken state. "Don't be. Just let me—"

"I love how caring you are," Liam confessed, staring at Ciara.

She looked up at him, wide-eyed. "You need some sleep. Now."

"Can I sleep in your room again?"

"Shawn would never stop teasing us if he woke up and found us in bed together," Ciara reasoned.

"He thinks we should be together."

Ciara's eyes widened. "What?" *If Shawn said something to Liam...*

"He—"

The bathroom door opened, cutting Liam off mid-sentence. Henry walked out, supporting Jenna, so she stayed somewhat standing. "I think Jenna and I will head home now."

Ciara nodded, eyeing Jenna who was struggling to keep her eyes open. "That might be a good idea."

"You alright with that one?" Henry asked, gesturing to Liam.

"I can handle Liam. And Shawn is already sleeping on the sofa. So, I've got this."

Henry nodded. "Good. We'll be back tomorrow to help with the mess."

"I can handle it, too. Don't worry."

"No need," Henry said.

"Thanks for coming."

Henry smiled and nodded. "Of course." He grabbed his and Jenna's coats before teleporting them to their shared flat.

Ciara turned to face Liam who stared at her. "Can you walk without tripping over?"

"Yes."

"Then, go to bed. I'll get you a glass of water. Okay?" Ciara said.

Liam nodded. He moved away from the wall and walked towards his room, swaying.

Ciara looked after him for a moment before she walked into the kitchen. She grabbed a glass and filled it with water. Taking the glass with her, she went to see if Liam had made it to his room. She couldn't see him in the hallway, but she couldn't find him in his room either.

She walked to her room to check if he was there.

And he was. He was lying on the bed in his underwear.

Ciara sighed and walked over to her bed. "Can you sit up?"

He sat up without answering the question. Ciara handed him the glass, and he gulped it down in one go. She took the glass from him and placed it on the bedside table.

"Did you notice you're in the wrong room?"

"Yes."

Ciara sighed. "And are you sure you want to wake up in the wrong room in the morning?"

"I want to wake up next to you," Liam slurred.

She chuckled at his drunken flirting. "Calm down, tiger. You're drunk."

Liam shrugged and lay back down.

"You'll get cold if you sleep on top of the duvet," Ciara pointed out.

Liam's mouth twisted into a confident smirk. "I saw you checking me out this morning when I walked out of the shower."

Ciara gaped at Liam's words. Sober Liam would never have said that. But his words still made her face heat up. Hoping he didn't notice her glowing red cheeks, she said, "Remember you just broke up with your fiancée? You were supposed to marry her in less than two months from now."

"Until she cheated on me."

"Well, I'm not planning to be your rebound relationship."

Liam's expression twisted into a frown. "Ciara, you—"

The doorbell rang, startling both of them.

After regaining her composure, Ciara sighed and stood up. "Someone must have forgotten something."

She left the room and jogged to open the door.

"Ciara!"

It wasn't what—or who—she had expected. The blonde woman threw herself at Ciara, wrapping her arms around Ciara's neck. She stank like a drunk, and mascara had run down her face. She was sobbing and swaying in her high heels.

"Iris," Ciara gasped.

"Can you ask Henry where Liam is staying, please?" Iris sobbed, clinging onto Ciara's shirt.

"I'm sure Liam is fine," Ciara said, unsure if she should have told the truth. "You should head home and—"

"I don't want to go there without him!" Iris sobbed. "I miss him so much!"

Ciara cringed as Iris's sobs echoed through the stairway. She shut the door behind Iris, with the woman still hanging onto her.

"Iris—"

"Can you please call H-Henry?" Iris gasped. Her grip on

Ciara's shirt released, and she fell to her knees, continuing to sob.

Ciara sighed. "Iris, calm down."

"No! Just call Henry!" Iris screamed. Ciara was glad she had placed a soundproofing enchantment on the flat for the party.

"How do you even know where I live?" Ciara asked, feeling a little helpless.

"I went through your medical records and found—"

"What's going on here?"

Both Ciara and Iris turned to look at Liam. He was still drunk, swaying a little. And he was wearing just his underwear.

Iris stared at her ex-fiancé wide-eyed and gaping. She scrambled up clumsily. Her gaze moved to Ciara and then back to Liam. She kept looking at them in turns.

The flat filled with tense silence. No one moved, and everyone was holding their breath.

The silence broke when the sound of hand hitting skin echoed through the flat. Iris's nails left a stinging pain on Ciara's cheek.

Ciara's hand flew up to her face.

Liam, still drunk, rushed to stand between the two women.

"So I was right!" Iris screamed at Liam, still sobbing hysterically. "You have been sleeping with her. You left me for her!"

Liam shook his head and clenched his jaw. "You're crazy," he spat at Iris.

"You didn't even want to marry me at first! You've been in love with her this whole time!" Iris yelled.

"Ciara has nothing to do with any of it!" Liam said, raising his voice.

"She ruined everything!"

"*You* ruined everything!"

"Your whole freaking family adores her! Your little sisters

are obsessed with her, and your little brothers can't shut up about her! And your mother doesn't find anyone but her good enough for you!" Iris screamed at Liam, pointing an accusing finger at Ciara.

His eyes hardened, and his voice turned cold. "What is your problem?"

"She is!" Iris's hands were shaking, and her eyes had turned red and puffy. "She stole you from me. She stole my life!"

Liam shook his head. "You're delusional."

"Why won't you believe me?" The anger in Iris's voice turned into despair.

"What the hell is this?" This time it was Shawn. Iris's screaming had been enough to wake him up. He was still drunk and could barely stand.

Ciara walked away from the couple, eager to get away. She went over to help Shawn stay upright. "Let's give them some privacy," she whispered to him, trying to pull him towards Liam's room.

Shawn didn't budge. Instead, he stared at the arguing ex-couple and pointed a finger at Iris. "Why is she here?"

"That's a brilliant question," Liam said, turning back to glare at his ex-fiancée.

"Liam, come home," Iris begged. She was still drunk, and her mood swings were getting worse.

"Shawn, let's go," Ciara hissed. She wanted no part in the argument.

Shawn nodded and let Ciara lead him to Liam's room. He stumbled onto the bed, and Ciara tried to ease the fall.

Iris and Liam continued to argue. Both Ciara and Shawn could hear the argument all the way from the flat door. At first, Iris was sobbing and begging for Liam to go with her. Soon, though, she started screaming at him again.

Shawn lay on the bed, unable to sleep. Ciara was sitting on the floor, hugging her knees.

"You sure he can handle himself?" Shawn slurred.

"I can't intervene."

Shawn's eyebrows rose. "Why not?"

"She thinks Liam and I are dating or whatever."

"Oh."

Ciara stayed in Liam's room. Shawn fell asleep within minutes, but Ciara still stayed there. She didn't want to interrupt the argument. She wanted no part in it.

Although, she already was a part of it. She thought back to the time she had talked with Liam outside his parents' house. She hadn't thought of him as her friend, but as something more. It had been wrong, and it hadn't been the only time. Even if she hadn't acted on her feelings, she was guilty of having them.

39

The argument was never-ending. Ciara didn't have a watch or her phone, so she couldn't check the time, but she thought she had spent at least an hour sitting on the floor.

Eventually she heard someone slam the door shut. She assumed Iris had left.

She didn't move, expecting Liam to come to his room. When he didn't turn up in five or so minutes, she went to see what had happened.

Ciara checked her room first, but Liam wasn't there. Then she checked the kitchen and the dining area.

He was sitting at the dinner table with a filled glass. Whatever was in the glass was clear, but Ciara wasn't sure if it was water or vodka.

"Are you okay?" Ciara asked softly.

Liam spun around in his seat, startled by her appearance. "I..." His eyes were glazed and puffy.

"You're not."

"It's nothing." Liam turned to look at his glass and raised it, but not to his lips. He just held the glass up, eyeing it.

"What just happened isn't nothing. She's your ex-fiancée, and she hurt you." Ciara cursed herself for her choice of words. "Unless you want to go back to her. Then I suppose she's your fiancée."

"Iris and I will never get back together." He sighed and turned to look at Ciara. "I mean, you saw her! How she was and…" He sighed again.

Ciara was unsure what to say. She didn't want to say anything insulting about Iris.

"A-and she slapped you!" Liam said, clearly upset.

"I'm fine."

There was a brief pause.

"I just want to get rid of her."

Ciara sat down. "Even if so, break-ups are never easy."

Liam said nothing, but he looked at his glass again.

"You loved her. You were planning to marry her. You won't get over everything in a month."

"I've never had a break-up like this," Liam mumbled. "My only other serious relationship was with…" He didn't need to say it. She knew.

"With me." Ciara nodded. "But you were already falling for Iris when we broke up. I suppose it made everything easier."

"How long did it take for you to get over it?" Liam asked.

Ciara shifted in her seat uneasily. "Months."

Liam's eyes grew wide. "Months?"

She chuckled, but there was no humour in it. "I was in love with you."

It took a while for Liam to form his next words. "H-how did you get over the break-up then?"

Ciara shrugged. "I suppose Theo helped me." She bit her lip. It hurt to say his name so casually. "Moving away helped too."

Liam's lips pursed together, his eyes solely on Ciara.

Ciara refused to look at him. Instead she stared at her hands, fiddling with her fingers. "I mean, I..." She cleared her throat and grimaced. "I moved away, because I heard you had a new girlfriend. I eliminated everything that could remind of you. Your house, your family, even Henry, and, well, my old life. I don't recommend that, though. It's probably the dumbest way to deal with a break-up. I should have just processed my feelings, but instead I ran away, because I didn't want to deal with them."

The room fell silent. Liam was mulling over Ciara's words, and she was struggling to keep her hands from shaking. Talking about their break-up so openly made her uneasy.

"How did Theo help you?"

"He helped me process my feelings and thoughts. We made photographs of most of the memories I had of you and me. You know, with magic. Then we burned them one by one. Well, I burned them, but he was there, too." Ciara paused to swallow a lump in her throat. She didn't want to cry, but thinking about Theo wasn't making it easy for her. "He was there for me. At first, as a friend. He wanted to be more since the beginning, I think. It took him all the way from July to March to convince me I should move on."

"It took you almost a year to move on to a new relationship?" Liam asked in disbelief. In his drunken state, he had no filter.

Ciara nodded. "Yes. So, the point is that you can't rush your break-up with Iris."

"I wish our relationship had ended differently."

"It was wrong of Iris to cheat—"

"I meant *us*," Liam said and reached to take Ciara's hand into his.

She finally looked up at him. "It's in the past. Besides, you were happy with her. U-until I came back, I suppose."

Liam shook his head. "Me breaking up with Iris had nothing to do with you. No matter what she thinks. Our problems started way before your return."

Ciara nodded, even though she wasn't convinced.

Liam finished whatever he was drinking with one gulp. Ciara observed him, and he noticed it, his lips curling into a smile. "It was water."

"Good."

"So Shawn is asleep in my room?"

Ciara nodded. "You can have my bed."

"We shared a bed last night."

Yes, and you left very quietly in the morning. Ciara wanted to say that out loud, but she didn't. She also wondered if she should have reminded Liam about the argument he and Iris had had, but she didn't do that either.

They ended up sharing the bed. This time, though, Ciara turned her back to Liam and stayed as far from him as physically possible without falling off the bed.

Liam was still drunk, even though drinking water had helped him clear his head a little. He fell asleep immediately.

Ciara waited for a while, hoping she could fall asleep, too. However, she couldn't.

Sharing a bed with Liam bothered her. She couldn't help but think about Iris and the argument from earlier. After that, there was no way she could sleep in the same bed with Liam.

When Ciara was sure Liam wouldn't wake up, she sneaked out of the room. It was stupid, but she went to the balcony and lit a cigarette.

She was stressed again.

The memories of what had happened with the witch hunters resurfaced. She couldn't erase the picture of that lifeless child from her mind.

She had been spying on the witch hunters. She had seen everything. They had killed the child in front of the parents. Ciara had tried to stop them from killing the parents, too, but she had been too late.

Perhaps it was mercy that the parents didn't have to live to tell the tale after such a trauma. Sometimes even Ciara wondered if dying would have been easier.

She had seen many people die. It came with her job. At some point, she had nearly become numb to losing colleagues, and she was even more used to seeing the bad guys suffer. Death had become mundane.

But she had seen a child die only a few times before. And it was never any easier.

Blowing out the smoke, Ciara's thoughts drifted to another dark corner of her mind. Liam—and Iris.

Ciara couldn't have caused it all, but her presence hadn't made it any easier. Iris had been jealous of her, and she knew that.

She should have buried his feelings for Liam and stayed far away instead of helping plan his wedding. It had been wrong of her, and she should have stayed out of it to begin with.

She had made another stupid mistake when she had let him move in with her. She had let him become a big part of her life.

A lot should have been done differently.

Once she had finished smoking the cigarette, she cleaned the entire flat. She wouldn't get any sleep, anyway, so she rather spent the time productively.

When the flat was cleaned, Ciara opened her presents. They consisted mostly of candles, vases, blankets, soaps, wine coolers, and wine.

One present also had a few pieces of paper attached to it. It was from Josh. He was the one helping Ciara with the witch hunters. The papers he had given her were filled with recent information. There were two lists: a list of locations and a list of recent murders and crimes.

Ciara read through the lists and then hid them in her kitchen cupboard. It was her only empty cupboard, and thus the best place for hiding the papers, because Liam wouldn't accidentally look in there.

At sunrise, Ciara sneaked into her room and grabbed a set of clothes. Then she took a shower and got dressed.

Once she was dressed, she needed another cigarette.

She was standing in the frosty morning breeze at the balcony, inhaling through the filter.

"I didn't know you smoked."

Ciara turned to look at Shawn. He looked pale, and his expression was enough to tell her he had a headache.

"I usually don't," Ciara said, bringing the cigarette back to her lips.

Shawn moved to stand beside her. "So why now?"

She shrugged. "How's your hangover?"

"Very much deserved, thank you for asking."

Ciara laughed. "Guess so."

"I saw Liam in your room. So where did you sleep?"

"In my room," Ciara lied. It wasn't a complete lie. She had tried to sleep there.

"So you two are finally dating?" Shawn asked, getting his hopes up.

Ciara laughed and shook her head. "No, absolutely not."

Shawn frowned, scratching his head. "Was I dreaming or was Iris here last night?"

"She was here. For real." Ciara sighed and brought the cigarette to her lips again.

"How did Liam react?"

"He cried after she left. They were screaming at each other for an hour at least. I'm surprised you could sleep."

Shawn furrowed his brows. "What was it about?"

"Based on what I heard, Iris thinks I'm the reason they broke up." Ciara raised the cigarette to her lips and inhaled deeply.

Shawn observed Ciara. "And you think she's right?"

"I don't know. I just think I should have stayed far away from them both." Ciara sighed. "What kind of an ex-girlfriend helps plan the wedding?"

"The kind that wants to be friends with their ex."

"Well, what if my wants just ruined their future together?" Ciara turned to look at Shawn.

"I doubt it."

Ciara shrugged. "Anyway, I'm the worst cook in the world, but I suspect you'd like something to eat. How does a sandwich sound?"

Shawn smiled. "That sounds good."

"And coffee?"

"Perfect."

Closer to ten, the doorbell rang. It was Henry. He was alone, because Jenna was still suffering from her hangover at home.

Henry looked around. "You cleaned up already?"

Ciara nodded. "If you had called, I would have told you to stay home with Jenna."

"She's been up all night, I think," Shawn said.

"Looks like you're back with the living," Henry joked, turning to look at Shawn.

"It was a rough night, but I feel much better already thanks to Ciara's amazing sandwiches," Shawn said and grinned.

"They were the most basic sandwiches ever," Ciara said.

"And still amazing."

Ciara shrugged. "If you say so."

"Oh, hey!" Shawn said, realising something. "When did you and Jenna leave last night?" he asked Henry.

"Late. Like really late."

"They just missed Iris," Ciara said.

Henry's eyes grew big, and he turned to look at his best friend with his mouth hanging open. "Iris was here?"

Ciara nodded. "She wanted me to call you to ask where

Liam was staying. Then Liam walked out of my room in just his underwear. Let's just say it was an eventful night."

Henry grimaced. "Ouch."

"Ouch, indeed."

"Why was he in your room in his underwear?" Henry asked, tilting his head to the side.

"My room is closer than his, and he could barely walk." Ciara shrugged. She knew it wasn't the truth, but it was close enough. She didn't want to go through the previous night's events again.

"He's still in your room?" Henry asked, pointing at Ciara's room's door.

Ciara nodded. "Probably."

A smirk crossed his face. "I have to do one thing."

Ciara and Shawn looked at Henry questioningly as he walked towards Ciara's room. After sharing a look, Ciara and Shawn followed him.

"This is for all the pranks!"

The two of them made it to the room's door just in time to see Henry use his wand to splash cold water at Liam. Poor Liam woke up screaming, instantly sitting up.

"Bloody hell," Liam cursed. "I nearly had a heart attack, Henry!"

Henry and Shawn were both snorting with laughter.

"You'd better dry the bed, Henry." Ciara pointed a finger at Henry and walked to her wardrobe to grab a scarf.

As Ciara was wrapping the scarf around her neck, Liam turned to look at her. "Are you going somewhere?"

She turned to face him, and her heartbeats grew faster and louder. But she didn't let anyone see the effect he had on her and nodded, keeping up a blank, neutral face—like a mask. "I have some errands to run."

"Oh."

"You, Henry, dry my bed before you leave," Ciara said, pointing at the dripping wet bed. "Shawn, feel right at home," she said, smiling at him. "I really have to go now or I'm going to be late." She walked out, striding towards the door.

"Late for what?" Liam asked, even though Ciara was already out of the flat.

Henry frowned. "It's barely even ten in the morning."

"Maybe she's avoiding Liam because she doesn't want to be slapped again," Shawn said and shrugged.

Henry's eyes widened with rage. "You slapped her?" he yelled at his brother.

"What? No! Are you out of your mind?" Liam exclaimed.

"Iris slapped her," Shawn corrected.

Henry's eyes widened again—this time from shock. "Really?"

Liam nodded, his jaw tightening. "Really."

Henry left after he had dried the bed. It didn't take long, thanks to magic. Shawn stayed a little longer. But eventually he had to go.

Liam was left alone. He didn't know when Ciara would be back home or what errands she had.

He had nothing to do, so he tried to kill time by reading a book. He had barely read the first chapter when the doorbell rang.

Sighing, he set the book down on the sofa. He walked to the door, wondering who it could be. He wasn't expecting company, but he twisted the doorknob and nudged the door open.

"Iris."

40

Ciara had a good memory thanks to having trained it a lot for work. She had read the papers Josh had given her twice to make sure she remembered each name and address.

She wasn't exactly running errands. She was on a mission, looking into the murders Josh had discovered. Her plan was to figure out if they had been committed by the witch hunters.

She found an eyewitness of the first murder on the list. She went to her house to ask her about what she had seen.

"You said you saw two figures leave the house. Correct?"

The elderly woman nodded.

"What did they look like?"

"They wore long coats. W-well, not exactly coats." The old woman hummed, thinking. The frown on her face made her appear much older, deepening her wrinkles. "Like cloaks, I think. I couldn't see their faces because of the hoods."

"Can you remember anything else? Even something

that might seem like a minor detail?" Ciara asked, writing down everything the woman said. She had a notebook that she was pretending to write in, but in reality she was using an enchanted pen that did the work for her. One she had enchanted just before the interview. Obviously the pen was out of the woman's view, behind the notebook.

"I thought I saw a flash in the living room," the old woman explained. "But I'm not sure. W-who would take a picture in the middle of a murder?"

Ciara furrowed her eyebrows. She had read the police reports that Josh had included with the list. She couldn't remember anything about a flash. "Did you mention this to the police when they asked you about what you saw?"

The old woman shook her head. "No. I-I think I just made it up in my head. M-maybe someone turned on the lights and then turned them off again. They didn't take any pictures, did they?"

Ciara smiled politely. "We have no evidence of any pictures. No camera, nothing. It was probably just the lights."

The old woman nodded, reassured. "That's what I thought."

But that wasn't what Ciara thought. If there had been a flash, it had likely been magic.

The second murder didn't have any eyewitnesses, but the third one did: a young girl. The girl's parents hesitated to let Ciara ask questions, but eventually they gave in. Ciara made sure to only ask bare necessities if even that, even though the girl hadn't been told that she had witnessed a murder. The girl thought the body had been a passed-out person.

Ciara asked the girl about a flash, and she could confirm that there had been one. Even if the witch hunters weren't behind the murders, the murders had to be connected.

Ciara interrogated six more eyewitnesses. There were even more murders, but some of them didn't have any witnesses.

They all had different stories, but everyone mentioned

seeing a flash. Even if the murderers weren't the witch hunters, they had to be people with magic—witches or wizards.

Ciara walked out of a block of flats, going through her notes.

"Excellent work."

She spun around to see a man leaning against the wall. She looked him over—a habit that came with the job.

He was a Caucasian man in his thirties. Dark brown hair and stubble. His eyes were an odd shade of blue. Based on his muscles, he was athletic. He was also tall—probably close to six and half feet.

Ciara didn't know him. For all she knew, he could have been a witch hunter. "Excuse me?" she said, reaching her hand into her wand pocket. Not that she needed the wand. But if the situation escalated into a fight, the wand could be useful.

"I've been following you."

She curled her fingers around the wand.

"Just today, so don't worry." He walked closer to Ciara, hands in his pockets. He didn't appear threatening. In fact, his posture was oddly relaxed.

"So you're stalking me?" Ciara asked, tilting her head to the side. "Aren't you supposed to keep that a secret if you wish to continue?"

The man smiled so wide his teeth showed. Ciara didn't miss the fact his teeth were so white they had to be bleached. She also spotted an expensive watch on his wrist, noting he had to be rich.

"Doherty always said good things about you. I can see why."

She released her grip on her wand when she heard her old mentor's name. "Doherty?" Her voice came out as a gasp.

Did he know Doherty or is he playing with me?

The man nodded.

"So, you've been following me all day. Now you choose to approach me. Can you get to the point?" Ciara asked impatiently.

"The head of the department, Gordon Frazier, was fired on Friday," the man said.

"I haven't been informed."

"I know. That's what I'm here for." The man stepped closer, so he was only an arm's length away from Ciara. "I'm Kellan Wolff." He reached his hand out.

Ciara eyed his hand but refused to shake it. She didn't trust the man. "I've never heard of you."

"I got Doherty's place after he died," Kellan said, pulling his hand back to his side. "I would have been your colleague if you hadn't been suspended when you were transferred."

Ciara nodded. "I'm not allowed back until next year."

Kellan smiled. "Yes, that's partially what I'm here for. But first things first...you want proof of Frazier's firing, I bet." He pulled a paper out of his pocket and unfolded it. It wasn't a non-magic, mundane paper but an enchanted one, so it was still creaseless.

Kellan handed the paper to Ciara. She took it and read it through. She made sure the magical seal was attached, and the signatures were correct. It was an official paper. At the bottom of the paper was the name of the next head of the department. *Kellan Wolff.*

"You're the new head of the department?" Ciara asked and handed the paper back to the man.

"I can give you more proof if you'd like," Kellan offered, folding the paper.

"That paper had the seal on it. All that's written on it is true. I believe you."

Kellan smiled and nodded. Then he shoved the folded paper back in his pocket. "I'm here to accept you to work early and to give you a promotion."

Ciara looked at the man as if he had gone mad. "Excuse me?"

"You heard right."

"A promotion? Based on what? I'm too young to be promoted."

"Your birthday is in two days."

Ciara shook her head. "Twenty-two is too young for promotion."

"Perhaps in America, and perhaps when Frazier was the head of the department," Kellan admitted. "But I make the new rules. I knew Doherty, and I knew about the secret group you had. I know enough to promote you."

"You want to promote me?"

"Yes."

"And would that mean I would be someone's boss?" She had never been the one to give out orders.

"Well, yes," Kellan said. "The current situation is a bit complicated. I am the actual head of the department, but Frazier remains as the head in the public image."

"To protect you?"

"Yes, and to keep him quiet."

Ciara nodded. "And I'd be someone's boss?"

"Your position is right below mine. You'll have your own team of well-trained hit wizards and witches, like Doherty had. But I will do most of your work as their boss at first, so you won't have to worry about any of that," Kellan told.

"What am I supposed to do then?"

"What you've been doing all day," Kellan said, gesturing to the notebook in Ciara's hands. "When you need help, you'll get it from your team."

"And when should I start?"

"Tomorrow, but I'll give you an extra payment for today and Friday, too," Kellan said. "Does that sound reasonable?"

Ciara nodded. "Yes."

"I'd like to meet you in my office tomorrow at nine."

"I assume it's Frazier's old office?"

"It is."

"Am I supposed to call you sir?"

Kellan chuckled and shook his head. "Please, don't. Kellan is just fine."

"Alright."

"Tomorrow at nine?"

"Tomorrow at nine."

"See you then."

"Wait. How did I not notice you?" Ciara asked before Kellan could leave, giving him a look of suspicion.

Kellan grinned. "A hiding spell." Then he vanished.

Ciara was done for the day.

And she would finally get to work again. The thought excited her, because staying at home didn't suit her. She missed the action. She also wanted to fight the witch hunters, and at work she could do it legally.

Even though she had only just met Kellan, she already had a feeling he took the matter more seriously than Frazier had. Kellan had also known Doherty, so Ciara could trust him.

Finally, things were working out.

41

"Iris."

"Hi. Um, c-could I come in?" She bit her lip, glancing behind Liam as if expecting to see someone.

Liam hesitated, briefly considering slamming the door shut, but then he nodded and let her step in.

Iris looked around. "Is Ciara home?"

"No."

She nodded and turned her full attention on Liam. "C-could we talk? I promise I'll behave."

Liam sighed but nodded. "You can hang your coat there."

Iris shrugged off her coat and hung it on the coatrack. Then Liam led her to the living room and gestured for her to sit down. They sat together on the sofa.

"I'm sorry I slapped her last night," Iris said, appearing to be genuinely contrite. "Although, I suppose I should say that to her."

"You should," Liam agreed. He grabbed the book he had been reading from the sofa and set it on the coffee table.

"I bought you that book, didn't I?" Iris looked at it with a small smile on her face.

"You did," Liam said and nodded.

Iris turned to face Liam. "I'm sorry about last night altogether. I was wasted, and I was acting awfully. It's no excuse, but I didn't mean to act the way I did."

Liam nodded. "I suppose I can forgive that."

Iris smiled, relieved.

"I was no more polite. In fact, I was awful to you, too. I'm sorry."

"I deserved it," Iris insisted.

Liam didn't know what to say to that. He couldn't forget Iris had slapped Ciara.

Iris hesitated but eventually found her voice. "Are you happy with her?"

"I'm not *with* her," Liam said truthfully. "I'm staying here until I can find a flat for myself. Henry and Jenna don't have enough room, and I don't fancy the idea of moving back in with my parents. So for now, I'm here."

"Oh." Iris was genuinely surprised, Liam could tell.

They sat on the sofa in silence. It wasn't purely awkward or uncomfortable, but it was different.

"I'm sorry I ruined our engagement and our relationship," Iris said, breaking the silence. "I should never have hurt you in such a way. I know it's too late now, and I know this doesn't make it any better. But I'm sorry."

"I can't say I forgive you. I don't think I *can* forgive just like that."

"And you shouldn't. What I did was horrible," Iris said, lowering her head in shame.

"You knew it would hurt me," Liam said. "I mean, you must have known. So why did you do it?"

"I-I don't have a complete answer to give you. I...I just know that I wanted you to feel jealous like I did."

"Jealous?"

"Ciara." Iris shook her head. "The way I said it last night

was wrong, but your family adores her. I can see why they do, and I shouldn't have expressed it the way I did. But your mother adores her. She's like a daughter to her. I know your mother liked me, but I was still jealous of the way she spoke about Ciara."

"You weren't around when she spoke about you. Just like Ciara isn't around when she speaks about her."

"I know. I just never really knew how to take it. I mean, your family talking about her so much. I get she was Henry's best friend first and foremost. I shouldn't have been jealous, I guess."

"I didn't even think about her until she came back last summer," Liam said.

"You did once," Iris said, a hint of accusation in her voice. "I know Henry was the one to suggest we should invite her to our engagement party. But I also know you hired an agent after she didn't respond to the invitation."

"I merely wanted to know if she was alive. For Henry's sake."

"But you never told me that."

Liam nodded. "I should have."

"Even then, I could have got the wrong idea."

"I forgot about her until I found out she was still alive and living in America," Liam said truthfully.

"Until she came back."

"She's just a friend."

"Maybe at first, but even now...just the way you speak about her." Iris frowned. "Please, be honest. Do you love her?"

Liam rubbed his hands together nervously. "I...I suppose I do."

"For how long?"

Iris deserved the truth—the whole truth. "I had barely broken up with her when we began to date, remember?"

Iris nodded. "You claimed to have liked me even before the two of you broke up."

"And I did."

"Does she know that?"

Liam hung his head. "I didn't know until last summer, but that's why she broke up with me. So we could be together."

Iris blinked. "For real?"

"Yes."

"I had no idea."

"I didn't love her back then," Liam said. "I...I had to open a vault in Peru. It was a while before Ciara broke up with me. There was this enchantment. I had already promised my boss I would get it open, so I had no choice. Or so I kept telling myself."

"What kind of enchantment?"

"I had to give up one of my memories. It could have been any memory, but I refused to choose one. I was stupid, and I let it be any memory. And as it turns out, it was the memory of the moment I first realised I loved Ciara."

"You stopped loving her, because you didn't remember," Iris concluded.

Liam nodded.

"How long have you known?"

"Since August."

Iris nodded.

"I wasn't going to act on my feelings. I could never have hurt you like that." Liam's voice became shaky. "I loved you."

"But I ruined it."

Liam knew Iris was right, but he didn't need to say it out loud.

"How did you find out then?" Iris asked.

"Find out what?"

"About the whole memory thing."

"I had a dream of the memory. Then, when I woke up, I just remembered."

Iris nodded. "Honestly, would you have married me while you loved her, too?"

"I loved you, Iris. So yes, I was going to marry you. I

was never going to act on my feelings for Ciara," Liam said, honestly. "It was wrong of me to feel the way I did, but I wouldn't have done anything about my feelings. I would have never..."

Iris nodded. "I suppose you can't control how you feel. And I can tell you feel bad about it."

"I feel bad and I did before, too."

"So when will you tell her?"

Liam shifted his gaze to her, eyes widened. "What?"

Iris sighed. "I still care about you. I still love you. But I know I can't fix what I did. I know you won't come home with me. I know you're done with me. So when will you tell Ciara about your feelings?"

Liam shook his head. "I don't know if I will."

"You should."

Liam turned to look straight into Iris's eyes. "I'm not over you, either, Iris. It'll take time."

"D-do you think we could be friends? A-are we good like that?"

"Yes, we're good."

"So when do you want to sell the flat?"

42

Ciara opened the flat door to be greeted by distant laughter. She recognised Liam's laughter, and she had a pretty good idea who the woman was.

She shrugged off her coat and hung it. She walked to the dining area, and her doubts turned out to be correct. Liam was sitting at the dining table with Iris—not arguing, for sure. It looked like they had ordered Chinese food together.

Liam looked up the second he noticed Ciara, his eyes fixing on her. "Ciara."

Iris spun around, her eyes wide with surprise. "Ciara!" she said.

Ciara slid her gaze from Liam to Iris. "Uh, hi."

Iris stood up and strode over to her. "I'm so sorry about last night. It was unforgivable of me to act like that."

Ciara smiled at her. "Don't worry about it. It's all good."

"I'm sorry."

"It's forgiven," Ciara said. "But, uh, I won't bother you any longer. I actually have work to do, so..."

"Are we good?" Iris checked once more.

Ciara smiled and nodded. "Absolutely."

She glanced at Liam but then tore her gaze away. She excused herself and left to go to her room.

Walking to her wardrobe, she started looking for her work clothes. She needed to do something to distract herself from her thoughts.

They're getting back together.

Ciara's room was a mess. She had emptied her wardrobe on the bed and the floor while searching for her work clothes.

Eventually she had found everything and packed her duffle bag that she always had with her at work. She had also packed her notes in that bag.

Ciara was placing her clothes back in the wardrobe, using a bit of magic to help her float them, when a knock interrupted her.

She took a deep breath, continuing to work. "Come in."

Liam could barely get the door open with all the clothes on the floor. He looked around the room. "Um, what's going on?"

"I had to find my work clothes," Ciara explained and continued to place her clothes back in the wardrobe.

Liam cocked his head to the side. "For what?"

"I'm going back to work tomorrow," Ciara said, barely stopping to glance at Liam.

His eyebrows rose. "I thought you weren't supposed to go back until next year?"

"Change of plans," she said and shrugged. Still, she didn't stop what she was doing. She didn't even turn to look at Liam.

"Are you sure it's a good idea?"

"Yes."

Liam went silent for a while, but Ciara paid no mind to it. She continued to put her clothes back in the wardrobe.

Liam shoved his hands in his pockets, watching Ciara. "Do you need help?"

"No. This won't take long."

"Have you eaten today?" Liam asked. "Iris and I already ate, but I could—"

"I ate with my boss," Ciara lied swiftly. She wasn't in the mood to talk with Liam. Not when she didn't even know how to lie to him.

"Oh."

"Did Iris leave or—"

"She just left."

Ciara nodded.

"I...was it okay for her to be here?" Liam asked uncertainly.

Ciara smiled and finally turned to look at Liam. "Of course."

He nodded hesitantly. "Good."

The following morning, Ciara walked into Kellan Wolff's office at precisely nine o'clock.

It was plain, decorated in beige and brown shades. The furniture was simple but likely more expensive than Ciara dared to imagine.

The dark-haired man stood up from his office chair and smiled. He looked impressed. "Just in time!"

"If I'm ever late, blame the bad guys," Ciara said.

He matched his office, wearing expensive-looking black jeans and a button-up shirt.

Kellan smiled and bit his lip. "I will then." He gestured to the chair on the other side of his desk. "Please, take a seat."

Ciara did.

"We need to go through your job description," Kellan said, also sitting down. "You've worked alone, too, right?"

"I have, but also in a team," Ciara said, nodding.

Kellan smiled. "Good. I need you to work alone for now. Mostly, at least."

"What exactly do I need to do?"

"Well, clearly you're a wonderful investigator. I'd like you to continue to do that," Kellan said.

"And what exactly do you want me to investigate?"

"For now, I think you should continue with the murders," Kellan said, leaning back in his chair. He kept his eyes on Ciara, scanning her every movement. "Does that sound good?"

Ciara nodded. "It does."

"If you find yourself in trouble, call your team for help," Kellan instructed. "Oh, and both a laptop and a phone are waiting for you in your office."

Ciara raised her eyebrows. "*My* office?"

Kellan smiled and nodded. "Follow me," he said, standing up.

Ciara stood up and followed Kellan out of the office. Hers wasn't far from his. It was just around the corner.

It looked fairly similar to his office, but a little smaller. On the desk, there was a phone and a laptop, like Kellan had said.

"Does this suit your needs?" Kellan leaned against the wall and crossed his arms over his chest while Ciara admired her office.

"I didn't even realise I'd have an office," Ciara said, walking over to the desk.

"The phone and the laptop only work with your DNA."

Ciara took the phone, looked it over and tried it out. "Good."

"So would you rather look around or meet your team now? They're in the training area."

"I'd like to meet them."

Kellan nodded, straightening up. "Wonderful."

"Ciara, meet your team!" Kellan said, leading Ciara into a vast hall with all sorts of training equipment.

There were enchanted targets for both boxing and spells, and even two duelling stages. On top of that, there was workout equipment from regular dumbbells to enchanted weights. The kind that changed their weight based on the user's needs. At the other end of the hall was a glass room for meetings.

There were six team members, five men and one woman. That didn't surprise Ciara; most of her colleagues had been men.

"Everyone, this is Ciara," Kellan introduced. "Your new boss."

A brown-haired team member took a look at Ciara. "Doherty has told us plenty about you, Miss. I'm Bill, the team's terrorism expert." He had a welcoming smile, but it didn't quite reach his eyes. He was older than Ciara, but not by much.

Ciara smiled. "Please, call me Ciara."

Bill nodded.

"Were all of you in Doherty's team?" Ciara asked.

The name silenced the room for a few seconds. Even Ciara herself was shocked, hearing the name come out of her mouth. She hadn't talked about Doherty since his death.

"Yes." "Yup." Some team members answered out loud, but the others just nodded.

"I'm Theresa, and I'm the hacker of the team," the only woman said and smiled at Ciara. Theresa smiled with her eyes, too. Ciara had already heard of her—on her mission with Doherty. "It's nice to finally meet you," Theresa said. The olive skin on her left arm was covered in black tattoos, matching her raven-black hair.

She looked like a woman no one would want to mess with, and Ciara couldn't wait to work with her. There were too few women working as hit witches.

Ciara smiled. "You too."

"I'm Declan, the linguist of the team," a black-haired, pale man said, offering Ciara a small, wary wave. He was undoubtedly the youngest of the team—and likely closest to Ciara's age.

"I'm Owen, the negotiator," a blond man said. He had to be the oldest, but he didn't look past forty. He didn't smile, but he gave Ciara a nod that she assumed was approval of sorts.

"I am River, curse specialist," a brown-skinned, brown-haired man said. He didn't smile. Instead, his jaw was clenched and his eyes were slightly narrowed.

"And I'm Niles, the trap expert," the last team member said. He smiled, brushing his hand through his red hair, and Ciara spotted the freckles covering his cheeks.

"We were all at Doherty's funeral," Kellan said.

"I'm sorry. I didn't pay enough attention that day," Ciara apologised, thinking back to the wretched day.

"Understandable," Bill said, nodding slightly.

"They all know about the secret group, too," Kellan said.

"It doesn't exist anymore," Ciara said.

"Then it's a good thing Kellan's our new boss. We'll finally get to prove ourselves useful," Niles—the trap expert with freckles—said.

"Frazier admitted the existence of the problem after you spoke with him," Owen—the oldest member and the negotiator—told Ciara. "But it didn't change much. Not nearly as much as it should have." He kept his eyes strictly on Ciara.

She felt as though she was being monitored. And she was.

Kellan nodded in agreement and turned his full attention to Ciara. "He only had us train more."

"Honestly?" Ciara asked in disbelief.

Owen nodded. "Yes."

"That's about to change," Kellan promised.

"Finally!" Theresa said, smirking with her hands on her hips.

"This team will only deal with the witch hunters from now on. If we need more help, the other teams will join us,"

Kellan said—mostly talking to Ciara. She suspected her team already knew.

"And if you need us to find you any information, just tell us," Theresa said to Ciara.

"Theresa is the best hacker I know," Bill—the terrorism expert with brown hair—said, pointing at the hit witch.

Ciara smiled and nodded in appreciation. "I'll keep that in mind. Thanks."

Ciara agreed to have lunch with her team and Kellan in order to get to know them better.

"So you've worked undercover, too?" Niles asked, brushing his red hair out of his eyes.

Ciara nodded. "I have a little, yes."

"So you dealt with the witch hunters in America, too?" Owen asked.

"Mainly yes," Ciara said. "I had other jobs here and there, but most of what I did had something to do with the witch hunters."

"And Doherty trained you?" Bill asked, looking up from his plate.

"Yes, he did."

"How long did you know him for?" Theresa asked, poking her food with her fork.

"Three years."

Kellan chuckled. "Stop bothering her with all the questions, and let her eat, guys."

"It's alright." Ciara smiled. "I'm the outsider."

"Not for long." Theresa flashed a smile at her.

Some of the guys nodded in agreement, but others seemed wary. Ciara could understand why. It was nothing personal. Eventually she hoped to prove herself to the team, though.

Trust was *everything* in their job.

For the rest of her workday, Ciara investigated the murders. It was nearly nine when she finished and went home.

"How was your first day?" Liam asked when he saw Ciara. He was on the sofa in the living room.

She smiled. "Hi. It was great. Well, busy but great."

"What time do you start tomorrow?"

"I'll probably start early. Around seven maybe."

"That early?" Liam said, surprised and disappointed. He and Ciara worked in the same building, but their working hours didn't seem to match.

"Yep."

"Will you work overtime tomorrow, too?" Liam asked.

"I honestly have no idea. I might have to."

"Hasn't the Hit Department heard of regular working hours?"

Ciara chuckled. "Not in Canada, nor the States. I doubt it's any different here."

Liam nodded.

"Anyway, I need to gather some files ready for tomorrow, so I'm gonna do that now," Ciara said, taking a step towards her bedroom.

"You're working from home, too?"

"Just for a bit."

"Have you even eaten today?"

"Yes." Ciara nodded. "Anyway, I have to get those files ready for tomorrow."

"Don't work too hard."

"It's fine, don't worry." Ciara walked to her room, eager to get back to work already.

43

Ciara spent her next day—her birthday, the 31st of October—at work, continuing the investigation. She interrogated a few more people and went through evidence material and her notes. She had to make sure everything matched.

Once she had finished for the day, she joined her team in training. It had been a while since her last time training with any colleagues.

They finished training by five. Bill had found out about Ciara's birthday, and the team offered to take her out for a drink or two. She couldn't say no to that.

It was a splendid chance to get to know her team. She felt more relaxed around them the more they talked, and vice versa. She insisted they should treat her as a friend or a colleague rather than their boss.

Being someone's boss was still new for her. She could hardly believe she had an entire team of her own.

She was proud of how far she had come at such a young

age.

It was past eight when Ciara opened her flat door. She was ever so slightly tipsy from the drinks.

"Finally!" Out of nowhere, Henry rushed to hug Ciara. "Happy birthday!"

"Whoa! Henry, wha—"

Jenna joined the hug, making it a group hug. "Happy birthday!"

Ciara couldn't help but smile as her friends stepped back, releasing her. "Thanks."

"Had to see you on your birthday," Henry said, grinning.

"Have you been waiting for me or what?" Ciara asked, shrugging off her coat and hanging it up.

Henry nodded. "Liam was waiting with us, too, at first. He let us in. But he had somewhere to be."

"You have clearly become a workaholic," Jenna said, crossing her arms. "Are you working over twelve hours a day now?"

Ciara chuckled. "I have to admit I didn't know anyone was waiting for me, so I agreed to get drinks with my new team. I barely know them, so I thought it was a good chance to fix that. Although I worked a bit overtime, too."

Jenna shook her head. "Of course you did."

"But at least I'll have a late morning tomorrow," Ciara said. She didn't have any set working hours. She was just below the head of the department, so it was enough for her to do her job and show up to work every weekday.

Henry and Jenna had brought cake, and they had some with Ciara before they had to leave. Liam still wasn't home, so Ciara was left alone.

She waited for a little while, but Liam was still a no-show. Eventually she went to bed, having nothing to do.

She woke up around nine the next morning. By then Liam had already gone to work, but he had left a note and a gift box on the dining table.

In the note, he wished Ciara happy birthday, not having seen her the previous day. Once Ciara had read the note, she opened the gift box. Inside it was her birthday present—a bracelet with a gem charm.

Ciara's cheeks warmed up. Even Henry had never bought her jewellery. Not on any occasion.

She finished her usual morning routine before heading to work. That day she worked with her team for a change.

They went through the addresses—the locations Josh had found for Ciara. They tried to figure out who owned those houses. As it turned out, one address was a warehouse.

Kellan agreed the team should check it out. It was Ciara's first mission as a boss. She kept thinking back to her mission with Doherty. This time she couldn't lash out like that. She was the one in charge.

The team changed clothes and geared up for the mission.

At the warehouse, Ciara ordered the team to split up. They made sure to keep their distance to the warehouse at first, going through the surroundings. The grounds were full of containers, and they had to go through all of them.

Theresa suggested splitting into smaller teams to cover more ground. Ciara considered it when they walked towards their first container, but eventually she said no.

She wasn't going to take risks like that. She didn't mind if they were slower if it meant they were safer.

No one questioned her decision.

Ciara walked to the container's doors and snapped her fingers. The doors flung open, revealing pitch-black darkness. Theresa used her wand to shine light inside.

Empty.

Ciara led Bill, Declan, and Theresa to the next container.

She let Bill open the door. This time Ciara shone some light inside to see what was in there.

The container turned out to be empty like the previous one.

Niles, River, and Owen informed Ciara that they hadn't found anything so far either. They were searching through the containers closer to the back of the warehouse.

The grounds were utterly silent, and it was making everyone anxious. It was like the calm before a storm.

Even Ciara felt her heart hammer in her chest, but it was under control. It was just her body's natural reaction to possible danger. She was ready to fight if it came to that.

Ciara kicked the next container open with Bill. A squeak made all of them—Ciara, Bill, Theresa, and Declan—cast spells inside the container.

Then Declan shone light inside. It was only a rat that was now unmoving from the spells they had cast at it.

Ciara sighed. "Next one."

There were a few more containers left. They went through each of them, because they didn't have room for mistakes. But they all turned out to be empty. They didn't even find any more rats.

The other half of the team finished right after. Ciara instructed them and her half of the team what was going to happen next. They would go inside, with Ciara's half going in from the front while the others entered from the back. That way they could surprise whoever was inside if they hadn't been spotted yet. They had been careful not to be seen while looking through the containers.

So far everything had gone as planned. Except for the possibly dead rat.

Ciara waited to hear from Owen before giving permission for anyone to enter the warehouse. He was observing the warehouse windows to see if he could spot anything.

"No movement. I'm at the back with River and Niles now," Owen informed the team, using a magical telepathic link. Each team member heard his voice inside their head. The link worked in a similar way to an earpiece.

However, the magical link was more trustworthy than any technological devices. The downside of the link was that it was also draining. That was why no one used telepathic links when they needed to talk to someone in their everyday life. Phones were invented for that.

"Let's move in," Ciara said via the link.

She pushed open the door and her half of the team ran into an enormous, empty hall. They were prepared for traps and enemies, clinging onto their wands as if their lives depended on them—because their lives did depend on them. Except for Ciara who didn't need a wand to cast magic.

Her heart beat unusually fast. It was her first mission back on the job, but it was even more importantly her first mission as the leader. She was responsible for the success of the mission and the wellbeing of the team.

No one was in the enormous hall. Still, the half of the team searched the hall for any evidence. They found two sleeping bags in one corner, but that was it.

"Someone's been here," Bill noted, keeping his voice low.

They still didn't know what was waiting ahead. For all they knew, someone could be listening to them.

"There's been an enchantment protecting this warehouse," Declan said, also keeping his voice low. "It was broken recently."

Ciara nodded. "Let's move."

There were two rooms ahead. Ciara decided they had to split again to cover both rooms. Ciara went with Bill, and Theresa went with Declan.

Ciara was the one to open the door again. Bill rushed in with Ciara right behind. The room was mostly empty, except for a table.

But what they found on the table was interesting. Herbs.

Glass shards covered the floor, sticking to Ciara's and Bill's shoes. It looked as though someone had left in a hurry, leaving a mess behind.

Ciara collected a sample of the herbs. She would deliver it to the lab at work. Whatever the herbs were, they weren't for cooking and they had to belong to a witch or a wizard.

Ciara moved to the next door, motioning for Bill to follow her. They listened carefully at the door before charging in.

Right then, the door across the room slammed open. Ciara and Bill raised their wands, ready to attack.

"Stop!" Ciara exclaimed, lowering her and Bill's wands.

It was just Owen. He, too, lowered his wand once he heard Ciara's voice.

"You checked the whole other half?" Ciara asked him.

Owen nodded. "We did."

"Someone's been here, but they left recently."

"And in a hurry," Bill added.

Ciara worried they had been seen; that they had been a few moments too late to catch whoever had been at the warehouse.

She didn't let it show to her team, but she cursed herself in her mind.

"You found nothing?" Kellan asked, forehead wrinkling. He and Ciara were talking alone in his office.

"We found a few sleeping bags and some herbs. And those weren't just cooking herbs."

"So what herbs are they?"

"The lab is running some tests. We should know by the morning," Ciara said.

"What about the other addresses?" Kellan asked, leaning back in his chair.

"We still need to check them."

"When?"

"We'll start tomorrow."

"Do you need more help?" The frown on Kellan's face eased a little. "There are other teams available."

Ciara shook her head. "No. I think everyone in the team knows what they're doing. They were great today."

The hard look in Kellan's eyes softened finally. "Doherty was an excellent mentor."

Ciara swallowed, unused to hearing his name, and nodded. "He was."

"Do you think we stand a chance?" Kellan still had that softer look in his eyes—something Ciara hadn't seen before. After all, he was her boss, and she barely knew him.

"Against the witch hunters?"

Kellan nodded, and Ciara saw worry flash in his eyes. "Yes."

"Well, we got rid of many of them in America. I don't see why that couldn't happen here," Ciara said honestly. "It's going to take more than a week, though. It'll probably take years."

Kellan nodded. "Well, it's a good thing we have you here."

Ciara smiled. "I'll do my best to help. Just like everyone else."

"Still, you have more knowledge and experience with the witch hunters. I hope that will turn out to be valuable."

"I hope so too."

"So you'll meet the team in the morning?" Kellan asked.

"Yes. We'll start working on the rest of the addresses."

"Good."

Back at her flat, the first thing Ciara did was check if Liam was home. He probably was. But his bedroom door was closed, so she decided not to bother him.

Instead she walked in the bathroom to get a nice, warm shower.

When she walked out minutes later with a towel wrapped around herself, she spotted Liam in the living room.

"Hi," he said when he heard her walk around the corner. "When did you come home? I didn't hear you."

"Just a moment ago," Ciara said, making sure her towel stayed in place by tightening her hold on it.

"So are you working overtime all week?" Liam asked.

"Probably," Ciara admitted.

Liam's expression twisted into a frown. "Are you trying to find the witch hunters?"

"There's plenty of other work to get done," Ciara lied and smiled at Liam.

He didn't need to know what she was doing. None of her friends needed to know. Henry and Mary would be the first ones to get worried—and for nothing.

"Good."

Ciara was about to head to her room to get dressed, but then she spun around to look at Liam. "Oh, I almost forgot! Thanks for the bracelet."

Liam smiled, his entire face brightening up. "You liked it?"

Ciara nodded and smiled. "It's beautiful."

"I'm glad you think so."

First in the morning, Ciara found out what the herbs had been. Blacknettle. It was a somewhat common magical herb used in various poisons. Even the lab couldn't tell which poison it had been used for. There were too many options.

Once her team was ready, Ciara left with them. It was time to check the next address on the list.

She walked in first. The house was eerily quiet. The light coming in through the windows was minimal, because it was a cloudy day.

Ciara and her team split into pairs, so they could check all the rooms. Because there were an uneven number of them, Ciara grouped with Bill and Owen.

The three went up to check the second floor. They ascended the stairs slowly, but still the old steps creaked.

Ciara walked to the first room on the left. She turned

back to see Bill and Owen waiting for her to open the door. She reached for the doorknob, twisted it and pushed the door open.

Cold air rushed out of the room, and the three of them looked inside. They could see nothing out of ordinary except for an open window, so they walked in. In just a matter of seconds, they had gone through the room, which appeared to be a bedroom.

Nothing odd except for the window. Owen shut it once they finished with the room.

They moved on to the next room, and Ciara felt adrenaline kick in.

She had gone through an endless number of houses and other locations in the past. It was rarely the first room that revealed anything, but they often found something as they went along.

She had seen what the witch hunters were capable of. She dreaded what might be waiting for them in the house. The worst scenarios were running through her mind, making her feel sick.

Ciara opened the next door, revealing a small bathroom. They could see it all without stepping in.

Splashes of blood covered the sink like red paint splatters on a white canvas.

Owen stepped inside to collect a sample. After he stepped out, they shut the door.

There was only one more room upstairs. Ciara walked to the door, shuddering at the thought of what might be inside.

It couldn't be good. The blood in the sink was enough to tell that.

She didn't know if Bill and Owen were prepared to see the horrors. She was used to them, and she hoped they were, too.

She was about to open the door, but she stopped, her hand already on the doorknob, and turned around. "See if there's more blood in the bathroom."

Both men looked at her. Bill tilted his head and was about to open his mouth, but Ciara didn't let him say anything.

"Just do it," she ordered.

They obeyed, leaving her alone at the door.

Once she was alone, she reached for the doorknob again. Cold shivers ran down her spine when she pulled the door open.

It was nowhere near an ordinary room. Not anymore. Shackles hung from the ceiling, and torture devices were scattered on top of a table. Drills, blades, and even magical objects. Ciara knew what each one of them did, even though she wished she didn't.

The worst part were the corpses hanging from the ceiling. Their skin had gone pale, and all their blood had poured out, forming a dried pool underneath them.

Ciara stared at the bodies, horrified by what those people had gone through. The stench made her feel ill, even though she should have been used to it.

The rotting smell had stayed inside the room until she had opened the door, thanks to an enchantment. Someone had tried to hide the bodies in there for as long as possible.

Using magic, she collected every magical object from the room. She used a spell to extract a photo of the room from her memory, so she could include it in the evidence. The objects she had collected, she hid inside an enchanted ziplock bag that seemed smaller on the outside than the inside. It also appeared as any other empty ziplock bag for non-magical people.

With one last look at the room and the corpses, Ciara shut the door. "We need to call the police."

By that she meant she would call a police department who in reality worked for the magical government, even though they worked in the non-magical police force. There were plenty of cases like that in the non-magic world; witches and wizards working in secret amongst them. Even some of the non-magic hospitals had witch and wizard healers working as doctors or nurses. Those healers were behind all the miracle recoveries and healings happening across the world.

Bill walked out of the bathroom, eyes darkened. "That bad?"

"You don't want to see it," Ciara said. "There are three corpses. I bet you can smell the stench."

"I can."

They found nothing else in the house. They were forced to wait for the magical police department to arrive before they could move on to their next location.

Eventually the police came. Ciara gave them the evidence she had, so they could investigate the situation more.

The next addresses were small flats, so the team split. Ciara went with Bill and Owen again, and the others—Declan, Niles, River, and Theresa—went together.

Inside the first flat, the trio split up, so they could search all the rooms. Ciara signed for Owen to take the first door and Bill to take the second.

Ciara stepped in first again. After all, she was in charge of the mission.

She watched each of her steps, heading for the third door. She only turned back to check on Bill and Owen.

They were both looking around warily, trying to see if there were any traps. Ciara could tell they were used to their work, so she didn't let herself be distracted by them.

She focused on the corridor ahead instead. She looked around, testing the walls on her way, but she couldn't find any kind of traps—magical or otherwise.

Eventually she stood in front of the third door. She breathed in, filling her lungs with air, and then exhaled slowly.

She reached for the doorknob and was about to open the door when she heard a sickening sound come from the first room, like a blade slicing through flesh.

Then came a bloodcurdling scream.

Ciara's eyes widened, and she froze. It took that split second for her mind to process what was happening. *Owen.*

She ran to the first room as fast as she could, past Bill.

She could see Owen lying on the floor with blood everywhere. Using a spell, she pulled Owen out of the room and shut the door tight. Then she locked the door with another spell.

"Bill!" she screamed out, trying to put pressure on Owen's wound. The problem was that the wound was too big.

Owen squirmed and howled out in pain again.

"Stay still!" Bill said to Owen. He tried to keep his voice calm, but it came out panicked.

Bill summoned a cloth with a flick of his wand and hurriedly wrapped it around Owen's abdomen. The blood soaked through the cloth instantly, covering Ciara's hands and clothes. Bill looked barely any better.

Owen stopped making any sounds just as Bill finished wrapping the cloth.

"Owen!" Ciara and Bill screamed in unison. They checked his pulse.

He was barely hanging in there.

"Take him to a hospital!" Ciara ordered Bill. "The closest one. He needs treatment now!"

Bill grabbed Owen and disappeared.

Ciara stayed on the floor, staring at the pool of blood.

She hadn't been careful enough. Owen was her responsibility, and so was whatever happened to him.

She didn't have time for a pity party, though. Snapping out of it, she grabbed her phone and warned Kellan and the rest of the team.

She waited inside, staying near the door, tormented by her thoughts.

She had already failed as a team leader. She had been the one in charge, and she had let Owen walk straight into a lethal trap.

That was all on her.

Kellan was the first one to arrive, opening the door and spotting Ciara.

"I'm such an awful boss," was the first thing Ciara said.

"It wasn't your fault," Kellan said to her firmly, patting her on the shoulder.

"His side was torn open by a spell," Ciara said, sickened by the image flashing in her mind. She had seen a lot of blood before, but it still made her feel sick from time to time.

Kellan eyed Ciara. "Is that why you're covered in blood?"

Ciara looked down. She hadn't realised how much blood there was on her. "Yes."

"We need to figure out how many more traps there are," Kellan said. "Niles is our expert with traps."

"I hope we don't find more bodies." She sighed, turning to look down the hallway.

"Don't hope too much for the best. They are terrorists."

"Trust me, I know what they are."

After the rest of the team arrived—excluding Bill and Owen—Niles was able to figure out the flat and its traps.

Once all the traps were disarmed, the team searched the flat cautiously.

It was a horror show.

In each of the rooms was one piece of a corpse. In the first room—the room Owen had stepped in—was a torso. Just a torso with purple veins showing closer to where the neck started. There was no blood around the corpse, so someone had cut it into pieces elsewhere.

In the next rooms, the team found limbs. Someone had even cut the fingers off.

There was one more room left unchecked when they found the head. The ears were cut off.

In the last room, there was text written on the wall using blood from the corpse. It said: *Stop or someone might get killed.*

Beneath the words was a pool of blood.

The murder looked like it could have been anyone's handiwork—even a non-magic's—but the message seemed clear. The witch hunters wanted attention, and it had likely been them. Such a horrendous murder was one way to gain attention.

It was enough for one day. The team hurried to the hospital to check on Owen. Kellan returned to the office to handle the paperwork. Ciara went home to wash the blood off before going to the hospital.

Luckily, Liam hadn't been home. He would have overreacted to Ciara's bloody hands and clothes.

"I need to see Owen Blake. I'm his boss, and he got injured at work," Ciara said at the hospital desk.

"He's with a healer. I believe his colleagues are waiting just outside his room. The doctors had to perform emergency surgery on him," the man at the front desk told Ciara. Then he gave her a room number and pointed her in the right direction.

She found the right room.

"How are you all?" Ciara asked her team. They had known Owen for a long time—years, likely—and they were undoubtedly sick with worry.

"The nurse told us to wait here," Bill said. "He should make it, but they said it's bad."

Ciara nodded. "I, uh, got permission to go in. I'll tell you if there's anything to know."

River nodded. "Thanks."

Ciara walked to the door, sighing, and then went in. There was a blonde-haired healer changing the medication going into Owen's cannula. Owen seemed to be unconscious.

"Excuse me."

The healer finished changing the medication and turned around to look at Ciara.

"Iris?" Ciara's eyes widened, but she recollected herself and gestured to Owen. "How is he?"

Iris smiled warmly at Ciara before turning to glance at Owen. "He should be fine. Eventually, I mean. It'll take a long while before he'll get the stitches out, though." Iris's smile faded. "Uh, I thought everyone was supposed to wait outside until the doctor gives permission to see him."

"I'm his boss, so the healer at the front desk told me I could come and see him," Ciara said. "It was a work accident."

Iris's eyes widened. "Oh! I didn't realise you were back at work."

Ciara smiled tightly. "I am. So, uh, can I meet the doctor? I need to make a report for work and I need to know more about his injury, so I can confirm paid sick leave for him."

She knew Iris could tell her most of what the doctor was going to tell her. But the rules were that she needed a statement from a doctor for her report. It was a requirement set by the magical government.

"I'll go get the doctor," Iris said and smiled.

"Thank you."

Ciara stayed at the hospital with the team for hours. They didn't leave until the hospital staff forced them to. It was eight by then. Ciara told everyone to go home, and she also told them to have the next day off. She promised to make sure they got paid for it, too.

Ciara couldn't go home, though. She had paperwork waiting at the office.

The report about the accident was the worst, but other than that she found the paperwork to be plain boring. It took her around two hours to finish, and then she packed her stuff, ready to go home.

As she was leaving, she noticed Kellan was still working. She walked to his office door and knocked. He flicked his wand to open the door for her.

Ciara stepped inside. "Owen should be fine, but it looks like he'll need a long period of sick leave. Bill was so quick that Owen got the treatment faster than usual."

"Was Owen awake? How was the team? I tried to make it to the hospital, but apparently a head of department has to deal with one too many things," Kellan said, glancing at the papers scattered on his desk. He sounded strained and was pale from worry. He had known Owen for a long time. They had been on the same team for years.

"Owen got some pretty heavy medication, so he was unconscious the whole time," Ciara said. "I told the team to take a paid day off. I don't think it would be smart to force them out to the field right after this. They all seemed a bit better when they heard Owen would be fine, but still."

Kellan smiled. "I knew I promoted you for a reason. That was good thinking."

Ciara nodded. "How are you?"

She knew no one had asked him. And Kellan didn't seem to be the type to share his concerns.

"Worried," Kellan admitted.

Ciara nodded. "He'll be fine."

Kellan sighed, relieved to hear it again. "I know, and that's good. I just can't help but think what could have happened."

"I get that."

"I know you lost your fiancé because of this."

Ciara bit her lip and nodded, an ache forming in her chest. "I-I did. About ten months ago."

"I'm sorry."

Ciara smiled, but it didn't reach her eyes. "I'm moving on. But I suppose his death made me more determined."

"I bet," Kellan said. "I wish this all could be over in days, because we have to risk our lives on this job."

"But you won't see the results until later," Ciara said, nodding. "And that sucks. Especially when everyone might not be there to see the end."

Kellan nodded. "Exactly."

"Will you be at work tomorrow?"

"I have to be, so yes."

"How busy is your schedule?" Ciara asked.

"Not that busy, I hope. Why?" Kellan furrowed his eyebrows.

"We triggered their traps today," Ciara said. "They won't stay at the other addresses for long now. From experience, I know that they are always alarmed when their traps go off."

"Meet you here at nine, then? We'll go see the rest of the flats together."

Ciara nodded. "Sounds good."

"Hello!" Ciara called out when she walked in. The lights were still on, so she knew Liam wasn't asleep.

"Hi!" Liam called back, coming out of the kitchen. "You stopped by at home earlier?"

"Oh, yeah. I did." Ciara shrugged off her coat and hung it up. "I had to get some clothes clean for tomorrow."

"So where were you? Until now, I mean," Liam said and leaned against the kitchen doorway, his arms crossed. "I get that you have to do your job, but it's dangerous to go after the witch hunters on your own on your free time."

"I'm not doing that," Ciara assured him. "I stopped by here during lunch. I was working overtime again."

He still had a doubtful frown on his face. "You sure?"

"Yes. One of us got injured today, so it was a bit crazy."

"Are you okay?"

Ciara smiled. "Yes. Everything is fine now."

Liam nodded, dropping his arms to his side. "Good."

"What time does your work start?" Ciara asked. "At nine?"

"Yes. Why?"

"We should go to work together," Ciara suggested. After all, they worked in the same building.

A smile spread onto Liam's face. "Sounds good."

44

Work didn't get easier for Ciara. The following weeks were unbelievably busy. Still, the team found no witch hunters. They were always a little too late to catch them, and she had no idea how that could be.

The team adjusted to working without Owen. After all, he was probably safer on his sick leave than he would have been at work.

He ended up having to stay at the hospital for weeks before the doctors allowed him to go home. He lived alone, which was common in their line of work, so he had to be recovered enough to take care of himself.

Liam suspected something, because Ciara spent hardly any time at home. Mostly she was working, but sometimes she went out for drinks with her team—especially after tough cases.

Liam didn't believe her, and he didn't have to say it out loud for Ciara to know. He knew she wasn't seeing her other friends, either. She didn't have the time.

She had to find the witch hunters, and that mattered the most to her.

The cold air bit at Ciara's cheeks, and the wind blew her hair all over the place. A regular November evening.

Ciara hurried to the right building and walked in. She sighed, welcoming the warmth, and headed for the stairs.

Walking up the last set of stairs, she spotted something on her door. She hurried to see what it was.

It was a note saying, *Someone who's alone and unaware might get hurt unless you stop.*

Ciara's eyes grew wide. She grabbed her phone and took a photo of the note before tearing it off and shoving it in her pocket.

She didn't realise her hands were shaking until she reached for the doorknob. She feared what she would find inside.

Not Liam. She was used to people getting hurt at work, but her personal life was different. She wasn't used to losing people outside work, not even after Theo.

She yanked the door open. "Liam!"

"Yes?" Ciara heard Liam ask from the living room. She could tell just by the tone of his voice he had been reading a book.

Ciara sighed in relief, unable to contain her smile. She closed the flat door, shrugged off her coat and hung it up. She walked to the living room, and her eyes settled on Liam. Warmth and relief filled her, and she wanted to hug him— but she didn't. "You don't mind if I invite a colleague over for a little while, right?"

"O-of course not," Liam said. "It's your flat."

"Even so, I thought it was polite to ask. I will, uh, call him. He...he had to stop by at home and, you know," Ciara rambled before she hurried into her room.

She dialled Bill's number the second she had her room's door locked. She had worked with him the most and, therefore, trusted him the most. The entire team had gained her trust, but this time she simply preferred Bill.

"Ciara?" he said when he picked up.

"Bill," Ciara said, her voice unusually shaky. She couldn't get a picture of dead Liam out of her mind, despite knowing he was okay. "I know you're not at work and this will sort of be work. But can you please come over?"

"Now?"

"Yes."

"Of course. What happened?" Bill asked, worried. Ciara could hear him shuffling around, getting ready.

"Someone left a note on my flat door, threatening to kill my flatmate," Ciara whispered. "He doesn't know and he can't know. So, how quickly can you get here?"

"Just give me the address."

She did, and soon she heard Bill's footsteps, running up the stairs. Then he rang the doorbell.

"I'm here."

"Great. Just a second," Ciara said and hurried to the door to open it for Bill. "Hey! You made it!" she said, pretending to be happy to hang out with a colleague.

Bill smiled. "Of course." He shrugged off his coat and hung it on the coatrack.

"I have the files and my laptop in my room," Ciara said, still smiling.

"Show the way."

Ciara and Bill stopped at the living room. Liam was still reading his book, sitting on the sofa, but he looked up when he sensed two pairs of eyes on him.

"Bill, this is Liam," Ciara said, gesturing to her flatmate. "And Liam, this is Bill."

Bill smiled. "Nice to meet you."

"It's nice to meet you, too." A brief smile crossed Liam's face, then his eyes fell on Ciara.

"Uh, we'll be in my room. We need to get some paperwork done."

"I'll try to be quiet." Liam nodded. "But, uh, have you eaten yet?"

"Actually no."

"I think I'll order Chinese. Is that good for both of you?"

"Sounds great," Bill said and grinned.

"What he said." Ciara gestured to Bill. "Um, thanks."

Liam smiled and nodded. "No problem."

Ciara pulled Bill to her bedroom, closing the door behind. She pulled the note from her back pocket and handed it to Bill.

He read it over twice to make sure he hadn't missed a word. "I don't think he's safe."

"I know." Ciara gritted her teeth. "What the hell am I supposed to do?"

It was new for her, not knowing what to do.

"Well, you should scatter around your laptop and files to make it look like we're not doing anything suspicious."

"Good thinking," Ciara said and spread paperwork over her bed. She also opened her laptop on the desk.

"And then you need to take a deep breath," Bill instructed.

Ciara took a deep breath, doing her best to calm down.

"So is he your boyfriend?" Bill asked, gesturing in the living room's direction.

"My ex from over three years ago."

Bill crossed his arms. "He looked rather jealous to be an ex."

"You're gay. Why would he be jealous even if he was interested in me?"

"How would he know I'm gay?"

"Good point," Ciara said. "Anyhow, he's just a friend. And his life is in danger because of my job."

Bill held up the note. "You took a picture of this?

"Yes. Before I tore it off the door."

"Send it to the rest of the team and tell them we need to

have a meeting bright and early. Send it to Kellan, too."

Ciara nodded and grabbed her phone. She did as Bill instructed.

"Liam would start suspecting something if you left the flat for no reason," Bill thought out loud.

"He would."

"So, when I leave, I'll stick around to make sure no one suspicious enters the building."

"You can't stay up all night."

"I'll call someone else to switch with me when I get tired," Bill said. "They want to kill your flatmate. I've seen them do worse."

"Well, they did kill my fiancé and mentor, so—"

Bill snapped his fingers in front of Ciara's face. "You're rambling. Stop that and start focusing."

"This is just a little too..."

"Personal?" Bill nodded. "Well, you and your flatmate were just threatened in your own home. I would be freaking out, too, if I were you."

Ciara and Bill pretended to have finished working when the Chinese takeaway arrived. That way Ciara could go to the door instead of Liam. She was prepared for the worse while he was still oblivious to what was going on.

But it wasn't a witch hunter, just a delivery girl.

The three of them ate together. Liam and Bill seemed to get along when they finally got the chance to talk.

Bill left after eating, but he was going to stay on watch outside the building.

"He seems nice," Liam said.

"He's great," she agreed. "And he's gay, if you're interested."

Liam rolled his eyes. "So is he on the same team or what?"

"He's in my team."

"In *your* team?" Liam asked, raising his eyebrow.

"Um...I might have forgotten to mention that I got

a promotion," Ciara said sheepishly. "I got...well, I got Doherty's job."

The name was still painful to say out loud.

"So, you're Bill's boss?"

Ciara nodded. "Yes, but I hate that term."

Liam chuckled. "You're honestly one position below the head of the department and you hate being called a boss?"

"Yes."

"You're one of a kind."

Ciara smiled.

She and Liam ended up watching a movie together. It had been Ciara's idea, because she wanted to keep an eye on Liam in case someone sneaked into the flat.

With Bill on watch, it was unlikely, but she didn't want to risk it. She was sick with worry, even though she trusted Bill with her life.

"So when does your work start tomorrow, *boss*?" Liam asked, teasing.

Ciara rolled her eyes. "At seven."

"I thought you were the boss."

"We have an early meeting. Bad guys get to sleep, but we don't."

"Even I get to sleep more than you do."

"Maybe I should have become a curse breaker after all," Ciara said, shrugging.

"It's not too late to switch." There was a hint of seriousness in Liam's voice.

"I think I'll stick to being the boss."

"Your choice."

C iara was the first one in the meeting room. River was watching her building, so he couldn't come.

Everyone else came early. They seemed to have taken the personal threat even more seriously than most cases.

"Do you have the note?" Kellan asked Ciara when he walked in as the last one to arrive.

Ciara took the piece of paper from her pocket and handed it to him. "My flatmate was alone at home, and this was on the door."

"But nothing had happened to him?" Theresa asked, frowning, as she sat down.

"No, he was fine," Ciara said. "I checked the entire flat again this morning, but I couldn't find anything."

"Would it help if he moved out?" Bill wondered out loud. "They targeted this threat at you, Ciara, even though they're threatening to hurt him. I think they want to get to you through him. He's just leverage."

"He's been looking for a flat for a couple of months now. I don't think he'll find one just like that." Ciara snapped her fingers to make her point clear.

"Tell him to move out," Declan said. "It's your flat."

"He'll notice something's off. Then he'll demand to know the whole truth."

"So wait..." Niles crossed his arms. "How do you know him?"

"He's my ex-boyfriend. We're friends now."

Bill grinned. "Well, there's nothing more awkward than having to meet your ex's new boyfriend."

"I don't have a boyfriend."

"Bill can pretend to be your boyfriend," Declan said, gesturing to Bill. "He's good-looking and everything."

Ciara shook her head. "Liam knows Bill's gay."

"Then Kellan." Niles grinned. "He has the looks."

Ciara turned to look at Kellan, wide-eyed. She had never dated her boss. And even though she had got to know Kellan better, they weren't *that* close.

"He has a point." Kellan glanced at Ciara.

"You meant your looks?" Niles asked, chuckling.

Kellan rolled his eyes. "Bill has a point," he corrected. "Liam will move out if he thinks you have a new boyfriend, and especially if that boyfriend hangs out at your flat," he said to Ciara.

"Does your job description include pretending to be a boyfriend, then?" Ciara asked Kellan, amused.

Kellan chuckled. "Well, I'm the boss, so I suppose I make my own job description."

"That's it then!" Bill grinned. "Saving lives and breaking hearts."

"Breaking hearts?" Theresa asked.

"Bill thinks Liam still likes me," Ciara said.

"Oh."

One of the team members was keeping an eye on Liam at all times. They took turns, so everyone had a chance to rest. But looking out for Liam was their primary focus that day.

Kellan and Ciara were mostly doing paperwork. And for once, they both left early, so they were home before Liam.

It turned out Kellan was an excellent cook, so he suggested they make dinner. Ciara warned him about her cooking skills before he let her do anything.

"So are you hungry or where did this idea come from?" Ciara asked. Kellan had let her make the salad, because it was unlikely she could burn it.

"Couples who cook together, stay together. He'll be jealous in no time when he walks in and sees us cooking." Kellan smirked, confident his plan would work.

"Uncomfortable, not jealous."

Kellan smiled, continuing to prepare the food. "Whatever you say."

Ciara sighed and turned to face Kellan who was working with his sleeves rolled up and his forearms showing. "This is going to be so weird."

She was unsure about the plan. She feared it wasn't going to work. Obviously Kellan was attractive. But with her feelings for Liam, lying wasn't going to be easy for her.

Kellan glanced at her. "I thought you were great at acting."

Ciara swallowed. "I've never had to act in front of him."

"Soft spot?" Kellan's eyes gave away he was teasing her, but he also wore a smug grin on his face.

Ciara rolled her eyes.

"He'll die if you fail. That should motivate you enough."

Ciara turned to glare at Kellan. "Can you not?"

"Sorry."

Ciara exhaled. "No worries." She inhaled, rubbing her hands together. "Just a bit nervous."

"A bit?" Kellan said, laughing out loud.

"How am I supposed to act like I'm dating my boss?" Ciara stopped working on the salad and turned her full attention to Kellan. "Besides, you're, like, twice my age."

"First of all, we have to pretend we've been seeing each other for a while now. Like since you started at work. That shouldn't be too hard, considering how much you're away from home." Kellan crossed his arms, turning to Ciara. "And second of all, I'm thirty-five, not ancient."

"Fine, Mr Thirty-Five. Still, I'm supposed to tell him I've been lying about being at work when I have actually been at work?" Ciara didn't like that. She wanted to keep Liam safe, but she didn't want him to hate her for lying to him.

"Yes, he needs to think we've been seeing one another in secret." Kellan nodded. "It might hurt his feelings, but he'll get over it."

Ciara sighed. "I hate lying to him."

"So, you sure you two aren't dating?"

Ciara huffed at Kellan who was smiling smugly at her. "He's a friend."

"Hope he doesn't punch me in the face," Kellan said. "Oh, and do you want to practise the kissing part?" Kellan turned to look at Ciara with a grin. "You know, so you won't be blushing like crazy when we have to do it in front of him?"

"Kellan!" Ciara scolded, wide-eyed.

Kellan laughed. "As if you wouldn't have kissed anyone undercover."

"That's different."

"So, do you want to try that kiss or—"

Kellan was interrupted when someone twisted a key in the door's lock. *Liam.*

"Use those acting skills," Kellan said, giving Ciara a serious look.

The door opened. "Ciara?" Liam's voice rang out, and he sounded confused.

Ciara took a deep breath and walked out of the kitchen to see Liam taking off his coat. "Hey, Liam. Your timing is perfect!" She forced herself to grin at him, finding it uncomfortable. "We're just about to finish making dinner."

"We?" Liam asked and hung up his coat.

"Well, uh, there's someone I want you to meet," Ciara said and gestured for Liam to follow her to the kitchen.

And he did.

"Liam, this is Kellan." Ciara smiled and let her hand slide into Kellan's hand, intertwining their fingers. "And, Kellan, this is Liam."

Kellan smiled at Liam charmingly. "Ciara has told me a lot about you. It's great to finally meet you."

He chose his words perfectly. Ciara couldn't help but wonder how many times Kellan had worked undercover. He had probably achieved some great work on his missions.

Liam smiled, but it seemed a little tight. "It's, um, great to meet you, too."

Ciara noticed the confused—nearly uneasy—look on Liam's face. "Can I talk to you for a second?" she asked.

"Sure," he said, his eyes fixing on her.

Kellan gave Ciara a quick kiss on her cheek, and she and Liam left the room.

"Um, sorry?" Ciara said a little uncertainly.

Liam glanced at the kitchen doorway before focusing his full attention on her. "About what?"

"I mean, I should probably have mentioned him before I brought him here so unexpectedly."

"It's your flat," Liam said. "It's fine."

"You sure?"

He nodded. "Yes. So, uh, how long have you been...you know?"

"Since I started working again. He's...well, he's my boss," Ciara said, biting into her lip.

"He's your boss?" Liam repeated, raising his eyebrows.

Ciara nodded. "Is it okay if he stays over tonight?"

Ciara and Kellan had agreed he should stay overnight. It was part of Kellan's master plan to make Liam move out.

"It's your flat," Liam reminded her again, shoving his hands in his pockets.

"Still, you live here too."

"Of course it's fine."

Ciara smiled. "Great."

Liam excused himself to take his bag to his room before dinner. Meanwhile, Kellan finished cooking and Ciara set the table.

Once Ciara was done, she walked back to the kitchen. "Kellan—"

Kellan leaned in to kiss Ciara's cheek, stopping her. "So far, so good," he whispered into her ear, brushing his fingers against the side of her neck.

She blushed from the intimacy of the whole thing.

"Now giggle and make it realistic," he whispered.

So she giggled.

As Kellan straightened up, wearing a wide smile, Ciara noticed Liam leaning against the doorway with his arms crossed.

"Liam, just in time!" Ciara said, hurriedly fixing her composure. "The food is ready."

"Great." Liam's voice was strained, but he tried to seem polite even as his eyes drifted to Kellan.

Ciara was glad it was Kellan who had to pretend to be her boyfriend. He knew how to talk to people and play his role. The dinner would have been even more uncomfortable without Kellan making conversation. But it was still odd to act like a couple, especially when he touched her arm.

But she stayed in her role. The role of a girlfriend.

Liam spent most of the evening in his room after dinner. He couldn't stand to watch Ciara and her *new* boyfriend. Kellan was continuously giving her a kiss or two and making her giggle. It appeared as though the guy couldn't keep his hands to himself. He kept wrapping his stupidly muscular arms around her every chance he got. His stupidly blue eyes were following her every movement like a lovesick puppy.

And Liam absolutely hated it.

Most of all, he hated that her bracelet's gem was glowing bright red whenever she was around the guy. It wasn't just an ordinary bracelet, and Liam would never have given it to Ciara if he had known she was seeing someone.

It was an enchanted piece of jewellery. People usually called it a love bracelet. The gem glowed when one was around the person they loved. If Ciara had only had a crush on the guy, it would have been some shade of pink, depending on the state of the infatuation.

However, it was *blazing* red.

Ciara was glad Liam spent most of his time in his room that evening, so she didn't have to act as much. She was still sitting on the sofa with Kellan's arm around her for most of the evening. After all, they had to be prepared if Liam walked out of his room.

The worst part for Ciara, however, was changing her clothes in the same room with her boss. Kellan politely looked away, and she did the same when he changed into pyjama pants. Still, it was weird.

"No shirt?" Ciara asked when Kellan told her it was okay to turn around.

"You have a love bracelet glowing bright red around that guy, so don't pretend you don't like abs," Kellan said.

"L-love bracelet?" Ciara stuttered. Wide-eyed, she turned to look at the bracelet on her bedside table. The gem wasn't red. It was clear. "It's not red."

"It was the entire time it was on your wrist and he was around," Kellan said and lay down onto the bed. He pulled the duvet up to his waist, making sure he *wasn't* hiding his abs. "You gonna stay up or what?"

Ciara was still standing next to the bed, frozen and staring at the bracelet. "Uh, no." She shook her head and lay down. "Are you sure?"

"About the bracelet? Yes. You're in love with the guy," Kellan said, amused.

"He gave me that bracelet."

"He's in love with you too, then." Kellan's tone gave away that he had thought so, but Ciara's words had confirmed it. "Now I almost feel bad for using the spell." Kellan's smile turned into a mild grimace.

"What spell?" Ciara asked, whipping her head around to look at her shirtless boss.

The grimace turned into a grin. "A spell to make it sound like we're having sex already."

"Kellan!" Ciara gasped loudly.

Kellan looked at Ciara, the amusement in his eyes growing. "That came out the wrong way for him, I bet."

Ciara's eyes widened. "Please, shut up."

"We can still pretend to break up if you're having regrets. We'll say it was break-up sex."

Ciara almost wanted to do that, but she shook her head. Backing away wasn't an option. "No. I..." She breathed out. "He needs to move out, so he'll be safe."

Kellan nodded, turning more serious as well. "I'm sure he'll be fine." It seemed as though he genuinely tried to comfort Ciara with those words.

"If this works, he will be." That thought was enough to help Ciara go along with the plan.

The following day, Thursday, Ciara went home with Kellan again. They left work early like the previous day, so they were home before Liam.

Liam came home when the two were eating, and Ciara asked him to join them. For a moment, Ciara could have sworn Liam hesitated, but eventually he said he would eat with them, but then he would have to go.

"You have plans?" Ciara asked, trying not to seem too interested.

"Yes. Nothing important." Liam smiled at her before his eyes drifted to Kellan.

Kellan turned to Ciara with a smile. He made sure Liam noticed him placing a hand on Ciara's thigh. "We have plans, too. Don't we, love?"

Ciara wanted to gag at the nickname. It wasn't that Kellan wasn't attractive or charming. Even she found his abs to be hot. It was the situation that made everything awkward.

She was in love with the other man in the room.

Liam left soon after the dinner. He didn't tell them where he was going, but he said he would be back later.

On Friday, Kellan had to stop by at his place before he could go to Ciara's flat, so she went home alone.

"Is your boyfriend working overtime or what?" Liam asked when she came home.

"He'll be here later," Ciara said. "He has to do a few things at home first."

"Okay." Liam nodded. "I, uh, have something to tell you."

Ciara bit her lip. "What is it?"

"I found a flat."

Ciara felt as though a weight had been lifted from her shoulders, but she kept her composure. "You're moving out?"

Liam nodded again. "Yes. I think I finally found the right flat. So I'm moving today."

"Today?" Ciara's eyes widened. She had been hoping for him to move out. It had been the goal of the whole pretend-dating. But she hadn't realised it could happen so soon.

"Yes. I just saw the flat yesterday, so it happened a little suddenly for me, too. I forgot to mention it yesterday. But, uh, I can leave some of my furniture here if you need it for now or—"

"No, no," Ciara said hurriedly. "It's fine. I can finally, uh, get furniture of my own."

Liam smiled and nodded. "Henry and Shawn are about to come over. They promised to help move my stuff."

Ciara had grown so used to living with Liam. The idea of waking up in an empty flat sounded awful.

"G-great. Um, I have some work...uh, stuff to finish on my laptop, so...I mean, do you need help or—" She couldn't believe she was stumbling over her words.

"No, we'll be fine. I should warn you, though, I accidentally mentioned your boyfriend to Henry."

Ciara grimaced. "So, he'll kill me?"

Liam chuckled. "Probably."

Ciara had just texted Kellan and her team about the situation when she heard Henry and Shawn arrive.

"Ciara!" Henry exclaimed.

Smiling, she walked out of her room. "Yes?"

"You didn't tell me! Or even Jenna!" he said, running to Ciara. "How could you do that to me?"

Ciara chuckled. "Um, can I tell you now? Yes or no, here goes nothing. I'm dating my boss."

Henry's eyes widened. "You're dating your own boss?"

"Yes."

"And you just got a promotion?" Henry asked, now frowning.

"How did you—"

"Liam thought I knew," Henry said and shrugged. "Tell me, are you dating him for the promotion or—"

"Henry!" Ciara scolded. "Of course not!"

"What is he doing?" Shawn asked, joining the conversation.

Ciara turned to smile at Shawn. "Hi, Shawn. He—"

"I'm being a jackass," Henry said.

"Exactly," Ciara agreed.

Kellan came up with an excuse for not showing up. He

didn't want to intrude after Ciara had let him know about the situation.

So Ciara told Henry—when he had asked—that Kellan had been forced to deal with a problem at work. No one suspected anything.

It only took a couple of hours for the guys to move everything from Ciara's flat to Liam's new place. Henry and Shawn went home after they had moved the last furniture. Liam came back on his own for a box of books and drawing equipment.

"Uh, here's your key," Liam said and handed Ciara the flat key. After all, it was no longer his to keep.

"Thanks." Ciara fiddled with the key in her hands. "Should I expect a housewarming party soon?"

Liam chuckled. "We'll see."

Ciara smiled at him, gazing into his hazel eyes. "I suppose I'll see you around."

"See you, Ciara." He gave her one last look, something foreign flashing in his eyes, and left the flat.

Ciara stayed still, staring at the closed flat door. When she was sure he wasn't coming back, tears formed in her eyes.

The tears—a mix of pain and relief—cascaded down her cheeks. She couldn't lose him like she had lost Theo. But pushing him away hurt.

Eventually Ciara walked to the living room. She stared at the blank wall where Liam's painting had been.

The flat was empty without him.

46

After Liam moved out, Ciara worked even more than before. She was avoiding her home, because she hated living alone. She also kept away from her friends in fear of putting them in danger.

Ciara didn't remember the last time she had seen Henry or Jenna. But it was worth it if it meant she didn't have to lose them. She was done losing people.

Kellan had tried to tell her to stop working so much, saying it wouldn't help. Ciara knew it, but she needed something to do with her time. Kellan eventually accepted it, but he continued to keep an eye on her. Ciara told him it would be temporary—only until they managed to get the witch hunters.

But she didn't know how long it would take.

It was two weeks after Liam had moved out when Ciara's crazy work schedule brought actual results. It was around five in the evening when she found a new address.

Luckily the team hadn't gone home yet, so they looked further into the location. They were all gathered in the meeting room—even Kellan. Niles had his laptop on the table and was searching for information on the address.

"It looks like a small manor," he said, frowning at the laptop screen.

Bill stood up and walked closer to see the screen. "That doesn't look small."

"Well, small for a manor," Niles said, shrugging. "Based on the photos I found, there are more than two ways in. There's the front door, a door at every balcony, and two back doors. It's supposed to have a basement, too. A building that old could even have an entrance straight to the basement."

"Alright." Kellan nodded. "Everyone ready in thirty minutes. I'll meet you all here," he ordered and left the room.

Theresa made her way over to Ciara. "Do you think we could find them this time?"

Ciara sighed. "Some of them, I hope."

They were going to be quick, so they had a better chance of catching witch hunters if there were any. This time the witch hunters wouldn't have time to escape.

"Will you finally stop training all night and every night if we catch them?" Bill asked, wrapping an arm around Ciara's shoulders.

She rolled her eyes. "I have nothing else to do."

"But when we catch these idiots who threatened your friend, you can start hanging out with him and the rest of your friends again."

"If we catch them."

"You just said you think we could find some of them in the manor. Don't be such a buzzkill."

"Finding them doesn't mean catching them. That won't be as easy."

Bill sighed. "Fair enough."

Kellan came back down to the training hall exactly thirty minutes later. By then everyone was dressed for the job and ready to go.

Owen was working from home with his laptop in case the team needed additional information while they were out in the field. It was late Friday evening, so the other teams had already gone home.

The team teleported near the manor, but far enough so as not to trigger any magic-detecting alarms. Still, just in case, they stayed unmoving and listened.

"Nothing," Kellan said when they had been listening for any alarms for long enough. "Now we need eyes on the building."

"I'll go," Ciara volunteered.

"Me, too," Bill said right after.

Kellan nodded. "We'll wait here."

Ciara and Bill sneaked closer to the house. They moved slowly to make sure no one saw them. They had to observe the trees, the bushes, and the house while remaining undetected.

Little by little they approached the house, eventually hiding behind some bushes. There appeared to be no lights on inside the manor, so they couldn't see much, but they spotted the entrance to the basement.

"I can't see anything inside," Bill whispered after they had been on watch for a while.

Their legs and backs were beginning to ache from staying still in such uncomfortable positions.

Ciara was eyeing the windows, trying to see any movement inside. Sighing, she almost turned to Bill to tell him they should go back to the others, but then she swore she saw something move. It could have been a hanging body—or a witch hunter.

Ciara's eyes widened. "Something just moved inside," she

whispered.

Bill cursed under his breath. "Do you think they noticed us?"

She shook her head the tiniest bit. "No. But we should tell the others. Let's go back."

"Alright."

Ciara kept her eyes on the windows and signed for Bill to run behind a nearby tree. She ran after him while trying to keep her eyes on the house and especially its windows.

It seemed as though no one saw them. But they weren't far enough from the house yet. And they were also going to have to keep their eyes on the trees on their way back. There could be witch hunters around—even outside—and they had no room for surprises.

Ciara waited a while to see if she saw anything through the windows. When she didn't, she signed for Bill to move. They ran further away from the house and hid behind another set of trees.

Not much longer and they would be far enough to run back to the others without having to hide behind bushes and trees all the time. Ciara gave Bill a sign again, and they ran.

They couldn't see the manor and its windows anymore, so they turned their full focus on the surrounding forest.

"We can run back," Ciara said. "Just keep your eyes on the surroundings. We don't know what could be out here."

They jogged back to the spot where they had left the others.

But the team was gone.

"Where are they?" Bill spun around frantically.

Ciara shushed him.

They heard a quiet thud. Ciara nearly cast a curse at the object that fell from the tree.

"Don't shoot."

She lowered her wand, seeing River hold his hands up.

"Just us." River smiled a little as the others jumped down from the trees.

"We didn't know if it was you when we heard footsteps," Theresa explained. "Probably Bill's heavy footsteps," she added with a teasing grin.

Bill rolled his eyes.

"We need to go in there," Ciara said, mostly expecting Kellan's permission. "The lights are out, so I have no idea what's inside, but something moved in there."

"Did you find a way in?" Niles asked.

Bill nodded. "We found the entrance to the basement."

"We should use that," Kellan said and turned to face Ciara. "Lead the way."

Ciara nodded and began to head back to the manor. No one dared to speak, following her all the way to the old wooden doors that supposedly led to the basement.

River cast a silencing spell on the doors to make sure they didn't squeak. Then he and Bill pulled them open slowly and carefully.

The team waited. Their hearts were thundering in their chests, expecting someone to emerge.

But nothing came from the darkness.

Ciara went in first. She wasn't planning to have any more accidents when she was in charge.

She tried to look around. Even after letting her eyes adjust to the darkness, she couldn't see much.

Her team and Kellan joined her.

None of them could see anyone in the basement. To be sure, Ciara lit up the room with a silent snap of her fingers. She had her wand in her hand, even though she didn't necessarily need it. She could have used her magic even without the wand. But if there was a fight awaiting inside, she preferred to have her wand in hand.

When the basement was lit up, the team could confirm it was empty. There were no corpses hanging from the ceiling or any sign of someone having brewed a potion in there. Nothing out of ordinary.

Once they had checked the basement, Ciara put out the

lights with another snap of her fingers.

"What now?" Bill whispered.

"Up the stairs." Again, Ciara was the first one to ascend. At the end of the stairs was a door. She waited for everyone to walk up before she pushed it open.

At first glance, they didn't see anyone, but it was just a matter of time. Ciara wished they would find someone alive rather than a corpse. Preferably a witch hunter.

Ciara's heart pounded wildly in her chest. Whatever was going to happen, she was ready. She just hated the waiting—the calm before the action.

Ciara split the team into smaller groups. Using hand gestures, she ordered Kellan and Niles to check the left side of the first floor and Declan and River to check the right side. Then she gestured for Bill and Theresa to follow her.

The manor was old, and the floorboards were creaky. The team had to use silencing charms. But then, it was eerily quiet.

Ciara headed to the bottom of the stairs, Bill and Theresa following her.

She couldn't hear Kellan, Niles, Declan, or River. But silence was better than fighting noises. So far everyone was okay.

But they certainly weren't safe. Not in that place.

Ciara feared it was a trap. No other address had shown so many signs of the witch hunters. It wouldn't have been the first time she had walked into an ambush. What made it worse was that she was the one in charge this time—even if Kellan was there, too.

Ciara stayed at the bottom of the stairs, listening. When she couldn't hear anything, she gestured for Bill and Theresa to follow. She stepped onto the first stair. It made a quiet squeak.

Moving her hand in the air, she put a silencing enchantment on the stairs. Luckily, no one seemed to have heard the sound from the first stair. Or if they had, they stayed hidden.

She moved up, one stair at a time, as quietly as she could. Bill and Theresa tiptoed right behind her.

She was awfully aware of how heavy her breathing was.

Her heart was beating rapidly, but that happened on most missions. It was her body's reaction to danger.

In fact, she felt unusually calm. It was just her, Kellan, and the team. She dreaded the idea of losing any of them, but she would rather lose one of them than Henry or her other friends. Just thinking about losing Henry—or anyone from her personal life—sickened her.

But it didn't mean she was willing to lose any of her team members. She would do anything to prevent even one of them getting hurt. Still, she was used to being in dangerous situations with them. She had got accustomed to the idea since she had first met them.

Losing people was part of the job. She had to accept it, despite how hard it was.

Ciara stopped in the middle of the steps again to listen to their surroundings. She couldn't hear anything.

She was just about to step on to the last stair when she heard a creak. Her hand flew up, and Bill and Theresa halted.

Ciara moved to stand as close to the wall as she could, listening. The only sound she could hear was her own heart beating. She held her breath to make sure she heard everything.

Just when she was about to take one more step, she swore she heard footsteps. They were quiet, but they were approaching.

Someone was upstairs.

Ciara waited patiently for the footsteps to come closer. Her heartbeats reminded thunder, her body preparing for the upcoming fight.

She could hear Bill's breathing become shaky when he heard the footsteps too. Ciara didn't dare to turn to look at him.

Her muscles tensed as the footsteps came even closer. She was dying to switch her weight from one leg to another, but she couldn't in case she made a sound.

She needed the element of surprise on their side. And she was praying no one downstairs ruined that.

The rest of the team hadn't made even one sound, and that was worrying her.

She could no longer hear Bill's breathing. Apparently he was holding his breath—probably afraid someone could hear his shaky breaths otherwise.

Ciara ran through the worst-case scenarios in her head as the steps came closer and closer. She could imagine the torn-up corpses they might find. She felt sickened by the thought, but she didn't let it affect her.

In her work mode, she didn't have room for feelings and emotions. There would be time for that after the mission.

The footsteps were no more than two strides away. Ciara closed her eyes for a second and prayed before the person took another step closer.

Just then there was a loud thud—like someone dropping a body. It came from below them.

Perhaps someone from the team had found something.

The person around the corner took a step back. Then there were more hurried steps, heading away from the stairs.

Ciara reacted instantly. Moving around the corner, she tripped the first person. The second man turned around, and she punched him in the face with a right hook.

She was about to send the man down the corridor, using magic, when she saw his face.

"Henry?" she hissed.

"Ciara?" Henry's eyes widened. His voice was unusually nasal, because Ciara had broken his nose with her fist.

"What the hell?" Ciara hissed. "You're not supposed to be here."

She turned to see Shawn on the floor at her feet. "He's not alone," he mumbled, slowly getting up.

"You checked this floor?" Ciara asked in a whisper.

Before anyone could answer, someone opened the door Ciara was standing beside. A hand nearly grabbed Ciara by her arm, but she punched it away. She tried to hit the man in the face when his fingers curled around her wrist.

"Wa—" Henry's nasal voice was cut short by a deeper voice.

"Ciara?"

Her eyes widened as he stepped closer, still holding onto her wrist. "Liam?" she hissed.

She turned to look at Henry and Shawn. She couldn't believe what a bunch of idiots they were.

"Yes, we checked this floor," Shawn said, rubbing his cheek, which was likely going to bruise.

Liam glanced at Shawn and released his grip on Ciara's wrist.

"Bill and Theresa, it's fine," Ciara said, still keeping her voice low. Both Bill and Theresa walked into view, revealing themselves to Ciara's friends.

"We also checked downstairs already," Shawn said.

So the building was safe. But unfortunately that also meant no witch hunters.

Ciara wanted to punch a hole in the wall, but she saved that for later. "Kellan, Niles, Declan, and River, come here!"

"Hugo! Jenna!" Shawn called out.

Ciara turned to look down the corridor. It was dark, so she shone light with a snap of her fingers. "What the hell are you doing here?" she yelled when she saw that Jenna and Hugo were there, too.

Right then Kellan jogged up the stairs with Niles, Declan, and River right behind him. "What is this?" Kellan asked, moving to stand beside Ciara and looking at her friends.

"I'd like to know, too," Ciara said, turning to look at the four guys and Jenna. "Are you out of your minds? It could have been dangerous in here! What are you doing?"

She had been avoiding all her friends to avoid exposing

them to danger. Still, they were doing it themselves.

"Liam can explain," Jenna said and moved to stand next to her boyfriend. "I'll take Henry home before he leaves his blood all over the carpet." She took Henry's hand in hers, and they teleported away.

Liam sighed, looking only at Ciara. "We reformed the group."

"We are already working to find the witch hunters. What's the point?" Ciara asked, clenching her hands into fists.

"Doherty caught more of them when working off hours," Liam said, defending their cause.

Ciara shook her head in disbelief, her jaw tight. "You are so stupid."

She couldn't believe how naïve they were. Especially Liam. She had forced him out of her flat—nearly out of her life—to keep him safe.

"They could be helpful," Kellan said thoughtfully, tapping a finger on his cheek.

"See? Even your boyfriend agrees," Liam said defensively, gesturing towards Kellan. His eyes stayed on Ciara but they narrowed.

Ciara didn't bother to reply. Instead, she turned to face Kellan. "No, they can't." She wasn't willing to discuss the matter.

"You two are dating?" Shawn asked, pointing between Ciara and Kellan.

"Not now," Ciara snapped at Shawn, but she kept her gaze on Kellan.

"We need help," Kellan tried to whisper, but Ciara wasn't hearing his point.

She shook her head. "It's illegal."

"I reckon you were in the group before Doherty died," Kellan bit back. "Besides, I'm the head of the department, so I make the decisions."

"This is against everything we've been doing recently," Ciara argued through gritted teeth.

"We'll talk about this later," Kellan said, dismissing Ciara. He even turned to look at Liam instead of at her.

Ciara wanted to yell at Kellan, but instead she sighed in frustration and rushed past her team down the stairs. Before she reached the last step, she teleported to her office. It wasn't anyone's home, so she could teleport inside the building.

She wanted to throw something at the wall. Her hands were shaking from frustration. Just as she was about to wipe everything down from her desk, Kellan appeared in her office.

"You can't be serious!" she screamed and walked up to him, poking a finger at his chest.

His jaw clenched, but he remained calm. "Ciara—"

"I just avoided them for weeks to keep them safe! Now you want to throw them to the wolves as if nothing!" she continued to scream. "That makes absolutely no sense, Kellan! They're not trained for this!"

"They looked like they were doing just fine." Kellan's voice was calm, but that only added onto Ciara's anger.

"Doherty died on a mission like that!" Ciara yelled at him. When the words really hit her, the tears started flowing down her face. She rapidly wiped them off as if they were burning her.

She couldn't lose everyone. She would lose her mind if she did. She wanted it all to end. She wanted Doherty back. She wanted Theo back. And she wanted the witch hunters gone. Preferably dead.

"Ciara—" Kellan took a step closer, only for her to raise her hand at him.

"Don't!" She took a step back, keeping her distance. "Have you not lost enough to realise what it's like?"

She was shaking even more—both from crying and the anger.

"They are already in danger because of their own actions. Wouldn't it be safer if they had all the information we have?" Kellan tried to reason. "I know how you feel, especially after

372

everything you've been doing for them. But even you can't make them stop what they're doing. No matter how much you wish you could."

Ciara walked over to her office chair and sank down on it, defeated. "Someone is going to die," she said, her voice breaking.

"The witch hunters will," Kellan said determinedly.

Ciara sighed shakily. She had seen so many colleagues die, but she had never lost someone she knew from outside work. Except Theo. She couldn't imagine losing Henry or Liam—or anyone else.

But there was nothing she could do.

She was too tired to fight. "They'll only join missions when it's absolutely necessary. And if there's something I say we should keep from them, you listen to me. Okay?"

Kellan nodded, seeming to agree with Ciara's terms. "Okay."

"Thank you."

"You should go home and get some rest."

Ciara nodded.

"Good job out there." Kellan turned around and headed to the office door.

Ciara leaned against the back of the chair before her muscles tensed, realisation hitting her. "Wait!" she blurted, making Kellan stop.

"Yes?" he asked and turned around.

"What was the thud?"

"What thud?" Kellan asked, furrowing his eyebrows.

"It came from the ground floor before I tackled Shawn and punched Henry."

Kellan shook his head, confusion washing over his face. "I heard nothing."

"It came from below us, so—" Ciara's eyes widened. "The basement," she choked out. "Is the team still there? Or the group?"

"The rest of the team." Kellan's eyes widened, too. "I-I

think Liam and your friends left, but—"

Ciara ran to Kellan, grabbing him and teleporting them to the front of the manor. They ran in, heading for the stairs. The team was still gathered at the top, unaware of the danger.

"We need to—"

Ciara was cut off by the basement door slamming open.

47

S pells were shot at the team. Ciara blocked two spells and blew one back at the witch hunters.

More of them were running up from the basement. They outnumbered the team. The odds looked awful. Ciara couldn't even count the witch hunters, there were so many.

"We need to go!" Kellan screamed over the chaos, throwing curses at the witch hunters.

It was a light show of curses and other lethal spells.

A witch hunter ran for the stairs while another backed him up, throwing curses at Ciara. The first witch hunter—a strong-looking black-haired man—was getting closer.

And most of her team was just behind her.

She threw a curse at the witch hunter who was trying to distract her and jumped onto the railing. She took a quick look at the one throwing curses at her only to see the witch on the ground. Then she turned her attention to the man about to grab her by her ankle. She kicked him in the face, snatched a knife from her belt and slit his throat.

Blood coated her hands instantly. She sheathed the knife and turned to see a bright light heading her way. A curse.

She dodged it, and it hit the wall behind her, making the structure crumble. She had to use a speeding spell to move herself higher up to avoid the wall falling on her.

At least the stairs were blocked.

Someone grabbed Ciara by her throat. She tried to claw at the hands. The fingers tightened around her throat, and she kicked behind her between her attacker's legs. She spun around and touched the man with her hand. Using her magic, she hurt the man enough to keep him still while she cut his throat with her knife.

She looked around, trying to see her team members. More witch hunters were coming upstairs, using floating spells and such, and she couldn't see everyone from her team.

But she could see Theresa fighting another witch hunter. Ciara cast a spell at the witch hunter, throwing her against the wall *hard*.

Theresa turned to look at Ciara, nodding in appreciation.

But it wasn't over.

A witch hunter tried to grab Ciara, but she dodged him. She sent a curse his way, binding him to the wall. Then another curse, making him drown in a water bubble.

Ciara spotted a man trying to sneak on Bill. Fighting another witch hunter in combat, Bill was too busy to notice. Ciara grabbed her knife and hurried to the sneaking bastard. Before the man could turn around, she swung her knife, slitting his throat.

Bill punched the witch hunter he was fighting. Then again. And again.

Ciara walked past him and cut the man's throat, not blinking once.

Theresa ran to Ciara and Bill.

Just as a curse approached the trio, Ciara grabbed both Bill and Theresa and teleported to safety.

They appeared in the training hall. Ciara and Bill fell on their knees, exhausted. Theresa leaned against a pole, sighing. Somehow she still had enough strength to stay on her feet.

A second later Ciara looked up. Only the three of them were back.

She forced herself to stand up. "Where—"

Niles and River appeared right in front of Ciara, clinging onto one another for support.

Ciara sighed in relief. She nearly rushed to hug the two when finally Kellan and Declan appeared.

Both Kellan and Declan stumbled onto the floor. A crimson pool formed around Declan in an instant.

"We need a healer!" Kellan screamed, barely getting onto his knees as he helped Declan lay on his back. "Now!"

Ciara ran to help them. "What happened?"

Someone had cut Declan's abdomen, and he bled onto the floor. His shirt and skin were sticky from the blood.

"He was hit by a curse!"

Ciara fell on her knees beside Declan, putting pressure on the wound.

He wouldn't get treatment in any hospital in time. Even if they got him there fast, it would take too long for a healer to get to Declan and help him.

"I'll take him to a healer," Ciara said.

Kellan nodded as if giving permission.

Ciara grabbed Declan's hand and teleported them to the Rosslers' house. She forced herself up and threw Declan's arm around her neck, so she could drag him to the door. He could barely keep himself on his feet, even with the help.

"You'll be alright, Declan. You'll be fine."

Ciara knocked at the door rapidly, hoping it conveyed urgency to whoever heard. In an instant, Jenna opened the door.

"Please, tell me Mary is home," Ciara pleaded.

"Mary!" Jenna screamed and hurried to help Ciara carry

377

Declan inside.

"What's going on?" Liam ran out of the living room. Seeing the two women struggling, he hurried to help.

The three rushed Declan to the bedroom, and Mary ran in right after.

"H-he was hit by a curse. Can you do something?" Ciara asked Mary.

"Yes." Mary nodded, already beginning to work on Declan. "Everyone but Jenna, get out now."

Ciara was too shocked to move, so Liam had to pull her out of the room. He closed the door after them to give his mother and Jenna privacy and to make sure Ciara didn't see what was happening.

Then he turned to Ciara whose gaze was fixed on the closed bedroom door. "What happened?"

"Y-you heard that thud at the manor, right?" Ciara asked, her voice nearly breaking. Slowly, her gaze fell on Liam, her eyes looking straight into his hazel ones.

He nodded.

"I thought it was someone from my team. I-I asked Kellan about it, and he hadn't even heard it. We realised it came from the basement, so we went back, because my team was still in there." Ciara leaned against the wall. "They rushed out of the basement. It was a trap and—"

"*Who* rushed out of the basement?" Liam asked, stopping Ciara's rambling and reaching out to brush his fingers against Ciara's upper arm.

"The witch hunters," Ciara whispered. "I grabbed Bill and Theresa, and Niles and River were right behind us. B-but Kellan and Declan..." Ciara shuddered. "Kellan grabbed Declan, a-and he was bleeding so much and—"

"Was Kellan hurt?" Liam asked.

"No," Ciara said, shaking her head. "I need...I need to tell them where Declan is."

Liam placed his hand on Ciara's arm to soothe her. "Send Kellan the address."

Ciara nodded and grabbed her phone. She sent the address to Kellan. Blood on her hands smeared her phone screen, and she realised she was covered in blood.

Liam noticed it, too. He led her to the bathroom and washed her hands. When the blood was gone, he took her to the kitchen.

He made her sit down and poured her some tea that had already been brewed. He flicked his wand to make sure it was warm. Then he placed the cup on the table in front of Ciara. "It'll help."

The doorbell rang. Ciara was about to get up, but Liam pushed her back down. He went to the door, knowing it was Kellan.

"Come in."

Kellan stepped inside, and Liam closed the door behind him.

"Is this your house?" Kellan asked.

"My parents' house," Liam told. "My mother is a healer. She's treating Declan."

"I suspect it's better to let her work without disturbance."

Liam nodded. "I'd say so." Then he gestured to the kitchen. "Ciara's over there if you—"

"You should talk to her," Kellan said, giving Liam a look he didn't quite understand. Liam didn't have time to think about it for long, because Kellan continued. "Who is making the decisions in your group these days?"

"We make them together, but you'll probably want to talk to my father," Liam said. "He's there." He pointed towards the living room.

"Thanks," Kellan said, nodding, and left for the living room to talk with Ray.

Liam returned to the kitchen to see how Ciara was doing.

"Kellan came?" she asked him.

"Yes," Liam said, nodding. "Did the two of you break up or—"

"Can we talk about it another time?"

"Of course."

"What is going on here?"

Ciara and Liam turned to look at Henry who was standing in the kitchen doorway. He had been upstairs, trying to stop the blood flow from his nose.

Ciara grimaced. "I'm sorry about the punch."

"I would have done the same thing," Henry said dismissively.

"You sure you could punch like that?" Liam asked Henry, laughing.

Henry rolled his eyes. "Of co—"

The bedroom door swung open. "We need to take him to the hospital immediately!" Jenna exclaimed.

Everyone rushed to the bedroom door.

"I'll take him," Kellan said.

"I'll come with you," Mary insisted.

"Ciara, go home," Kellan said before he left with Mary and unconscious Declan.

"Is he allowed to boss you around even on your free time?" Henry asked Ciara when his mother and Kellan were gone.

Ciara shrugged.

"Who's the younger guy?" Jenna asked.

"Declan. He's in my team."

48

Shortly after Kellan and Mary left to the hospital with Declan, Liam took Ciara home. She had told him she would be fine on her own, but he insisted.

Liam helped Ciara take off her jacket and noticed the dry blood on it. "You should wash this."

Ciara sighed. "Blood?"

"Yes."

Ciara grabbed the jacket and went to the kitchen to throw it in the washing machine.

Liam followed her at first, but he stopped in the living room. He looked around to see how much the flat had changed. But he couldn't see any new furniture.

He walked to his old room. He was shocked to find it completely empty—just like he had left it when he had moved out.

"Liam?" Ciara called, walking out of the kitchen.

Liam turned to look at her. "You know, most people already have Christmas decorations in their homes, but you don't even have furniture yet." He walked back to Ciara, still looking around.

"I haven't been home much."

"So, you've been at Kellan's place," Liam said, thinking he knew what Ciara meant.

Ciara shook her head and chuckled, but her gaze lacked emotion. "I've never been at his place."

Liam furrowed his eyebrows. "Never?"

"Never."

"So, you, uh, broke up?" Liam stammered.

"We were never dating, to be honest. We just had to pretend for work."

Liam scrunched up his nose. "Seemed pretty real to me. Unless your job description includes having sex with your boss."

Ciara closed her eyes and hid her face in her hands to avoid eye contact with Liam. In her head, she was going through ways she could repay Kellan for the sex sound spell.

"So it wasn't just pretending?" Liam asked bitterly.

"No, it was just pretending." Ciara opened her eyes, looking anywhere but at Liam. "He, uh...it was some stupid spell Kellan came up with." She grimaced. "Guess it did its purpose, because we got you to move out. It was Bill's idea, actually. It was stupid, but it worked. I mean—"

"Wait," Liam said, stopping Ciara. "You wanted me to move out? Why didn't you just say so?"

"I didn't *want* you to move out. I *needed* you to move out," Ciara corrected. "There was a threat and—"

"What threat?"

"There was a note taped to the door. Someone threatened to hurt you," Ciara said, gesturing towards the flat door. "You were already here, and I saw it when I came home from work."

Liam paused, opening his mouth and then closing it before he found the words. "You pretended to date Kellan to make me move out?"

"It was Bill's idea."

"I thought you were Bill's boss."

"Kellan liked the idea."

"Well, no man in their right mind would say no to that," Liam said as if stating the obvious.

Ciara bit back her smile, her cheeks turning pink. "Right."

"So you've been working on the witch hunter case more than you let on."

"You can't lecture me about that after what you've been doing behind my back," Ciara said defensively. "For me, it's just my job."

"Not just me," Liam reminded.

Ciara crossed her arms. "Doesn't make it any better."

"Josh has been helping us."

"What?" Ciara exclaimed.

Liam had expected that. "He was helping you out originally, wasn't he?"

"How do you know that?"

"Just a lucky guess."

"So, for now, who are part of the reformed group?"

"Like I mentioned, Josh is helping us. Besides that, there's me, Henry, Jenna, Shawn, Hugo, my parents, a few of their friends, and Iris. Remember Hannah, Eric, or Tony? They are back in the group too."

Ciara flinched at Iris's name. "So I suppose every one of them is trustworthy."

Shawn and Hugo were new to the group, but Ciara could trust them. Eric was the one who had lost his brother, and Ciara could also remember Hannah and Tony. Iris was the only one she wasn't sure she could trust.

"They are," Liam assured.

Ciara nodded. "Anyway, you can go home or whatever. I need to write a report and who knows what else." Ciara froze and her brows furrowed, realising her laptop was in her office. "Or, actually, I'll do that tomorrow at the office."

"So you're okay?" Liam asked. "I can—"

"I'm fine. I'll hear about Declan's condition tomorrow and I'll call everyone in the morning."

"You're just worrying about everyone else and looking after them. That doesn't mean you're fine," Liam said.

"I'm fine. But I'll feel better once I hear about Declan."

Liam nodded. "Call me if you need anything. Anything at all."

"I'm fine."

"The offer still stands."

"Alright."

Liam and Ciara said their goodbyes, and Liam left.

Ciara took a deep breath, standing in her empty-feeling flat. She walked to the kitchen and grabbed a bottle from her liquor cabinet. Using magic by snapping her fingers, she popped the cork off. She raised the bottle to her lips and took her first sip—or rather, a big gulp.

On her way to the balcony, she snapped her fingers to float her cigarettes from the nearby table to her hand. Sitting down on the floor of her balcony, she set down the bottle beside her. She took one cigarette and placed it between her lips.

She used magic by snapping her fingers and lit up the cigarette. She inhaled, then took the cigarette away from her lips.

Blowing the smoke out, she reached for the bottle. The liquid warmed her throat.

It brought back memories of Doherty. She had once sworn him she would never develop the bad habits of her colleagues—drinking and smoking—but she couldn't keep that promise anymore.

She was losing her mind, and she had no other way to cope. She was losing her grip on herself. For the first time, she was slipping, letting people get too close, too fast and too easily.

She cared too much, and she was losing her focus on the thing that mattered the most—ending the witch hunters and their terrorist acts. Theo and Doherty deserved to be avenged.

Kellan had no right to choose her friends' fate, and she was livid. He would have felt the same in her position. But he was her superior, and she didn't have any power over him.

She blamed herself for what had happened to Declan. If she had paid more attention to the details at the manor, he wouldn't be at the hospital.

She didn't know if Declan was going to make it, and it was driving her insane.

All she wanted was to stop her friends—to keep them out of harm's way.

But she was powerless. The only way she could have stopped the others would have required her to use controlling curses on them, and that was out of question.

No matter how many times she inhaled with the cigarette between her lips, she didn't feel any better. No matter how big of a gulp she took from the bottle in her hand, it didn't help.

But she didn't know what else to do.

Ciara woke up to loud banging at her door. She sat up, only to realise she had fallen asleep on the kitchen floor.

The air was freezing cold even inside the flat. She quickly realised why. The balcony door had been open all night. She raised her hand and moved it from left to right, shutting the door lazily.

She stood up, shuddering from the cold.

The banging continued.

Ciara headed to the door but tripped over something on her way. Turning to look, she saw the whiskey bottle. "Fuck!" she cursed, watching the contents spill all over the kitchen floor.

She moved her hand in a wavelike motion, and the bottle was standing upright again with all the whiskey from the floor cleaned up. She grabbed the bottle and placed it on a kitchen counter before she continued her way to the door.

This time she made it and opened the door. But it was Kellan, and she wasn't in the mood to see him.

"See you on Monday," she said grumpily and tried to close the door, but Kellan didn't let her.

Instead, he let himself in, closing the door behind him. "You've been drinking."

"How about you don't judge my decisions, because I'm not allowed to judge yours?" Ciara crossed her arms and glared at her boss.

"Fair enough, I guess," Kellan said. "Anyway, Declan is recovering well. He woke up this morning."

Ciara frowned, even though she was delighted by the news. "What time is it?"

"Three in the afternoon."

Her eyes widened. "Fuck!"

"I've already dealt with Declan's sick leave and the report."

Ciara pressed her lips together. "Of course you did. Don't want me to report the fact you want to cooperate with an illegal organisation, huh?"

Kellan rolled his eyes. "You didn't answer any of my calls. Oh, and we're having a meeting with the team in thirty minutes."

"Thirty?" Ciara exclaimed. "I was just asleep!"

"More like passed out," Kellan said, giving her a long look.

Ciara shook her head disapprovingly. "I'll be ready in ten."

"Five."

"Eight," she said firmly before walking to the bathroom.

Kellan and Ciara were on time but were the last to arrive.

"Next time we have to be more thorough when we search

a building," Kellan said. "We could have had a chance if we had done so yesterday."

"There were too many of them," Ciara declared. She had learned Kellan hated to be disagreed with, but she didn't care anymore. He was mostly a good guy, but some of his crap couldn't be agreed with.

"They could have been using a multiplying spell to fool us," Kellan said defensively.

"It was a trap. It would have been impossible for us to have beat them last night," Ciara said, leaning back in her chair and playing with a pen. "They were waiting for us."

"Or your friends," Niles said.

"With whom Kellan wants to illegally cooperate," Ciara said, turning to glare at Kellan.

"Doherty did what they were doing. He died doing it," Kellan said firmly. "If this reformed group is his legacy, I'll take it."

"Doherty died *because* of that stupid group," Ciara disagreed, shaking her head.

Kellan sighed.

"We won't need their help," Bill tried to reassure them.

"Yes, we will," Kellan said. "The witch hunters are ahead of us, like Ciara pointed out. We'll need everyone who's willing to help."

"This is our job, not theirs. We have other teams," Ciara argued.

"Your friends are doing their part willingly," Kellan said. "And I will not stop someone who's willing to help. So if you don't want your friends to be involved, make them stop. I doubt you'll be able to do that, though."

Kellan was right, and Ciara hated him for it.

"If it makes you feel any better, they were doing great yesterday," Theresa said.

"They even got away unharmed, unlike our team," River said. "They've done these things before."

Ciara sighed, refusing to say anything.

"They're working with us for now." Kellan turned to look at Ciara. "Okay?"

The team nodded, even though Kellan was expecting Ciara's answer. But she stayed quiet.

"Okay?" Kellan asked again, raising his voice.

"I thought I didn't have a say in this," Ciara spat out.

"You don't."

"There you go," Ciara said, throwing her arms up. "But I'm not going to ask for their help. That's going to be on you."

Kellan nodded. "Very well then."

49

Ciara went straight home from the meeting. She shrugged off her coat but didn't bother hanging it. Kicking off her shoes along the way, she walked to her bedroom. She went straight to bed to warm up under the duvet, because it was still freezing cold.

Just when she was comfortably snuggled inside the duvet, her phone beeped. She grabbed it from her bedside table. Seeing Liam's name on the screen, she opened the message.

Do you think we could go to Ollie's Pub for drinks tonight? Let's say at 7? It's the one I got wasted at when you and Jesse came to the rescue.

Ciara had been planning to stay in bed for the rest of the day. She was still hungover, and it was too cold to do anything in her flat.

But she was willing to change plans for Liam.

Meet you there at 7!

Ciara sent the message, and she didn't have to wait long to hear from Liam.

Great!

She jumped up from the bed and hurried to get ready. She wasn't wearing any makeup, and she needed to change her clothes.

🍁🍁🍁

Ciara was ready to leave at half past six. Her jumper warmed her even in the cool flat. Her trousers hugged the curve of her bottom nicely, and her boots looked fabulous.

She was about to walk out of her bedroom when she realised her bracelet was on the bedside table. She pondered if she should wear it.

Liam had only asked to meet her as friends, no matter what his actual feelings for her were. Even if there was a hidden meaning behind the bracelet, she wasn't sure if she wanted to find out yet.

Still, she wore the bracelet. But she hid it under her jumper's sleeve.

On her way out, she grabbed her coat from the floor and threw it on, then locked the door and left.

She didn't walk to the pub. Instead, she used magic to teleport nearby. Otherwise she would have been late.

It wasn't seven yet when Ciara made it to a spot near the pub. It was more remote, so non-magic humans didn't see her when she appeared out of nowhere.

Ciara walked the rest of the way. Her hand was on the door handle when she halted.

She could see Liam through the window. He was already sitting at the bar.

But he wasn't alone. Iris was sitting next to him, and they

were laughing together. The scene looked cut straight from a romantic comedy, and it made Ciara's stomach twist.

Something invisible tightened around her chest. She was no longer excited about spending time with Liam. It would be the three of them—not just her and Liam.

It was enough of a confirmation for Ciara. The two were a couple again. Perhaps Liam had even invited her to tell about their reaffirmed wedding.

Ciara hadn't expected Liam to ask her out on a romantic date, but seeing him and Iris together hurt. Her heart ached as if someone was carving it with a knife.

She turned around and walked away. She was acting like a ridiculous teenager with a stupid crush on a guy who liked someone else, but she didn't care.

It had already been a bad day, and it was only getting worse. Ciara couldn't have made herself act happy, and she didn't want to walk in there and make a fool of herself.

She messaged him an apology, telling him she couldn't make it because of a sudden flu. Then she prayed he wouldn't be angry about it—even though she wasn't sure he even cared.

Ciara teleported to the first place she could think of.

It wasn't her flat. She had hated the flat ever since Liam had moved out. It was too big for her to live there on her own.

The place she had thought of was a beach.

It was ridiculous. She and Liam had gone there when he had first visited England since he had moved to Peru. It had been their first official date.

The beach looked different. Last time, it had been summer. In the winter, freezing wind blew across the beach. Ciara had to use a heating spell, despite her thick coat.

She sat down onto the sand, for once not caring if her clothes got dirty.

There was one place she would have preferred over the beach—Theo's grave. But it was an ocean and a continent away, and she wasn't strong enough to teleport that far. The longer the distance, the more exhausting the teleportation was. And teleporting across a continent or across the Atlantic was simply impossible.

She grabbed her phone from her pocket. There was already a message from Liam, but she swiped it away without reading it.

She had never felt so alone.

She had talked to Liam about a lot of things when they had lived together, but she couldn't confide in him anymore. He made her feel the way she used to, even if he didn't know that.

She couldn't call Henry either. Not to talk about Liam. He would eventually mention it to his brother.

Ciara couldn't call Jenna either, because she couldn't risk Henry hearing. She also didn't trust Jenna not to tell Henry.

The downside of her best friend being her ex-boyfriend's brother. It was no surprise Henry had felt shut out when she and Liam had been dating. But she had never realised it. Not back then.

Evie and Mia were out of question, too. Evie and Ciara hadn't talked in a while, and Mia loved gossip.

As for Jesse, Ciara hadn't talked with him since she went back to work. He was keeping distance from her, and she had no idea why.

Ciara had never missed her own mother so much. She was dying to call her, but she couldn't risk her wellbeing like that. Her mother was the only person she could still keep safe.

It was nearing eight in England, and Ciara was still staring at her phone screen. As she noticed the time, she realised it was nearing noon in Vancouver.

She hadn't talked to Estella—Theo's mother—in a long while. But she didn't know who else to call, so she dialled her number.

It took a while before Ciara heard the first beep. By then

she already regretted calling Estella.

After the second beep, she wondered if Theo's mother would even pick up.

Just as she was about to tap the red phone icon, Estella picked up. "Ciara, hi!"

"Hi." Ciara hadn't realised she had been crying until her voice broke. She was shaking, and her cheeks were wet from the tears.

"What's wrong, dear?" Estella asked, her voice rising with worry.

"I...I'm sorry for bothering you."

"Nonsense," Estella scoffed. "I told you to call me if you ever wanted to. It's great to hear from you. But I can tell something is wrong right now."

"I just...I fear I made a mistake by moving here," Ciara said shakily.

"What makes you say that?"

Ciara laughed humourlessly. "It's stupid."

"It's not stupid if it makes you cry. Now, tell me."

Ciara hugged her knees with her other arm. Even with the warming spell, she felt cold. "I told you about Liam last time, remember?"

"Yes."

"I think my feelings for him are back. Or I-I know they are. At first, I refused to get my hopes up, but then his fiancée cheated on him and they broke up. He...he moved in with me for a little while after the break-up and I...I..." Ciara stayed silent, fighting back the sobs. It was ridiculous to cry over Liam and Iris's newfound relationship. It shouldn't have come as a surprise.

And out of all people, Ciara was crying about it to the mother of her deceased fiancé.

"What did he do?"

"I think they're back together. Liam and his ex-fiancée. Or fiancée now," Ciara said, and her voice broke again. "I feel so stupid! I don't know if I should even be over Theo yet

393

and—"

Estella shushed Ciara. "There's nothing stupid about love. Don't you dare think your feelings are ridiculous. And as for Theo, I'd be worried if you weren't moving on. He'd want you to move on."

"I just feel so alone here," Ciara said, swallowing down her tears. "I don't know what's wrong with me. I keep snapping at people. I-I cried in front of my boss and—"

Estella shushed Ciara again. "You're stressed."

"I...went back to work."

"You're still trying to find the rest of the witch hunters, aren't you?"

"Yes."

"It's no wonder you're stressed," Estella said. "It'd make anyone stressed with your experience. And yes, I heard about Doherty. I'm so sorry you had to go through that."

Ciara shuddered. "I just want this all to be over."

"Oh, Ciara! If I were there, I'd give you a hug."

That made Ciara smile briefly, but the tears were still streaming down her cheeks.

"I know you feel weak right now, but being sad doesn't make you weak. It shows you care."

Ciara gritted her teeth. "Caring as a hit witch isn't an option."

Estella sighed. "You're being too hard on yourself. And I'm sure you're not as alone as you feel. If you spoke to your friends about this—"

"They all know Liam too well."

"Then you must call me every time you need someone to talk to about this."

"I'm sorry I haven't called you often enough," Ciara apologised guiltily.

"It's alright. But it's nice to know you haven't forgotten about me."

"That could never happen."

"Good," Estella said. "Now, tell me about this boy who

broke your heart again."

Ciara looked at the crashing waves and sighed. "It was just a stupid misunderstanding. He gave me a love bracelet for my birthday. I didn't even realise it at first, but then someone pointed it out to me."

"He gave you a love bracelet?"

"Yes."

"Is the gem still attached?"

"Y—" Ciara placed her phone down and put it on speaker. She pulled her sleeve up to see the bracelet. She touched the gem, and it instantly shattered into tiny pieces in her hands. "N-not anymore."

"Oh."

"What does that mean? I didn't even know love bracelets did that."

"I've heard the gem breaks if your heart breaks."

"Wonderful," Ciara said, sarcastically. "A broken heart wasn't enough, so now I have a broken bracelet."

50

Ciara finished the phone call with Estella around eleven. It took her a little longer to leave the beach, because she sat there alone for a few minutes. Once she had fixed her makeup, she headed home.

It was right before midnight when she walked up the stairs to her flat. She was searching for her keys from her coat's pocket. When she found them and pulled them out, she looked up.

Liam was sitting on the floor beside her flat door. "Ciara." He stood up.

Ciara frowned. "What are you doing here?" She hadn't expected to find Liam at her door. She had been planning to just go to sleep.

His frown matched hers. "I came here after I got your message. I thought I'd come check on you, but you weren't home."

"You've been here the whole time?" Ciara moved to open her flat's door. She didn't even glance at Liam while doing so—too afraid to meet his gaze.

"I left for a little while, but then I came back." Liam's gaze was fixed on Ciara, but her eyes were solely focused on the doorknob.

"Oh." She turned the key in the lock until it clicked.

"Look, I was worried. Where were you?"

"I took a walk," Ciara lied, casting her gaze down. She let Liam in and then stepped inside, closing the door.

Liam crossed his arms. "Did you walk a marathon?"

"No. I was on the phone with someone."

"Did you notice any of the messages I left? Or any of my calls?" Liam's voice held a hint of accusation.

Ciara could feel his eyes on her, but she didn't meet his gaze. "No. Sorry." She shrugged off her coat and hung it. "But as you can see, I'm fine."

"Why are you trying to avoid me?" Liam asked, exasperated.

"I'm not," Ciara lied.

"Why would you cancel our plans and say you're sick then?" Liam sighed in frustration. "Did you go after the witch hunters alone?"

Ciara rolled her eyes. "No."

She walked to the kitchen, thinking about getting a glass of water. Liam followed her. She spotted the whiskey bottle on the kitchen counter and shoved it back in her liquor cabinet.

"You've even forgotten your jacket in the washing machine," Liam said and pursed his lips together. He clearly hadn't missed the half-drunk whiskey bottle, either.

Ciara had completely forgotten about the stupid jacket, and it was probably ruined already. It had been wet in the washing machine for a day. In her mind, she cursed herself, but she didn't let it show.

"I had to hurry to work, so I forgot it," she said dismissively.

"What's wrong?" Liam took a step closer to Ciara. "You won't even look at me, and I can tell you're trying to get rid of me."

Ciara's shoulders tensed. "Maybe I just want to be alone," she said, trying to appear indifferent.

"I know it's not that!" Liam snapped, throwing his arms up in frustration. "Something is wrong. Are you still angry about the whole reforming thing?"

"Of course I'm angry about that!" Ciara snapped back, gripping the edge of the kitchen counter.

"And that's why you're avoiding me? Yet first you agreed to see me."

"Why does it matter so much?" Ciara huffed out.

"Because I absolutely hate that you're avoiding me," Liam confessed desperately, taking another step closer to Ciara.

She felt bad for making him feel that way. Still, she couldn't tell him that he had broken her heart.

"Look, I'm sorry. I just had the whole evening planned and—"

"I'm so sorry I ruined your and Iris's announcement then," Ciara huffed, annoyed.

"My and..." Liam tilted his head. "What?" he asked, his voice rising a little. "What does Iris have to do with any of this?"

Ciara sighed sharply. She really needed a cigarette. But she would have to walk past Liam to get to the balcony, and he would try to stop her.

"She's your girlfriend. Or fiancée. I don't know how it works in your situation." Her already broken heart was beating fast with anxiety.

"What?" Liam exclaimed. "Why would you think that?"

"It's obvious." Ciara rolled her eyes. She couldn't believe Liam was acting so clueless.

"How is it obvious? Because I'm not with her!" Liam said, raising his voice.

"If you say so. But even if so, I don't see what's the problem. I'm sure you had a nice evening with her." Ciara's voice was bitter, but at least she finally turned to look at

Liam.

Liam furrowed his eyebrows and gaped at Ciara. "Why do you think Iris would have been there?"

"Now you're just playing dumb," Ciara accused sharply. "I saw her!"

"What?" Liam exclaimed. "You didn't even show up!"

"I was at the door, but then I changed my mind," Ciara admitted, tapping her foot impatiently. She needed to get past Liam to get to the balcony for that cigarette.

"I don't get..." Liam frowned, trying to look for words. "Why would you..." Liam shook his head, and that was when his gaze settled on the bracelet on Ciara's wrist. "It's broken." Both his voice and his eyes softened.

Ciara's eyes widened, realising the bracelet wasn't hidden under her sleeve anymore.

"Who were you with? W-why would it break like that? They don't break unless..." Liam didn't finish the sentence, but the concern on his face grew.

"You knew it was a love bracelet?" Ciara asked breathlessly, staring at Liam.

If he knows, does that mean...

"Of course I knew," he said, scratching the back of his neck. "You were with Kellan?"

Like Kellan had mentioned to Ciara, Liam had seen it glow bright red when Kellan had been around.

"No," Ciara said and walked past Liam. She made her way to the little table next to the balcony door where her cigarettes were.

Ciara reached out to grab the pack, but Liam took her hand into his to stop her.

"Please, don't," he pleaded and grabbed her other hand, too.

Ciara wanted to take the cigarette pack, but she couldn't. Not because of Liam's hold—which she could have easily freed herself from—but because she was too flustered by how close he was standing.

"Please, tell me what's wrong?" Liam pleaded.

Ciara took a deep breath. "I don't want to talk about it. Okay?"

"Can you at least tell me where you were?" Liam's voice softened, becoming soothing.

"I was outside." She would never tell him where she had been exactly. It would have been too humiliating. "I was, uh, on the phone with Estella."

"Estella?"

"Theo's mother."

Liam paused. "H-how is she?"

The two of them had rarely talked about Theo. And somehow neither of them seemed to want to change that.

"She's fine. I should call her more often."

"How is she spending Christmas?" Liam asked.

"With her friend's family."

"What about you?"

"I don't know."

"I'm going to my parents' place. Come with me."

Ciara hesitated. "Are you sure?"

"Yes."

She had no Christmas plans, and she had spent the holidays at the Rosslers' house in the past. Henry, Jenna, and the other Rosslers would be there too.

Taking a deep breath, Ciara said, "Okay."

"Did you see Kellan today?"

"He picked me up for work. We had some stupid meeting."

"So he's more than just your boss," he said, his voice shaky.

"A friend, maybe." Ciara swallowed, afraid to say her next words out loud. But she knew that if she didn't say them right then and there, she'd never work up the courage to say them. "The gem breaking had nothing to do with him," she said breathlessly, hoping Liam knew what that meant.

Liam went silent. "So..." He struggled to find his voice. "So it wasn't glowing because of him."

"No."

There it was. Her confession. He finally knew, and all he did was let go of her hand.

She was about to apologise for ruining everything, but Liam pivoted her around to face him. Her hand flew against his chest, and she stumbled onto him. Her breath hitched from the sudden closeness.

He reached out his hand to cup her face, and her heart fluttered in her chest. His fingers brushed down her cheek, leaving her skin tingling, and they stopped below her jawline. He gently raised her chin, so she finally met his gaze.

She could have sworn his breath hitched when she gazed into those hazel eyes she had missed for so long.

"C-can I stay over tonight?" His voice was husky, hooking her in.

Ciara's heart thundered in her chest, and she lost her voice for a second. She knew what the question meant—the hidden meaning behind it. "Y-yes."

His breathing was heavy—even shaky—and hers matched it.

His eyes flickered between her eyes and lips as he slowly wrapped his left arm around her waist. His eyes flickered back to her eyes as if asking for permission—asking if he could go on.

His gaze fell back down on her lips, and he brought his face closer to hers. His warm, uneven breaths hit her skin, sending pleasant sparks throughout her body.

He looked back up into her eyes, asking for permission one last time. She nodded slightly, and her heart went wild.

She wanted his lips on hers. No, she needed them. She was done waiting and...

His right hand slid to the back of her head, entangled in her hair, and he leaned in, his lips finding their way to hers.

Finally.

The kiss was tender. Gentle.

Ciara's hands gripped his shirt possessively, pulling him

harder against her. The gentleness was gone.

Liam's lips were rough from the cold winter weather, and his stubble scratched Ciara's skin. And she was hooked in the eager kiss.

His hand dropped from her hair. She nearly pulled away, dissatisfied with the loss of contact, but then she heard her cigarette pack being shoved off the table behind her. His hands travelled under her thighs, and he hoisted her onto the table, not breaking the kiss.

His hands moved with a will of their own, sliding up her thighs to tug at the hem of her jumper. He broke the kiss, staring deep into her eyes, and pulled the restricting piece of clothing off her. The second the jumper hit the floor, Liam's lips were already back to exploring Ciara's lips, hungry and demanding.

She wrapped her arms around his neck, entangling her hands in his hair. She had wanted to run her hands through his hair for *so long*. And it was every bit as good as she had imagined.

They kicked off their shoes and socks in a hurry, their hands dancing on each other's skin. He teased her, tugging at the hem of her top.

She grinned against his lips and unbuckled his belt. His shirt went off, flying, and hers was next.

His muscular arms wrapped around her, and he pulled her off the table against his chest, their half-bare bodies touching. Ciara's knees went weak, but his powerful arms kept her where she was.

He pulled her to the bedroom eagerly. They hit every piece of furniture and wall possible on their way, throwing off the rest of their clothes.

By the time her back hit the soft mattress, his lips had found their way to her neck and from there continued exploring every inch of her skin. "Ciara." His voice was heavy and warm against her tingling skin.

"Liam," she moaned.

Ciara looked around, trying to spot the person she was most excited to see. But she couldn't see Liam anywhere.

"Ciara!" Henry called out, rushing over to her. "He's leaving for Peru."

"I know he is. Wait..." Ciara's eyes widened. "Right now?"

Henry only had time to nod before Ciara rushed through the crowds. She ran out of the tournament area, forgetting all about the cheers and her victory.

For a moment, she thought she was too late, but then she spotted him walking away.

"Liam!"

He stopped dead and spun around. "Ciara?" he said, seeing the girl run to him. "What are you doing? You just won. You should be celeb—"

Ciara cut him off by wrapping her arms around his neck and pulling his lips to hers. For a moment, he stood frozen. When he finally came to his senses, realising his long-time crush was kissing him, he put his arms around her waist and pulled her closer.

The kiss was sweet and short, even though it felt like an eternity for both of them. They were out of breath from excitement when they pulled away.

"I know things have been...weird between us. And I know you'll be in Peru soon, so I thought I'd...I had to do that before it was too late," Ciara rambled.

Liam smiled. He reached to touch her face and ran his thumb over her lips to make her stop talking. "I'm glad you did."

Relief washed over Ciara, and she couldn't help but smile.

"I-I don't know how, but I want to make this work," Liam said, moving a few strands of hair behind Ciara's ear. "I-I can come visit as often as possible and—"

Ciara smiled and pecked Liam's lips. "So you want to make this official?"

"A thousand times, yes."

51

S oft fingers brushed against Ciara's bare skin, and her eyes fluttered open. It was already bright outside, meaning she had slept in.

It was no surprise after the previous night. The mere memory of it set Ciara's heart ablaze.

"Morning." Husky, deep, morning voice. Ciara smiled, hearing it.

She rolled onto her back, eager to see Liam and unable to control her smile. "Morning."

His smile matched hers, and it was the best view she had woken up to in a very long time.

"Have you been up for long?" She eyed his long, brown hair, remembering how soft it had felt between her fingers.

"A little while," Liam admitted.

Ciara turned to lie on her right side, properly facing Liam. They were both smiling like lovesick puppies, replaying the night's events in their heads.

Ciara's gaze travelled from Liam's eyes to his lips. She

was about to suggest another kiss, but then her eyes settled on something on the bedside table behind him. "Where did that come from?"

Liam's eyes widened when he realised what she was talking about. He reached to grab the sketchbook, but Ciara was faster. She snapped her fingers, and the sketchbook appeared in her hands.

"That's cheating," Liam complained.

She opened the sketchbook where there was a pencil as a bookmark, revealing a drawing. A drawing of her sleeping form with the duvet covering just the right places.

"You still draw?" Ciara asked, mesmerised by the work of art.

"Sometimes," Liam said sheepishly, biting his lip.

Ciara flipped to the previous page as fast as she could, knowing Liam wouldn't let her see more drawings if it was up to him.

"Do—" He was too late; she had already seen the drawing.

Another drawing of her. An enchanted one. It was moving like a non-magical video. In it, she was talking and smiling. She assumed it was from her housewarming party from the end of October.

"How long have you been drawing these for?" Ciara asked, entranced.

Liam snatched the sketchbook from her hands. "For a while."

Ciara grinned, turning to face Liam. "So are there more drawings of me?"

His cheeks turned a light shade of pink. "Yes."

"Let me see."

"Not now."

Ciara sighed theatrically. "Fine." She sat up, not caring the duvet was no longer covering her.

"Where are you going?" Liam asked, struggling to keep his gaze from travelling down. Without looking away, he placed the sketchbook back on the bedside table.

"I'm going to take a shower," Ciara said and stood up. "Wanna join?"

"Yes!"

Ciara dried her hair with a hairdryer. Liam had already gone to make breakfast.

Once Ciara finished drying her hair, she sneaked into her room to get dressed and then tiptoed to the kitchen doorway. She leaned against the doorframe, admiring the view of Liam making pancakes.

"What's the occasion?" she asked, grinning.

Liam turned to look at her, not hiding his wandering eyes, and chuckled. "I got to wake up next to you."

"Why didn't I get pancakes the last time that happened?" Ciara teased, walking over to where Liam was and jumping to sit on the kitchen counter.

"That was different."

"You left quietly in the morning."

"I didn't know how you would have felt waking up next to me after that night," Liam said, his eyes flickering between the pancakes and Ciara.

She wouldn't have minded. In fact, quite the opposite. "I wouldn't have been disappointed, if that's what you're wondering."

Liam's crooked grin gave away his amusement. He continued to cook the pancakes, stealing glances at Ciara.

Ciara was biting her lip to contain her smile. She hadn't felt so happy in a long time.

Liam poured uncooked batter onto the pan and moved to stand between Ciara's legs that were hanging off the edge of the kitchen counter. He pushed her hair from her shoulder and placed a soft kiss on the side of her neck. She shivered from the feeling of his breath on her skin.

Liam noticed, and he smiled against her skin. He placed one more lingering kiss on the same spot before he pulled away, facing Ciara. "I'm glad you let me stay overnight."

Ciara bit her lip. "Me too."

Turning to check on the pancake on the pan, he noticed Ciara still had the broken bracelet on her left wrist. He moved his fingers over it at first, tracing it. Then he gripped at it and snapped it.

"Liam!" Ciara gasped, wide-eyed.

He placed a kiss on her lips to silence her. Pulling away, he said, "I'm buying you a new one."

"So you can be jealous again when I happen to be in the same place with you and some other guy, huh?" Ciara teased.

Liam rolled his eyes and threw the bracelet into the rubbish bin. "My plan didn't exactly work out."

"But weren't the results *eventually* what you had hoped for?"

Liam smiled widely. "After a few setbacks, yes."

Ciara hummed in agreement.

Liam flipped the pancake and turned to look at Ciara again. "I'm glad you're not into Kellan after all."

Ciara scrunched up her nose. "He's too old for my taste."

"And way too good-looking, too?" Liam asked, not buying it. "Have you seen the guy?"

"I have, one too many times," Ciara assured him. "And I'm not one bit attracted to him."

Liam's face turned more serious. "Did you argue with him or something?"

"In a way, I guess." Ciara shrugged. "I'm sure there will be a meeting handling it on Monday."

"And are you still angry with me?" Liam asked and moved to stand between her legs again.

Ciara sighed, looking straight into his eyes. She could only hope he saw her point—saw how worried she was. "I hate that you reformed the group. It's dangerous."

"You put yourself in danger every day at work," Liam said, the look in his eyes mirroring Ciara's.

"But it's my job. It's different."

"How so?" Liam asked, raising his hand to brush the side of her face. "Because I worry about you every single day when you go to work."

"I have more experience."

"It doesn't make it any safer," Liam said with his worried gaze glued to her eyes.

But I would rather be the one in danger. "Fair enough."

"So are you ever going to furnish this flat like you were planning to?" Liam asked Ciara.

They were lying on her bed—this time clothed—with Liam's arm wrapped around Ciara.

Ciara placed her hand on his chest. "I don't know."

"You don't know?"

Ciara shrugged slightly. "I'm never home."

"Is this the moment you reveal you have a boyfriend after all?"

Ciara rolled her eyes. "I'm working, training, or getting drinks with the team all the time."

"And nothing else?" Liam asked.

"This flat is way too big for one person."

"I thought you liked this flat, because it was neither too small nor too big."

"I changed my mind."

"When?"

"After you moved out," Ciara admitted.

Liam recollected the other night when Ciara had told him about the threat. "So you didn't want me to move out?"

"I had to make you move out, because I thought that way you wouldn't be involved with the witch hunters through me, and therefore you'd be safe. Clearly, I was wrong. You're involved with the witch hunters anyway," Ciara said, huffing.

"Well, your plan was..." Liam paused, swallowing, "effective."

Ciara cringed, rolling onto her back. "Oh, my God," she

groaned. "It wasn't my plan. Bill came up with the whole dating thing, and Kellan...ugh..." Ciara hid her face in her hands.

Liam chuckled at her expression and gently peeled her hands off her face. "I'm glad it wasn't real."

"Me too!"

Liam grinned and placed a kiss on Ciara's forehead.

"Anyway, how do I not even have your new address yet?" Ciara asked, eager to move on from the topic.

Liam chuckled, scratching the back of his head. "Right."

Ciara turned to look at Liam, tilting her head. "Have you been keeping it from me on purpose?"

"Let me explain," Liam said. Ciara nodded, urging him to continue. So he did. "When I moved out, I thought you and Kellan were together. Dating." He scrunched his nose up from the mere thought. "I hated seeing you with him and even more so hearing—"

"Let's not talk about that!" Ciara pleaded.

"Anyway, I just wanted to move out as fast as I could. And I didn't actually find a flat. I, uh, lied about that." He scratched the back of his neck again. "Shawn's flat is too small. Same goes for Hugo's flat. Henry and Jenna, same thing. I also didn't want to move back to my parents' place, because Mum would have made a hassle out of it. Sure, she means well, but I wouldn't stand it for days, not to mention weeks."

"So are you living under a bridge or what?" She had no idea who else Liam could live with.

Liam chuckled, but it sounded nervous. "Iris and I sold our flat, and she already has a new one. I've been staying there."

Ciara frowned to hide how disheartened she was. "Okay, so..." She hesitated a moment. "You live with your ex-fiancée." Her frown deepened at her own words. "Who, might I add, cheated on you. But you're saying there's nothing going on between you and her?"

Liam looked into Ciara's eyes. "There is absolutely nothing going on between me and Iris."

Liam's words didn't convince Ciara, and he could see that.

"Honestly," he said, more serious. "I haven't forgotten that she cheated on me. I could never be with her after that, and I could never trust her in a relationship again."

"But you still have feelings for her."

"No, I don't," Liam said instantly.

"You were dating for over three years." Ciara sat up, because she no longer felt comfortable in Liam's arms. "You broke up less than three months ago. Not that long ago you were still crying over her."

"If you mean what happened after the housewarming party, that was like two months ago," Liam said in his defence.

"I doubt you're over the break-up yet."

Liam sat up, too. "Why would I be here if I wasn't? And how long did it take you to get over our break-up?"

Ciara sighed. "Are we having this conversation *again*?"

"A-again?"

"We had this conversation two months ago. Remember?"

"No, I don't remember." Liam shook his head. "After the housewarming party?"

Ciara nodded.

"I was drunk."

Ciara sighed, refusing to raise her gaze to Liam.

"Besides, I started dating Iris a month after you broke up with me."

"That's different. You already liked her before we broke up."

"I've had feelings for you since August."

This time Ciara turned to look at Liam in disbelief. "Great! So now I'm a home-wrecker." She stood up and walked out of the room.

"Ciara!" Liam exclaimed, running after her.

She went to grab her cigarettes. They were no longer on

the table, and she couldn't see them on the floor either.

She spun around to look at Liam. "What did you do to my cigarettes?"

"Ciara—"

"Just answer me!"

"I threw them away when you were in the shower," Liam said.

"I'm gonna go get new ones then."

Ciara headed for the flat door, but Liam stopped her midway by wrapping his arms around her.

"Let go of me!"

"No, Ciara. Wait," he said desperately. "Just let me explain everything to you. There are things you don't know!"

"So you've been sleeping with Iris post-break-up and now you needed some change?"

"I would never use you like that!"

"Yeah, well, I feel used!" Ciara snapped at him, pushing him away.

"Because you don't know everything yet!" Liam said, raising his voice.

"I feel like I don't want to know any more than I already do," Ciara huffed out, annoyed.

"Just listen. Please," Liam begged.

Ciara said nothing. She didn't even look at him.

"Before our break-up, I had to open a vault in Peru. There was an enchantment protecting it. The only way to get to the vault was to give up a memory. I had promised my boss I'd get that vault open, and I didn't think one memory could be worth so much. I could have chosen a memory, but because I couldn't pick one, I decided to give up any memory I had." Liam's words were hurried, scared Ciara would stop listening. "The vault cost me both you and our relationship."

Ciara turned to look up at Liam.

"It took the memory of the moment I first realised I *loved* you," Liam said. "I didn't even look twice at Iris before I lost that memory."

411

"Why didn't you just break up with me when you fell for Iris?"

"Because I felt like I owed you for making you wait for me for so long already. It wasn't like I didn't care about you at all, because I did. I just didn't love you."

Ciara didn't know what to say.

"My feelings for you had nothing to do with what happened between me and Iris," Liam swore. "I broke up with her because of the cheating."

"Which you've already forgiven."

"No, I haven't. I just don't want to fight with her, it's easier that way," Liam said. "And yes, I am staying with her right now, but that doesn't mean I would want to get back together with her. She was my absolute last option."

"Before me."

"Because I couldn't stand seeing you with Kellan, thinking you're in love with him!"

Ciara stared at the floor, refusing to meet Liam's eyes. She trusted Liam. He was telling her the truth. She just couldn't bear the overpowering jealousy gnawing at her heart. It was the kind of jealousy she had only felt once, and it had been over three and a half years since that time.

"Is it so hard to believe that I love you?" His words were a mix of desperation, pain, and longing.

And love.

But Ciara wasn't ready to fall back into his arms yet.

"So why was Iris at the pub last night?"

Liam looked Ciara in the eyes. "She was there to give me a pep talk." He grew nervous when she turned her gaze away again. "I was planning to spend a nice evening with you, a-and at the end of it, tell you how I feel until the next guy snatches you out of my reach again. I swear that's all—"

With two swift strides, Ciara was standing in front of Liam with her arms snaking around his neck. She had to tiptoe to lean in. It was a sweet kiss. She only let her lips linger on his long enough for him to register what was happening and wrap his arms around her waist.

"I'm sorry." She felt ridiculous for overreacting—for not listening in the first place. "I didn't know about the whole memory thing." She shook her head, still trying to process everything Liam had just told her. He had loved her for as long as he had had a memory of that love. "And I didn't know about your plan for yesterday. And I'm sorry for overreacting when you mentioned Iris. I mean, she drove me into moving to another continent and I—"

"You moved to America because of Iris?" Liam's eyes widened at the revelation, but he still didn't move his arms from around Ciara.

Ciara bit her lip and nodded. "Because of your relationship with her. But I already told you that when...you were drunk."

Liam blinked, staring at Ciara with his mouth open. It took him a moment to form any words. "You moved to America because of *that*?"

Ciara's hands slid down to his chest. "I didn't think I could face her. I didn't want to see you two together. She was the reason you didn't love me anymore, and why I broke up with you. Or so I thought anyway."

Liam blinked, looking at Ciara. "So it's my fault you're working as a hit witch?"

"That's a little far-fetched, but technically yes," Ciara said. "I didn't want to become a curse breaker, because that could have meant crossing paths with you. Then I was offered the job in Canada, and it wasn't a hard decision to make at the time."

Liam stared at Ciara for a moment before he pulled her tightly against his chest, hugging her. He buried his face in her hair, inhaling the scent of her caramel shampoo. "I'm sorry about everything. Both from years ago and today. In fact, I'm even sorry about throwing your cigarettes away."

Ciara slid her arms around Liam to hug him back. "I'm sorry, too." She bit her lip, having a hard time containing her smile. "And I don't think I'll need those cigarettes for much longer if you stick around."

Liam chuckled and pulled away enough to see Ciara's face. He smiled at her, and they stayed like that—in silence—gazing into each other's eyes.

It didn't last forever, and eventually Liam became serious again. "Can you believe I'm over Iris? Because I am. You would never be a rebound relationship."

"I believe that."

"Good."

Ciara smiled at Liam. "You know, I usually use cigarettes as stress relievers." Ciara nearly burst out laughing from Liam's confused expression. "But since I don't have them anymore..." she continued suggestively.

He caught onto what she was implying, smiling both with amusement and excitement. "I think I know exactly how to relieve stress," he said and pulled Ciara back to the bedroom.

52

O n Monday, Liam insisted on walking Ciara to her office. He had picked up some of his stuff from Iris's place the previous day, and he had stayed overnight.

"So this is it," Ciara said when they reached her office door.

"Aren't you going to invite me in?" Liam asked, smiling at Ciara. "Or wouldn't your boss like that?"

Ciara shook her head and rolled her eyes, while smiling. "Fine, come on in." She unlocked the door and opened it. "But just for a moment, because I have actual work to do."

Liam grinned as Ciara let him in. "Of course."

She showed Liam her office. He only stayed a few minutes before he had to leave, giving Ciara a goodbye kiss.

Ciara worked without distractions for nearly an hour before Kellan walked in.

"Kellan." Her jaw tightened. After all, she and Kellan

weren't on the best of terms.

Kellan shut the office door. "I'm sorry I was harsh on you," he said, not bothering with greetings.

"I overreacted," Ciara said dismissively. She was in a *much* better mood than she had been the previous week.

"Which is understandable. I literally asked you to put your friends in danger. Even though that same danger has already cost you a fiancé, a mentor, and who knows how many colleagues." Kellan shook his head. "I had no right to do that."

The mention of Theo made Ciara's eyes burn. She cleared her throat, forcing words out. "Still, you were right. They won't stop, no matter what we say or do. We'd have to arrest them to make them stop."

Kellan nodded.

"I'm sorry for the way I acted."

"It's okay."

The two of them ended up coming to an agreement. They were going to ask for the reformed group's help when there was no other choice. Ciara knew it would be more often than she liked, but she had to accept it.

It turned out to be one of the first days Ciara didn't work overtime. She went home with Liam when he got off work.

Just like the day before, they eventually ended up cuddling in her bed.

"So do you think we should tell people?" Ciara asked. The thought had been bugging her since the morning.

"That we're together?"

"Yes."

"Why wouldn't we tell people about it?" Liam asked.

"You were originally supposed to marry Iris like last week."

Liam looked down into Ciara's eyes. "Originally, yes. But you're forgetting that I broke up with her three months ago.

She's in the past."

"You're not afraid of what people will think?"

Liam shook his head and smiled at Ciara. "Henry will probably be excited. Jenna, too. And so will Gabe, Polly, and Poppy. I mean, it'll be hard handling their excitement, but I think it'll be worth it." Liam grinned, and Ciara seemed to relax at his words. "Shawn will tell us he knew this would happen. Hugo will probably agree with him."

"And what about your mother?" For Ciara, Mary's opinion was everything.

"She adores you."

"But—"

"Are you worried Mum will think differently of you now that we're dating?" Amusement twinkled in Liam's eyes, and he chuckled. "I know she won't. She'll be over the moon when she hears. So will Dad."

Ciara bit her lip, still uncertain. "If you say so."

"I know so. And you know it, too. We've dated before, remember?" Liam raised an eyebrow at Ciara, smiling at her.

"How could I ever forget the best time of my life," Ciara flirted.

Liam grinned and placed a kiss on her lips. "So do *you* think we should tell everyone?"

"It'll be Christmas Day in a week. I suppose they'll find out eventually, anyway."

"We could surprise them for Christmas," Liam suggested.

"Henry will kill us if we keep this from him for a week."

Liam shrugged as if he didn't care. "He'll get over it."

"Well, if he asks, I'm going to tell him this was your idea."

Chuckling, Liam nodded. "Alright."

"I see you and Liam...made up," Bill teased Ciara at work on Tuesday. He had seen Liam walk Ciara to her office door. He had even been there to witness the goodbye kiss.

Ciara tried to contain her smile. "You could say that."

Bill grinned. "So, happily ever after, is it?"

Ciara rolled her eyes and cast a few spells at Bill.

He blocked each one of them. "I ship it."

"Clearly."

Bill tilted his head as if he were observing Ciara. "Why are you so tense?"

Ciara's face was twisted into a semi-permanent frown, and her stance was unusually tense.

She sighed. "I'm waiting for a call. We might have a new lead."

"Ah. That explains a lot."

The pair continued to train. It didn't ease Ciara's mind, though. For once, she dreaded the idea of having to work overtime.

She was used to working extra time, and it was part of the job. But she wanted to spend time with Liam during her time off.

Just as Bill and Ciara were about to finish for the day, her phone rang. As she had hoped, it was Josh with new information about the witch hunters.

Ciara was forced to inform Liam she would have to work overtime. Bill stayed with Ciara, but the rest of the team had already gone home.

They were working in the meeting room. She had her laptop open, and they were going through the places where witch hunters had possibly been spotted.

"They were seen here," Ciara said, scrolling through a restaurant website until she found the exact address. She pressed the map to see the location.

When she did, she gasped.

"That's right next to your flat," Bill realised.

Ciara read through a few lines on the file Josh had sent her. "This was just hours ago!"

"They know where you live. But we already knew that."

Ciara nodded. "They're trying to scare me."

"What are you going to do?"

"Change my plans on asking Liam to move back in with me."

"Doesn't he have a new flat? Maybe you should move in with him temporarily. Even if they're just trying to scare you, this is a serious threat." He pointed at the laptop screen.

"He's staying with his ex, so that's out of question."

Bill's eyes widened. "His ex?"

Ciara nodded.

"So, a hotel? You'd get the expenses covered by work."

Ciara leaned back in her chair and turned to look at Bill. "The least of my worries right now is money."

"Well, I don't think it's safe for you to stay at home."

Ciara sighed, looking between Bill and her laptop. "You might be right."

"The problem is that most hotels are booked for the holidays."

"I know," Ciara sighed. "So I'll probably live in my office and—"

"No," Bill said, cutting her off. "We'll figure something out."

"Can you call Kellan and ask him to come here? Oh, and also tell the team that there's new information, but we'll handle it," Ciara said. "I need to call Liam to tell him to stay away from my flat."

"Of course," Bill said, grabbing his phone from the table. He walked out of the room to give both himself and Ciara some privacy.

Ciara dialled Liam's number and held the phone to her ear. She didn't have to wait long for him to pick up.

"Hey. Did you get off work already? I thought you—"

"You can't go anywhere near my flat, okay?" Ciara said hurriedly. Her mind was already swarming with the worst scenarios.

"What is going on?" Liam asked, worried.

"I'm not sure yet. Just promise you won't go to my flat or anywhere near it, okay?"

"You have to tell me why."

Ciara sighed. "The witch hunters have been seen there. We already know that they know where I live, so it's unlikely to be a coincidence. There are shield and protection enchantments on my flat. They'll block anyone I wouldn't let in."

Liam went silent. "Are you sure you wouldn't let in any of the witch hunters?"

"I wouldn't let in strangers. Not with everything going on."

"R-right."

"I'll have to figure out where to stay. The hotels are booked for the holidays—"

"We can stay at my parents' place," Liam said. "In my old room."

"Are you sure?" Ciara asked hesitantly. "Because it wouldn't be fair to bother your parents."

"We're spending Christmas there, anyway. Besides, Mum will be excited to have us over for a little longer."

"You need to ask her first."

"And when she says yes, you'll agree, eh?"

"Yes."

"I'll call her in a minute," Liam said. "But what are you going to do now?"

"I need to talk to Kellan. We might go check my flat."

"I should come, too."

"No," Ciara blurted.

"Ciara—"

"Please, don't," she pleaded. "There's probably nothing in there, and I'll just grab my stuff."

"And if there is—"

"We'll be careful," Ciara assured. "Owen can keep in contact with us, so he'll inform you if something goes wrong."

"Ciara."

She could hear the worry and hesitation in his voice, and warmth filled her chest.

"My flat is protected, so I doubt we'll run into anyone. And I know I'll be able to concentrate better without you there."

"I'll go crazy, not knowing if you're safe or not."

"It'll be over in minutes."

"Ciara—"

"Please, Liam."

Ciara heard him cursing under his breath. "Alright. Just meet me right after, okay?" he said.

"Of course."

"At my parents' place."

"First, call your mother. Then send me a text if she says we can stay there. Okay?"

"I will."

"I love you. Bye." Her eyes widened, realising what she had said. She hurriedly tapped on the red phone icon, hanging up.

She had barely regained her composure when Bill walked in with Kellan.

"The situation?" Kellan asked.

Ciara and Bill showed him all the data they had received from Josh. Ciara told Kellan about her plan, and Kellan agreed on both checking the flat and having Ciara stay elsewhere until she could go home safely.

Ciara then called Owen and asked if he could help. His job was to keep an eye on the security cameras near her flat while keeping an immediate contact to Ciara, Bill, and Kellan.

The three geared up, changing their clothes and leaving everything unnecessary in their offices. Or in Bill's case, the meeting room.

53

Ciara, Bill, and Kellan used magic to get to the right block.

Ciara looked around, keeping her eyes moving, so she was aware of her surroundings. She didn't move her head, though. It would have looked too obvious if someone was watching.

They made it to the right building without seeing anything—or anyone—suspicious.

They took the stairs. On their way up to the right floor, they only saw one of Ciara's neighbours. On the upper floors, they could also hear people closing flat doors.

Nothing seemed out of ordinary.

Until they got to the flat door. Once again, there was a note.

Soon.

That was all it said.

Kellan snapped a photo of it, and then he let Ciara take it off the door. Ciara observed it, flipping it in her hands.

There wasn't any more text on the back. It was just a one-word message.

Thanks to magical features, Kellan could check the note for any fingerprints with his phone, based on the photo he had of the note. The system, however, didn't find anything in the database.

Ciara kept the note, folding it and shoving it in her pocket. Then she unlocked and opened her flat door.

They went over the entire flat but found nothing out of the ordinary. They told Owen it was safe once they were finished.

"They are planning something," Kellan said when he walked into Ciara's room, scratching the side of his neck.

Ciara was in there packing. Even though they had found nothing in the flat, it wouldn't have been safe to stay there.

Bill walked in, too. "How are they always ahead of us? I mean, even this. They're playing with us."

"We have to figure that out," Ciara said while throwing her stuff in her bag.

"But not before the holidays," Kellan said. "We should all take some time off."

Ciara froze and turned to look at Kellan. "After that note? Something is going to happen soon."

"I'm staying hopeful enough to say the witch hunters will celebrate Christmas as well," Kellan said. "We'll all have to be on alert throughout the holidays, though."

"We could find them before Christmas. Then—"

"No," Kellan said strictly. "They're ahead of us, so it's too risky. Besides, we all deserve to spend Christmas with family and friends."

Ciara couldn't disagree with that.

It was unlikely they were going to get ahead of the witch hunters. They didn't even know what their source of information was. And the team deserved a break after the rough few months.

Once Ciara was done at her flat, she switched off the lights and locked the flat door. She, Bill, and Kellan enforced the security spells to make sure they were still working.

They left, using magic again to get back to their workplace. Each of them grabbed their stuff from work and headed home.

For Ciara, that meant the Rosslers' place. Liam had spoken with his mother, and he and Ciara were going to stay with his parents for however long they needed to.

It was raining when Ciara appeared in front of the Rosslers' house. She used a magical shield as an umbrella. If she hadn't, she would have been soaking wet in an instant. Ciara walked up to the front door and knocked.

The door swung open. Mary, smiling widely, stood there. "Come in, come in, dear," she said joyfully. She let Ciara in and closed the door behind her.

Ciara smiled at Mary. "Thank—"

Mary cut Ciara off by pulling her into a bone-crushing embrace. "It is so wonderful to hear about you and Liam! I am so happy for you two!"

Ciara chuckled as Mary let go of her and stepped away. "I'm glad you think so," Ciara said, relieved by Mary's reaction.

"Of course I do!" Mary was trembling with excitement, and her smile looked like it could be stuck permanently. "And it's so great you're staying here for longer! We haven't seen you in such a long time. At least not under good circumstances. I mean, I suppose your reason to be here could be better, but well—"

"Mum, stop rambling," Liam said, descending the stairs.

Ciara turned to look at her *boyfriend*, smiling. He walked up to her and wrapped his arm around her. Looking down at her, he kissed the top of her head.

"I'm glad you're fine," he breathed out.

"There was nothing to worry about." Ciara gazed into Liam's eyes and placed a comforting hand on his forearm.

"Oh, look at you two!" Mary gushed.

"Mum," Liam groaned.

"But you're such a cute couple. Even years back you were!" Mary said, smiling. She took a deep breath and calmed herself. "Anyway, I'll have dinner ready shortly."

"We'll take Ciara's bag upstairs," Liam said and took Ciara's things from her.

"Of course. No hurry," Mary said, grinning.

Liam and Ciara walked upstairs to Liam's old room. Looking around, Ciara noted he had already unpacked some of his stuff. His laptop was on the desk. The closet was also open, and Ciara could see some of his clothes in there.

She smiled, looking around the room.

"What are you thinking about?" Liam asked, setting Ciara's bag down next to the bed.

"This room has a lot of memories." Ciara thought about all the wonderful memories—including their first time on that very bed.

Liam smiled. "Good ones especially."

Ciara agreed.

Gesturing to Ciara's bag, Liam asked, "Is it okay if I help you unpack later?"

She nodded. "Do you know the last time I was here? In this room, I mean."

Liam tilted his head to the side, thinking. "When we were dating?"

Ciara shook her head. "In July, when Henry and I stayed here for a weekend. The weekend your parents stayed at a spa." It had also been the weekend Ciara had first heard about the group and had remet Doherty.

"I completely forgot about that," Liam admitted.

"It feels like ages ago."

"It does." Liam set his hands on Ciara's waist and pulled her closer to him. He pecked her lips and pulled away,

425

smiling. "So do you think we should make some fresh memories in this room or—"

"Liam!" Ciara hissed, wide-eyed. "It's your parents' house."

"If you think I'll be able to keep my hands off you the whole time we're staying here, you'll be surprised."

"You could at least try to control your urges during the day."

Liam kissed Ciara's shoulder. "If you insist."

"I do!"

Chuckling, Liam raised his head from her shoulder and kissed her lips.

"Dinner's ready!" Mary called from downstairs.

"We should go." Grabbing Liam's hand, Ciara pulled him downstairs.

Ray had just come home from work. He found out about the new relationship when he saw Ciara and Liam walk down hand in hand. His face was priceless, and he was as thrilled as Mary.

After dinner, the four of them were in the living room. The conversation had turned more serious than earlier at dinner. The television was on, but no one was watching it.

"So do you have any news on the witch hunters?" Ray asked.

"Josh could tell us that some witch hunters had been spotted near my flat. They know where I live, so it was unlikely a coincidence. We checked the flat, but we only found one note." She had Kellan's permission to share information with the group, so she didn't hold anything back.

Liam's brows furrowed. "What note?"

"It was on the door like last time," Ciara said. "There was just one word. 'Soon.'"

"Soon?" Ray checked, frowning.

"Yes. We suspect they're planning something. Kellan

426

thinks they won't make an appearance until after Christmas, but the team will be on alert throughout the holidays."

Liam turned to look at his father. "We should warn everyone in the MPG."

"The MPG?" Ciara asked.

Liam chuckled. "It's short for Magical Protection Group. I know, uncreative, but it's better than no name at all."

"It works."

Liam nodded.

Mary sighed. "Let's hope we get to have a peaceful Christmas," she said, and everyone nodded in agreement.

54

"I wish I didn't have work in the morning," Liam murmured, brushing a few stray hair strands behind Ciara's ear.

They were lying on his old bed, facing one another. It was already late, and Liam's parents had been asleep for some time.

"*I* wish I had to go to work in the morning," Ciara said, chuckling. She didn't remember the last time she had had a proper Christmas holiday. But she agreed with Kellan that the team deserved time off. And they didn't get chances like that often.

Liam smiled. "But would you rather go to work or lie in bed with me all day?"

Ciara pretended to think, tapping her cheek. "That's a tough one."

"Workaholic."

Ciara chuckled. "I'd stay in bed with you all day, silly," she said and wrapped her arms around Liam, welcoming his body warmth.

Liam smiled and pecked her lips. "You know, I didn't get to say something on the phone earlier today."

"What do you mean?"

"I love you, too." He looked deep into her eyes, and she felt as if she was melting. The feeling wasn't as thrilling as their first kiss the previous week had been, but it was just as good—if not better.

A blush crept up onto Ciara's cheeks, thinking back to the call. She had just hung up on Liam, fearing his reaction. "I wasn't sure...you know...I mean...you and...uh, Iris and..."

Liam shushed Ciara, brushing his finger across her lips. "I don't love Iris. I did once, but that's in the past. I love you, Ciara Veronique Jareau. I would never have stopped if I hadn't given away that memory."

His voice held so much love that it was overwhelming for Ciara. She had missed the feeling he gave her. But finally, he was hers, and she was his.

Ciara smiled at Liam, brushing her fingers on the side of his face. "Well, who knows what could have happened if you hadn't lost that memory. We could have broken up because of some stupid fight or...well, anything. Either way, we wouldn't be right here, right now."

Liam smiled, but a hint of sadness flashed in his eyes. "And you would never have been with Theo."

Ciara froze, surprised to hear his name. They hadn't talked about Theo.

"Is it wrong to mention his name?" Liam asked worriedly.

"No." Ciara shook her head and paused. "No, it's not."

She didn't want to forget Theo. Even if she was with Liam, she still grieved. It had been nearly a year since his death. She was moving on, but it didn't mean she would forget.

"How do you feel about...well, everything now that it's almost Christmas?" Liam asked, knowing it was Ciara's first Christmas without Theo.

"It feels like all that happened ages ago." Ciara rolled onto her back, staring at the ceiling. "I miss him here and there. But if everything hadn't gone this way, I wouldn't have so many other things in my life. Like I wouldn't be here with you." Ciara turned to look at Liam. "I would be in Canada."

Liam nodded. He took Ciara's hand into his and squeezed it. "I'm glad you're right here with me. Although, I wish you had never gone through everything you have."

Ciara smiled at Liam. "I'm glad I'm right here, too."

"How did you spend last Christmas?"

"With Theo and Estella." Ciara turned to look at the ceiling again. She felt uncomfortable talking about Theo while looking at Liam. "It was a traditional Christmas, I suppose. Christmas dinner and presents with family. Estella was at our house. And no, I didn't cook."

"You had your own house?"

Ciara nodded. "Estella and I sold it after Theo died. I lived on rent after that."

"So you owned a house, and you were engaged. It's going to be a different Christmas this year."

Ciara turned to look at Liam. "I don't mind one bit. I've always loved spending Christmas here. I'll get to see your siblings. I can help your parents, except with cooking. I get to see Henry and Jenna, too." Ciara smiled. "And I get to be with you. So it's going to be great."

Liam smiled. "I think this might turn out to be the best Christmas in a while."

"Why do you think so?" Ciara turned to her side again to look at Liam.

"Because I'll get to spend it with my family and you."

Frowning a little, Ciara asked, "What about your last Christmas?"

"We were at Iris's parents' place on Christmas Day," Liam said. "It was great at the time, but it's not the same."

"We were both engaged back then."

Liam's expression turned into a smug grin. "You know, I still have time to get a ring if that's what you're implying."

Ciara chuckled. "Or perhaps you should slow down a little."

"You don't want to be engaged to me?"

"Less than a week after we started dating again?" Ciara shook her head. "I love you, but my answer would be no."

Liam chuckled. "Guess I'll have to wait."

Ciara smiled but shook her head. "You're impossible."

"And you're cute when you pretend not to care about my nonsense," Liam said, grinning.

"You'll never get enough sleep if we keep talking through the night."

"I'll just grab an energy drink or—"

Ciara brought her mouth to Liam's and kissed him. Short and sweet. "You need to sleep," she said and pulled away.

Liam smiled. "If you insist."

"I do."

He wrapped his arms around her, holding her close, and she rested her head on his chest.

"Good night, beautiful."

"Good night, handsome."

Mary was also on her Christmas holiday, so she was home when Ciara woke up. Liam and Ray were both at work.

For most of the day, Ciara helped Mary with cleaning the house. Magic made it a lot faster and easier, so they were done before Liam and Ray arrived. Even the dinner was ready before the two came home from work.

The following day, Ciara and Mary went grocery shopping for Christmas. Ciara had suggested splitting the list, so they would be faster, and Mary had agreed.

It was a busy day at the supermarket. Everyone was buying food and drinks for Christmas, so it was bustling with people.

Ciara had already picked up almost everything on her list; she just needed olive oil. When she found the right aisle, she grabbed the first bottle she could reach. As she was about to place it in her basket, she realised there was something attached to it.

A note. It looked just like the previous ones. Even the handwriting was the same as on the last one. The only difference was the location.

Someone was following her.

Ciara's eyes widened. She shoved the note in her pocket and switched olive oil bottles in case it had been tampered with.

She looked to her left and right, just in time to see a hooded figure dash out of her sight. She dropped the shopping basket and ran. Dodging a few other customers, she got out of the aisle.

But by then the hooded figure was gone.

It had been a witch hunter. There was no other explanation.

Ciara had to find Mary. She went back to where she had dropped the groceries and grabbed them. She was nearly jogging, trying to find Mary, when she bumped into someone.

"Ciara?"

She looked up. "Jesse?"

He smiled down at her, his hair ruffled—likely from the wind outside. "Christmas shopping?"

She glanced at the basket in her hand. "Uh, yes. I'm helping Liam's mother get everything. I swear, the grocery list was infinite." She tried to force a smile, but most of her focus remained on her surroundings and the people passing by. She couldn't spot the witch hunter, though.

Jesse chuckled. "I bet."

"You're shopping pretty far from home." Jesse lived closer to central London, and they were closer to where the Rosslers lived farther from the city.

He shrugged. "They have a better selection here."

"How are you spending Christmas?" Ciara kept glancing around. The witch hunter could still be around.

"With my parents. You?"

"With the Rosslers." Ciara nodded and took a step to leave. She had to find Mary.

"Cool. Well, I'll leave you to shopping then," Jesse said and smiled, probably noticing that Ciara wasn't focusing on him. "Merry Christmas, Ciara."

"Merry Christmas." With a wave, she hurried to find Mary. Luckily Mary had finished getting everything from her half of the list by the time Ciara found her.

She didn't tell Mary about the note in case it made her worry. And she knew Mary would have told Liam who would have also been worried.

But Ciara kept eyeing their surroundings. She was half-worried and half-disappointed when she didn't find the hooded figure in the crowd.

Ciara didn't look at the note until later when she was alone. Mary was cooking dinner downstairs, and Ciara was upstairs in Liam's old room.

It was two words this time.

Very soon.

Ciara tried to scan the note for fingerprints or other evidence, but, like last time, there was nothing.

She sent a photo of the note to Kellan and dialled his number.

"Ciara, I know you hate having time off, but—"

"I got another note," she said, keeping her voice down. She didn't want Mary to hear.

That was enough to worry Kellan. "What? At the Rosslers' house?"

"No. At a supermarket."

"They're following you?" Kellan hissed.

"They *were* following me, for sure. I sent you a photo of the note. See it?"

After a brief silence, Kellan said, reading aloud, "Very soon."

Ciara hummed. "So am I supposed to wait for them to attack or what?"

She was slowly going crazy with worry and anxiety.

"They're just trying to mess with you. Besides, we're ready if something happens."

"You expect me to do nothing?"

"For now, yes. We'll work on this after Christmas. We will solve this," Kellan said determinedly. "You just have to accept that everything can't happen instantly. In fact, I reckon you said that to me originally."

Sighing, Ciara said, "I truly hate the holidays."

"I know," Kellan sighed. "Try to enjoy the time with your friends. And be careful."

"You, too."

Liam and Ciara were staying up later than Mary and Ray. They were cuddling on the living room sofa, watching a comedy show.

"Tomorrow is my last day at work this year," Liam said.

"I know," Ciara said and looked up at her boyfriend.

"I wish today had been, because now I won't be able to come pick up Gabe, Polly, and Poppy with you and Mum."

Ciara bit her lip. "Do they know we're together?"

"They'll find out tomorrow," Liam said, grinning. "The girls will freak out."

"In a good way?"

"Of course." Liam smiled at Ciara reassuringly. "You should have seen Poppy when I first saw you since your return. I was filling the glasses, and, well, if it weren't for Poppy's comment, the whole house would have been flooded. She looked amused for sure. Maybe even excited."

"Because of the flood?"

"Because of my reaction to seeing you."

"You were in love with Iris back then."

"Even if so, you looked stunning. You still do. You always have done," Liam said, gazing at Ciara.

"Now you're just being cheesy," Ciara said, but she couldn't help smiling.

"Still, it's true."

The following day, Ciara went with Mary to pick up Gabriel, Polly, and Poppy from school.

The school hadn't changed at all. The building was a large old manor with towers and a huge garden. Ciara had never appreciated how beautiful it was. Not until now. After all, she no longer had to spend most of her year there.

School had been fun for her, but she had never been the most enthusiastic student. She didn't miss her school years, but it was nice to recall the memories.

Liam and Henry's younger siblings were surprised to see Ciara with their mother.

"Why didn't Henry come?" Gabriel asked once they were home.

"He's at work, I think," Ciara said.

Polly's eyes widened. "You don't know for sure?"

"To be honest, I don't."

They were still standing in the hallway.

"Ciara is staying with us for now because of some problems at her flat," Mary told her children.

"In our room?" Polly asked excitedly, turning to Ciara.

Mary chuckled, but she didn't say anything.

"I'm staying in Liam's room," Ciara said.

Poppy pouted. "But I thought he would spend a few nights here, too."

"He will," Ciara assured.

Poppy's eyes widened. "Don't say!"

"Say what?" Polly asked.

"Are you two dating?" Poppy squealed.

Ciara gaped at the girl. She couldn't believe Poppy had figured it out just like that.

"You are!" Polly squealed, getting enough proof from Ciara's expression.

Ciara bit her lip. "We are."

Mary smiled at the scene before she left to prepare dinner. Gabriel excused himself to his own room. The girls pulled Ciara to the living room.

"For how long?" Poppy asked before they made it to the sofa.

"Not even a week."

"So did he ask you out on a date?" Polly asked, grinning, when the three sat down with Ciara in the middle.

Ciara chuckled. "Not exactly." There was no way she could tell them the complete story.

"Wait, what about your other boyfriend?" Poppy asked, crossing her arms.

"My other boyfriend?" Ciara asked, confused.

"Kellan."

Grimacing, Ciara said, "That was actually just for work."

Poppy's expression turned into one of understanding. "Undercover?"

"Sort of."

Polly giggled. "Poor Liam! He was so jealous."

"So which one of you confessed first?" Poppy asked, grabbing Ciara's arm.

"I'm honestly not sure," Ciara admitted.

"Was it romantic?" Polly asked, grabbing Ciara's other arm.

"Girls, please, stop pestering my girlfriend." All three turned to look to the doorway where Liam was casually leaning against the doorframe, a slightly amused smile on his face. His hair was tousled, and his sleeves were rolled up to his elbows.

"Liam!" his sisters exclaimed and rushed to greet their brother.

Ciara couldn't help but smile, watching Liam hug his sisters. She stood up and moved a little closer, but she made sure not to disturb the precious moment.

"Gabriel is upstairs! I'll go get him!" Polly said before rushing to the stairs.

Liam turned to look at Ciara, a one-sided smile on his lips. "Hi."

Ciara moved to stand beside him. "Hi."

He wrapped his arm around Ciara and pulled her closer to kiss her lips.

"You two are sickeningly cute," Poppy said, amused.

Ciara blushed at the comment.

"I know," Liam said, smirking, while he still had his arm wrapped around Ciara. He didn't drop it until Gabriel came downstairs.

Later, while Liam was hanging out with his siblings, Ciara excused herself to her room. She had a gift to send off before Christmas. She wanted to be sure the present would reach its destination on time.

It was a small present for her mother, to make sure she knew Ciara was thinking about her, because it wasn't safe for Ciara's mother to come back to England.

Ciara placed the wrapped present on the bed, making sure the card was attached. She smiled, thinking about her mother's warm smile.

"Merry Christmas, Mum," she whispered and used magic to send the present away.

55

"It's so great to have most of the family here even before Christmas Day!" Mary beamed.

The delicious scent of the meal filled the kitchen. Mary had loaded the table with food, even though it wasn't even a Christmas dinner.

For Ciara, the situation was like déjà vu. She was once again sitting beside Liam at the familiar table. The twins—Poppy and Polly—were giggling together. Mary was telling Ray off for eating before everybody else. Gabriel was talking with Liam and Ciara about his studies.

The only ones missing were Henry and Jenna.

It wasn't like an exact copy of Ciara's memories, but she had spent dozens of dinners at that table with the same people. What made it even more similar to the past was Liam's hand resting on her thigh.

It was as if the past three and a half years had never happened. Everything felt so familiar—so domestic. The Rosslers' place had been like a second home for Ciara.

"What are you thinking about?" Liam asked. Gabriel was shovelling food onto his plate, so he was briefly distracted from the conversation.

Ciara's smile widened, and she glanced at Liam. "I'll tell you later."

Seeing Ciara smile like that made Liam smile, too. "Okay."

"Oh, I have a question for you, Ciara!" Gabriel said.

Ciara turned to look at him. "Go ahead and ask."

"Were your grades good when you graduated?"

"They weren't the best, but they were better than average. So, I suppose they were good," Ciara said.

"Were Liam's grades better?" Gabriel asked.

Liam smirked cockily. "Of course they were."

"Gabriel, in case you didn't notice back then, your brother was the biggest swot ever," Ciara said, grinning.

Gabriel chuckled. "You're probably right."

"He even tutored me."

"He did?" Poppy squealed.

"Don't raise your voice at the dinner table," Mary scolded Poppy, even though she was still smiling gently.

"I did," Liam said proudly. "On potions."

"I was the worst at potions courses," Ciara told.

Gabriel's face brightened. "So I still have a chance of becoming a hit wizard!"

Mary's eyes widened. "Wouldn't it be better to become a curse breaker like Liam?"

"What if I really, really want to become a hit wizard?" Gabriel asked.

Ray frowned and turned to look at his wife. "The kid has to make his own decisions," he said, even though Ciara had a feeling he didn't like the idea of Gabriel becoming a hit wizard any more than Mary did.

Mary sighed heavily and turned to Gabriel. "I will not support your choice to become a hit wizard. But your father is right. It's still your choice."

Gabriel smiled.

"But think it through more than twice," Ciara said seriously. She hadn't thought it through more than once. She didn't regret her career choice, but she would prefer to see Gabriel in a safer job.

Gabriel nodded. "I will."

"Ciara could even get you a position," Liam said. "She has her own team and office, and she's only one rank below the head of the department."

Gabriel's eyes widened, and he grinned. "Really?"

"I could take you into my team for training," Ciara said, nodding. "But after that, I would preferably have you moved onto another team. One that doesn't handle some of the most dangerous tasks. My boss, the head of the department, would likely agree with me."

Gabriel's eyes were glistening with hope. "Really?"

"We'll talk about it once you graduate unless you change your mind," Ciara promised.

Gabriel grinned. "Great!"

Ciara glanced at Liam who was smiling at her. She couldn't help but blush, seeing the dreamy look on his face.

"What?" she mouthed at him when no one was looking.

Liam just smiled. He briefly glanced at his plate, but soon his gaze was back on Ciara. "Nothing."

🍁🍁🍁

"Y-you two are together?" Henry's face was priceless when he and Jenna arrived on Christmas Day. His eyes were wide and his mouth hung open. Pointing between the couple, he asked, "How did this happen? Again!"

Jenna rushed to hug Ciara. "This is wonderful!"

Henry blinked a few times, finally regaining his composure. Soon he smiled a little. "Honestly, Liam, stop stealing my best friend over and over again," Henry said light-heartedly.

Liam chuckled. "Not anytime soon, buddy."

Henry shook his head, smiling. "Unbelievable."

Shortly after Henry and Jenna's arrival, it was time for the Christmas meal. Mary had prepared everyone a perfect Christmas dinner. There was everything—roast turkey, roast vegetables, cranberry sauce, Brussels sprouts, and more.

"Don't eat yet!" Poppy screamed when everyone was about to start eating.

"What? Why?" Mary looked between the table and her daughter.

"I need a picture for Instagram!"

Everyone burst out laughing. Poppy sighed and shook her head. Then she snapped a photo of the table. After a few more photos, everyone was allowed to start.

It was the kind of Christmas Ciara liked. The food was delicious. The house was decorated beautifully with floating baubles, dancing candles, and swaying tinsel. Everyone was chattering joyously.

And no one spoke a word about the witch hunters. No one even thought about them.

"It's so rare to have everyone here on Christmas Day." Mary smiled, watching her husband, her children, and her sons' girlfriends eat the meal she had prepared for them.

Liam smiled at his mother. "We should definitely make it a tradition."

Mary grinned. "Next time, we'll have Jenna's parents come over, too. And your mother, Ciara."

Ciara smiled. "That'd be nice."

Once everyone had finished dessert, it was time to gather around in the living room to open the presents. It took a while for everyone to find all their own presents and open them.

"I have one more thing for you," Liam whispered to Ciara, wrapping his arm around her.

"Naughty or nice?" Ciara mouthed after checking no one was looking.

Liam chuckled. "Nice."

"What are you two giggling about?" Henry demanded to know, pointing an accusing finger at the couple.

"Inside joke." Ciara shot a grin at Henry. "You wouldn't get it."

Henry pretended to be hurt, placing his hand over his heart. "My heart!"

Jenna snorted. "Your heart is fine."

Later in the evening, Ciara leaned against the kitchen doorway, watching Liam fill his wineglass. She let herself admire the view. He had his sleeves rolled up to his elbows and his hair was tousled, lacking any hair products to keep it neat. She couldn't resist the urge, and snapped a photo of him with her phone.

He turned to look at Ciara. "Did you just take a photo of me?"

Ciara grinned. "Maybe."

Liam chuckled, placing down the wine bottle and walking over to the doorway. "You're impossible."

"I can't exactly draw you with my drawing skills, so I need to have something."

Liam had given Ciara one of his drawings for Christmas. They had both been in that drawing together, hugging, and she loved it.

Liam smiled. "I still have something for you."

"Something nice, I think," Ciara said, amused.

"I think you'll like it."

Ciara smiled. She snapped her fingers, making a bunch of mistletoe appear over their heads. She looked up, and Liam followed the gesture. They looked back at each other at the same time. He pulled her closer to him with his free arm—he still had the wineglass in his other hand. He let his lips linger right above her lips, teasing her, before he finally leaned in.

They didn't pull away until they heard someone walking down the stairs. They turned to see Poppy.

"Can I have some wine, too?" she asked.

"Not until you're eighteen," Liam said.

Poppy placed her hands on her hips. "So you've never drunk alcohol at a school party?"

Ciara had a hard time holding in her laughter.

"I was the responsible one," Liam said.

"He was," Ciara confirmed.

Poppy frowned. "But—"

"No."

"Boring." Sighing, she left back upstairs.

"In three years!" Liam called after her.

"Boring!"

"I remember who was acting not-so-responsibly at school parties," Liam said smugly, sliding his gaze to Ciara.

She cringed. "Oh, God, no."

"I had a wonderful Christmas," Ciara said, smiling and lying in bed with Liam.

Liam grinned, turning to look at her. "Your Christmas is missing one more thing."

"What do you mean?"

"Something nice." Liam grabbed his wand from the nightstand and flicked it in the air.

Just then a love bracelet appeared on Ciara's wrist. It was identical to the one that had broken.

Ciara looked at it in awe and turned to smile at Liam. "You'd better not break this one."

"Never."

56

Ciara woke up to her ringtone on the first of January. She and Liam had spent New Year's Eve with Shawn and Hugo, and there had been drinking involved, so she had a terrible hangover.

At first Ciara struggled to open her eyes and reach for the phone. But when she saw the caller ID, her eyes widened, and she instantly picked it up.

"Kellan!"

"Looks like the witch hunters didn't celebrate yesterday."

"What do you mean?"

"They started killing non-magics, using magic, at midnight. There's a group of them staying at an old empty warehouse near Reading."

"They killed non-magics? *With magic?* W-what's our plan?"

"For now, we need to have a meeting. Preferably with the MPG. Somewhere other than work."

"I'll send you an address soon. I just have to check

something," Ciara said.

"Hurry."

"I will."

She hung up. Turning to look behind her, she noticed Liam wasn't there. She snapped her fingers to change her clothes and freshen her breath. Then she bolted downstairs.

Liam and his parents were in the kitchen. When Ciara made it to the doorway, Liam turned to look at her. He smiled at first, but his expression changed when he saw how pale she looked. "Is everything okay?"

Ciara shook her head. "Do you think we could have a meeting here? The MPG and my team. It's important."

Liam's parents shifted their gazes to Ciara. "Of course. Is everything okay?" Ray said.

"No." Ciara struggled to get the words out. "There were massacres last night."

Ciara grabbed her phone and sent the address to Kellan and the team. Ray was the one to inform the MPG.

Within an hour, everyone was in the Rosslers' living room. Ciara was leaning against the wall near the doorway while Kellan stood next to her.

Kellan explained to everyone everything he had told Ciara.

"And we're sure it's not a trap?" Ray asked.

"We're not," Kellan said. "In fact, we've rarely been able to track them this easily. I believe this is what they were implying in those notes."

"Notes?" Henry's eyes moved between Kellan and Ciara, looking for answers. "I thought there was only one note this month."

Ciara sighed. "One last month, two this month. Someone was following me at the supermarket. Whoever it was left me a note."

Kellan continued to explain the details of the upcoming

mission.

Meanwhile, Liam moved to stand next to Ciara. "You didn't say anything about another note."

"Not now. Okay?"

Liam nodded, but his frown didn't fade.

The MPG and Ciara's team had come up with a plan. They were going to split into smaller groups, so they could cover more ground and more entrances. After all, the warehouse was huge.

Everyone had two hours to get to their positions.

Ciara hurried upstairs when the meeting was done. She wanted to be ready early.

Liam ran after her. "Ciara."

"Get ready." She didn't mean to sound bossy, but she did.

"We have two hours."

"Well, I'd like to be early."

Liam sighed. He knew there was no changing Ciara's mind when she was in working mode.

Ciara undressed herself and grabbed her working clothes: black leggings for mobility, and a tank top, and a tight sweater. She had flat knee-high boots that she could run in and that were great for hiding knives too. She pulled her hair up into a ponytail, so it wouldn't get in the way.

She hid the knives in her boots and shoved her wand in its pocket.

Once she was dressed, she grabbed her lucky charm from her bag. It was a rare magical object, and she only had one of them. It had been a gift from Theo.

Ciara walked over to Liam who had just finished changing. She didn't say anything, slipping the lucky charm into his pocket.

"What was that?"

Ciara looked up at him. "A lucky charm."

Liam's eyes widened. "A lucky charm?"

Ciara nodded.

Liam's surprised look twisted into a frown. "Nothing's

446

going to happen."

"Just leave it there, okay?" Ciara pleaded.

Liam grabbed her hand. "I will. But I'll be fine either way."

Ciara swallowed and closed her eyes. "I just want to be sure."

Liam cupped Ciara's face, and she fluttered her eyes open. "We have each other's backs. Nothing will happen."

Ciara took a shaky breath. "I know. It's just..." She shuddered at the thought of what she was about to say. "It's Theo's death's anniversary."

Liam's breath hitched. "I'm sorry."

"This day is just a bit too much of a repeat from last year and—"

"This won't be like last year," Liam said firmly.

Ciara clung onto Liam, wrapping her arms around him. She was already trembling with anxiety. Her throat felt tight, and she was cold, as if running a fever.

Liam hugged her. "Everything's going to be okay."

He hated seeing her like that. But knowing how dangerous the mission was going to be, there were no comforting words.

Ciara and Liam were in the same group with Theresa, Bill, and Iris. In any other case, Ciara would have felt uncomfortable with Iris around. But with the task at hand, she had more important matters on her mind.

The group was already at their assigned spot.

"Is everyone ready?" Kellan asked through a magical telepathic link. It was the same kind of link as they used at work all the time. A secure way of communication between the groups.

"We're ready," Ciara said. She had been assigned as one of the leaders.

"We're ready, too," River said. In his team were Jenna, Hannah, and Eric. Hannah and Eric were the old members who had also wanted to join the reformed group—MPG.

"Same here," Ray said. His team consisted of four of his friends—Vincent, Laura, Dominic, and Deanna. They were all members of the MPG. Everyone on the mission, except for Kellan and Ciara's team, were.

"Yep. Same," Shawn said through the link. He was in the same team with Hugo, Niles, and two other MPG members, Grace and Felix Burnham.

Kellan's team consisted of Henry and two MPG members, Tony and Victor.

"If you see, hear or find anything, you know what to do," Kellan said through the telepathic link. "No unnecessary risks. Safety before bravery. Good luck, everyone." He paused. "Let's do this."

That was their cue to enter the warehouse. Ciara stepped in front of the entrance and unlocked it by touching it. She led her team inside.

Liam stayed right behind Ciara, not hiding his worry. He had also volunteered as a team leader, but Kellan had picked Ciara. Ciara knew Liam hated it, but he hadn't complained.

The first room appeared to be empty, but the team looked around to be sure. They tested the space for any enchantments.

"We ran into two witch hunters," Shawn informed them through the link. "We had to kill them."

Ciara's team finished checking the first room, but she signalled for them to wait after she heard Shawn's voice.

"They're using spells to trick us," Kellan warned through the link. "They can form hallucinations that look like actual people."

"Is everyone okay?" Ciara asked through the link.

"So far, so good," Kellan said.

"We found sleeping bags," Ray informed. "Why are they using sleeping bags when they could just summon a bed?"

Ciara pursed her lips together. "They've always used sleeping bags here in Great Britain."

"We found their lab," River told. "I'll collect samples."

"Good," Kellan said.

Ciara led her team to the door. But she was the one to open it in case it was a trap—like the one Owen had walked into.

She couldn't imagine the same happening to Liam.

The second room appeared to be empty, too. It had stone walls and a concrete floor. Ciara investigated the walls to make sure there weren't any hidden passages. The others looked around and checked the room for enchantments or curses.

"We checked our second room and there's still nothing," Ciara reported through the link.

"That's odd," Kellan said. "Are you absolutely sure?"

"Yes."

"Be careful. It could be a trap."

"We'll keep you updated."

"Good."

After the second room, Ciara and her team continued to a corridor as planned. They had the floor plan of the warehouse, so they had planned each team's paths beforehand.

Ciara held her wand up, lighting up the corridor so they could see what was ahead. The corridor wasn't long.

Or it wasn't supposed to be.

The problem was that the floor plan didn't match the reality. The corridor split into two.

Ciara blinked. Then she shone light both ways to make sure it wasn't a hallucination.

But it turned out the floor plan had been inaccurate.

"The floor plan doesn't match our part," Ciara told the others. "We must split up."

"Are you sure?" Kellan asked. "The hallucinations—"

"This isn't a hallucination."

"The floor plan was old," Theresa said through the link. She had been the one to find it as she was the best hacker. "Maybe the warehouse has been modified since then."

"Could be," Kellan agreed. "Ciara, do what you think is best."

"Are you sure splitting up is a good idea?" Iris asked Ciara—not using the link.

"We don't really have a choice," Bill said, looking between the two corridors.

Ciara didn't like the idea, but Bill was right. "Liam and Theresa with me on the right. Bill and Iris on the left. Bill is the leader."

They let the other teams know about their split and then they continued their own ways.

Liam stayed right behind Ciara. "We might be walking into a trap."

Ciara bit her bottom lip nervously. "Keep your wand ready."

"Already do."

"Good."

The corridor was longer than the last. It seemed endless. Ciara's heart was pounding in her chest. She was expecting to walk straight into an ambush.

After a while, Ciara signalled for Liam and Theresa to stop. She used a revealing spell on the corridor to see if it was a hallucination. Either it was powerful magic or it was real, because the spell did nothing.

They continued. Ciara ran her hands along the wall to check for any hidden passages.

A little further on, the corridor widened. Liam moved to stand beside Ciara.

"Our corridor is widening. What about you, Bill?" Ciara asked through the link.

"Same narrow corridor," Bill told.

"No traps so far?" Kellan asked.

"Nothing so far," both Ciara and Bill confirmed.

Ciara, Liam, and Theresa followed the corridor until they found a wide set of double doors.

Ciara stepped in front of them. She reached out to touch

the rough surface, but didn't push. She glanced at Liam and Theresa who stood behind her, wands ready and waiting for her to open the doors.

"I bet this is a trap," Ciara warned them. She turned to face the doors and pushed them open.

They couldn't see anything inside, so Ciara walked in. The ceiling was higher than the corridor's, and there was a window up there. Somehow the lights were on, too. The other rooms hadn't had any lamps. There wasn't even supposed to be electricity in the building.

And worst of all, the room was a dead end.

"Something's not right," Ciara said, turning to look at Liam.

Theresa leaned against the wall near the door, looking around. She checked her nails casually. "Looks like a trap to me."

"W—"

The doors slammed shut, revealing a figure hiding behind them. "Ten points for the right answer."

Ciara's eyes widened, staring at *him*. Blood drained from her face, and her entire body went rigid. Coldness hit her, and her hands started shaking. "*No.*"

I t had to be a cruel joke. Ciara didn't *want* to believe her own eyes.

"Hi." He looked straight at her with his all-too-familiar grey eyes. He was smiling a little, showing the dimples that Ciara had been so used to seeing. All that had changed was his hair. It was shorter than it had been when he had died.

Ciara tried blinking, but he was still there. She tried again, but it wasn't a hallucination. Then she blinked again, but it only made her feel dizzy.

"Thanks, Theresa." Theo turned to look at the black-haired witch. "Go after the blonde girl and the guy."

Theresa nodded, heading for the door.

"What?" Ciara found her voice, and her eyes snapped onto Theresa.

Theresa smiled sheepishly at her. "Um, sorry? It was too easy not to fool you. I mean, sleeping bags? You honestly thought we use those? Nope, all planted to make it look like we had actually been there."

"Theresa's on the witch hunters' side. She's coming for Bill and Iris," Liam said through the link. "And Theo is here."

Theresa turned to face Liam, pouting. "You just ruined my fun."

He didn't say anything. He stood right beside Ciara, ready to pull Ciara behind him and to use his wand.

Ciara had trusted Theresa. She had spent hours working with her. She had even hung out with her outside work. Theresa had done all the hacking for the team.

She had even found the floor plan of the warehouse.

She had found the floor plan.

And she had modified it.

Ciara had suspected nothing. Not even once.

"Have fun," Theresa said to Theo and walked out.

Ciara turned to look at Theo, shaking with shock. "How?" It was an effort to keep her voice from breaking.

Theo frowned. "No welcome back?"

"Y-you're with them." Ciara felt as if she couldn't get enough air. As if she was choking. "Y-you're killing people. You're lying to people. You're—"

"I'm sorry you had to spend a year without me," Theo said, sounding sincere. Like the Theo Ciara had known. The Theo she had agreed to marry. "But it had to be done."

"Why?" Ciara rasped out.

"For the greater good."

"Killing innocents isn't good!" she screamed at Theo. Her breathing was shaky, and the room was swaying. But she couldn't pass out. Not with everything going on around her.

Theo pursed his lips together. "We're not doing it for fun, *Ciara*."

She shut her eyes tightly. "You're just a hallucination. You're dead. You died a year ago."

"Even your new boyfriend can confirm I'm real." Theo sounded smug.

Ciara's eyes flew open. His posture matched his voice. She stared at Theo, not quite understanding his words.

His lips curved into a smirk, and he nodded at Liam. "Ask him."

Ciara turned to look at Liam, the words stuck in her throat. "What is he talking about?"

Liam's eyes glistened with regret. He opened his mouth, struggling to find the words. "I didn't want to tell you, because—"

"What is he talking about?" Ciara raised her voice, demanding answers.

Liam looked at Theo, unable to make eye contact with Ciara. "He killed Doherty."

The horror struck her. Her gaze flew back to Theo. She was about to scream.

"He saw it happen," Theo said, gesturing to Liam.

Ciara turned to look at Liam, subconsciously taking a step back. "You've known for months?" she spat at him.

They had both lied to her.

Liam tried to apologise, but he was cut off before he could speak.

"He didn't tell you. No idea why." Theo shrugged dramatically. "Jealousy, maybe?"

"Shut up!" Ciara snapped at Theo.

Theo's face hardened. "Enough fun, then. I want you to come with me, Ciara."

Ciara shook her head. "No, Theo."

She was furious at him, but also shocked he was alive. Even relieved. She wanted to cry and rush into his arms. And at the same time, she wanted to cast a killing curse at him for everything he had done.

He had put her through hell.

Theo lost his composure, hearing his name slip off Ciara's lips. "You're on the wrong side, Ciara," he snarled through gritted teeth.

Ciara shook her head. "I don't think so."

"You don't believe in the good of all?" Theo asked, taking a step closer to Ciara and Liam. His eyes were mostly fixed

454

on Ciara, except for a few cautious glances at Liam. "Because I know you do. You hate how the government mindlessly makes decisions, even deciding what's good and what's not."

"It's the law!"

"An ancient law. A law for inequality and injustice," Theo said. "We don't kill for nothing. We are fighting for our rights. For the rights of everyone. This is a war against injustice."

"You're killing innocents, Theo!" Ciara screamed, her voice breaking. She couldn't believe *her* Theo was capable of such violence.

"We wouldn't have to if society acknowledged what's wrong! The same problem in every country of this world. There's no equality for us, no matter where we go." Theo looked at Ciara with desperation. "We're not free. We can't live our lives as we wish. You know that. You know that very well. You know how cruel the system is. You know better than anyone. You know the system makes it right to punish someone for accidentally using magic in front of a non-magic person. How is that right?"

Ciara clenched her jaw. "Accidents are rarely accidents."

"There are genuine accidents that people are punished for."

Ciara shook her head. "What you're doing is wrong."

"We're fighting for freedom. We do what we have to. We don't have a choice."

"There's always a choice!" Ciara yelled. "Like you could have chosen not to fake your death! Do you have any idea what your mother is going through?"

"You're just angry because you still care," Theo said challengingly. "You brought up my mom because you still care. You hate the fact that you care about a *witch hunter*."

"No. I—"

"Theresa escaped," Bill announced through the telepathic link.

"The warehouse is swarming with witch hunters!" This time it was Hugo.

"Get out safely! Now!" Kellan ordered.

"We need to go, Ciara," Liam said quietly. He tried to grab her hand, but she didn't let him.

"Why did you fake your death?" Ciara asked Theo.

"You do care." Theo's lips curled up. "It was the best way. No one knew I switched sides. I had useful information, and it stayed useful for a while, too."

"You could have told me!" Ciara cried out.

Theo furrowed his eyebrows, seeming regretful. "I did now."

Ciara was shaking. She wasn't sure if it was anger or shock.

"Why did you kill Doherty?" she demanded.

"He saw me. He would have told you. And he was becoming a threat, anyway." Theo turned to look at Liam. "I tried to kill him, too." He returned his gaze to Ciara. "I was unsuccessful. Although it looks like I finally got my opportunity."

Ciara jumped in front of Liam. "No."

"We can't get out!" Jenna screamed through the link. "We're trapped."

There was invisible pressure on Ciara's chest. "Someone help them!" she ordered through the link, panicked.

"Ciara, come with me," Theo said, his voice silky smooth.

"No."

Theo sighed. "Fine. Since this isn't working as I hoped, I have to change tactics."

The doors opened behind Theo. Theresa and a tall, muscular witch hunter guy walked in, dragging Iris and Bill with them.

Blood flowed out of Bill's nose, covering his shirt. He had cuts on his face. He had taken quite a beating.

Iris didn't look much better.

Ciara's eyes widened, realising what Theo was doing. "Don't."

Theo turned to look at her.

"Please, Theo." She looked him in the eyes, begging him

to stop. She prayed he would see the pain he put her through.

"Don't kill them?" he asked.

Ciara nodded, praying Theo would listen.

"Then come with me." Theo held out his hand, fingers twitching.

"And do what? Kill more people? More innocents?" Ciara hissed. She looked at her fiancé in disgust.

"Only if it comes to that." Theo let his hand drop to his side, a bitter smile forming on his face.

"Ray's hurt! It's bad!" Dominic, the MPG member, yelled through the link. "Where's Iris?"

"Iris and Bill are injured and held prisoners," Ciara informed him through the link.

Liam stood frozen behind Ciara. He had gone pale, seeing the state Iris and Bill were in. Hearing about his father just made it worse.

"Theresa," Theo ordered.

Theresa flicked her wand, making a knife fly out of her left boot and right towards Iris.

"Don't!" Liam screamed. He was about to run forward, but Ciara stopped him.

Ciara had cleared her head a little. She couldn't risk having Liam in the same position as Bill and Iris.

The knife hit Iris's abdomen. She cried out, and her face contorted in pain. Liam winced.

"She'll bleed out if this takes too long," Theo said, looking grim.

"Just stop!" Ciara yelled at him. "You're hurting people as if they're nothing to you!"

Theo sighed and turned to look at Liam. "Liam, how about a switch?" Theo gestured to Iris. "You get your lady over here back, still alive, and you return my fiancée."

Liam's fists clenched. "Not a chance."

"How about we gut your ex, then?"

"Don't even think about it," Liam snapped.

"They killed Eric," River said through the link. Eric—

Ray's friend and the one who had already lost his brother to the witch hunters.

Everything was failing. The witch hunters had set a trap for them, using Theresa. The mission had been doomed from the beginning.

"Theo, stop this!" Ciara was growing more desperate. Almost desperate enough to consider Theo's offer.

She didn't see any other way out.

Jenna and River were trapped with one of Mary's friends, Hannah. Bill and Iris weren't too far from being killed, either. And for all Ciara knew, Ray could have been dying, too.

One of them was already dead. How many more would die before they got out?

"How does this help you?" Ciara asked Theo.

"I *need* you on our side."

"I'm never going to become a killer like you!"

"We are fighting for freedom. You just can't see it yet," Theo said calmly. As if he truly believed it himself.

"Theo, please, stop this," Ciara begged. "This...this isn't you." She had to gasp for air. Her chest hurt, as if someone were crushing her lungs.

Theo looked at Ciara solemnly. "I'm sorry about this." He flicked his wand in the air.

At first, nothing happened, but then Bill screamed. He fell onto his side, writhing in pain.

"Stop!" Ciara screamed, forcing her feet to stay where they were. "Stop! Stop!"

"Henry's injured," Kellan said through the link.

"Ray's unconscious. There's a pulse, but it's looking bad."

"Hannah's dead," River announced. That meant it was only him and Jenna. Half of their team had been killed.

"Shawn was hit!" Hugo screamed through the link.

"Bill is..." Liam couldn't find the right words to describe Bill's condition.

"Can anyone get out of here? We need help!" Kellan shouted through the link, but no one responded.

Out of nowhere, Bill stopped screaming, and the room became silent. His eyes closed, and he stopped moving.

Ciara couldn't see his chest rising.

She screamed, and the door shattered into shards of wood. Everyone except her was thrown against the shaking walls, and a part of the ceiling fell down.

58

The whole warehouse shook as if in an earthquake. Liam managed to get up, but he struggled to stay on his feet. He tried to get to Iris and Bill while covering himself with shield spells as pieces of the ceiling fell down.

Theo leaned against the wall, looking at Ciara in amazement.

Theresa and the other witch hunter tried to stand up, but they fell back onto the floor, unable to stay on their feet.

Ciara was floating in the air. Her screaming seemed never-ending, her hands clenched into fists, and her eyes shut tight.

It felt as though hours passed, even though it was only minutes. Ciara's screaming ceased, and she fell limp to the floor.

The building stopped shaking.

Liam rushed to help Iris and check on Bill. Once he was standing in front of Bill and Iris, he gripped his wand, flicked it and sent both Theresa and the other witch hunter flying against the wall behind them. The guy was knocked unconscious.

Theo saw his chance and rushed to Ciara. He gripped her hand and brought his other hand to her face.

Liam glanced at Ciara after making sure Iris was still conscious. His eyes widened when he saw Theo leaning over Ciara, but he was forced to turn his attention to Theresa who attacked him with curses.

"Ciara!" Liam exclaimed, duelling Theresa. He was too busy blocking curses, so he couldn't turn to see if Ciara had reacted to her name being called out.

He wasn't sure what had happened. Ciara was special, having the ability to harness magic without a wand. But it had to be more than that. Because what they had witnessed was even more rare than wandless magic.

Ciara's eyes fluttered open, as if she were waking up. She looked up at Theo who was leaning over her. "Please, Theo, stop this madness," she begged tiredly.

Her outburst had weakened her.

Theo looked into her eyes, his gaze softening, and brushed her hair off her face. "I'm doing what's right. If you'd just see that, Ciara..."

It broke her heart to see him like that. Her fiancé. The man she had thought was dead.

She had loved him. She had loved him so much.

But she couldn't accept what he was doing. He was one of the witch hunters. He had killed innocents.

Ciara gripped Theo's hand. "Theo, please."

"I can't," he said and looked at her with sorrowful eyes.

"Did you leave the notes?"

His brows furrowed. "The *note*."

One note. He was lying again. It had been him the entire time—even at the supermarket.

Ciara closed her eyes, and tears began to form. She knew what she had to do, but she wasn't sure if she could do it. Even the thought sickened her.

"Jenna's bleeding out!" River screamed through the link in panic. "I need help!"

She had to save her friends before it was too late.

Theo cupped her face. "Come with me, and I'll tell everyone to leave the warehouse. Every last one. Then, this will all make sense."

She became unusually aware of her and his every breath. His heart beating. His warmth—the warmth she had longed for in the past year.

Estella's face flashed in her mind, and more tears cascaded down her face.

"Theo." Her voice broke, and her hands shook.

"Ciara," he breathed out, gazing into her eyes.

She looked into those beautiful stormy grey eyes, memorising every last detail. The little speckles of silver painted on a stormy sky.

She let her eyes wander, memorising all of his face. His flawless olive skin. His high cheekbones. His dark eyebrows. His thick eyelashes. His distinctive Cupid's bow.

She looked back into his eyes. They stared at each other in silence, forgetting everything going on around them and blocking out the sounds of duelling for a second.

Ciara wanted to stay there forever.

But she couldn't. She snapped her fingers, and her knife flew from her boot into her hand. For a split second, she hesitated. Then she pushed the blade into his abdomen. She cried out as if she was the one in pain, feeling the warm liquid coat her hand.

Theo's face contorted in pain, and he hissed. His eyes didn't leave Ciara's, and he touched her shoulder, his palm against her skin. He whispered something inaudibly and cast a spell, still gazing at her.

His eyes shut, and his hand slid away from her shoulder as if he was slipping—dying—before he teleported away.

Ciara sat up, her muscles screaming to give up. But she forced herself upright and onto her feet. She wanted to fall back onto the floor. She was tired, but she couldn't tell if it was the outburst or stabbing her fiancé that exhausted her so.

Theresa gave up, seeing Theo was gone, and ran off.

"Take them to safety," Ciara ordered Liam and stumbled out of the room.

She had barely made it halfway down the corridor when she heard River's voice through the link. "They're leaving."

Ciara ran. Somehow she stayed upright despite her exhaustion. She forced herself to rush down the stone corridors and through the concrete rooms.

She found River's team. Jenna was on the floor, barely conscious. River was kneeling beside her, pressing onto her wound to keep the blood from pouring out.

There was one dead body in the room Ciara didn't recognise. The two others she did.

Eric lay lifelessly on the floor in a pool of his own blood. His throat had been sliced open.

Hannah had seemingly been killed with a spell. She hung in an unnatural position, and it looked as if her neck had been snapped. Her eyes were still wide open.

"Take Jenna to a hospital," Ciara ordered River. "I'll handle Eric and Hannah."

River nodded and teleported himself and Jenna out of there.

Ciara stood alone in the room, devastated. Then she heard running. She raised her wand, knowing wandless magic wouldn't work in her exhausted state. But she lowered it when she saw Kellan and Henry.

Ciara looked her best friend over, noting a nasty cut on his arm. It was wrapped with a piece of clothing.

"Henry!" she cried out and ran to hug him.

Henry hugged her back the best he could while eyeing the room. "Where's Jenna?"

Pulling away, Ciara saw Henry's wide eyes and pale face. "River took her to the hospital."

"Is she—"

"Go."

"But—"

"Go," Ciara said firmly.

Henry didn't have to be told a third time. He teleported out.

"We need to deal with the bodies," Kellan said, looking at the aftermath of the bloodshed that had taken place in the room.

"I can't teleport."

Kellan's eyes widened, and he looked unusually worried. "What happened?"

"I'm just...drained. Can you take them to the Rosslers' place?" she asked, gesturing to the bodies of Eric and Hannah.

"But someone needs to—"

"I'll make sure everyone gets out," Ciara said.

Kellan nodded. He floated the two bodies to lay side by side. Touching both, he teleported away with them.

Ciara continued to run through the warehouse. Next she ran into three people from Ray's team: Laura, Dominic, and Deanna.

"Where's Ray?" she asked instantly.

"Vincent took him to the hospital."

Ciara sighed in relief. "Go to the Rosslers'."

The three did as they were told. Then Ciara continued on.

There were a lot of corpses scattered around the warehouse. Ciara was happy they had all been witch hunters. Still, she checked every one of them.

The only team left in there was Shawn's. But at least Ciara hadn't found any of them among the dead.

She had to run through the entire warehouse and out until she finally found them—except three were missing.

Hugo rushed to her. "Ciara!"

"Where are Shawn, Felix, and Grace?" she asked.

"At the Rosslers'. Shawn was injured," Hugo said.

Ciara nodded. "That means everyone's out."

"We should go," Niles said.

"I can't teleport," Ciara said sheepishly. "Long story."

Hugo offered his hand, and she took it.

"To the Rosslers' place," she instructed. Both Niles and Hugo nodded, teleporting to the Rosslers'.

Ciara and Hugo rushed inside to see what was happening, but only Kellan and Shawn were there. Niles followed them in.

It turned out everyone was at the hospital.

Mary had treated Shawn and then rushed to see her husband. She had taken the younger Rosslers with her. Liam had taken both Bill and Iris to the hospital, so he was there, too. Henry was at the hospital, both to be treated and to see Jenna. River was also there, having taken Jenna. Mary's and Ray's friends—the ones still alive—had also gone there.

"We killed more of them than they did us," Kellan said, but those words brought no comfort to Ciara.

"This isn't a victory," she said and leaned against the wall, exhausted.

"I wouldn't expect victories until the very end of this war," Kellan said solemnly.

Ciara nodded.

At least they knew more. They had better chances preparing in the future. They no longer had to guess how the witch hunters always escaped. It had all been Theresa's doing. She had kept the witch hunters informed of their every move.

But none of that comforted Ciara.

"Someone needs to check on Bill at the hospital. I don't even know if he's..." Ciara shook her head, refusing to say the words out loud.

"Niles and I can go," Kellan offered.

"Good."

Kellan and Niles left.

Shawn walked closer to Ciara and Hugo. "You alright,

Ciara?"

She shook her head. "I need to do something," she said and ran upstairs.

In Liam's room, she started throwing her things in her bag mindlessly. She had no idea what she was even doing.

She didn't come to her senses until she reached to take the bracelet from the nightstand.

Except it was beyond broken. It wasn't just the gem that had shattered. In fact, none of it had *shattered*. The entire bracelet had turned to ash.

Apparently that happened when someone killed her own fiancé on the anniversary of his faked death.

Even if Theo had turned out to be a bad guy, Ciara had still missed him. She had loved him. She had grieved his death.

And this time she had been the one to kill him.

As she thought back to the moment, she realised her hand was still covered in his blood. She sprinted to the bathroom and threw up.

She was shaking, and she was struggling to keep her hair off her face. Her cheeks were wet with tears, and she couldn't see through them.

I just killed Theo, she kept thinking over and over again until she was chanting it in her head.

When Ciara finished vomiting, she rushed to the sink to wash off the blood. She kept rubbing at her fingernails, trying to get all the blood off her hands, but it kept staining the water.

She hated red.

Her hands were still shaking. She had to look up, but the view in the mirror wasn't any better. All colour had drained out of her face. Her eyes were red, and tears ran down her cheeks.

And there was something on her chest, just below her left shoulder, where Theo had touched her. A burnt witch hunter mark, like a branded tattoo.

59

Ciara sat on Liam's old bed. Her eyes were sore from crying. She was still exhausted, but she had gathered enough strength to send her enchanted bag to her flat.

She would have teleported herself, too, if she had had the strength.

When she had gathered herself somewhat, she went downstairs.

Shawn and Hugo were in the kitchen. She could hear them talking, so she made her way there.

Hugo's eyes widened. "You look..."

"I know."

Shawn frowned. "What happened at the warehouse?"

"A lot." She didn't want to think about Theo—or the possibility of him being dead.

Shawn nodded. "Are you okay?"

Ciara shook her head. There was no point in lying. Shawn had asked only to be polite, but he knew she wasn't.

The three fell silent. Ciara looked towards the front door. She wasn't sure who she was expecting, but she wanted something to happen. She wanted action—anything but having to think.

"Liam knew," she said out loud. She didn't look at Hugo and Shawn. They had probably known, too.

"We knew too," Hugo said. "He told after we reformed the group."

"He didn't—" Shawn's talk was cut short as Ciara turned to look at him sharply.

"Can we not? Not now." She didn't want to hear any excuses.

Shawn nodded and looked down.

Ciara's presence made everyone in the room uncomfortable. She wouldn't feel any better alone, but she couldn't handle the tension.

"I'm going," she said

"Where?" Shawn asked.

"Just out." She left through the front door.

The chill air hit her skin. It was freezing, but there was no snow on the ground. Ciara breathed out, and it looked like smoke in the air.

She cast a warming spell, luckily having enough strength for that.

Then she started walking.

She tried not to think about Theo. Even thinking about her injured friends was easier.

She was worried about Jenna, wondering if she would even make it. The two had been friends since their first year at school. Jenna had been there for Ciara too many times to count. She felt guilty for not being there for her. But she couldn't go to the hospital, in fear of running into Liam.

And she couldn't even teleport.

Ciara didn't know if Bill was alive. He was her closest friend in the team, and she regretted failing him.

If she had gone with Theo, a lot would have gone

differently. But she couldn't make herself do it. Not after everything she had been through because of the witch hunters.

Ray had also been severely injured. Ciara didn't know how bad it was, but she feared the worst.

And Theresa had stabbed Iris. It couldn't be good, especially with Liam so worried.

Her Liam.

Or at least he had been. Jealousy gnawed in Ciara's chest, but at the same time she didn't want to see him. She was furious at him for lying to her. He had known about Theo for months and hadn't told Ciara. He had even talked to Ciara about Theo.

But others had known, too. Had lied, too. Ciara wasn't sure if everyone but her had known.

And it hurt.

She had mistakenly trusted all of them when she should have only trusted herself. She couldn't tell truth from lie anymore. Not after all the lies.

She had never missed Doherty so much. He would have told her the truth. She could have trusted him.

But he was dead, for real, and she had no one.

No one to trust. No one to offer her a shoulder to cry on.

She had no one to talk to. There wasn't a single person she could trust. For all she knew, Mary and Ray had hidden the truth from her, too. Perhaps even Henry and Jenna.

Liam had told everyone but Ciara, and it hurt.

Even Theo had lied to her.

Her entire life was a big lie.

Exhaustion hit Ciara. Exhaustion from merely using a warming spell. So she sat down on the cold ground.

Ciara needed someone to talk to. But she couldn't call Estella. She wanted to—even just to tell her what had happened—but she didn't dare to. She had just killed her son, and there was nothing Ciara could say or do to make it right.

There was nothing she could do to make it right for herself, either.

She sat and let her tears fall. She had been on many missions that had ended in the worst ways possible, but none of them had left her a mess like this one.

She had never had to kill someone she loved—not even to save other people she loved. She had killed Theo for the lives of people who had lied to her.

Nothing could make that right. Not even in her own mind.

Theo smiled at Ciara. "I'm really glad we got to meet again."

Ciara bit her lip, trying to contain her smile. "Me too."

"Really?" His eyes shone with surprise.

Ciara chuckled and nodded. "Yes, really."

Theo grinned. "T-that's great...to hear, I mean." His cheeks reddened.

Ciara smiled, noticing it. She took a sip of her drink to keep herself from smiling more. "I'm glad you invited me over tonight."

Theo still hadn't stopped smiling. But hearing Ciara's words made him relax, and he eased against the sofa cushions. "Yeah. Me too."

"I-I was so worried about you." Theo's hands were shaking as he cupped Ciara's face. His caress was even gentler than usual. "You were hit with that spell and...and...and then—"

"I'm fine." She took his hands into hers, peeling them off her face and giving them a comforting squeeze. "I'm fine," she repeated, noticing how much his hands were still shaking.

"Thank God," Theo mumbled and pulled Ciara into a loving kiss.

Ciara was the one to pull away. "Everyone's looking," she hissed, even though she was smiling.

Theo chuckled and pecked her lips. "Let them watch."

"Theo!"

Theo took a deep breath, setting down his glass.

"Is everything okay?" Ciara asked, turning to look at him instead of the movie they were watching.

He scratched the back of his neck. "It's just...you know...I've been thinking."

"Thinking about what?" Ciara asked worriedly.

"This is going to be the most unromantic way to do this," Theo warned.

"Screw romance. Just spit it out," she encouraged.

Theo laughed. "Alright then. If you insist." He smiled at Ciara, gazing into her eyes. "I want you to move in with me." He paused, waiting for Ciara to say something back. When she didn't respond within a few seconds, he began to panic. "Unless you don't want to, of course! Or...or if you want to, I don't know, like—"

Ciara grabbed Theo's hands and smiled at him. "I'd love to move in with you."

Blinking, Theo asked, "Really?"

Ciara chuckled and pulled Theo closer to give him a short but sweet kiss on the lips. "Yes."

"I love you!" It was a spontaneous response, but it was true.

She was taken aback by the confession, and it took her a moment to regain her composure. Before she said anything, she made sure she had thought it through. "I love you, too."

Theo grinned.

Theo and Ciara were walking along a beach. It was November, so it was cold. But nonetheless, the view was beautiful.

Theo had his right arm wrapped around Ciara to keep her warm. His left hand was in his pocket, making sure the black velvet box didn't fall out.

He was afraid she could hear his heart drumming in his chest. He was shaking from nerves.

He knew they were a great couple, and they loved each other. They had talked about getting engaged in the past, but he wasn't sure if she was ready for that step. He hoped she was, though.

He wanted to commit to her for the rest of his life.

Once they reached a cliff with a beautiful view of the sea, they stopped. Ciara waved her hand, using magic to shield them from the strong wind.

Theo swallowed. "I have something for you."

Ciara turned to look at him, tearing her eyes off the beautiful view. "What is it?"

Theo smiled. He let his arm drop from around her and went down on one knee. "Ciara Veronique Jareau, I am utterly in love with you and I want to spend the rest of my life with you if I can. Will you marry me?"

They were both surprised—but for different reasons. Theo couldn't believe he had said the words just the way he had planned.

And Ciara hadn't expected the question. She stood frozen, her eyes widening and her face going blank.

Theo had no idea what she was thinking until he cleared his throat and she finally reacted.

Her face lit up. "Yes! Yes. Of course yes!"

Theo chuckled. Swiftly, he slipped the ring on her ring finger and stood up. "It fits. I was hoping you'd like it, but if—"

"I love it, Theo!" Ciara said, astonished. "It's beautiful."

Theo smiled. "That's a relief."

60

It was hours later when Ciara finally gathered herself and walked back to the house.

She didn't know if anyone would be there. Most had probably gone home or were still at the hospital, waiting to hear about their friends and family.

Ciara hoped they were all *just* injured. She didn't want to think about the worst scenario. They had already lost more than enough.

She hadn't known Eric and Hannah well, but she had met them before. They had been good people who hadn't deserved to die. They had once had lives—careers, family, and friends.

Even though Ciara could handle Eric's and Hannah's deaths, she wasn't sure what she would do if she lost someone she had known for years. Like Jenna. Or Ray.

She felt sick, thinking about Bill. She hadn't known him for long, but they had become fast friends. But it wasn't just that. Bill was different than her past colleagues, because he was also in her team. She felt responsible for his fate.

When Ciara finally made it back to the house, she saw the front door had been left open. Even if no one was home, Ciara could just walk in.

She rushed inside and listened. The house was silent. There wasn't even odd creaking coming from upstairs.

Ciara's anxiety kicked in. She had no idea what was going on. The thought of someone having attacked the house crossed her mind, and it made her sick.

Even the thought of blood made her want to vomit.

A thud echoed through the house. It came from upstairs, so Ciara tiptoed there. She didn't want to make any noise, so she couldn't run up the creaky steps.

As Ciara got closer, she heard more sounds. All coming from Liam's room.

Ciara wasn't ready to face him. She would rather have faced a witch hunter. *Please, be a witch hunter.*

She was disappointed when she opened the door.

Her eyes scanned the room. It didn't look like the same room she had been in only a few hours before. Clothing and other items had been thrown around. There was even paper shredded on the floor.

It was a mess.

"Ciara."

She turned to face Liam hesitantly.

How could he have kept it all a secret? How could he have lied to her through everything? There had been so many chances to tell her. They had talked about Theo. Yet he had never told her the truth.

His eyes were bloodshot, and his shoulders were slumped forward. His hair was all over the place—he tended to pull at it when he was worried or anxious.

He looked nothing like the usual charming Liam.

Or perhaps Ciara couldn't see him that way anymore. After the numerous lies. She had trusted him blindly, and she knew not to do it again.

"I thought you—"

"What's going on at the hospital?" That was all Ciara wanted to hear from him. She didn't want his pity or his excuses, and she didn't want to hear more lies.

"Jenna's stable. According to the doctors and healers, she'll be fine."

It felt like the weight of the world had been lifted off Ciara's shoulders. The relief was so overwhelming her knees nearly gave in beneath her.

Liam cleared his throat, trying to keep his voice from breaking. "Iris keeps slipping into unconsciousness."

Ciara hated the jealousy gnawing at her heart. She wanted nothing to do with Liam after what he had done.

"Bill...they don't know."

Just like that, the weight of the world came crashing back down onto her. She felt nauseous again, but there was nothing left for her to throw up.

"And Dad..." If he hadn't done what he had, the heartbreak in his voice would have been enough for her to rush to his arms. "It's bad." All colour drained from his face, and he stared into nothingness.

An invisible hand wrapped around Ciara's throat, strangling her. She felt as if she was running out of air.

"Ciara—"

"Don't!" she snapped, raising her hand, when Liam tried to step closer. "Don't."

"Your bag and your—"

"They're at home," Ciara said, staring at Liam blankly.

Why did he have to be the one to do it? Why did he have to break her heart again?

"You know it's not safe to—"

"I don't care." Ciara shook her head. "Anywhere is better than here." *With you.*

"Ciara—"

"No."

"I'd feel much better if you stayed. Just for tonight," Liam pleaded desperately. He no longer had the right to hug her, and he seemed to realise that. He had to keep his hands clenched at his sides to keep himself from clinging onto her.

"No."

"Ciara—"

"No!" she exclaimed sharply. Then she could no longer keep the tears at bay. She was so overwhelmed by everything.

Liam went silent, having no idea how he could make things right.

"You had no right." Ciara shook her head, shuddering. "No right to keep that from me." She tried to blink her tears away, but it was no use.

"I know. I—"

"Then why did you?" Ciara screamed at him.

"I didn't want you to be hurt."

"Does it look like you succeeded?"

"I didn't mean to hurt you!" He looked at her with desperation. She was slipping through his fingers like sand.

"How could you think it wouldn't hurt me?" Ciara yelled, her voice cracking. "You told everyone. Everyone but me. They all knew!" The tears made Liam just a blurry spot in her vision. Her entire body was shaking, and she had to grip onto the doorframe to stay on her feet.

"You didn't deserve what he did to you!" Liam yelled at Ciara.

"You were just prolonging the wait," Ciara spat at Liam. "I don't even know what for!" She had had enough of him. "For your own fun?"

"Don't be stupid! You know it's not like that!"

"I'm done," Ciara said, her eyes turning cold. "At least Theo had the decency to apologise."

"You're kidding me." Liam was fuming, having been compared to a serial killer.

"It would have been best if we had never started this. I wish we hadn't," Ciara said coolly and turned around. It was her time to leave.

"I can't believe you would think to leave me like this."

Liam's voice held so many emotions Ciara couldn't make out all of them. Sorrow, anger, and more.

"My father might die any minute. Just like Iris...or Bill. And all you can think about is yourself!"

"And maybe none of that would have happened if you hadn't been lying to me all this time!" Ciara retorted and then snapped her fingers.

The doorframe morphed into air, and the block of flats she lived in came into view. She ran up the stairs, tears blurring her eyes. Unlocking her flat door with a spell—and with the last of her energy—she rushed in, ready to fall onto her own sofa.

Finally, she was alone.

She didn't make it to her sofa—barely even made it to her living room—and instead let herself fall onto her knees, exhaustion hitting her like a brick wall. She closed her eyes to keep new tears from forming.

It was the worst day of her life, and it couldn't get any worse.

Or so she thought.

Her eyes snapped open when something sharp and cold was pressed against her neck. "Get up." Male voice. Familiar.

Her words caught in her throat, her eyes widening. *No way.* She did as she was told, slowly standing up, with the knife still pressed on her throat.

"Now that your fiancé isn't here to keep you safe, we have some unfinished business."

How did he know? Was Theo truly dead?

"Jesse—"

"Let's talk about my American cousin whom you killed two years ago." She had never heard his voice sound so cold. "And don't be so surprised. I told you something would happen *soon*. Or, *very soon*."

Theo hadn't left the last two notes; Jesse had.

GLOSSARY

MPG: Magical Protection Group, the reformed group working against the witch hunters (see below)

HIT WITCH / HIT WIZARD: someone working to catch dangerous witches and wizards along with other criminals, excluding non-magics

CURSE BREAKER: someone working to break curses

WITCH HUNTERS: terrorists who want the secret of magic to be revealed to non-magics

NON-MAGICS: people without magical abilities

CRASHBALL: a magical sport reminding volleyball

ACKNOWLEDGEMENTS

This book is the final result of dozens of stories thrown away and years and years of writing. Thank you to everyone who helped me on that journey.

But especially thank you...

To my mother who has always encouraged me to write stories. Thank you for all the help and hard work you put into this book for me.

To my sister who was the first to read the finished version of this story and who couldn't put the book down for hours. You have no idea how excited I was to see someone read this book so eagerly.

To my father who never fails to wonder how I can sometimes write day and night. Your amazement is inspiring.

To my fiancé who pushed me into finishing this book. Thank you for telling me I wouldn't finish this book. Because if you tell me I can't, I can, and you know that better than anyone.

To all my friends who were as excited as I was when I told this book would be published.

To my editor whose criticism was unbelievably inspiring.

To all of you who were part of this book's journey from the first word to what it is now. Thank you.

ABOUT THE AUTHOR

Senja Laakso had a childhood dream; she wanted to write about magical fantasy worlds And that's what she does now.

She also wants to help other writers and authors make their dreams become the reality, and that's why she hosts The Creative Writer Podcast.

Senja lives in Finland, the country known as the land of a thousand lakes. To hear more about Senja, follow her on social media, check out her podcast and subscribe to her newsletter.

www.senjalaakso.com
Instagram: senja.laakso
TikTok: senja.laakso

CPSIA information can be obtained
at www.ICGtesting.com
Printed in the USA
BVHW081322211021
619527BV00007B/83